BANTAN'S ISLAND PERIL

By

MAURICE B. GARDNER

WILDSIDE PRESS

To my brother

WILFRED

TABLE OF CONTENTS

PART I

ILLUSTRATIONS

Six black and white page illustrations and
colored jacket design by Jim Cawthorn.

BANTAN'S ISLAND PERIL

Bantan's Island Peril

PART I

NAO—OF AMO ISLAND

Rippling muscles moved in harmony beneath bronzed smooth skin as a handsome young giant was methodically plying a paddle, and the canoe in which he knelt skimmed across the calm surface of the mighty Pacific Ocean. So accurate the paddler's strokes, hardly a bead of perspiration was to be seen on his forehead. His thick, dark hair was pushed back in pompadour style. His body was naked save for a loin cloth. His dark eyes appeared blank, without expression.

Darkly tanned as his flawless skin was, a casual observer at first would have guessed he was of native origin. However, a closer view of the young man's well formed features would reveal he was no native, but in reality a white man. He was quite young—in his early twenties—and possessing the body of an Apollo. Upon his right temple was a blood-red birthmark about the size of an American twenty-five cent coin. So, too, had his father been marked.

To one who had not known of him previously, it might be alluded this bronzed young giant was known as Bantan—a native name meaning white child of the sea born of unknown parents. His real name was Arthur Delcourt. His origin being of American parents, he had been marooned in the equatorial Pacific when three years of age, and he had been found

11

and adopted by the mateless chief of Beneiro Island. His adventures in the past are well known. His near-future ones are to follow.

That same morning when awaking on Beneiro Island, Bantan had been aware of the heaviness of his head, the dullness of his reasoning faculties, and that he had no memory of his past. Instinct was not to be denied, however. He was definitely aware of his hunger. From the cliff top where he had slept soundly through the night, he returned to the beach over a well worn trail, gathering fruit.

Passing through the charred remnants of the Beneiro village, a frown creased his brow, and a strangeness appeared in his dark eyes—as though his blanked mentality endeavored to arouse him of his connection with it and his association with the inhabitants in past days. With a shake of his head he returned to the beach where he partook of his breakfast. Afterwards, he placed the uneaten fruit in the canoe.

Standing undecidedly for a moment, Bantan returned to the edge of the destroyed village, and for many minutes stared about at the charred embers as though mesmerized by the devastation. There was something tangible at what he looked. His slightly injured brain was aware that the people who had lived in the destroyed village must have taken up their existence elsewheres. Since he could not recollect his connection with them, that portion of his reasoning faculties which was undamaged enlightened him that were he to seek them, perhaps they could establish his identity, and thereafter all would be well with him. At last, with a shake of his well formed head and a shrug of his broad shoulders, he returned to the canoe. He instinctively knew what it was and for what purpose intended.

He looked out at the gentle surf and the shimmering water beyond. Within him a stirring was aroused. Without further delay he launched the canoe into the foaming water. Quickly he took up the paddle and, plying it with strong strokes, presently had reached the calmer surface beyond. Where he was headed— what definite objective—he could not know. It was the adventurous spirit of his nature that impelled him to act as he did.

All that day Bantan paddled, being unrewarded by sight of land. At night he ensconced himself in the canoe's bottom upon a pallet of grasses and slept the entire night through as would an untroubled child in its soft crib. The gentle lapping of wavelets against the canoe's sides lulled him to sleep.

Awaking and performing ablutions from the water at the side of the canoe, he then partook of his morning meal. Before taking up his paddle, he stood upright. Shading his eyes from the glare of the rising sun, he surveyed the horizon. No sight of land was to be seen anywhere. Hardly a cloud was present in the blue canopy above. Kneeling, he then took up his paddle and proceeded to paddle westward—the same course he had set the previous day.

Whatever passed in his mind, one could not guess, for his features were inscrutable. With the rising sun at his rear, he had no need to shade his eyes. As an automaton he paddled, pausing only when he wished to scan the horizon more intently or partake of fruit.

Bird life had ceased to appear since the afternoon of the previous day. Several sea gulls had flown overhead, going in a diagonal direction to the canoe's passage. At intervals flying fish rose from the serene surface and sped through the warm air to drop back into the water again. At times one would flit near Bantan, but none struck him or landed in the canoe.

In the distance to his left, porpoises were to be seen sporting in the water; but at no time did one approach the canoe and its lone occupant. To his right, a large turtle swam, leaving slight ripples to mark its passage.

Sharks, feared denizens of the deep, could not have been hereabouts, for there was no tell-tale sign of a triangular fin cutting the surface. However, in case of necessity, he was armed with a steel dagger sheathed at his right hip. Cached in the canoe's bow was a bow and a number of sturdy arrows. There also was an automatic and a belt of cartridges—a grim reminder of the fierce conflict Bantan had had with the Nipponese in the recent war in the Pacific. There could be no telling what unknown dangers might beset him in the future; and complying with his better judgment, he had included the automatic and the belt of cartridges with his bow and arrows when he had departed from Marja Island. He had been normal then and in full possession of his reasoning faculties, while now he suffered from amnesia.

With the passing hours Bantan relaxed his vigilance. Unknown to him near the rear of the canoe had appeared a triangular fin, indicating a shark was trailing. At first it had appeared some fifty yards distant, but with passing minutes had drawn as close as ten feet from the canoe.

The paddler's eyes now concentrated upon the distant horizon. Could it be that he sighted a landfall? Overhead, from westward toward which the canoe was moving, two sea gulls were winging their way. They were in apparent strength, for as the canoe passed they made no attempt to land. They shrieked raucously at the lone occupant. Bantan watched stoically as they passed, then resumed his attention to the front.

Meanwhile, to his rear, the trailing shark made no effort to come closer. It seemed content to follow the canoe at a respectable distance for the present.

On the western horizon a definite shape was slowly becoming apparent. It seemed to reach into the heaven, breaking the natural skyline of water. At first the bronzed young giant could not determine other that it was a landfall. As the hours passed he was fully aware of the volcanic cone that towered high in the heaven, but now he began to distinguish a blur to the front of the first detected land mass.

To the rear of the canoe, still unknown to the paddler, the shark trailed. It would come within ten feet, then drift to about fifty yards, but once again approach to the nearer distance—never closer. When the paddler paused to eat fruit and cast the refuse overboard, then would the triangular fin move swiftly as the voracious creature devoured the remnants of Bantan's meal.

As the hours of the tropical day passed, and the nearer the canoe drew to the land mass, so, too, did the sun reach his zenith, then gradually slope westward. When the dazzling rays began to annoy the paddler, he would lower his head and less often would glance toward the land mass still many miles distant.

Mile after mile the canoe covered the trackless water, constantly drawing nearer the island. Shading his eyes with his hands, Bantan stared intently westward. Though the distance was still great, he could distinguish lush foliage to the front of the mountainous peak. The sight of the verdure-clad island made the young man happier. Naturally, the first thought to enter his mind was: If the island was inhabited, who were the occupants and what was their mode of living? Could they be the ones he sought to aid him in establishing his lost identity?

The sun in the heaven before him shimmered upon the water with such glaring intensity that he could scarcely keep his eyes open to look at the island in the distance becoming nearer. It was at last with un- fathomable relief that he watched the molten mass sink behind the towering volcano. He now could look toward the island without squinting his eyes.

The trees had taken definite shape, and a stretch of sandy beach could be clearly seen at the edge of the foliage, circling the island as far as his eyes could fol- low. With a smile upon his lips, Bantan was about to resume paddling when he paused to look astern. His sharp eyes at once detected the triangular fin that cut the water a short distance from the canoe. Upon the instant he knew it for what it was; that part of his reasoning faculties had been undamaged.

"A shark!" he exclaimed. "Trail me at your risk. I have no fear of you."

Partaking of several plantains and some figs, he cast the peels into the water. The swift movement of the fin proclaimed the shark was hungry, for it devoured the swill ravenously.

The bronzed young giant resumed paddling, but now and again he kept a watchful eye upon the trailing shark. While in the canoe, Bantan had no fear of the shark, feeling it would not attack him unless infuriated by hunger. In that event, he would have a fore- warning.

As the dusk of the tropical night descended upon the ocean, Bantan welcomed the coolness that was now ap- parent with the setting of the sun. His steady paddling continued without pause. Following the dusk, an al- most impenetrable mantle of darkness enveloped the ocean, and the lone occupant of the canoe could scarcely distinguish the bow. Myriads of stars appeared in the canopy above, but their feeble light did little toward illuminating the world below, so many billions of miles distant.

By continuing his course, Bantan knew he could not go astray. By concentrating his attention before him, the looming volcano could be distinguished, silhouetted against the western sky.

Not forgetting the presence of the trailing shark, the now grim young man would intermittently pause in his paddling and listen with sharp ears. With each stroke of the paddle he anticipated striking the sea monster. Instinctively he now wondered if it had been wise to not have disposed of the shark while it had been daylight. Had he done so, however, it was not improbable the spilling of blood might have lured others from the depths to harass him further.

An hour passed during which the canoe continued its way without interruption. The paddler at last desisted in his efforts to look toward the eastern heaven. A silvery effulgence was spreading upward toward the waterline.

With increased paddle strokes now because of the chill of early evening, Bantan propelled the canoe to greater speed. Before him in the westerly heaven the looming volcano silhouetted against the star-shot canopy seemed near at hand—yet several miles must still separate him from the island to the front of it.

Bantan's keen nostrils quivered now. What was it that he smelled? The slightly acrid odor that assailed his delicate nostrils proclaimed that it was smoke. He knew now the island must be inhabited, for the presence of smoke was indicative to cook fires.

More intently the paddler strove to peer into the looming darkness, but nothing could be seen. Then he felt something had bumped into the rear of the canoe.

With the thought of the trailing shark, he jabbed the paddle tentatively here and there, but he could not touch the sea monster. Once again he resumed paddling. Within a few minutes something bumped against the canoe again—this time upon the prow of the opposite side.

It was apparent the shark's hunger was beginning to assert itself. The sea monster was changing its tactics. From waiting and biding its time, it had decided to take the initiative, hoping by bumping against the canoe it might upset the water craft and proceed to victimize the lone occupant when he was spilled into the water.

Bantan placed the paddle in the bottom of the canoe. His lips tightened as his fingers clasped the handle of the dagger sheathed at his hip, and withdrew it. He disliked the thought of being compelled to engage the shark in darkness; but if the encounter became a necessity, then he would be forewarned and, likewise, be prepared.

The young giant now crouched in the middle of the canoe. His left hand rested against the gunwale. His right hand, clasping the dagger, rested with knuckles against that side of the canoe. Not a muscle moved, not a tendon quivered.

Repeatedly the shark bumped against the water craft—each time attacking in a different place. Or, could it be, another had joined the first, and together, they were determined to victimize the occupant?

Bantan might have sought the automatic and with it discharge shots at the menacing sharks before they might damage the canoe with land so near. He was no coward, and what he decided upon was indicative of good judgment. Groping in the bottom of the canoe, he sought the fruit that still remained.

Plantains were tossed into the water separately, so

as to prolong the feeding. One was tossed to one side of the canoe, and the second upon the other. Following each tiny splash he would hear a surge of water, indicating the shark had been aware of food being thrown to it.

While doing this, the canoe was unmolested further. The sharks—Bantan guessed now there must be two of them—seemed content to be fed thusly. Presently the last of the fruit was tossed overboard. In the act, the young giant looked toward the eastern horizon, and he was relieved to observe the moon rising above the water skyline. Her silvery effulgence lighted the ocean beneath, and the eyes of the young man quickly scanned the water about the canoe. There was no immediate sign of the sharks.

Bantan's eyes were then directed toward the western horizon, and the lush foliage of the island was distinguished with clearness. To its rear the volcano loomed majestically, the rays of the rising moon reflecting upon the barren cone.

Quickly sheathing his dagger, Bantan took up the paddle. His chilled body was grateful that he exercised again, and the canoe seemingly leaped forward in response to his mighty strokes. Constantly his eyes looked about the water for sign of the sharks, but he could not see them. Perhaps the fruit he had tossed into the water had satisfied their ravenous appetites for the present; but of course he could not be certain of the near future.

To his sharp ears now came the sound of the distant surf. As the moon completely cleared the horizon, her effulgence became much brighter. The strip of shimmering beach could be clearly seen.

Once again the bumping against the canoe was to be felt. The young giant jabbed the paddle at the disturbance in the water and was happy to realize his action had had some effect, for the shark darted away. The creature on the other side then bumped against the canoe. Bantan quickly thrust his paddle on this side—futilely—then with seemingly renewed strength plunged it in the water with straining arms. In response, the canoe leaped toward the first of the outer breaking waves.

With still greater strength Bantan paddled, and the canoe continued to respond nobly. In a concerted action, both sharks attacked the canoe simultaneously. The stout little water craft trembled momentarily, but its progress was not to be halted with the occupant's goal so near at hand. A mere hundred yards now intervened to the safety of the shore.

Bantan jabbed to each side of the canoe again, and the second time was rewarded to feel the tip of the paddle strike one of the sea monsters. So quick his nerve reflexes, at the next moment he thrust a second time in the same place. To his dismay the paddle entered the shark's yawning mouth. Sharp teeth closed upon the blade with a vicious snap, splintering the end, and it was torn from the paddler's hands, strive though Bantan did to wrest it free.

The canoe was almost overturned in the brief engagement, but the young giant quickly righted it. He withdrew his dagger from its sheath. With a savage expression overcoming his face, he looked to one side and then the other. He was almost determined to leap into the water were one of the sharks to be seen, and give it battle.

A short distance from him he now saw the paddle floating upon the surface. It was too far to reach, but a daring scheme occurred to him. With one hand, and then the other, shifting the dagger accordingly, he managed to maneuver the canoe toward it. In one quick movement he snatched up the floating paddle. Not a moment too soon was he, for a swirling of water indicated the shark was near at hand, and then he heard a snapping of toothed jaws less than a foot away. He jabbed at it with his dagger, but missed.

Quickly sheathing his weapon, Bantan again plied the damaged paddle with redoubled strength. As the canoe moved forward, the young giant was relieved to presently feel the surf reach for the water craft. With expert strokes, the canoe was guided through the tumultuous water to presently touch the sandy beach. Bantan lay down the paddle and agily leaped out. Laying hand upon the bow, he dragged the canoe to the very edge of the foliage.

For a few moments he stood there, motionless, filling his lungs with the sweetness of the air incensed with perfumed flowers and lush vegetation. Almost with reluctance he exhaled. His delicate nostrils were also aware of the acrid scent of smoke, and he knew he must reconnoitre and learn of this island's inhabitants before they became aware of his presence. Instinctive nature imparted a wariness to him.

Bantan's first objective, therefore, was to circumambulate the shore until he neared the village. Keeping close to the foliage, but not so close that he might brush it, the young giant started on his way. Since he had landed upon the eastern shore of the island, the rising moon illuminated the sand so that he had no difficulty. The many rocks that he passed were easily side-stepped. Occasionally hermit crabs scurried away as he passed.

When he had walked for nearly half an hour, all the while the acrid smell of smoke was becoming stronger, he knew the village could not be much farther. He came to a sudden stop. About a hundred yards ahead he glimpsed canoes beached near the edge of the foliage. While Bantan looked, a figure stole from the foliage and approached one of them.

Without hesitation, though his very manner seemed stealthy, the man drew the canoe to the edge of the water and in another moment launched it into the surf. Taking up a paddle, he plied it dextrously, guiding the canoe without mishap beyond the surf. In the calmer water beyond, he set his course—which was away from the silent watcher who remained close to the foliage a short distance from the landing.

The young giant momentarily wondered what the paddler was about at this hour of the night. Since it was none of his business, he resumed his way. But it was only a few steps that he took, for now there appeared from the foliage another figure. From the manner of dress, Bantan realized this person was a woman. He could see the long hair falling about her shoulders. The girl stood upon the beach, her attention directed upon the moving canoe. With lowered head, she turned. For a few moments she seemed undecided; then, still with lowered head, she walked slowly along the beach in Bantan's direction.

The watcher assumed she was in a quandary as to where her mate was going. There was the possibility she was an unloved, loving girl, and suspected her beloved one was on his way to a secret rendezvous with the one he really loved.

Drawing closer to the foliage, Bantan watched the girl as she walked slowly in his direction. It was easy to determine that she was mentally distressed, for her shoulders were bowed as though she bore the weight of the world upon them. Time and again she would wring her hands. The spring had gone from her footsteps—she walked in the manner she might when she would have attained three times her present age.

The silent watcher was aware that the girl was young and very comely. Her bosom was modestly covered with a halter, and though her mid-section was bare, a dress encircled her hips and extended almost to her well rounded knees. Sandals encased her small feet. As she drew nearer, he could hear the muffled sobs issuing from her lips.

Bantan's heart instinctively softened toward this unknown girl. He was tempted to emerge from his place of concealment and go to her and offer what consolement he might to mitigate her sorrow. But he stayed his impulse, realizing as a stranger to her, she might become frightened and think he meant her harm.

To one side of him in the foliage the young giant heard a furtive movement. He cocked an ear in that direction. It sounded like an animal threading its way toward the beach—in the direction nearest the approaching girl. Concerned for her safety now, he cautiously stole along the shore, hoping to intercept the animal were it bent upon attacking the helpless girl.

The beast was now silent, having reached a vantage spot. The approaching girl had not heard the stirring of the animal, so numbed her faculties were in grief. With a long-drawn sigh escaping her lips she came to a halt. Lifting pain-filled eyes that glistened with tears toward the rising moon, her mouth opened and the anguished words she uttered, the silent watcher could understand, for she spoke in a language that was similar to the one Bantan had learned when he was a boy—the Beneiro!

"Why must Amar forsake my love for another?"

"Amar," Bantan reasoned, must have been the warrior who had launched the canoe and paddled away from the island.

Then, suddenly, the animal at the edge of the foliage dashed out to the beach to leap upon the unsuspecting girl. A terrible squeal issued from its slavering jaws.

The girl turned quickly with horror to behold the wild boar about to leap upon her. The scream in her throat was checked, for at the same instant she saw a nearly naked giant with gleaming dagger clutched in his right hand appear as from nowhere and leap toward the wild animal before it could touch her. So close they had been she could feel the breeze stirred by their movements.

The surprise of the attack combined with Bantan's hurtling weight crushed the wild boar to the sandy beach. A muffled grunt escaped its jaws. It was the last sound the wild animal would ever utter, for at the next moment the young giant's dagger was buried unerringly into its savage heart. Cleansing the bloody dagger on the beast's coarse hair, he returned it to its sheath. The life blood spurted from the wild boar's heart in gushing streams as the victor of the encounter quickly arose to his feet. The engagement had taken mere seconds. With a friendly smile the young man looked toward the girl.

Dazed by the suddenness of the conflict, the girl stood there as though frozen stiff. She hardly breathed, and her hands were clasped tightly to her heaving bosom, as though to stifle the wild pounding of her heart. But she was poised to dart away if needs be, for she was only too familiar with the law of her people in regard to strangers—especially one from Ono Island—if it were from there her champion had come.

Bantan spoke to her in the Beneiro tongue.

"I am happy to have slain the wild animal that would have harmed you," he said in friendly tones.

The girl's hands dropped to her sides and she emitted a long-drawn sigh of relief. Hesitatingly, for she was still fearful of the stranger, she took a few steps in his direction. Her right hand now pressed her breast.

"Thank you for sparing me from injury and possible death," she said in a relieved tone of voice. She drew closer to her savior and studied his features that the rising moon illuminated with clearness. She had no fear of him now—only curiosity which is, more or less, inherent in all women. "You are a stranger upon Amo Island, are you not?" she asked.

"Yes, I am a stranger," was his reply.

The girl continued her appraisal of the young man's handsome features with the aid of the moon's soft effulgence.

"My name is Nao," she introduced herself, stressing the vowels with the accent upon the "a." "By what name are you known, and from where did you come?"

"Name?" Bantan's eyes reflected his wonder. He shrugged his shoulders. "Something has happened to me, Nao," he explained. "I have no knowledge of a past existence and other people. I do not know by what name I am called."

The girl studied him a moment as though in disbelief that what he told her could be true.

"Why have you come to this island?" she then asked, shuddering visibly as she remembered the law of her people.

He again shrugged his shoulders and shook his head hopelessly.

"I do not know, Nao," he answered truthfully.

"But you came just in time to spare me from the wild boar," she murmured. "How strange that should be. A moment before I cared little whether or not I lived. Now—"

While Nao had been talking, Bantan moved so that
the rising moon no longer shone directly in his face.
He and the girl now stood facing each other, and the
moon's effulgence lighted the opposite side of their
faces. His keen eyes detected the misty pathways
where tears had flowed down her rounded cheeks. A
gentle breeze wafted to his nostrils the pleasing aroma
of perfume that emanated from her—a perfume obtained from juice squeezed from sweet-smelling flowers.

"You have been crying, Nao," he said softly.

The girl lowered her head as though ashamed of
her sentimentality.

"It is true," she murmured hardly above a whisper.
She raised her head and looked up at him gratefully.

"It is not good for one so young to be sad," he
added.

"I do not like to be sad," she answered, shaking her
head slowly. "But—but there are times in one's life
when all does not go well." With her words she again
lowered her head.

Bantan's heart filled with compassion for the unhappy girl. Suspecting the nature of her sorrow, he
was considerate enough not to press her for details.

"Nao," he said. With the utterance of her name,
the girl lifted her head and her now luminous eyes
sought his questionably. "You have told me this is
Amo Island," he added. "The villagers are known as
Amo people?"

"That is so," she answered in a friendly tone. "The
volcanic island is called Aoono. The islanders to the
west of Aoono are called Ono people."

He was surprised to learn that there was still another
island upon the other side of the volcanic one.

"Did the people of Amo and Ono Islands always
live apart?" he then asked.

"A long time ago, so our forefathers have told the story," she answered, "the people of both islands lived upon this one. But there was trouble as to whom was to be the ruler, so two factions were founded. There was much discontent among the people and that led to bitter quarrelling. At last the people on one side so badly defeated the other that they took up their living upon the other island which they named Ono."

"When I have known the people of Amo Island," Bantan said after a short silence, "I must go there and know of them."

Nao shook her head sadly.

"It is not as easy as that," she replied. "Strangers are not welcome upon either Amo or Ono Island."

"Not welcome?" he asked with surprise.

Again she shook her head; there was no need of spoken words.

He looked toward the shimmering ocean, remaining silent.

Nao became compassionate. Impulsively one of her warm hands touched his arm.

"You are not to be unrewarded for sparing my life," she said in a low voice. "I could not be so ungrateful. I shall speak to my father about you. He is close in the councils of the chief. I hope you will be an exception."

A smile of relief touched his lips as he turned to meet her soft eyes.

"I do not consider myself an enemy of the Amo or Ono people," Bantan declared. "I am a stranger, it is true; but I come as a friend."

"Oh, I hope very much you will be accepted as a friend of the Amo people," she said tremulously. "I must now return to the village. It is getting late. My parents will be wondering where I am. You will remain here until morning?"

"My canoe is a short distance from here," he answered. "I shall be there."

"I'll surely see you in the morning," she said with a gentle smile.

As the girl turned, Bantan recollected the wild boar he had slain. It would be a shame to allow the flesh to be devoured by hermit crabs.

"Wait, Nao," he said "May I carry the wild boar to your hut? Your family may wish to cook and eat it."

The girl smiled as she turned about to face Bantan.

"It would be a shame to have it wasted," she agreed, nodding.

The young giant bent. In a moment, with no apparent effort, he straightened with the carcass of the wild animal slung over a broad shoulder. Walking side by side, it was several minutes before either spoke. While Bantan looked straight ahead, at his side Nao was appraising and comparing this handsome stranger with Amar, the chief's son, whom she had loved since she was a little girl, and she was aware that Amar suffered by comparison. She experienced a qualm of shame at this realization; but considering how Amar had been slighting her affections for the past many moons, perhaps the advent of Bantan might alter matters to the best of all concerned.

"You carry the animal as though it were a cloud," she observed admiringly.

He smiled, revealing his perfect set of strong, even white teeth.

"I must not forget to cook some and bring it to you in the morning," she said with a shy smile.

"I would like that," he said.

When they reached the landing, Nao turned to her companion questionably.

"Show me where your hut is, Nao," he said, "I will carry the wild boar to your very door. Maybe your father will be convinced I am a friend of your people."

"Our hut is near the landing," the girl answered. "There it is." She indicated the hut with a slender hand.

Following the direction she pointed, Bantan saw a well-shaped, sturdily built hut before which a cook fire was smoldering. Several other huts also in line with Nao's had cook fires smoldering before them, but no one seemed to be astir. The occupants of the village had not all retired, however, for up one of the village lanes, the young giant saw several natives walking about.

The girl led Bantan to the very door. With a smile she paused and turned to him. The young giant placed the carcass of the wild boar at her feet.

"After I am away," he suggested, "you may tell your father of the animal that might have killed you. I hope it is good eating."

"Thank you again," she murmured with shining eyes.

Bantan slowly walked to the beach. Pausing there and turning, he saw that the girl was watching him. He waved. She answered similarly with smiling features, then he disappeared from her view.

With glowing eyes, Nao opened the door and called to her father and mother. In a few minutes her parents, having been aroused from deep slumber and rubbing their eyes, appeared at the door.

"What is it, Nao?" her father asked with apparent irritation.

"Look—meat for tomorrow," his daughter answered.

The eyes of Nao's father widened at sight of the wild boar lying inert at the girl's feet. Her mother uttered an amazed cry of delight. Quickly the man knelt and rested a hand upon the carcass.

"It is still warm," he murmured.

Maro, Nao's father, and Luno, her mother, were not easily surprised after living some forty-odd years. But the sight of the slain boar at their daughter's feet did arouse their curiosity.

"You did not slay and carry it here, Nao," her father declared. "You would not have strength enough to do so. Who killed it and how did it come hither?"

The girl smiled reflectingly. With a wistfulness that betokened more than mere gratitude, she related how the handsome stranger had been timely in sparing her from injury and possible death.

Luno watched the girl's eyes as she spoke glowingly of the giant stranger, and in her heart she understood the radiance that welled from within her daughter and was so obviously revealed.

But Maro was made of more sterner material. He did not see the possibility of romance, as his mate did.

"A stranger!" he said in cold tones. "Nao, you know strangers are not permitted upon Amo Island."

The girl's smile vanished and her dark eyes were imploring.

"But, father, I had nothing to do with his coming here," she murmured. "After he slew the wild boar we talked a short while. His language is much the same as ours. He told me he came as a friend, and hoped to be accepted as such. You must see and speak with him. He has suffered some injury to his head, for he doesn't remember his name or the people with whom he lived."

"You know, Nao, it is the law of Amo Island that

strangers are not welcome here," Maro reminded his
daughter sternly. "I did not make that law. Long
ago our forefathers made it law that strangers are
forbidden upon our island."

"But, father, he saved my life," the girl protested,
and tears were threatening. "If a stranger risks his
life to save the life of an unknown girl, doesn't that
prove he is friendly?"

Luno drew near her daughter and placed a comforting arm about her shoulders. She looked appealingly
at her mate.

"Maro, a stranger saved our daughter's life," she
reminded him.

"The law is the law," the girl's father repeated.
"If I would remain in the good graces of Tomara, our
chief, I must report the presence of a stranger upon
Amo Island."

Luno now intervened.

"But Nao's life was at stake," she remonstrated.
"Nao is our only living child. The stranger is a friend.
He should be thanked and accepted as a friend in our
village."

"Why were you wandering along the beach at
night?" the girl was then asked by her father in a stern
voice.

Nao sighed deeply.

"My father should know I am not blind that Amar
seeks forbidden love upon Ono Island," she replied.
"Tonight I followed him to the shore and watched him
paddle away. In my grief I unknowingly wandered
along the beach without thought of danger. Were it
not for the stranger, I might be seriously injured—perhaps dead."

The muscles of Maro's jaws tensed at his daughter's
words. Too well did he know of Amar's infidelity

toward his only daughter's affections. In a loving father's estimation no man is too good for a worthy daughter, even though that one was the son of To-mara, the chief and God of the island, and one day would succeed his father. His jaw now relaxed, and though no smile came to his lips, the words he uttered made the girl joyful.

"Tomorrow morning, Nao," he said, "I will go with you to meet the stranger."

"Thank you, father," the girl answered with respect.

Her mother smiled happily.

Maro then knelt to gather up the carcass of the wild boar in his arms. Nao secretly smiled with amusement as she heard the expulsion of air forced from her father's lips when straightening with his load. When it was deposited inside the hut, Luno and Nao wrapped the flesh in breadfruit leaves. Thereafter, all prepared to retire.

Though Maro and Luno had no difficulty in falling asleep at once, Nao could not do so. Lying upon a soft pallet of sweet-smelling grasses in her apartment, she reviewed time and again the brief scene when Bantan had leaped to her protection and slew the wild boar. And each time her maidenly heart beat faster. With flushed cheeks she realized even Amar had never caused her heart to beat as fast as it did when she visualized the handsome features of the stranger.

*   *   *

Bantan returned to his canoe. For the first time he realized how wearied he was. Rearranging the grasses in the bottom of the canoe, he ensconced himself there-upon and, feeling of the sheathed dagger at his right hip, he gave a sigh. Almost at the next moment he was fast asleep.

He slept the night through without disturbance, waking as the sun cleared the horizon. Arising and stretching, he went to the water's edge and entered the gentle surf. With powerful overhand strokes the young giant drew himself into the calmer water beyond. There he swam awhile before returning to the beach.

Bantan was now aware of the gnawing pangs of hunger, and without delay set out to procure his breakfast. A variety of fruits were soon gathered. Presently, his hunger satiated, he returned to the canoe and awaited the promised coming of Nao and her father.

The sun was some distance above the horizon when, looking toward the distant shore, Bantan saw a native warrior, tall and broad of shoulders, with a slender, well-shaped girl at his side, walking in his direction. It must be Nao and her father. He also noticed the girl carried something in the crook of one arm, and he surmised it to be the piece of cooked meat she had promised him.

As they drew closer, the bronzed young giant unquestionably recognized the girl as Nao. In the silvery moonlight of the previous night he had realized the girl had been comely; but now, in the daylight, he was aware he had underestimated her comeliness. She was truly beautiful. Tucked in the glossy sheen over her ears were frangipani flowers.

Her features were oval and of a much lighter hue than the Beneiro and Marja women—testifying to her true Polynesian origin. Her forehead was high and her eyes were large and dark brown. Her nose was small and straight; her lips were not pronounced, and were red as though kissed with roses. He was also aware that no ornaments encircled her neck or wrists.

Nao's companion was fully as large as Bantan. He wore a loin cloth and sandals encased his feet. His body was tanned deeply. His hair was black, being a trifle long, and was pushed back in pompadour style. He walked erect and there still was a spring in his footsteps.

As the older man and the girl approached, Bantan arose from the side of the canoe where he had been seated. A friendly smile touched his lips. The girl had been smiling for some little while before she neared her savior of the previous evening. Having looked upon Bantan by moonlight and finding he was handsome, now, in the daylight, she could hardly suppress the increased palpitation of her heart, for the bronzed giant was something akin to a demi-god. Deep was the sigh that was emitted from her lips, and greater the glow that radiated in her dark eyes. She convinced herself she was not wrong in comparing Bantan with Amar—and the latter suffered by comparison, even though he was a chief's only son. Last night by the silvery moonlight she had studied Bantan's handsome features and noticed that they had not the bitter lines that Amar's possessed, nor the cruel, thin lips. She realized only too well that bitterness impressed upon a man's features was not in harmony with compatability.

Now, as father and daughter confronted the bronzed young giant, the girl turned to the older man whose features were very stern.

"Father, this is the stranger I told you about," she announced.

The older man nodded his head curtly, acknowledging the introduction, but no smile of welcome touched his lips. Wordlessly, with narrowed eyes, he appraised the stranger.

Bantan still smiled. He stretched a hand toward Nao's father; but when Maro did not extend his to clasp the proffered hand, the younger man made no comment, for he realized it was possible the people of Amo Island did not shake hands in greeting.

Nao handed Bantan the foreshank of the wild boar, which was wrapped in breadfruit leaves. It had been cooked earlier in the morning, as had the rest of the flesh.

"I promised you this last night," she said with a shy smile. "I hope you like it."

Bantan unwrapped the foreshank. Sinking his strong teeth into the succulent flesh, he tore off a piece which he chewed and swallowed with seeming relish.

"It is very good," he said with a broad smile, looking first at the girl, then shifting his attention to the silently watching older man.

While the bronzed giant continued to eat, Maro spoke at last. His tone of voice was somewhat harsh, and his features were expressionless.

"My daughter has told me how you spared her from an attack by a wild boar last night," he said. "As her father, I wish to thank you, for Nao is very dear to her mother and me. She is our only living child. She has told you that strangers are unwelcome upon Amo Island. Long ago our forefathers made this law. I cannot change the law, for I am only one."

Having spoken, Maro shrugged his shoulders.

Bantan continued eating the cooked meat. It was very tasty. He could not recollect when he had ever eaten cooked flesh that he enjoyed so much.

Nao watched him silently with flushed cheeks. One hand was pressed firmly against the left side of her bosom—as though she might stifle the erratic pounding of her heart.

Maro continued speaking, but his tone of voice now was less severe.

"Because of my obligation to you, stranger, I would offer you the freedom of our village and the island. You could remain as long as you wished.   I am only one, however.   Knowing Tomara, my chief, as I do, and his son, Amar, I have every reason to believe were you judged by the council over which they preside, you would be condemned to death—if for no other reason that you are a stranger."

The bronzed young giant paused in his eating to lift steady eyes to meet the older man's.

"Since I came in peace," he replied, "the least the council should decide is that I be allowed to leave in peace."

Maro shook his head ruefully.

"It is not that easy," he said.   "The council of Amo can be wrong in their judgment of a stranger.   I know —you have come in peace.   Those others who would judge you may ask: For what reason did you come here, since no one is invited to Amo—not even the people of Ono Island.   It would be difficult to convince others of your peaceful intentions when they are not obligated to you—as I am."

"You suggest that I leave the island while I have the opportunity?" Bantan asked.

Maro nodded, then turned to Nao. Her dark eyes were misty, and the silent appeal that could be read therein her father could easily understand. With stern features Maro shook his head.

Bantan had now finished eating. He tossed the clean-picked bone away and drew the back of a hand across his greasy lips.   His eyes were steady as he looked at Maro.

"I would be punished by your people for being a stranger and coming here uninvited?" he asked.

Maro's stern lips relaxed.

"I wish that were all," he answered. "The council of Amo shows no mercy toward a stranger. Once, when I was a young man, I remember of a strange white man marooned upon our shore. He was found unconscious. He was brought to the village and revived. I was not on the council then, but well I remember his fate. Through the sign language he tried to talk to the members of the council, but to no avail. The fact that he was a stranger was guilt enough. He was condemned to die—and die he did. Would you like to know how he died?"

Bantan nodded.

Maro turned until he faced the looming volcano.

Bantan's eyes remained unchanged in expression.

"He shouted and tried to break free," Maro added. "Two warriors had to hold him."

"Then he was cast into the crater to his death," Bantan concluded.

Maro nodded. Words were unnecessary.

In Bantan's heart the injustice of the people of Amo Island toward strangers was unwarranted. It was reasonable that they should punish a stranger should he betray an extended welcome. But to condemn one to death just because he was a stranger was a matter that should be remedied. Alone, he realized he could not alter the belief of people so instilled with hatred toward strangers. He wished that he might be able to correct their attitude so that in the future strangers might come to this island without danger of being condemned to death. He lifted his dark eyes to solemnly regard the girl and her father.

"Maro, your people are wrong in condemning people because they are strangers," he declared. "Your law is an unjust one. From the time you were a child, and you were taught that law, it is only natural you would

believe it just when you became a man." Bantan now
shook his head sadly as he added: "It is too bad that
people must be as yours are—especially, since knowing
you and Nao. I have the feeling that the other villagers might be as human."

Maro shook his head.

"Were I not obligated to you, stranger," he said,
"I would be as eager to condemn you for being a
stranger. I would be on the council that condemned
you to death in the crater of Aoono."

Bantan's solemn eyes shifted to Nao. Her features
were as gentle as could be, and her dark eyes were filled
with fear for his safety.

"You know I am right, don't you, Nao?" he asked.

She nodded her head.

"Whatever the teachings of my people," she answered, "in my heart I know you speak the truth.
There is no guile in your eyes, and no evil is stamped
upon your face."

Bantan's eyes seemed to change. A determined expression replaced the other. Reading this new light
in the bronzed giant's eyes, and understanding the nature of it, Nao muffled the sob that might have found
its way to her lips.

"No," she warned, shaking her head. "I can read
in your eyes what you are thinking. Please, if not for
your sake, then think of father and me. We would be
judged as guilty as you for not reporting your presence to the chief."

Bantan's eyes shifted to the girl's father.

"That is true?" he demanded.

Maro nodded his head slowly.

The bronzed young giant shook his head impatiently;
then, as a sudden thought occurred to him, he quickly
looked at Maro.

"Do you suppose you were seen when you came hither?" he asked.

The semblance of a smile touched Maro's lips.

"I don't think so," he answered. "If we had been seen and anything was suspected of us, we would have known it by now."

Remembering his damaged paddle, Bantan reached into the canoe, and bringing it forth, showed it to Maro.

"My paddle was damaged by a shark last night," he said. "It is hardly fit to use for a long trip. Could you give me another?"

The girl's father nodded.

"I can furnish one to take its place," he answered.

Nao's eyes brightened.

"I could bring it to you when the villagers are having their siesta," she said to Bantan, and then looked at her father for his approval.

Maro shrugged his shoulders and then nodded.

"You must be careful, Nao," he warned.

"I will, father," the girl promised. "No one will see me when I leave the village with the paddle."

"Then there is nothing more to be said," the girl's father said to Bantan.

"I suggest you both return to the village," Bantan then said. "I shall remain in hiding during the day. When night comes and Nao has brought me a paddle, I will leave your island. No one will have known that I have been here."

Maro heaved a sigh of relief.

"That would be best," he agreed.

Nao knew she would never forget Bantan had been to Amo Island. With a sad smile she bravely tried to conceal her true feelings. She turned to her father and reluctantly indicated she was ready to leave. Over a shoulder she called softly to the bronzed young giant.

"Goodby."

"Goodby, Nao," Bantan answered.

Maro and his daughter returned along the beach in the direction they had come. Several times Nao cast a fleeting glance over a shoulder to see Bantan still watching them. Each time that she turned to look ahead she fought down the stifling sensation that persisted in her throat.

When they had disappeared around a bend in the shoreline, Bantan shrugged his shoulders. Then, aware that the canoe was openly exposed to a possible roving villager, he concealed it in the foliage.

The young man was in a quandary. He had never run from danger in his life. It is true there had been times when discretion had played the better part of valor, and he realized its value in determining what course to take—especially if it be of a precarious nature. After moments of debate, he decided to reconnoitre.

Moving with stealth, Bantan's footsteps brought him ever nearer to the village of the Amo people—without being apprehended—until he reached its outskirts. There a convenient tree was observed. Drawing himself up about thirty feet from the ground, the bronzed giant ensconced himself in a comfortable crotch and satisfied his curiosity concerning the village.

In construction, the huts were similar to those upon Marja Island. They set in lanes without too much distance between them. A garden plot was alongside each hut, and there taro and yams were cultivated. These two tubers were a staple product of the villagers at meal times. Being able to obtain a view of the entire village from his vantage place, Bantan ob-

served the much larger hut located in the center, and
he assumed rightfully that was where the chief and his
immediate family lived.

What form of deity the people worshipped interested the watcher in the tree; but looking carefully,
he saw no idol. Could it be their only form of worship
was Tomara, the chief—that he was the God of the
Amo people?

Bantan now allowed his eyes to rest upon certain
members of the village. Before some of the huts native women tended fires over which earthen pots were
placed and preparations for the noon day meal were
in process. A savory aroma was wafted to the silent
watcher's nostrils. Young girls assisted their mothers
in the meal preparations.

Nearby, warriors were squatted upon their haunches
in the shade of their respective huts awaiting the time
when the meal would be prepared.

In various groups nearly naked children played
games—boys and girls alike being participants. So
eager and whole-hearted their interest in their contest,
none asked or gave quarter. Loud was their shrieking.
Time and again their parents would admonish them
with threats of dire punishment unless they were more
quiet.

The length and breadth of the village Bantan
looked, but he saw no sign of Maro or his daughter.
They, being the only two he knew, he would recognize
at once. The watcher in the tree remained a short
while longer before deciding to return to the shore
where his canoe was hidden. As the villagers were now
partaking of their noon day meal, the young giant
realized he was hungry, so lowering himself from the
tree, he retraced his way, gathering fruits, meanwhile.

When Bantan reached the concealed canoe, he was

not greatly surprised to find Nao awaiting him. She was seated in the canoe, but as she heard the bronzed giant approach, she arose to her feet with a happy smile enwreathing her features.

"You have brought me a paddle, Nao?" he asked.

With his words he deposited the fruits he had gathered into the canoe. He realized his question was unnecessary, for he saw the slightly used paddle that the girl had placed there.

She nodded in answer to his question, then a deep flush mounted to her cheeks.

"I also have saved the other foreshank for you," she added. "You seemed to enjoy the meat I brought earlier, so I thought you would like this as well."

He thanked her with a smile.

"Your father doubtless instructed you to return to the village at once," he added.

Nao smiled shyly and shrugged her shapely shoulders.

"I don't think he would mind if I lingered a short while," she said. "After all, it isn't very often that a stranger comes to Amo."

Bantan shrugged his shoulders and a wry expression touched his lips.

"An unwelcome stranger," he commented.

The girl shrugged her shoulders and smiled winsomely.

"Aren't you going to eat the meat I brought you?" she asked.

He nodded, then proceeded to unwrap the breadfruit leaves.

"Have you eaten?" he asked.

She nodded.

"I will eat one of these," she said, reaching for a

hand of plantains Bantan had brought. She broke
one free and peeled it.

With seeming relish Bantan ate the foreshank of
the wild boar. Its succulent flesh was as delicious as
the other he had eaten earlier in the day. Nao nibbled
daintily upon the plantain. They exchanged favoring
glances while they ate and spoke a few words concerning the food they were eating. When he had
finished and tossed the bone to one side, the young
giant drew the back of a hand across his greasy mouth.

"That was very good, Nao," he said with a sigh.
"How can I thank you for being so considerate—to an
unwelcome stranger?" he added with hesitation.

The flush of the girl's cheeks deepened and she shyly
avoided his direct glance.

"You wouldn't be unwelcome—if I had anything
to say about the law of Amo Island," she murmured.

"It is kind of you to say that, Nao," he said. "I
wish your island law would permit me to remain longer.
But if I must go away—I must." He shrugged his
shoulders.

"You could wait another sun until you are more
rested," she suggested. "After paddling several suns,
you have not had time to be completely rested. Do
you plan to continue paddling until you reach another
island where you would be more welcome?"

Again he shrugged his shoulders.

"If only I could remember who I am," he murmured.
"Then I would know for certain what to do in the
future."

"You will remember," the Amo girl assured him
comfortingly.

Bantan looked toward the girl and found that her
eyes were filled with a mistiness that did not conceal
the luminosity of her soul's yearning.

"Nao, you look at me strangely," he said, his voice arousing her from the seeming trance she was in.

The girl smiled as she shook her head, but the glowing light in her dark eyes did not vanish. It radiated stronger. She reached out a trembling hand and placed it upon the back of one of his.

"I—I—don't know what to say," she confessed in evident agitation. "And even if I knew what to say—I—I—would be afraid that I might offend you—were—were I to say it."

The bronzed young giant arose to his feet with a shrug of his shoulders. With a laugh to banish whatever vexing problems troubled, he turned to the island girl. Nao was looking up at him now with a perplexed expression in her dark eyes.

"Come, Nao," he said, reaching for her hands and drawing her to her feet. "You must not remain here longer. You may be missed in the village. It is best you return at once."

The girl appeared hurt by his almost rude dismissal.

"You will not leave tonight?" she asked quickly, her bosom rising and falling rapidly. "I shall see you again— before nightfall?"

He regarded her gravely. Though he wanted to tell her it was best that she did not come to see him again, he didn't have the heart to do so. An admonition was dismissed at that moment—something he later might have reason to regret.

"If you wish, Nao," he agreed.

With new hope and the glow in her luminous dark eyes once more radiant, the girl reached for his hands and held them a long moment while her eyes rested upon his searchingly—as though she might read in his what she wished to know.

"Thank you," she murmured fervently.   "I shall come to you shortly before sundown."

She released his hands and took her departure before her strangely acting heart made her do something that would be most unbecoming to a member of her sex.

Bantan watched Nao as she hurried on her way. Upon several occasions she turned and waved to him, and he acknowledged by waving in return.   Then at last she disappeared beyond a bend in the shoreline.

With a shrug of his broad shoulders, the bronzed young giant returned to the canoe, and seating himself at its side, he realized his emotions were becoming disturbed.   As his thoughts were of the strangely agitated island girl whom he had known only a day, he realized she was infatuated with him.   He did not question this fact.   And then he asked himself the extent of his feelings toward her.

Since he had no memory of his past existence, Leona Brown, Kalma, and Wanya were unknown to him. Upon the occasions he had been in Nao's presence, instinctive nature could not be denied.   Only too well had he been aware of the pleasurable warmth that had pervaded his inner being, even to the extent of increasing the palpitation of his heart and a radiant glow entering his eyes when he had looked at her.   Inhibition, transmitted into him from past generations of fine ancestors, had not permitted him to reveal by word or action that as a man he desired her for the woman that she was.

With a shake of his head, Bantan strained his reasoning faculties that had been undamaged in a vain effort to recollect his true identity.   Many were the cogitations that came into his mind that he weighed and at last was forced to discard in futility.   So earnest his endeavor to break down the barrier that separated his present existence from the one he tried to recollect, he became aware of a roaring sound in his ears and needles of pain stabbed within his head.

At last, wearied from the mental conflict, Bantan flung himself upon the ground at the side of the canoe and buried his face upon his bronzed arms. For many minutes he moved his head back and forth as the roaring in his ears continued and the sharp pains in his head gave him no relief. But at last the roaring sounds faded and the head pains seemingly numbed him with the result he slumbered.

In his dreams the beautiful Amo girl and himself were alone in the world. They dwelt in sublime happiness without thought or worry of anything else. Life was very pleasant in this ethereal land, thus was it of any wonder that a smile touched the lips of the sleeping young man when he finally awoke?

*   *   *

Even by the time Nao reached the landing, her cheeks were still flushed and her heart beat strangely. Her poor brain was in a turmoil. Never in her entire life of seventeen years had she felt like she did now —never had her affection for Amar reached such a culmination of ecstacy as did her self-acknowledging love for the handsome stranger. Just to look at him and be near him was enough for her otherwise unruffled heart to hammer against her bosom with such intensity that it might explode. And, strangely, she was happy beyond words to express the slightest trepidation because of her happiness.

In this highly agitated state of emotion, Nao had eyes for no one as she was about to pass several warriors who were working on the bottoms of their canoes. Ordinarily, the girl would pause and exchange pleasantries—but not on this day. Literally, she was walking on clouds.

Shocked, as though doused with ice-cold water, the girl came to a standstill. Her name was sharply spoken. Without even looking toward the speaker, she knew it had been Amar who addressed her.

"Nao!"

Turning slowly, her self-control evident now, the girl looked at the sinister features of Amar, only son of the chief, Tomara. He was fully as large as Bantan. His hair was quite short and pushed back in pompadour style. About his neck was a necklace of beautiful sea shells. His loin cloth was of an unique design as were the sandals he wore. His features were well molded and would be considered handsome were it not for the thinness of his lips that were touched with an ironic smile. His eyes were narrowed and the dark depths were hard.

"What is it that you wish, Amar?" Nao asked, averting her eyes from his strangely piercing ones.

Amar drew near the girl with unmistakable displeasure unmasked upon his features. Reaching her, he took one of Nao's hands in his large one and squeezed it intentionally until the girl tightly clenched her lips to prevent the cry of pain she might have uttered.

"You would have passed without speaking to me, Nao," he said in apparent indignation. "Does Tomara's son deserve such an oversight from a common village girl?" He drew himself haughtily erect when he had spoken.

"I did not see you, Amar," the girl answered truthfully, looking up at his leering features for a moment, then quickly averting her eyes. "My hand," she said, trying to withdraw it from his strong one; "you are hurting it."

For another moment Amar held her hand tightly, then his grip relaxed.

"I did not realize I held your hand so tightly, Nao," he said mockingly. "Forgive me."

As he released her hand, the girl rubbed it with the other. Then, without another word, she resumed her way to her hut, notwithstanding the grins of amusement the other warriors bore upon their faces.

Amar made no effort to speak further or stop her. As the girl passed him, the trace of a saturnine smile touched his lips. The chief's son had observed the girl's flushed cheeks before he had spoken to her. Being able to read a girl's heart through the expression of her eyes, he had not missed the glow that had radiated in them for the object of her thoughts. Could it be that Nao had been secretly meeting some warrior of the village—for the reason a warrior and a maiden meets in secret?

Last night Amar had not been too successful with his *amour* during a clandestine meeting. Today, for that reason, he was in a vile mood. As a means of gratifying his injured vanity he was on the lookout, causing any one distress who might be a little more successful in the ways of the heart.

*   *   *

It was an hour before sundown when Nao, with more cooked meat from the wild boar wrapped in breadfruit leaves clasped in one arm, left her hut and went to the deserted landing. Blithely walking along the beach, she did not see the piercing eyes that watched her from the concealment of a nearby palm tree.

With a cruel smile upon his thin lips, Amar lost no time in following the girl, but kept himself in a position ready for concealment in the event Nao turned to look backward. Several times the girl did cast glances to her rear until the landing was beyond view, but she did not see the sinister figure that furtively trailed her. Her vigilance now relaxed, with cheeks flushed and madly beating heart, she almost broke into a run so that she might reach Bantan the sooner.

The handsome stranger's features kept recurring in her mind over and over again much like a happy refrain that seemingly knew no ending, nor would Nao wish it otherwise. This state of happiness she was in superseded anything that had ever been blissful in her past life. She hoped it would continue without cessation; but that, she realized only too well, would be hoping for too much in this mortal life—so susceptible to misfortune that most individuals experience at one time or another.

Now at last she was drawing near where the canoe was concealed in the foliage. She would know the familiar setting of trees with the clump of lush ferns at one side so long as she might live. With some trepidation she parted the foliage, but eagerness was in her eyes.

"Stranger," she called softly; and, a moment later, when she received no reply: "Stranger—are you here?"

She heard a stirring within the foliage and her fast-beating heart nearly skipped a beat.

"Nao?" Bantan asked; his questioning of her name was needless, for he had recognized her voice. Instantly his dream recurred to him, and manfully he suppressed the flush that threatened his cheeks.

"It is I," the girl replied.

In a few moments Bantan and the girl confronted each other. At sight of the leaf-wrapped parcel she held in one arm, the bronzed giant smiled.

"You have brought more cooked meat?" he asked.

She smiled shyly and handed it to him. Accepting it with thanks, he unwrapped it, then seated himself.

"You are very good to a stranger," he murmured; and as he spoke he lowered his head to bite into the meat.

For that reason Bantan failed to observe the unmistakable love-light that glowed radiantly in the girl's dark eyes. She stretched a timid hand to caress his dark hair, but withdrew it quickly and pressed the hand to her heaving bosom. They were silent while he ate. Meanwhile, she nibbled upon a plantain which she obtained from the canoe.

Finishing his meal and drying his lips, Bantan arose to his feet and looked gratefully at Nao. He was strangely fascinated by her loveliness. The girl arose, her hands dropping to her sides, and she looked up into the bronzed giant's steadily regarding eyes. Was this to be the moment she awaited? She felt strangely delirious. Her breathing seemed to catch in her pulsating throat. Her heart throbbed madly. A warmth pervaded her entire being.

"Nao—" he said with a slight hesitation, as though unsure what he wished to say. "Nao—I—I have been thinking—"

"Yes?" Her voice was a mere whisper and for a brief moment her eyes closed. She sighed deeply. Then she heard the breath catch in his throat. Her eyes opened quickly. A strange light had appeared in his, and she now saw that he was not looking at her but at something that had arrested his attention beyond her. "What is it?" she asked, her fear at once apparent in her wide-opened eyes.

"I saw a face at the edge of the foliage behind you, Nao," he whispered. "You must have been followed."

He stepped around her quickly, and in another

moment emerged in full view of the beach. True, Nao had been followed. A native warrior, fully as large as Bantan, was studying him curiously, but failed to recognize him.

Amar, only son of Tomara, stood there proudly with hands akimbo. He looked every inch of the chief he one day would be acclaimed. His right hand was close to the handle of the stone dagger sheathed at his hip. A mocking leer now possessed his features.

Before either spoke, Nao followed in Bantan's wake and at once recognized Amar. She moaned in despair. Too well did she realize the happiness she had experienced—brief as it had been and so near fulfillment —had been too sweet to last.

"Amar!" she cried.

The mocking smile on Amar's face turned to bitterness as his eyes shifted to the fearful girl.

"Nao, you know the law of the village in regard to a stranger," he said accusingly.

"He saved my life last night from an attack by a wild boar," the girl defended her savior. She spoke swiftly. "He has come to Amo Island as a friend. He knew nothing of our law. When I told him strangers were unwelcome here, he understood. He was going to leave tonight."

"The stranger will not leave tonight," Amar hissed, shifting his attention to the bronzed giant. "He will go with me to the village to be judged by the council."

Bantan drew erect. His dark eyes blazed with defiance.

"I will not go anywhere with you if I do not wish," he said; and with his words he took an aggressive step toward the chief's son.

Amar's features registered his outraged surprise.

"You would dare talk back to *me*—the chief's son?" he demanded with incredulity.

None of the island warriors would have dared defy Amar. But it was not a member of the Amo village that confronted the chief's son now and cringed before him as would be expected of one of his father's subjects. Amar now realized how stupid he had been to have lacked foresight of having several warriors accompany him to effect the capture of the giant stranger. He salved his pride with the knowledge that he could not know it was a stranger that Nao was going to meet in secret.

"Nao, go to the village and summon warriors to take this stranger a prisoner," he commanded the girl. "I shall remain here and see that he does not get away."

Nao looked pitifully at Bantan and moaned beneath her breath. She could not be instrumental in his capture and condemnation to a certain, horrible death.

"I cannot!" she cried, shaking her head.

"You refuse the command of the chief's son?" Amar demanded imperiously. "Then you shall share his fate!" Turning to the bronzed giant, he motioned impatiently. "Come, let us go to the village. You are my prisoner."

Bantan's eyes had narrowed to mere slits, and his lips were tight-pressed. A grimness possessed his features.

"Do you think I am so foolish to go to my death without a struggle?" he demanded. His right hand hovered over the handle of his dagger.

Amar wet his dry lips with the tip of his tongue. The chief's son was no coward, and when he saw his bluff had failed, he drew the stone dagger sheathed at his right hip. That was the signal for which Bantan awaited, for now he drew his steel dagger, ready to meet the chief's son in combat.

"Since you are a stranger," Amar hissed, "I should

know you would be stupid and resist me. But," with
a derisive laugh, "I shall not kill you. Aoono is not
to be cheated."

"Be careful, stranger," Nao cried in warning to
Bantan.

The bronzed young giant flashed a smile to the distressed girl, and he would have assured her with words
that he had no fear of the chief's son. That moment
of detraction was what Amar awaited. With a muffled curse he leaped forward, his right hand describing
an arc, and Bantan was to be the object of his descending dagger.

Nimbly, the bronzed giant stepped to one side. A
half-smile touched his lips, enraging the chief's son
further because of the failure of his aim. Again Amar
leaped at the stranger, feinting with his dagger hand,
hoping to confuse his opponent. But Bantan was not
easily fooled.

The two adversaries stood several feet apart. Their
knees were slightly flexed, the muscles of their legs
tense. Their left hand was held before them, while
the dagger hands made a slight waving motion. Glaring defiantly at the chief's son, Bantan now became
the aggressor. Warily he inched his way toward his
enemy, and when Amar's nerve failed him against
holding firm, he retreated a step, then another, as Bantan steadily moved toward him. As the bronzed giant
continued to move forward implacably, Amar retreated
steadily backward—in the direction of the foaming
water's edge.

Realizing Bantan had the better advantage, the
chief's son tried to maneuver his opponent into the position he was. They moved about briskly for a few
moments, their daggers slashing at each other, but not
drawing blood. When they watchfully faced each

other, their positions were the same—except that Amar
was closer to the water's edge than before. The
water washed to within ten feet from where he stood
on the defensive.

Amar's dark eyes glared with intense bitterness.
Thus far the two formidable combatants had not
physically come together. Their conflict had been of
a feinting nature, except that Amar slowly gave ground
before his opponent's slow, but steady, advance.

Back, ever backward, the chief's son retreated while
Bantan's feet moved ever forward down the beach—
an inch at a time, sometimes two—but never pausing
or giving ground. Once an inch had been gained, it
was not surrendered. Because of the sloping beach the
bronzed giant had the advantage, since he looked down
upon his opponent.

Amar became determined once again to reverse their
positions. He feinted with his dagger hand, but his
opponent did not fall for the ruse. Quickly, then, the
snarling chief's son feinted again. Quick as lightning,
Bantan seized the wrist of the dagger hand, imprisoning it. He thrust his dagger at Amar, and only by a
speedy backward twist did the chief's son escape the
dagger's point. At the next moment his quick left
hand grasped Bantan's wrist, imprisoning it, as his
own was.

The two giants, having imprisoned the wrists of
their dagger hands, came face to face with each other.
A scant six inches separated their faces. Amar was
snarling in fury, whereas Bantan's face was inscrutable
save for the half-smile that still touched his lips.
Amar's breath was coming in labored gasps, whereas
Bantan's giant chest moved rhythmically to his steady
breathing.

"Stranger!" The chief's son spat at this adversary,

spraying his face with spittle. Had Amar used a more
vile epithet, the manner in which he uttered the word
"stranger" could not have been more meaningful.

Bantan said nothing in reply. With the back of a
hand he quickly brushed his face. His dark eyes narrowed more so. Then Amar strove mightily to force
his opponent up the beach. For tensed moments he
exerted all his strength, but could not budge his equally
powerful opponent a scant inch. When he failed at
this, he attempted to turn him about in a wrestling
movement, and in this, too, he failed to alter the situation.

It was Bantan's turn now to bear heavily against
the chief's son. Though Amar was powerful, he could
not withstand the bronzed giant's increased pressure.
A half-step backward he was compelled to retreat.
Another half-step followed. Then, with a resurgence
of strength, Amar managed to hold back his opponent—but for moments only. Great beads of perspiration stood upon his forehead—evidence of the
mighty resistance he put up. Great exhausts of air
were forced from his tortured lungs, to be replaced
with gasping, renewed breaths, that were sharply
drawn because of the extreme physical endurance to
which he was in opposition.

Amar strove mightily to free his imprisoned dagger
hand, but in Bantan's merciless grip, such was impossible. The bronzed giant paused once in his relentless
advance to concentrate upon thrusting his imprisoned
dagger hand toward Amar's chest. With equal
strength his enemy prevented the fulfillment of this
hope. Perspiration profusely streamed down the face
of the chief's son, but, strangely, Bantan did not perspire too noticeably.

Once again the bronzed giant marshalled his great

strength in forcing Amar backward again, and this time the slow, steady retreat of the chief's son did not halt until he had been forced into the water—the breaking surf rolling above his knees.

All the while they struggled, Nao watched with fear choking in her bosom. She drew her breath in labored gasps as though she were in physical stress instead of a mental one. To the very edge of the beach she had come, anticipating every move, and sighing with relief as she saw Bantan slowly, but surely, besting his equally powerful adversary.

The straining battlers tentatively groped with their feet to find more secure footing. Being forced backward, Amar's foot had dislodged a round stone that was now directly in the path of Bantan's forward-moving feet. His first intimation of this obstacle was when his toe stubbed against it. He quickly raised his foot to place it forward. It was then a redoubled surge of strength in resistance on Amar's part caused the bronzed giant to quickly seek footing. The back of his heel came down suddenly upon the rounded stone, and his foot slipped out from under him. Bantan lurched, and while he tried instantaneously to recover his equilibrium, his grip on Amar's wrist loosened for the fraction of a moment that the chief's son awaited.

Amar was quick to take advantage of Bantan's misfortune. With a quick twist he freed his dagger hand. Muttering a gasping snarl of triumph, he pulled on his opponent's imprisoned dagger hand, further upsetting his already off-balanced adversary. The bronzed giant was falling into the foaming surf on his left side. Amar was in the act of thrusting surely with his dagger. While falling, with alertness Bantan's left hand cupped water and dashed it into the leering Amar's face, momentarily blinding him with the salty spray.

Nao Watches Bantan and Amar

Crying in rage, Amar blindly tried to plunge his
dagger into his opponent, and oversweeping his point
of equilibrium, he fell upon his side into the surf a
moment after Bantan had. His grip upon his opponent's wrist was broken in the fall.

The bronzed giant was first to reach his knees. His
eyes had not been subjected to the salt water, thus his
vision was clear. The sight of Amar's bowed head at
his left side as he struggled to arise from the foaming
water, inspired Bantan to act upon the spur of the
moment. He raised his left hand to his shoulder and
brought its edge down hard upon the nape of Amar's
neck. With the thudding contact the chief's son
grunted explosively and fell forward into the swirling
water, unconscious.

Quickly Bantan sheathed his dagger, then made certain his unconscious enemy no longer clutched his stone
dagger. Arising to his feet, he reached down and
grasped Amar beneath the arm pits and dragged him
out of the water. Up on the beach near the edge of
the foliage he released him. The chief's son remained
inert, his breathing stertorous.

The now smiling girl was at Bantan's side, and as
the victor of the contest looked down at her, the pride
Nao felt for him at his ability to best the chief's
powerful son was clearly reflected in her dark eyes.
Unashamedly she clutched both of his arms, her admiration too great for words to express.

Bantan's answering smile turned to perplexity as he
looked down at the unconscious Amar.

"What am I to do with him, Nao?" he asked.

A look of disdain replaced the proud expression in
the girl's eyes.

"Amar would not hesitate to kill you were you in
his place," she answered with flashing eyes. "If you

let him live, he will hunt you down.. You will not be
spared any mercy. I know Amar. And what of me?
I would be condemned by the council for meeting you.
Aoono would claim two of us then."

Bantan appeared to be thinking deeply. His brow
furrowed, so great his concentration. Then a slow
smile touched his lips.

"Nao, I think I have solved the problem," he said.
"Would you like to come with me? I know not what
the future holds; but if you remain here, you surely
will be condemned to death."

A happy smile enwreathed the girl's features for a
moment, then it faded gradually as Nao was thinking
deeply.

"My father and mother would miss me," she said.
"But, if you permit Amar to live, they would miss me
more, for Aoono would claim me." Now her perplexity cleared as revealed by the shy smile that touched
her lips. She added: "The choice I make is that I will
go with you—where, does not matter, so long as we
are together."

"That solves everything, Nao," Bantan answered
with a smile.

"May I slip back to the village and tell my father
and mother of my choice?" she then asked. "And
there are a few treasured belongings that I would like
to take with me."

He nodded in agreement.

"My father and mother love me very much," Nao
added in extenuation. "And I love them very much,
too. I would not be happy away from them unless I
were to tell them I am going with you of my free will,
then they will not have to worry about me."

He nodded in understanding.

"While you are gone, Nao," he said, "I shall bind

Amar so he will not threaten our future. Then I shall provision the canoe and be ready to depart when you return."

The girl smiled sweetly.

"Tell your father to notify some one to come after Amar a little while after we have left," he suggested.

With a nod the girl was on her way.

From the foliage Bantan obtained vines and bound the still unconscious Amar's hands and feet. Without loss of time he gathered various fruits which should last two persons until they had reached some other more hospitable island. The young giant then withdrew the canoe from its place of concealment onto the beach, then awaited the return of Nao. With interest he watched a patch of white cumulous clouds reshape themselves in the passing minutes.

Lying upon his back, Amar at length recovered consciousness. Slowly at first he opened his eyes. The bonds about his wrists and ankles somewhat restricted the blood circulation and hurt him. His hate-filled eyes caught sight of the stranger resting against the side of his canoe. At the same moment Bantan observed Amar's baleful eyes watching him. He did not speak, however. He waited for the chief's son to do so.

Twisting and turning uncomfortably, Amar at last broke the silence.

"Stranger, you have let me live when you might have slain me," he said in cold tones.

Bantan nodded, but uttered no words.

"You do not realize the humiliation you have perpetrated against the chief's son, stranger," Amar continued accusingly. "Being a stranger upon our island and unaware of our customs, you could not know. I should feel grateful that you have let me live—but

I don't!" He hissed between his teeth, so great his rage. "Being the chief's son, and one day to be acclaimed the chief and God of the village, do you think I could ever forgive this insult?"

"You should be grateful that you are alive, Amar," Bantan said. "The reason I have bound your hands and feet is to insure my safety in leaving your inhospitable island. Nao is going with me."

Amar cursed beneath his breath. His dark eyes were never more filled with consuming hatred.

"Stranger, I vow by the sacred bones of my ancestors that I shall search and find you," he promised. "Then you will know what it is to have insulted Amar."

Bantan's patience with his defeated enemy was becoming exhausted.

"Amar, you have said enough," he warned. "I don't care to hear any more from you."

The chief's son became silent, for the warning expression upon the bronzed stranger's face disclosed his mounting displeasure.

Looking along the beach, Bantan's eyes lighted. He could now see Nao running daintily toward him. She carried a grass bag in which he assumed her treasured possessions were packed. In due time she reached the canoe which was ready for launching. Although she was breathless, she was smiling happily.

"I am ready," she said.

Aware of the girl's presence, Amar started cursing again. Nao looked down at him for a moment. She shuddered at sight of the hate-contorted expression upon the face of the chief's son. She placed the bag containing her possessions in the bow of the canoe, and indicated she was ready to leave.

Bantan nodded. He drew the canoe to the edge of the water. Motioning for Nao to step within, the girl did so, seating herself near the bow and bracing her hands upon the gunwale to each side.

Amar's dire threats of reprisal were still to be heard as Bantan launched the canoe into the gentle surf and, leaping within, took up his paddle and plied it with dexterity until the calmer water was reached. No longer could he and the girl hear the chief's son cursing them.

In the fast-settling dusk, Bantan looked at Nao and smiled. The girl's answering smile was of confidence. She knew she had no reason to worry or fear anything while with the handsome, bronzed stranger, so complete her trust in him. In truth, Bantan represented life to her.

PART II

PRISONERS ON ONO ISLAND

The stars in the heaven were twinkling brightly. No breath of air stirred. The chill of the evening air had now changed, and there was a noticeable humidity that was almost stifling. The broad expanse of the mighty Pacific Ocean was calm and very dark. In the northeast sky just over the horizon ominous masses of thunderheads were making an appearance. Distant flashes of lightning could be seen, and low, intermittent moaning sounds were audible.

A canoe was moving across the darkened surface in an easterly direction. To the west the distance between Amo Island was increasing as Bantan plied his paddle with methodical strokes. By this time several miles had been covered.

It was so dark the young giant could hardly see the girl sitting in the bow of the canoe, facing him. Her fragrance was wafted to his nostrils. Some few minutes had passed since they had spoken, and now the girl sighed.

"Nao, you are awake?" he softly called.

"Yes," she replied; "I am awake."

"I heard you sigh deeply," he added.

"I have reason to sigh," she answered.

"Have I forgotten to tell you what a brave girl you are?" he added.

"Because I trust you—a stranger?" she said with a light laugh.

"That was what I meant, Nao," he agreed.

"Under the circumstances I had no choice of doing what I am," she reminded him. "Certain death would have been mine had I remained upon Amo Island. With you, I am alive—and, strangely, I have no fear of the future. Two nights ago when I went to sleep, little would I have dreamed that I would now be fleeing with a stranger from the only home I had ever known."

There was nothing Bantan could say in reply.

Nao remained silent for several minutes before speaking again.

"Since I was a young girl I always had admired Amar, the chief's only son," she said. "But one does not always remain a child, and for many, many moons it seemed I realized I loved Amar. Every time he looked, smiled, or spoke to me, I would feel exalted. I now know it was my imagination that made me feel that way, for he did not seem to care in any especial way for me. For many moons I knew he had affairs with other girls in the village, and recently I learned he had been going to Ono Island. One hears of things like that, however secretly they are conducted. Amar was courting the daughter of the Ono Island's chief. Perhaps there was hope, that were he to mate with her, friendship would exist between the two islands. Yes, Bantan, I *thought*—" and she emphasized the word "—that I was in love with Amar. But I now know the difference between imaginative and real love."

Bantan did not speak. His attention had been arrested by a flash of sharp lightning in the northeastern sky, and to his alert ears came the distant rumbling of thunder.

"Nao, we are going to have a storm!" he exclaimed. "It would be certain death to continue in its direction. We shall have to return to Amo Island. It may be morning before we can leave in safety."

The girl caught her breath sharply, for she realized if they were apprehended, Aoono would claim them.

"Do what you think is best," she murmured tremblingly.

Quickly the paddler reversed the canoe's course. The stars were his only guide. With mighty strokes he sent the canoe back in the direction of Amo Island, and he earnestly hoped they could reach its sanctuary before the tropic storm broke in all its untamed fury.

Bantan realized it would have been suicidal to attempt to battle storm-tossed water in the canoe, and he was fortunate to have observed the oncoming storm when he did. In his mind there was the hope he could cover the intervening distance to the island that had so recently been quitted, for one could never determine the speed tropic storms are inclined to travel.

The darkness was fairly impenetrable, but there was one guide that was not to be overlooked. The looming volcano dimly could be seen silhouetted against the stars. Keeping this constantly as his goal, Bantan plied his paddle as he never had before, and the little craft responded nobly.

There was a stirring in the air now. The light breeze was rippling the until-now serene surface of the ocean. In the northeastern heaven the ominous masses of thunderheads were rapidly advancing from beyond the horizon. The lightning was more vivid and the thunder boomed louder.

The anxiety Bantan felt of their chances toward reaching the island before the tropic storm overtook them combined with the speedy strokes of his paddle brought great beads of perspiration upon his forehead. Rivulets rolled to his eye sockets, and then down his cheeks. Never had he paddled so furiously as now. His haste had never been so needy. Constantly were his eyes upon the looming volcano, and with the passing of desperate minutes he had the satisfaction of knowing he was drawing much closer to the island than when he had paddled away.

Nao was trembling in fear, and when a particularly brilliant flash of lightning streaked from the rolling storm clouds, she covered her eyes with her hands. She shuddered as the subsequent crash of thunder rolled in the heaven.

"Do you think we will reach the island before the storm breaks in all its fury?" she asked in low tones that trembled a little.

"I never paddled a canoe so fast as now, Nao," he replied.

The breeze was becoming fresher and the wavelets were growing in proportion with each passing minute. So speedily the canoe was skimming across the surface, as yet none of the wavelets washed over the sides. As the minutes passed it was only a question of when they would do so.

As the steadily increasing breeze shifted, so, too, did the waves that were slapping against the left side of the canoe, and thus were forcing the little water craft slightly off its original course.

Bantan plied his paddle mightily and he realized each minute's grace was precious to the life of Nao and himself. He was thankful the stirring breeze had relieved the humidity of the air, for with less difficulty he breathed.

Nao turned from where she was seated and her keen eyes detected the looming volcano silhouetted against the stars.

"Aoono is not too far away," she murmured encouragingly.

"But still not close enough, Nao," he answered.

Bantan's eyes swept the heaven, and he saw that now over a third was covered by the rolling thunderheads. The ominous masses seemed to advance more rapidly even as he looked. A vivid flash of lightning appeared from them and buried itself into the bosom of the distant water. A deafening crash of thunder followed almost immediately.

"The storm is getting much closer," Nao murmured fearfully. And then in a braver tone of voice, she added: "I have heard it said that death by drowning is not a bad way to die."

"Don't speak like that, Nao," the young giant admonished. "We are not going to die. We have much to live for."

In the darkness a sweet smile overcame the girl's face.

"Oh, how I hope so!" she sighed.

The brisk wind that had been blowing ceased abruptly. The elements always provided a warning. It was the calm that precedes the storm's breaking. The air again became humid. The profusely perspiring paddler desperately gasped for air with mouth open now to renew his consuming energy.

Another glance at the heaven overhead revealed over half was covered with the rapidly advancing storm clouds. A few pattering drops of rain fell, then subsided temporarily.

Bantan felt positive the storm would break before he could beach the canoe. Looking ahead, for a few desperate moments he endeavored to locate the looming volcano in the darkness that enveloped the ocean surface. That part of the sky fortunately had not as yet been reached by the rolling thunderheads, thus stars still could be seen.

With dismay, Bantan realized that his course had

deviated somewhat. He was now headed directly
toward Aoono Island, whereas the volcanic island
should have been slightly to his right. He realized
the beating waves had forced him off his true course.
With renewed strength he wielded his paddle, hoping
to return the canoe to its original one. The island
could not be more than a half-mile away now.

Tentative gusts of wind swept across the ocean's
surface and in seconds small wavelets increased considerably in size. The little canoe began to pitch and
toss, and many strokes of Bantan's paddle lost their
full efficacy. Squalls of great raindrops dotted the
ocean surface, heralding the storm's first attack, and
in moments Bantan and Nao were drenched. The
pelting rain did well to arouse the paddler's need of re-
served strength with which to wield his paddle. From
the bow he heard the girl utter a moan.

"We are near the end!" she called to him.

"Not yet, Nao," he shouted encouragingly.

"Anyway," the girl added, "I do not regret going
to my death with you. I would have preferred that
we had the opportunity of living our lives together in
the future."

Bantan did not answer to this. In these last
moments before the tropic storm broke in all its fury
and enveloped the canoe and its two occupants, he was
forcing the stout little water craft with every ounce of
strength at his command, thereby conserving the little
energy required for conversation for the last supreme
bid for success in his undertaking.

Again an ominous calm overcame the ocean beneath.
The squalls of rain ceased, and the humidity was all
but enervating. Sharper was the lightning that speared
the rolling heaven, and almost deafening were the
crashes of thunder that snapped loudly, then rever-

berated, and rolled overhead with nerve wracking effect.

A grim smile touched Bantan's serious features. In his heart there was the triumphant exultation that he was going to win through in safety.

Nao was terror-stricken. With each passing moment she expected a mighty gust of wind to overturn the canoe and sweep her and Bantan to their death into the chopping water. She wondered momentarily what unknown force restrained the storm's breaking.

As Bantan looked toward the looming volcano, so near ahead of them, he saw the rolling storm clouds blot out the last of the stars. No longer the volcanic cone could serve as his guide. Inky darkness prevented this except when a flash of lightning would momentarily light up the tableau of sky and water. In the lull the paddler thought he could hear the sound of the turbulent surf, but strain his eyes to their utmost as he did, he could not penetrate the blackness ahead.

A favoring flash of lightning revealed the white-capped waves near at hand, but to his dismay he realized the canoe was past Amo Island. There was no hope of landing upon the shore of that inhospitable island. He would not care about landing upon the volcanic island, for he believed no shelter could be obtained there. As a last resort the paddler decided he would have to beach the canoe upon the shore of Ono Island, for there at least the foliage would offer some manner of refuge.

And then the pent forces of the storm were unleashed in all its titanic fury. The wind descended upon the surface with shrieking intensity, whipping up mountainous waves. The heaven opened flood gates and water deluged down upon the immensity below. The lightning was blinding; the subsequent crashes of

thunder were deafening.   It seemed all hell had been
let loose.

And the canoe containing Bantan and Nao?

The first mighty blasts of wind nearly overturned
the stout little water craft.   With the dextrous use of
his paddle, Bantan prevented a near catastrophe.

"Brace yourself against the sides of the canoe,
Nao!" the young giant shouted to the girl.

"I am!" was the now confident reply.

Then came still more deluging rain.   The canoe
commenced to toss erratically.   Looking ahead of him,
Bantan saw a brilliant flash of lightning reveal a
tableau of waving trees and swaying foliage.

"We're in the surf, Nao!" Bantan shouted.   "Be
brave! We'll soon be on land."

He could not hear the girl's reply, owing to a
gust of shrieking wind.   With his paddle the young
giant managed to keep the canoe from overturning, but
it was a herculian task.   Water dashed over the sides.
Several inches already covered the bottom.   It would
be surprising that it did not founder before shore was
reached.

Above the fury of the wind and the rain, to Bantan's sharp ears came the pounding of the surf upon
the beach.   Seconds alone counted now—moments of
continued good fortune.

Watchfully, fearfully, Bantan expected the wild
wind to overturn the canoe, and only by constantly
paddling on the opposite side to the wild wind did he
manage to keep the water craft on a straight keel.
There were moments of frantic tossing and pitching,
and then the prow scraped onto the sandy beach.

"We've grounded, Nao!" he shouted.

Quickly placing the paddle in the bottom of the
canoe, Bantan leaped out and gripped the bow with

both hands. He held firm, and presently, with widespread feet braced in the sand against the pull of the undertow, felt its force lessen.

Drenched, her hair plastered over her face and neck, Nao drew herself out of the canoe. The wild wind, lashing rain against her and Bantan, imbued them with renewed strength.

"Follow me, Nao!" Bantan shouted his directions to the girl.

The girl bowed her head to escape the brunt of the wind-driven rain, and her hands followed along the canoe until she had reached the stern. She clutched it firmly. Bantan started toward the foliage, dragging the canoe after him. Nao followed. Into the wildly swaying foliage the young giant forged unmindful of the whipping branches that spurred him to greater effort. About ten feet from the beach where the foliage was less dense, Bantan paused.

"Are you all right, Nao?" he shouted to the girl.

The girl answered to the affirmative but was very much drenched from the heavy rain.

"I'm going to turn the canoe over to empty it of water," he said in a loud voice so that she would know what he intended doing.

Bantan grasped the paddle in one hand, not wishing to lose it, and with the other overturned the canoe. The bag containing Nao's drenched personal belongings were whipped away and scattered hopelessly upon the darkened beach by a mighty gust of wind that almost loosened the canoe from the man's firm grasp.

While in the act, with his back to the savage, wind-driven rain, a brilliant flash of lightning revealed the tableau just ahead—a clearing! At sight of what was to be seen, joy welled in Bantan's heart. About twenty feet ahead of him a dilapidated hut stood. In that brief moment of revealing light, the young giant noted the walls seemed stable enough even though a portion of the roof had caved in.

"Nao, there is an old hut ahead," he called to the girl. "It will provide shelter from the storm."

Again gripping the bow of the canoe, Bantan dragged it along, with the girl following and clinging to the rear. Moments later they were searching for the door, and it was to be found upon the right side facing away from the wall nearest the beach. The canoe was dragged through the opened doorway and the drenched girl followed in its wake. Leaving the canoe to one side of the door, Bantan reached for Nao's hand, and together they sought the driest spot the interior of the old hut offered. In the Stygian gloom, lighted at intervals from sharp flashes of lightning that came through the gaping hole in the roof, through which rain poured, the man and the girl came to a pallet of old grasses near the wall farthest from the door.

While Bantan slumped to it with a sigh of relief, Nao drew to one side and wrung her dress in several places, squeezing the water from it. Presently she groped her way to her companion's side. Damp though their scant clothing was, they were thankful their fate was not worse. The girl pushed her wet hair over her shoulders while Bantan smoothed his back in pompadour fashion.

"It is hard to believe we have survived," Nao murmured.

"But we have!" he said with exultation. "We were fortunate to have found this old hut. At least it shelters us from the wind and the rain."

At Bantan's spoken words, a great gust of wind-driven rain fairly caused the hut to tremble. The two occupants fervently hoped the old structure would withstand the mighty blasts.

"This is much better than being out in the storm," the girl said after a short silence.

"Much better, Nao," Bantan answered. "Even though by morning the storm will have died down, the ocean will be too rough to attempt to resume our way."

"So long as the Ono villagers don't find us," Nao said, "we will be safe."

For moments they were silent, listening to the wild fury of the storm. Coconuts could be heard dropping to the ground. Limbs from other trees could be heard snapping from the mother trunk and crashing to the earth beneath. One limb fell near the abandoned hut, just missing a corner, and the two occupants were thankful it had not crashed against the roof or walls. After this had occurred, one of the girl's hands sought her companion's and she sighed.

"Poor Nao," he murmured compassionately. "I am afraid you may regret having known me. We've had a rough time of it so far."

The girl laughed softly.

"I don't seem to mind anything at all—now," she said. "Even the loss of my belongings doesn't seem to bother me."

"I'm sorry that had to happen, Nao," was his rejoinder.

One of Bantan's arms went about her shoulders protectingly and he drew her closer to him. The girl rested her head against his broad shoulder.

"Would you believe me if I told you something?" she asked, her warm breath fanning his cheek.

"What, Nao?" he murmured.

"I don't think I have ever been so content—as I am now," she confessed.

He inclined his head and placed his cheek against hers, and for a long while they sat thus, not speaking a word—seemingly content that they were together and sheltered from the storm. Outside, the fury of the storm reached its peak, then slowly began to subside.

With the passing minutes Bantan became aware Nao was breathing gently and she had become lax, slumping against him. Gently he eased her back on the pallet of grass. For a few moments she stirred and he thought she was reawaking, but then with a deep sigh she remained still. From her lips was to be heard incoherent mumbling.

For a little while he remained awake, listening to the gradually subsiding storm, then he, too, stretched himself near the sleeping girl, and in a few moments was fast asleep.

Time and again during the night while in deep slumber, Bantan's muscles writhed, and an unusual roaring throbbed in his ears. Sharp pains stabbed within his head. Strangely, he did not awake. A short while before dawn he heaved a deep sigh and thereafter slept peacefully.

Bantan's first intimation that morning had come was when he heard the noisy twittering of birds. Opening his eyes, he saw that the interior of the hut was light. Sunlight streamed in through the gaping hole in the roof. When he moved he grimaced because of the stiffness of his muscles. In a moment he arose to a seated position and looked about him wonderingly.

A quizzical expression appeared in his dark eyes. He had been dreaming of Marja Island, also Kalma and her father. His dreams included Wanya, his foster sister, and Beneiro and Skilda, his foster parents. He looked about the interior of the hut, and he shook his head as though unable to believe his present position. He recollected his return to Beneiro Island and his subsequent capture by the Waneiro women under the leadership of Mazona. It had been a blow upon the head from Mazona's club that had caused his amnesia.* Now, clearly, he recalled everything, including Nao. With a sudden start he wondered where she was.

"Nao?" he called softly. And when he did not receive a reply he called again to the girl.

He arose to his feet, stretching, then walked to the doorway and looked outside to survey the havoc the storm had wrought the night before. Mighty branches from trees were strewn about the dilapidated hut, and only by a miracle one particularly large branch had just missed a corner in its descent. Coconuts were strewn profusely about the ground. Vapor from the moist earth was rising upward in response to the warm rays of the rising sun.

Hearing a crackling of twigs from the front of the old hut, Bantan softly stole around the corner to behold Nao approaching with arms ladened with several varieties of fruit. The girl looked radiant, her features bright and smiling. Her lustrous hair had been neatly combed. She appeared none the worse for her harrowing experience of the previous night. At sight of the bronzed young giant, her smile became radiant.

"Nao!" he exclaimed with a cheery smile.

"You're a sleepy head," she chided him. "I've bathed and combed my hair, and even gathered our breakfast.

"While you prepare it I'll take a quick swim, Nao," he said. "Are we anywhere near the Ono village?" he asked as an after thought.

---

*Note: See *"Bantan Valiant"*

"I heard no sounds," the girl answered with a shake of her head.

Bantan's keen nostrils quivered. The acrid scent of smoke was very faint, so he was positive they were a considerable distance from the village of the Ono people.

"We won't have to worry for a while, Nao," he assured her. "The scent of their cook fires is very faint."

"Do you mean that you can smell the cook fires of the Ono village from where we are?" the girl asked with a shake of her head and a perplexed expression in her dark eyes.

"That's right," he said with a smile.

Nao could only shake her head.

"It's beyond me," was her only comment.

Bantan went to the beach and indulged in a quick swim. He kept his eyes alert for any possible inhabitants from the Ono village. When he returned to the hut, feeling much refreshed, he found that Nao had prepared the morning meal and was awaiting him. Seated opposite each other in a squatting fashion, the man and the girl smiled to one another and proceeded to partake of their matutinal repast.

As they ate, Bantan mentally compared Nao with Leona Brown, Kalma, and Wanya. Knowing the girl but two days, strangely it seemed he had known her a long while. There was no denying Nao was very attractive, and the peculiar circumstances that had brought them together was almost unbelievable, considering the sequel that was now in effect.

It is to be wondered if Kalma's dear spirit would rest contented to know that Bantan had found a girl who would be capable of taking her place in his heart. It was not that any one could really do that, but only as a reasonable substitute. He convinced himself that

Kalma was not of selfish spirit, even in death. They had loved one another very dearly. The fact that she had taken her own life rather than be defiled by their enemy proved her truthfulness to Bantan. Believing him to be dead, it was the taking of her own life in the hope her spirit would join his in that other world beyond the grave. The young giant had since forgiven Kalma because of the circumstances that had prevailed at that time. He was positive had she known he was alive she would have refrained from taking her life only as a last extremity.

The young giant was aroused from his reveries at the sound of the girl clearing her throat. With a shake of his head he looked at her. She was studying him curiously.

"Yes, Nao?" he asked.

"Your thoughts seemed far away," she remarked with concern in her dark eyes.

He nodded slowly.

"They were," he admitted.

"Were—were they too precious to tell me?" An humble appeal was to be detected in her tone.

"No, Nao, I think I should tell you," he answered. "Then, perhaps, you may understand if, sometimes, my thoughts seem far away."

Her steady, questioning eyes importuned him to speak further.

"Memory of who I am has returned to me," he said. "This morning when I awoke I was aware I had been dreaming of where I had come from and the friends that are mine."

The Amo girl heaved a sigh of relief.

"I'm so happy," she murmured. "Please tell me your name."

"It is Bantan," he replied. "It means white child

from the sea born of unknown parents."

"Bantan," Nao crooned. Again she repeated the name. A smile touched her lips. "I like the name Bantan very much."

"If you wish, Nao," he added, "I'll tell you all about the people with whom I have lived since I was found by Beneiro, who is my foster father. Would you care to listen?"

"Of course, Bantan," the Amo girl murmured assuringly, "I want to know all about you."

And so Bantan told Nao of his life with the Beneiro, and later of Mr. Brown and his lovely daughter Leona, who had come in search of him. * As a result of inherent pride he had deserted them, but subsequently had come to know of Kalma while suffering from amnesia, and who, with her American father, a doctor, had cared for him. When his lost memory had been restored to him he realized he loved two women, one a white girl and the other an island goddess. ** He added how the white girl had returned for him, but realizing his state of feelings toward Kalma, she had sent him back to the island goddess. He then related how the coming of a new enemy had prevented his marriage to Kalma, and believing him dead, she had taken her own life rather than be defiled by the leader of the enemy.*** He went on to state he had left Marja Island after the enemy had been eventually vanquished, and thus he had come to Amo Island after an event upon Beneiro which had resulted in another amnesia spell overtaking him. He did not forget to speak of Wanya, his foster sister, and he sighed deeply as he remembered the last occasion of their being together.

---

*Note: See *"Bantan of the Islands"*
**Note: See *"Bantan and the Island Goddess"*
***Note: See *"Bantan Defiant"*

"She loves me very much, Nao," Bantan concluded. "But I, feeling she is like a sister to me, could not return her love. As a result, though Kalma is no longer of this world, my thoughts often are of her."

Nao's smile was an understanding one.

"You loved Kalma very much, Bantan," she divined.

"More than words can tell," he admitted.

"And when you come to know another girl," she added, "your thoughts go back beyond the grave and you wonder if you are being fair to Kalma's memory. Isn't that the truth?"

He nodded solemnly.

A sad smile touched Nao's lips.

"I think I can understand how you feel, Bantan," she said. "Do you wish to tell me more about her?"

With a strange sadness in his breast, Bantan told Nao all that she wanted to know about the Marja Island goddess. He evaded no questions that she might ask. After some little while had passed he seemed to feel relieved that he had unburdened himself to this seemingly understanding girl, for he could easily determine Nao was not jealous of his former sweetheart's memory.

A little later he dried the moisture in the automatic. Nao seated herself beside him. The questions she asked about civilized man's weapons were simple and direct, but the eagerness with which she asked her questions were indicative of an active mind. Bantan answered all her questions to the best of his ability. She even insisted that she be permitted to assist him. In these little helpful ways Nao hoped to impress Bantan of her willingness to share the trivial things in life with him before undertaking the more vital ones. There was no restraint between them, and when there was occasion to laugh they did so together whole-heartedly.

While they dried and polished the mechanism, Bantan stressed the potency of the little glittering shells with the blunt grayish blob on the end. When the pieces of metal were dried and polished, Bantan explained how the pressure of the forefinger upon the trigger released a spring that permitted a hammer to descend upon the cap on the end of the cartridge, detonating it. He called to her attention the safety latch and for which purpose it was used.

"Were we upon Marja Island, Nao," he added, "I would show you how the automatic works. But here, with enemies not too distant, they would hear the report and would investigate—and find us."

Nao's intelligence was evident and she rarely had to have any particular subject explained a second time. The information Bantan relegated to the girl pertaining to the automatic, he informed her this in turn had been imparted to him from Kalma's father, who had passed the earlier years of his life in America.

"Do you ever regret you did not return to America when you had the chance, Bantan?" Nao asked with steady eyes upon his.

He shook his head.

"I should regret that I didn't," he answered; "but in my heart I find it hard to convince myself. I had been told much of life in America by Leona Brown and her father, also by Kalma's father. Sometimes I was afraid to go to a land that differed so much from the life I had always known here." With a shrug of his giant shoulders, he added: "That is in the past. I didn't go."

The girl's smile was warm.

"I'm glad you didn't, Bantan," she said. "Had you gone to that faraway land you call America, who would have saved me from the wild boar?"

Nao's smile was so infectious that he could not repress the one that touched his lips.

"That is true, Nao," he agreed.

"And we wouldn't be together as we are now," she added.

"That, too, is true," he answered.

Both laughed heartily. Then Bantan suggested a swim and Nao readily agreed. They arose, and hand in hand went to the shore. While they swam in the calm water beyond the surf, the girl proved to be an excellent swimmer. Her actions reminded the young giant of Wanya's capability at swimming.

Unknown to the bronzed young giant and the girl, two pairs of startled dark eyes had watched them emerge from the hut and go to the shore. When the man and the girl had passed from view, the owners of the startled eyes looked at one another in amazement. With a nod they parted the screening fronds of a magnificent fern that concealed them and stealthily walked to the doorway of the hut.

They were two youths from the distant Ono village. They were about eleven years of age. For some time they had been coming to this abandoned hut where previously an old hermit by name of Zema had taken up his existence following some minor difference of opinion with the other natives. Zema was considered somewhat demented, and the villagers had not protested when the old hermit wished to pass his declining years without interference. As a matter of fact they were relieved when he had left the village.

Ulo and Lato, the two youths, had often come to visit the old hermit, and it was they who had found him dead one morning—having died of natural causes during the night. They returned to the village with the announcement of their discovery. Later, several warriors returned and buried the old hermit.

The two youths seldom came to the old abandoned hut after Zema's demise. This morning, however, after the previous night's storm, they met and decided to go and see if the storm had completely wrecked the dilapidated hut. They had come and discovered it had weathered the storm remarkably well, but at present was being occupied by a bronzed young giant and a lovely girl. Having heard them speak, and recognizing their speech, Ula and Lato assumed that they were from Amo Island, since they did not recognize them as members of the village.

At the doorway of the hut their inquisitive eyes peered within. The canoe at once arrested their attention, and examining it hurriedly, they realized it was not as the canoes upon the Ono landing, therefore, must be from Amo.

"Ula, we must return to the village and report our discovery," Lato said.

"We must do that, Lato," his companion agreed.

With stealth they left the vicinity of the abandoned hut, and only until they had reached a considerable distance from the old hut did they break into a run for the distant village.

Two young boys running into the Ono village was not a rare spectacle, but when announcement of their discovery was made known, then there was cause for excitement. Within a few moments after their arrival, a warrior, the father of Ula, hurried to the hut of the chief with the information that a strange, bronzed man and a beautiful girl had been seen in the vicinity of the abandoned hut the hermit Zema had occupied.

Roko was in his late forties and inclined to obesity. His graying hair was cut short and inclined backward. His features were round and flabby, his eyes dreamy, his mouth weak, and his chin was surrounded by a layer of fat. He wore a sack-like robe upon the breast of which was embroidered a likeness of Oom, the idol. A narrow band of *tupa* cloth encircled his forehead in the center of which was fastened a beautiful red stone not unlike a ruby. The chief had been suffering from ennui for some moons, and the news that the father of Ula brought roused him from his seeming inertia.

"Maho, take five warriors with you and capture them," Roko directed. "Exercise caution, for we want them alive. Your son and Lato will be well rewarded for their discovery."

Bowing in reverence, Maho departed from the chief's hut. In a few minutes six warriors, armed with stone daggers and stone-tipped spears, were off on their mission.

Thus it was as Bantan and Nao were partaking of their noon day meal, they were unaware that watchers were screened in the surrounding foliage, awaiting a signal from Maho, their leader, to leap upon them.

Maho was looking at the seated young giant, and he realized he would not be an easy capture. The girl would not be too difficult. Word was passed around to the warriors in hushed whispers that Tolu would attend to the girl, while the five others were to concentrate their attention upon the man.

Bantan and Nao had no intimation of the eyes that watched their every movement. Partaking of their noon day meal in the shade of a giant barringtonia tree a short distance from the old hut, they were happy as could be. An observer would have suspected they were honeymooners, for their glances at one another were of a shy nature.

They were discussing the best possible time to leave the island for Marja, when, unknown to them, a signal flashed among the silent watchers.

The six warriors left their spears where they were, and from as many directions they were dashing toward the seated couple enjoying their meal. Nao's surprise was so overwhelming that she had no opportunity of reaching her feet before Tolu seized her. Despite her fierce struggle, she was no match for the sturdy warrior who imprisoned her arms, rendering her helpless.

"Bantan!" she shrieked.

Bantan, however, was more active, his reflexes swifter. He managed to reach his feet and looked at three of his adversaries. But before he could draw a dagger, an unseen and unsuspected enemy from his rear leaped toward him and imprisoned the right hand, preventing its withdrawal of the dagger. Turning about quickly, and dragging the warrior with him in the movement, the bronzed giant prevented the three warriors from leaping upon him, since the warrior he swung about struck two of them, hurling them backward, and just missing the third. This warrior maneuvered about and imprisoned his flailing arm.

The fifth warrior delegated to help subdue Bantan leaped for his legs and wrapped his arms about them. The bronzed giant lurched, tried to pull one leg free, and failing, tried the other—but was powerless. He sought again to free his imprisoned right hand, and then the left, but with no success. The effort, combined with a tug from the warrior holding his right arm, pulled the bronzed giant off balance. His legs, imprisoned in a seeming grip of steel, could not be spread to brace himself. As a result, he went down with two of the recovered warriors on top of him.

Writhing mightily, Bantan strove with every ounce of strength at his command to be free of the seeming tentacles that gripped his arms and legs. For tense minutes the struggle went on, and finally the bronzed

giant was rolled over upon his back, and four warriors
held him down, one capturing each of his arms and
legs.   Lying there, his massive chest heaving as a
result of his futile struggle, Bantan looked up at the
leader of the warriors.

"Why are we taken captives?" he demanded of
Maho who, now having procured his spear and holding
it menacingly, was looking speculatively at the prisoner.

"You and the girl must be from Amo Island," he
said with a knowing leer.   "We are not friendly with
the Amo islanders.   Since you and the girl are now
upon Ono Island, that is sufficient reason for your capture."

"But we have done no harm," Bantan protested.
"We did not intend to come here. The storm last night
compelled us to land and seek shelter. We intended to
leave before the coming night."

Maho laughed aloud at the captive's protest.

"Strangers who come to Ono Island and are captured," he answered, "need not worry about leaving.
It was fortunate the storm compelled you both to seek
sanctuary here. Too long has the village lacked excitement. Now we should have some."

With his words Maho turned and walked to the
abandoned hut and looked within. Espying the canoe,
he paused to examine it. A cursory examination revealed it was unlike the canoes of Ono Island, and
where it had originated was from none other than Amo.
Yet, upon closer examination, he realized it differed.
He did not observe the automatic and belt of cartridges
carefully concealed in the bow, covered with grass.
He did, however, see the bow and arrows. These he
took with him when he returned outside. When he
confronted the now standing prisoner he examined him

more critically. Observing the dagger sheathed at his right hip, he snatched it from the prisoner.

"Your canoe is not like ours or the Amo village," he said. "Nor, do you look like a native. Who are you, and from where did you come?

"I am a white man, born in faraway America—far across the ocean," Bantan replied. "The most of my life has been lived upon Beneiro Island. You would know nothing of that island?"

Maho shook his head.

"Where did you get these?" he asked, indicating the bow and arrows.

"I made them," the bronzed giant replied. He noted Maho had not found the automatic and the cartridge belt, and he fervently hoped they would remain unfound. He entertained the almost hopeless possibility that he might one day be in a position to have use for them.

"You will be questioned further by our chief, stranger," Maho said. He turned and beckoned Tolu to come forward with the girl captive.

"What is your name and from where do you come?" he demanded, when the girl was brought before him.

"My name is Nao," she replied. "I come from Amo Island."

Maho laughed, exposing his unusually large white teeth.

"Roko, our chief, will be pleased to know we have an Amo prisoner," he remarked; "and a very beautiful one, too." Then, with a signal to the warriors holding Bantan prisoner: "Come, let us return to the village. Roko will be impatient to see his captives."

The girl's fearful eyes managed to catch Bantan's attention.

"I am sorry your choice in going with me has resulted in this, Nao," he said to her with a sorrowful shake of his head.

"I don't regret it," the girl moaned. "I should have known my happiness was too precious to last.".

In silence, thereafter, menaced by stone-tipped spears, the two prisoners were marched in the direction of the distant village. Hopeless indeed was their predicament, and even Bantan's slumped shoulders gave evidence to his despair. If there could be any hope —that was one thing. But how could there be any in his present position?

Time and again during the march to the village Nao, who was in the lead, would look back at Bantan. When she would catch his attention she would smile bravely, though in truth she was terror-stricken. In return, he would smile, but in his heart he knew he could offer her no hope. Each time that she smiled to him, he had more reason to admire her bravery. More determined he became to make a break for freedom. But each time he felt like suiting to action this determination, a glance at the menacing stone tipped spears and the eyes of those who carried them, dispelled the rash plan from his mind. A break for freedom would result in failure—possibly death.

It was nearly an hour later when the search party returned to the village. At sight of the two captives, the villagers called to one another in turn, spreading the word of the successful return of the search party. Boys and girls darted about the captives and shouted in glee. Some of the more daring boys picked up branches and sought to reach a closer proximity to the captives so that they might whip their legs. Maho shouted threats of dire punishment to them if they didn't desist.

From the edge of the village, Bantan and Nao had

observed the imposing totem-like idol that towered above the huts. Now that they stood near it, both looked up at it with awe and respect for what it represented. Oom, the deity of the Ono villagers, was fifty feet in height. Its base was a large, white, rounded rock ten feet high and eight feet in diameter. Upon this was set twenty stones of a similar diameter but only two feet in height, one on top of the other, and fastened securely enough so that the strongest gales had failed to topple the idol in the several centuries that had passed since its construction. Upon each stone above the base had been carved the features of a lesser god. The artisans of the time had been patient and had performed their work with the utmost skill.

Upon the top of the twentieth stone had been placed another exactly twice the size of the smaller stones featuring the lesser gods. Upon this had been carved another face. Closer examination would reveal that the top stone duplicated a part of each of the twenty smaller featured stones, and this composite face was the God of all the lesser gods.

While Bantan and Nao studied the idol with interest, Maho instructed his warriors to keep constant watch over the prisoners while he informed Roko of his successful mission. Entering the chief's hut, he found Roko seated in his throne chair which set upon a dais. The chief appeared expectant and his eyes lighted as he saw Maho enter. The warrior bowed in reverence, then straightening, he smiled.

"We have captured the strangers, O Chief," he announced. "It was as Ula and Lato said. There was a man and a girl. Shall I have them brought in for your inspection?"

"At once, Maho," the chief answered with an impatient movement of his hands.

"It shall be as you wish, O Chief," and bowing respectfully, Maho turned and went outside.

In a few moments Bantan and Nao were ushered into the chief's hut to behold the ruler of Ono Island seated upon his throne, awaiting them. Guards stood at either side. The bronzed giant noted the furnishings of the huge room consisted of several rattan chairs and a table. About the walls hand-made clay vessels were attached, each being filled with sweet-smelling flowers.

At sight of the two prisoners Roko's interest was instantly aroused. Looking firstly at the girl, his breathing became rapid, stertorous. An unholy gleam appeared in his eyes that until now had been dreamy. The haughty manner Nao looked at the enemy chief was clearly indicative that she entertained no fear of him.

The chief then shifted his eyes to the bronzed young giant at the girl's side. Bantan stood tall and straight, and defiance gleamed in his dark eyes. As he looked at the chief, he could understand that he was considered an inferior being, for a supercilious sneer now possessed Roko's mouth.

"You and the girl are strangers upon Ono Island, are you not?" the chief interrogated in a rather high-pitched tone of voice.

"That is true," Bantan replied. Before the chief could ask another question, he quickly added: "Since we are strangers, why have we been taken captives? We have done no harm to any of your people."

An expression of annoyance overcame Roko's features.

"Prisoners do not ask questions," he said angrily. "They need only answer the questions I ask."

Nao's hand sought Bantan's and clasped it tightly. Looking at her he smiled encouragingly.

"Who is this girl and what is she to you, prisoner?"
Roko then asked with asperity.

"She is mine," was the bronzed giant's answer.

Roko smiled evilly as his eyes shifted to the girl
captive.

At Bantan's reply, Nao heaved a deep sigh and her
dark eyes radiated her feeling toward him.

"Woman, does this man speak the truth?" the chief
demanded of Nao, though he well knew what her
answer would be, for he had seen the lovelight in her
eyes for the bronzed giant.

The girl looked proudly at the chief with head held
high.

"It is true," she answered.

"From where do you come?" the chief then asked
of the girl.

"I am from Amo Island," was Nao's reply.

Roko nodded his head.

"And you, stranger," he demanded, shifting his attention to Bantan; "from where do you come?"

"From faraway America," was Bantan's reply. "I
am not a native by birth. I am a white man."

Roko had never heard of America, and since he had
never seen a white man, it was of small importance to
him that Bantan was of white origin.

"Then you did not come from Amo Island?" he interrogated. "Yet the girl does. Are you lying to
me?" The chief's voice rose to a high pitch near a
breaking point.

"It is true what Bantan says," Nao said, hoping to
mollify the chief's antagonism toward the bronzed
young giant.

Roko shifted his attention to the girl. He was
smiling again.

" 'Bantan'?—you say his name is," he said with apparent interest. "That is a native name."

"Bantan was born in America," Nao explained; "but he lived the most of his life upon Beneiro Island."

The chief shifted his attention to the bronzed giant. His eyes were accusing.

"Why didn't you tell me that?" he demanded.

Bantan shrugged his broad shoulders. The interrogation was becoming tiresome and there was no sense to it. He met the chief's eyes defiantly.

"You told me I was to answer questions," he replied. "You did not ask my name."

Roko's eyes glinted angrily.

"You are insolent," he said. "Maho, take him to the prison hut. I wish to question this girl further—alone."

Nao's hand clutched Bantan's and the sorrowful expression in her eyes would have impelled the young giant to defy the chief and all his warriors if it could have helped matters any. Maho gripped an arm while another warrior held the other.

"I will be all right, Bantan," Nao murmured in a brave little voice. "I do not fear the chief."

Bantan shuddered because of his helplessness, and in that moment his eyes rested upon Nao's he observed a tear roll from her misty eyes, leaving a moist pathway upon her cheek. Bitterness surged through the bronzed giant. He turned glaring eyes to the chief.

"If you so much as harm a single hair of her head, I'll find a way to kill you!" he said in icy tones.

Although Roko smiled, a chill raced up and down the length of his spine, for there was something in the bronzed stranger's eyes and tone of voice that clearly indicated were he in a position to carry out his threat, the result would not be an idle gesture.

"Take him away, Maho," Roko shouted in an effort to masquerade his craven fear. "Have two guards posted outside the door of this hut—just in case the girl captive becomes violent."

In another moment the chief's hut was empty except for Roko and Nao. The girl was bravely fighting back the tears that threatened.

The chief smiled unctuously.

"Come, do not be frightened," he said in appeasing tones. "Come closer. I would talk with you further. You interest me."

Tossing her head back, Nao straightened her drooped shoulders with defiance and took several steps toward the chief.

"Come closer," Roko said softly. "You still are too far away."

Nao took two more steps, then halted. She was about six feet from where the throne stood in which Roko reposed, leaning forward a trifle.

When the girl refused to budge another inch, even though the chief insisted, Roko suddenly burst out into hilarious laughter. The girl looked at him strangely, but she was still unafraid.

"You love Bantan very much," he said when his laughter ceased. "I could read your devotion for him in your eyes when he was taken away."

"I love him very much," Nao replied in all honesty. "If I had not loved him I would not have left Amo Island."

Roko nodded, his eyes possessing a faraway look.

"It must be wonderful to be young and in love," he mused. "How I have wished I were young again and experiencing my first love."

Nao regarded the chief with surprise to think he could be sentimental. Vaguely she tried to understand what his objective was. Though her inner sense of respect and decency rebelled, she decided to humor him.

"But you were young once and must have experienced love then," she said in a low voice. "You are cruel to torment me this way by taking my man away from me."

An expression of annoyance crossed Roko's features, but that did not lessen the increasing glow in his dark eyes that rested constantly upon the girl, as though he were hypnotized by her beauty. Meeting his eyes, Nao inwardly shuddered at what she read therein.

"What is your name?" the chief asked then.

"I am called Nao," she replied.

" 'Nao,' " he repeated. "It is a nice name. Yes, I like it very much." He nodded complacently. "It is very becoming to your beauty."

With his words Roko seemed about to arise from his throne, but a moment later he sank back and sighed.

"Nao, won't you come closer?" he asked, his voice dropping to a purr.

The girl refused to budge from where she stood. She was as close to the chief as she cared to be.

A look of displeasure crossed Roko's face, and as he was in the act of arising from his throne again, the door suddenly opened. The chief's eyes were expressionless as he looked at his only daughter entering.

Nao turned and looked at a beautiful girl about her own age standing inside the doorway. Her manner was regal and her well formed features were to be considered beautiful despite her supercilious manner. A headband fashioned from soft cloth encircled her head and at the center of her forehead a pretty red stone was fastened in the band. A halter with an unique

design embroidered thereupon covered her prominent
bosom. The brilliant piece of cloth that was wrapped
tightly about her hips and extended half way to her
well rounded knees accentuated the voluptuousness of
her slim figure. The fingers of her right hand were
idly pressing the exquisite necklace of small sea shells
about her neck. Her sensuous lips parted and the wet
tip of her tongue moved over them.

"Lori," the chief said in a flat voice.

Roko's daughter was appraising Nao. Her dark
eyes went from the top of the girl's head down to her
feet, and then back to Nao's face.

"This is the girl captive, father?" the princess asked.

Her father nodded.

Lori's eyes brightened with interest.

"What are you going to do with her?" she then
asked.

"I haven't decided," was the reply accompanied by
the shake of his head.

The princess approached the captive, and walking
slowly about the silent girl, a cruel smile touched her
lips. There was something about the haughty captive
that Lori admired—perhaps it was her defiant spirit
—something the princess possessed. In her sadistic
mind perhaps she would enjoy breaking the girl's spirit
until she cringed and begged for mercy. She was well
aware she needed some new recreation to enliven her
otherwise dull existence.

"May I keep her until you have decided, father?"
the princess said with a note of unmistakable pleading
in her tones. "If she doesn't behave, I'll have her
beaten. She looks too proud—for a captive."

Roko shook his shoulders hopelessly. Ever since his
mate had died two years before, Lori's wishes had—
could not—be denied. The girl was a great deal like

her mother—selfish—her wishes always came first. At first, when his mate had died, Roko had been happy. But the passing moons had brought him under Lori's domination. With a final glow in his eyes that faded, the chief's eyes shifted to his daughter.

"She is yours, Lori," he said resignedly.

Nao felt relieved and she sighed at the chief's decision in favor of his daughter.

"Thank you, father," the princess said sweetly. Then the sweetness vanished from her tone and manner. Turning to Nao, she spoke a single word that was imperative: "Come."

The girl captive cast a final glance at Roko and realized the disappointment he suffered at seeing her go. With shoulders still squared and her head proudly held high, she followed the princess of Ono Island out of the chief's hut.

From the prison hut directly across the lane separating the chief's hut, Bantan was watching through the single, barred window. His attention was fascinated by the carvings upon the village idol. As he saw Nao follow the chief's daughter, he could not restrain the impulse to shout to the girl.

"Nao!"

The girl turned instantly in the direction from which her name was shouted and her heart was saddened to see Bantan's smiling face from behind the barred window. As she turned, so, too, did Lori, at hearing the girl's name spoken.

"He was the stranger taken captive with you, Nao?" Lori demanded.

"He is Bantan," the girl replied.

" 'Bantan'," the princess repeated. To herself she admitted the name was pleasing. Again she murmured the name, "Bantan." She decided with a nod that she liked the name very much.

"Come, Nao," Lori said, "I would look upon the prisoner."

Together they walked to the barred window. Nao's eyes were moist as she looked at Bantan, but his dark eyes were gladdened by the sight of the Amo girl. To his nostrils was wafted a strangely pleasing perfume that emanated from the beautiful girl at Nao's side. It reminded him somewhat of that which Kalma had used when she lived.

Lori was studying the bronzed giant's handsome features with more than mere interest. Her breathing quickened as evidenced by the fast rise and fall of her bosom. The cruelty of her lips was relieved by a gentle smile. It was this smiling face and strangely glowing eyes that Bantan looked at and studied for a moment. Gratitude was in his heart toward this beautiful girl who had spared Nao from an unknown fate at the hands of the chief. Though her smile appeared friendly enough, he had reason to wonder at the strange glow in her dark eyes. The words of gratitude upon his lips could not be withheld, and speaking them, he knew she would understand their connotation.

"Thank you."

Lori's glowing eyes did not waver. She seemed hypnotized by the handsome bronzed giant.

Nao looked quickly at her in the strange silence that prevailed, and what she read in Lori's eyes made her shudder. She firmly pressed a hand to her fast-beating heart.

Then, with an effort, the princess removed her eyes from Bantan, and turning to Nao, spoke one word in a pleasing tone of voice that still was imperative.

"Come."

Without a word Bantan and Nao parted, but the expression in their eyes was most eloquent.

Lori did not utter another word until they reached the hut next to her father's that she occupied. The girl captive knew that the princess was disturbed inwardly, for her long, slender fingers with exceptionally long nails clenched repeatedly. Once she caught sight of one of the palms where the nails had pressed intensely. She noticed how indented it was.

The hut the princess occupied was rather sumptuously furnished with rattan furniture and finely woven mats with all sorts of unique designs embroidered thereupon. Hand-fashioned urns of clay, gaily painted, were numerous, and each were filled daily with sweet-smelling flowers. Upon a dais at the opposite side of the hut from the door set a spacious bed. At its foot crouched a young native girl with impassive features. Lori looked toward her imperiously and indicated the door.

The slave girl wordlessly arose and bowed, then hurried past the princess and the girl captive without looking either way. Outside the door, which she closed as she passed out of the hut, she squatted with features that were unchanged. Her ears were strained, however, to overhear the conversation within.

Lori flung herself upon the bed and stretched upon her stomach, her chin pillowed upon the back of her hands. She beckoned to Nao to come close and be seated upon the floor near her. The girl captive did as she was bid. The princess apparently was deep in retrospection, and for all the attention she paid Nao, she might have been alone. Lori's thoughts were of the handsome bronzed giant. At last she roused herself with a visible effort and turned her attention to the girl captive.

"Nao, are you mated to Bantan?" she asked.

The girl captive slowly shook her head.

"We have only known one another less than three suns," she replied.

"Yet you love him very much," the princess murmured.

Nao's eyes glowed.

"I love him so very much that because of him I left my home and my friends," she answered truthfully.

The shadow of a smile touched Lori's lips. The moist tip of her tongue slowly traversed her upper lip and then the lower. A strange gleam possessed her half closed eyes.

"You know, Nao," she said then, "all strangers who come to Ono Island must die."

The girl captive nodded her head as she closed her eyes.

"The law of Ono Island is the same as that of Amo," Nao said, opening her eyes that were a trifle misty. "If Bantan and I had not left Amo when we did, we would have been condemned to die. At least Aoono has been cheated of us."

"Death upon Ono Island is not pleasant for a stranger," Lori resumed.

Nao shuddered, but did not speak.

"Only I have the power to sway my father in his judgement toward a prisoner," the princess added.

Nao's eyes were pleading as they sought the strangely regarding ones of Lori.

"You could spare Bantan's life?" she murmured hopefully.

The princess nodded her head and closed her eyes. When they presently opened a smile touched her thin lips.

"And I could spare you, too," she added. "But —there would be conditions."

Nao remained silent, hardly drawing a breath.

"You, Nao, would have to sacrifice your love for Bantan," Lori resumed. "I saw the manner in which my father looked at you. He has been stricken by your beauty. You have the choice of becoming his slave."

The girl captive shuddered at the crafty bargain the princess was presenting to her.

"I cannot say how long you will continue to please him," Lori added. "That would be your problem."

"But under what conditions would you spare Bantan's life?" Nao asked with a sudden chill gripping her heart.

The princess shrugged her shoulders in evident displeasure at the girl captive's question.

"That does not concern you," she said sharply.

Nao raised her head proudly and she arose to her feet.

A strange light blazed in the eyes of the princess.

"Sit down, Nao!" she commanded. "I did not tell you to stand."

The girl captive remained standing, apparently unheedful of the command of the princess. Her head bowed and her shoulders quivered. She had believed she could cope with Lori and was thankful when the princess obtained her release from her father, the chief. Now she realized how hopeless her position was.

"I told you to sit down, Nao!" the princess all but shouted.

The Amo girl captive still remained standing.

A cat could not have moved as swiftly as Lori did. In an instant she was upon her feet, standing at the side of the silently suffering girl captive. A maniacal

light gleamed in the flashing eyes of the princess. Her
beautiful features were contorted in rage.

"You defy me?" she shrieked.

Still Nao did not answer—did not raise her head
to look at Lori.

With a scream of unmitigated rage, the princess
drew back her right hand and, with all the might she
could muster, slapped the silent girl captive upon the
side of the face, knocking her down. Even before Nao
had struck the floor, Lori was upon her, pulling the
girl's hair with one hand and repeatedly slapping her
face with the other. Nao offered no resistance, and
this passivity further enraged the chief's daughter.

"Weakling!" she shouted. "How do you expect to
hold the love of a man like Bantan—if you do not fight
for him? Do you think he would admire your craven
spirit?"

Nao's dazed eyes merely stared at the princess, but
she made no effort to speak or offer resistance.

With an exclamation of disgust, Lori arose to her
feet. With blazing eyes and heaving bosom she hurried to the door and flung it open.

"Sela, summon a warrior to take this girl captive
back to my father," she commanded.

The slave arose, bowed, and was off at a run.

The princess returned to the captive girl who now
lay upon her stomach with her face resting on her
arms. Her long, lustrous hair covered her features
completely. Lori stood over her, shaking with a
demoniacal rage.

"Perhaps you may learn to fight back at my father,"
she snarled. "He may give you more reason to fight."

With her words the princess drew back her sandalled
right foot and kicked at the prone girl's ribs.

Nao's dazed senses had cleared now. She had never

been the type of girl who sought quarrels. She had
lived peacefully. But as she had lain upon the floor
she realized almost every sense of decency had been
violated. And when Lori planted the kick in her ribs,
that was the final physical abuse she intended to suffer.
With a chilling sensation gripping every fiber of her
being, she leaped to her feet, sweeping the hair from
her eyes as she did so. She looked for her tormentor.
There, she was standing in front of her, gloating at
her seeming helplessness.

For once in her life—be it the first and last time—
Nao was sternly resolved to put a temporary halt to
the torment she had been compelled to endure. The
insults, both mental and physical, rendered from this
girl—whether princess or no—she realized her punishment could be no greater were she to retaliate.

She leaped for Lori with hands outstretched and
fingers claw-like. The princess had not anticipated any
such outburst of spirit from the hitherto passive girl
captive, thus she was taken by surprise. One hand
gripped her hair, the other was at her throat, and
before the tiger-like leap of the girl captive, the princess
was forced backward, falling, with Nao astride her.
Lori struck the back of her head against the floor with
a loud thump, rendering her unconscious.

Feeling the princess grow lax beneath her, Nao arose
to her feet in amazement. She was free! That one
thought dominated for the moment. Alert, she dashed
to the door, and opening it, peered outside. She had
not forgotten the slave girl had gone to fetch a guard
to lead her back to the chief's hut. Looking toward
the prison hut, she saw the two guards posted there
were not looking in her direction. Quickly she stepped
outside and dashed around the corner of the hut.

Nao steadied her quivering nerves. She realized

she must be calm if she were to succeed in the daring scheme that was conceived in her mind. She must forsake the dear thought of imparting to Bantan its nature, for she felt if they were to live, it was her duty to rescue him from his present hopeless plight when opportunity favored.

She thought of the civilized man's weapon that was hidden in the canoe in the old abandoned hut—the automatic. Bantan had explained to her how it operated. She couldn't forget so quickly.

Nao was thankful this was the hottest time of the tropic day, for the majority of the villagers were taking their siesta. The excitement at the capture of the two strangers had passed, and the villagers were normal again—would remain so until the time of sacrifice drew near, then a near hysteria would possess them.

Through a practically deserted village the girl passed without being recognized. Reaching the landing—it also being deserted—she remembered from which direction she and Bantan had been marched. Without a moment's hesitation she was on her way as speedily as her legs would take her.

Were she to take the shortest route through the island's interior, the passage through foliage and underbrush would retard her progress, in addition to the whipping of the branches against her body. She decided upon the slightly longer route, keeping close to the foliage. At first she walked rather rapidly, and looked to her rear time and again. At last she broke into a run, and later slowed down to a fast walk while recovering her spent breath. Alternating in this way, she covered the distance much sooner than she would have anticipated. The footprints upon the sandy beach she and Bantan had made earlier in the day when they had gone swimming made her realize she had reached the vicinity of the old abandoned hut.

In a few moments she had penetrated the foliage to where the hut stood. As she neared the door, she hesitated, for to her alert ears came the sound of youthful voices. She picked up a broken branch some six feet in length and an inch in diameter. Clasping it tightly in her right hand, she approached the doorway and peered inside.

Ula and Lato, who had discovered the strangers, had returned. The chief had promised them the canoe as their reward, and the youths had lost little time in coming to claim it. At the moment Nao peered within the doorway, they were examining the canoe thoroughly. They had come only a few minutes before the girl.

Lato had been scouring the interior of the forepart, and with the discovery of the automatic and the belt of cartridges, he uttered a cry of delight and called to his companion, who was looking in the rear of the canoe—which was nearest the doorway.

"Ula, look what I've found!" Lato shouted.

Ula did not reply, for at that precise moment Nao had brought her stick down upon the youth's head with a resounding smack, and Ula's presence of mind was blackened temporarily.

Hearing the sound, Lato looked up with surprise. His curiosity turned to fear, for the grim-faced girl was eyeing him with intentions that boded him ill. At once the youth recognized her as the girl captive; but thoughts of what she was doing here when she should have been confined in the village he had no time to reflect upon at the present. With a cry of distress, he dropped the automatic and belt of cartridges, and

backed away fearfully.   He gave a terrified look at
Ula's inert form lying upon the ground.

Nao followed him, grim of purpose.   The only exit
from the hut other than the door was the gaping hole
in the roof.   But Lato had no means of escaping that
way.   Furtively he backed away from the approaching
girl with the menacing stick clutched in her right hand.
Lato's eyes looked this way and that, then he dashed
hither and yon, but always Nao was close to him.   He
could not shake her, for she implacably followed his
every step—his every movement.   She seemed to sense
what he was going to do next.

It was inevitable.   Nao finally cornered him.   When
Lato saw there was no escape, he dropped to his knees
and begged for mercy.   But Nao had no mercy to
spare him, for her life and that of Bantan's were at
stake.   With glinting eyes the girl whacked the youth
across the head with the stick, and Lato's senses were
blackened.

Nao was to take no chances.   Quickly she sought
pliable vines and bound, first, Ula's wrists and ankles,
and then Lato's.   She would have nothing to worry
about them for a while.   Returning to the canoe, she
examined the automatic and belt of cartridges and
found they had not been tampered with.   The paddle
still rested in the canoe's bottom.   Glancing toward
the bound Ono youths she nodded.   Then laying hand
upon the canoe, she dragged it through the doorway.
It was not too heavy, and Nao was a strong girl.
After a brief rest, she dragged it through the underbrush, leaving it at the edge of the foliage.

Returning to the hut, she saw that the Ono youths
were as she had left them, though Ula was slowly recovering consciousness.   He was groaning as Nao
paused to look at him, and he was moving a bit.   But

Lato, in the corner of the hut, was still unconscious. Nao realized she had given him an extra hard clout.

In her mind the Amo girl was planning the strategy she was to employ. It would be several hours before sundown, so she had time to spare. She utilized some of this to provision the canoe. Time and again she would return to the hut to check on the bound prisoners. Both had recovered their senses now. Examining their bonds, Nao was satisfied to know they had not been tampered with. The youths regarded their captor in wide-eyed wonder, but they offered no remonstrance, nor asked for mercy, for one look at Nao's stern features forbade that request.

*   *   *

In his prison hut, Bantan had remained standing by the barred window after seeing Nao accompany the chief's daughter to her hut. Feeling the Amo girl was in safe hands that would be merciful, the bronzed young giant then squatted upon his haunches. His usual impressive features were blank. What was to be his fate he could not even conjecture.

It was not long before he heard shouts of excitement outside. Quickly he arose and peered through the barred window. Looking in the direction of the shouting, his eyes were directed to the hut of the princess. The slave girl had returned with a guard. Entering, they had found the chief's daughter unconscious. Leaving the slave girl with her, the warrior had run into the village shouting for attention. Watching intently, Bantan immediately became aware that something out of the ordinary was wrong.

During the minutes that passed, the watcher saw a warrior dash to the chief's hut, and in a moment Roko appeared and hurried to his daughter's hut and disappeared within. Presently the chief reappeared at the doorway. He looked with fearful eyes toward the prison hut, and seeing the captive peering through the window, a look of relief overcame his face. As he continued to stare at Bantan, an expression of rage grew within him.

Maho was now coming toward the chief. Bantan's eyes gleamed as he recognized the handle of his dagger sheathed at the warrior's right hip. How he would have liked to have it in his possession! But what concerned the prisoner most was the cause of the excitement in the hut of the chief's daughter.

Roko and Maho were talking in low voices, but their eyes would look toward the prison hut repeatedly. Then Maho nodded, having obtained his instructions, and left the chief, who returned to the interior of his daughter's hut.

Still keeping watch at the barred window, Bantan presently saw a couple of warriors with shovel-like implements starting to dig a hole in the square between the chief's hut, that of his daughter's, and the prison hut. After some little time had passed and the hole seemed deep enough, two more warriors appeared carrying a freshly cut pole some six inches in diameter and twelve feet in length. One end was placed into the cavity, and holding it upright, a couple of warriors shoveled dirt back into the hole, pausing every few minutes to tamp the dirt more firmly about the base of the post.

When this task was completed Maho, with two warriors, approached the prison hut. All were armed with stone-tipped spears. The door was unlocked and the leader of the men beckoned to the prisoner to step outside. Bantan had no choice but to obey. A warrior seized each of his arms, and he was marched to the post.

Surrounded by dozens of Ono warriors now, many of whom were armed, Bantan realized the futility of making a break for freedom. He did not seem so much concerned about himself as he did the Amo girl. Where was she? The thought that Nao had effected an escape did not occur to him.

As Bantan was bound to the post, many of the Ono women vilified him, while children approached closer and spit at him. Some of the more daring boys searched for branches and whipped his legs.

One of the warriors wrapped many pliable vines about the captive, from his shoulders, pinioning his arms to his sides, down to his knees. When he was completely bound, Bantan's eyes were defiant. Not a sound of protest had escaped his lips during the proceedings. His lips were tight-pressed, for knowing the native mind, he realized a captive who gave no indication of suffering was held in awe.

From the hut of the chief's daughter, Roko and Lori now appeared. A glance at the princess revealed she had not yet fully recovered from the blow she had suffered upon the back of her head when she had been overwhelmed by the infuriated Nao. Her features were very pale, and her eyes still appeared stunned. Her father had a supporting arm about her waist. As they approached the bound prisoner, the villagers drew back, forming an aisle for them to pass.

Roko's features were possessed of false courage. The bound giant was unable to harm him. Confronting Bantan, a mocking smile was upon his lips. He looked down at his daughter.

"Lori, the prisoner escaped death upon Amo Island and cheated Aoono of a victim," he said. "But we, of

Ono, know best what to do with a captive, don't we?"

The girl's smile was a faint one. Despite what Nao had deservingly done to her, the princess could not dismiss the fact from her mind that Bantan was handsome and attracted her. As she looked at the captive's handsome features, now soberly composed, and his tousled hair, she smiled hopelessly.

"It is a shame that you must die, Bantan," she murmured, sadly shaking her head.

Angered by his daughter's compassion, Roko withdrew his arm from about her waist, and took another step toward the captive. He swung his open right hand, and dealt Bantan a hard slap upon the face. He would have repeated the act had the princess not stayed him.

"No, father," she pleaded. "A brave man should not be insulted that way. To be tortured is one thing —but he doesn't deserve to be insulted."

Bantan's rage was mitigated by the words of the chief's daughter. The glare in his eyes vanished as he shifted his eyes from the chief to the girl. Though no smile of gratitude came to his lips, an expression of respect was to be read in his dark eyes.

Roko's rage was lessened. A mocking leer now touched his lips.

"Look well about you, captive," he jeered. "When the sun sinks beyond the horizon of water, then shall you know the death the Ono people can inflict upon a captive."

"Come, father," Lori said, taking one of her father's arms. "It is bad enough that he must die without insulting him further." A look of sadness was in her eyes as she reluctantly removed them from the handsome bronzed giant.

Bantan could not determine the extent of the at-

traction he had for the chief's daughter, though he did
wonder at her strange manner toward him.   With a
shake of his head to dispel such a thought, he then
began to worry about Nao.   Was she still in the hut
of the chief's daughter?   That was where he last had
seen her go.   There was the matter of the excitement
that had prevailed.   What had caused it?

Now his attention was arrested by the boys who
whipped his legs with branches.   They shouted in glee.
Their mothers still vilified him, and he paid them no
attention, either.

Bantan closed his eyes and rested the back of his
head against the pole to which he was bound.   He
smiled inwardly at the recollection how he had tricked
his binders, for when they had bound him, he had
exerted his muscles to their greatest expansion. Though
he had been bound tightly, when they had finished he
had gradually eased his strained muscles so that he
was not too uncomfortable and his blood circulation
was unrestricted.   His fingers, meanwhile, began testing the strength of the vines, and his strong nails were
chafing them in the hope of wearing them through, for
while life was his, hope of freedom was ever present.

His face still smarted from the slap the chief had
dealt him, and the hope that one day he might repay
the blow was not entirely dismissed from his mind.

The village women finally desisted in their vilifica-
tions, for they had the evening meals to prepare.   The
children, however, remained to torment the bound captive.   There was nothing Bantan could do but bear the
trifling punishment compared to what unknown horrible tortures he might be subjected to before death
at last relieved him of his agonies.

Shortly before sundown the bronzed captive was entirely alone.   The children had deserted him to join

their elders at the evening meal. With renewed vigor and without danger of apprehension now, Bantan's fingernails worked at the binding vines. So urgent the need of taking advantage of his present position, great beads of perspiration stood upon the young giant's brow. The fingers of both hands simultaneously were concentrating on the vines at each side of him. They were not too stout, but of a stringy texture that required each strand to be cut through with his fingernails. At last a vine upon his right side had been gnawed through, and in a few more seconds a vine on his left had been severed.

Had he several hours to concentrate upon his task, Bantan did not doubt he might free himself. The fact remained he had only minutes to himself now, for already some of the villagers were finishing their evening meal. As yet none approached him. With a resurgence of vigorous hope he resumed work on his bonds.

In the western heaven just above the water horizon the blazing orb that lighted the day was commencing to sink. Already the lower edge of the flaming red ball was disappearing amidst various cloud formations of varying beauty. The heat of the tropic day had passed and now the air was comfortable.

Bantan's fingers were never more busy in all his life. With desperation he sought to sever more of the confining vines, and though two more were gnawed through, he doubted that he would be able to break free. However, he would test his bonds. With surging muscles he exerted every ounce of strength to snap the others in a mighty effort, but there were too many of the stout little vines encircling him, and his strength, mighty as it was, was incapable of breaking them.

Looking about the village as far as his limited position would permit, he noted some of the natives were
now deserting the vicinity of the cook fires.   Their
evening meal had been consumed, and some were coming in his direction.   For the time being no especial attention was given the bound captive.   None even
bothered to inspect his bonds, for there were matters
to be attended prior to his sacrifice.   From the edge of
the village branches were gathered and brought before
the prisoner.   In the minutes preceding the settling of
dusk the pile grew higher as they heaped the branches
all about him.

Up above his knees, and as more firewood was
brought, the level of his waist was reached.   Higher
still, as the minutes passed, until they had heaped the
firewood up to his shoulders.   While these proceedings
were taking place, with each moment's advantage, Bantan's fingers were still busy at his bonds.   A couple
more vines were severed.   It seemed hopeless, but he
was not to give up while there remained the faintest
glimmer of hope in these last minutes.

In the western heaven the blazing red sun had completely slipped beneath the water horizon.   The
sky above was red, pink, and orange, and the hues in
the cloud formations were as no artist dared aspire to
paint with genuine duplication.   Rapidly, thereafter,
the dusk increasingly settled.

All of the village huts had been emptied of their occupants.   About the bronzed captive the women and
children were dancing and shouting in glee, for the
time was fast approaching when the ceremony would
commence.   Several tom-toms had been brought near
by, and their beaters were awaiting the appearance of
the chief and his daughter.   When they appeared,

then would the tom-toms start to beat in announcement that the death-dance was about to begin.

None of the villagers could know that Lori, in her
father's hut, was purposely delaying the sacrifice of
the handsome bronzed captive, to whom she had become strangely attracted.   Though Roko appeared
impatient, his daughter made no effort to hurry, even
though the coming of night was near at hand.

"But what about Nao, father?" the princess asked.
"Why hasn't she been recaptured?"

"Have no worry about her, Lori," her father assured the girl.   "Several warriors have gone to the old
abandoned hut where the two strangers were discovered by Ula and Lato.   In all probability the girl
went there.   The warriors should be back any time
now with her as a captive again."

"The little spitfire!" Lori muttered.   "I never
thought she had the spirit to fight back."   She rubbed
the back of her head which still was tender.   Then,
once again, her thoughts were of Bantan.

The chief regarded his daughter in silence.   It were
as though he anticipated what she was going to say.

"Father, why must Bantan be sacrificed so soon?"
she asked.   "We could keep him captive until the night
of the next full moon; and to conclude our Full Moon
ceremonies we could then sacrifice him."

Roko shook his head impatiently.

"Lori, it would be sacrilegious of us to include the
sacrifice of a captive during our Full Moon ceremonies," the chief reminded his daughter.   "The Ono
people expect the captive to be sacrificed tonight.   We
must not fail them."

Lori sighed deeply.

"It is a shame that the handsome bronzed captive
must die," she murmured.   "If we were friendly toward

him, in return, perhaps he could tell us much about the island from which he came."

Roko was adamant. Not even his daughter was going to postpone the death of Bantan this very evening. The chief could not forget the chill in the bronzed captive's eyes that boded him no good. The sooner he was dead, the better for his peace of mind. For once Roko was to assert himself to his daughter—who was so very much like her mother when she had lived.

"Come, Lori," he said sternly. "We cannot delay any longer. Already dusk is setting."

The princess shrugged her shoulders and she sighed deeply. Reluctantly she arose, signifying she was ready to join her father in witnessing the death dance. She shuddered at the thought of the conflagration that would consume the handsome bronzed captive and thereby remove him forever from the sight of the attracted princess of Ono Island. Though it was sacrilegious of her to think in the manner she did, in her heart Lori secretly hoped Bantan might in some miraculous manner escape his predestined doom.

As the chief escorted his daughter from his hut, that was the signal Mobo, the leading tom-tom beater, awaited . He thumped his drum in announcement that the death-dance was to begin.

Kolo, the witchdoctor, garbed in mask and ceremonial costume, now appeared from his hut, followed by two slave girls who held his sacred trailing robe from touching the ground. With pomp and dignity, he approached the bound captive. Through slits in his mask his eyes glared at the captive, who stared at him coldly. Kolo uttered gutterals which only witchdoctors are supposed to comprehend, and the motions described by his bony hands no one could possibly understand.

For perhaps two full minutes this ritual lasted, then

raising his masked head he appeared to be invoking the blessings of their idol, Oom. With a triumphant shout in his high-pitched voice, he lowered his head. Turning, he passed through the aisle the villagers prepared for him. The tom-tom of Mobo, meanwhile, had been sounding with single strokes that had been very light, and yet distinctly heard above the hush that had settled upon the village.

But now the strokes increased in sound and tempo. A group of flower-decked girls danced about the bronzed captive with sinuous movements of their lithe bodies moving to the tempo of the single tom-tom that Mobo was stroking. With a signal now, the other tom-toms joined the leader's, and faster was the tempo of their strokes. A group of nearly naked warriors joined the dancing girls in an outer circle, going in an opposite direction to which the girls danced. Faster and yet faster the tom-toms sounded, and the girls and the warriors kept time as they whirled and leaped high, and then bent low, crouching almost to the ground, before again leaping high with hands stretched to the heaven.

When some few minutes had passed and an accelerated series of sounds that almost blended in one continued rhythm, the tom-toms ceased with a suddenness that left one gasping. At once the dancers ceased their frenetic gyrations and retired. The moment of expectancy had come. The eyes of the villagers were opened wide. They awaited the torchbearer who would come with a blazing brand to ignite the branches that surrounded the bound captive. That would be the signal for the present hush to be broken.

During the proceedings, Bantan had continued to sever more of the encircling vines about him. He had lost count of those his stout fingernails had parted, and though the ends of his fingers were raw and tender, still he persevered in his objective, hopeless though it seemed. But hope was an element that was not easily extinguished in the young giant's bosom. Life was dear as he breathed deeply and exhaled slowly. Though he worked at his bonds unceasingly, his eyes never failed to keep close watch about him in the settling dusk. One warrior in particular—Maho—his eyes were trained upon, for he possessed Bantan's dagger. The bronzed giant's eyes would gleam as he looked at it sheathed at the warrior's right hip.

From the doorway of the chief's hut, Lori's breathing was rapid and her bosom rose and fell in evidence to her pent emotions. In her heart she could barely resist the temptation to seize a dagger from a nearby warrior, dash to the handsome bronzed stranger, sever his bonds, and beg him to flee. It all seemed preposterous that she, the princess of the Ono village, could feel so attracted to the captive; and yet she could not deny the fact he appealed to her strongly—almost to the point of defying her father and the entire village.

She caught her breath painfully, and a choking sob escaped her lips as she saw a warrior approach the bound captive with a burning torch. He touched it to various places, holding it for a moment, until the flames began to feed greedily upon the firewood that surrounded the post to which the bronzed captive was bound. A hush still prevailed in the village.

What was that?

Two warriors, followed by two boys—Ula and Lato—appeared from the foliage. They were shouting, attracting the attention of the villagers at once.

In that brief instant Bantan felt his moment had come, for the acrid smoke of the flames billowing about him was choking in his nostrils and throat. With a silent prayer to the God Who once before had answered him, the bronzed giant again exerted his full strength in the hope of snapping the vines that still encircled him. His mighty muscles bulged. The cords of his neck stood out boldly. His mighty chest heaved. His lips were drawn to thin lines and his eyes were closed in that brief moment of terrific strain. He felt and heard some of the encircling vines snap to his herculian effort. A more hopeless man might have desisted in vain endeavor for freedom long since—but not Bantan.

With smoke from the rapidly spreading flames billowing about him, and the heat being keenly felt, a final, stupendous effort he made. His face mirrored the strain to which he was subjecting his powerful muscles in this last bid for freedom—and the extenuation of life's liberty. One last, concentrated surge he made, lunging forward as he did so, and a gasp of relief escaped his parted lips. The remaining bonds, weakened, parted as though a knife had severed them.

Bantan's gleaming eyes caught sight of Maho, who was in possession of his dagger. He was standing nearest to him. Pushing the burning brands away, he stepped from the post, and relieved himself of the severed vines. One leap he made toward Maho, and the warrior, too surprised to react, was relieved of Bantan's appropriated dagger. The warrior did have presence of mind, however, to leap aside, shouting wildly as he did so, before his assailant could harm him.

The attention of the villagers shifted to the shouting Maho, and when they saw that the bound prisoner had in some miraculous manner freed himself of his bonds, they voiced their rage. They started to close in on the

Bantan Breaks Free

bronzed giant who stood there defiantly with his dagger clutched in his right hand. Now that he was free, if only for brief moments, Bantan was ready to die fighting—but not before he had given a good account of himself.

Suddenly, above the increasing rage of the villagers, there came a staccato report from the beach. A warrior upon the outer circle moaned, clasped his side, and toppled to the ground with blood streaming from a small wound. His companions bent to examine him with dismay. Arising quickly, they looked toward the shore.

The determined figure of a lone girl was running toward them. In the settling dusk they could see that both hands carried a strange, metallic object which she held before her. A whisp of smoke was arising from the end of the hollow tube.

At the sound of the report, Bantan's heart leaped with joy. It must be Nao with the automatic. He could not see her because of the many villagers who had been closing in upon him. They stood now in amazement, as though hypnotized by the sharp, staccato report that had been heard.

At the doorway of the chief's hut, Roko was greatly disturbed by ensuing proceedings. Something was happening in the vicinity of the post where the bound prisoner was supposed to be burning by this time. The flames from the firewood were leaping high. But the howling dismay of the villagers was not the exultant shouting that should have been were the prisoner being consumed by the flames. He must investigate the meaning of the strange report he had heard. Then he paused, a chill racing the length of his spine. Another sounded—and then another!

Lori could have cried aloud with joy. Her breath

caught in her throat. Perhaps some miraculous power was going to preserve the handsome Bantan's life after all when things had looked so ominous for him. Her sharp eyes could see that he was not bound at the post and the flaming tongues were not consuming him. But the matter of the strange reports she heard—could this be the mysterious power that was saving him?

Nao steadily advanced toward the threatening villagers, and after two more bullets were discharged from the automatic's smoking muzzle, felling two more, mortally wounded, the rage of the villagers turned to fear. What strange power was this that barked from the distance and villagers would sink to the ground, moaning in pain? With howls of fear they turned and tried to push their way backward.

Bantan, meanwhile, took advantage of the pandemonium. With his dagger menacing any who came close to him, he was fashioning an aisle through the villagers in the direction of the beach.

One warrior turned and was determined to master this frail girl who had inspired all with such fear. Again a staccato report was heard. The warrior clasped his hands to his burning side and fell to the ground, writhing in agony.

The grim-faced girl was still advancing into the village with the automatic pointed before her. As though by magic an opening appeared in the midst of the confused villagers and a lone, nearly naked figure leaped forward with a happy shout upon his lips. In the fast-settling dusk Bantan saw the girl with the automatic pointed in his direction, and he could not be sure she would recognize him. And then he stumbled and pitched to his knees, his outstretched hands saving him from falling flat.

Simultaneously another staccato report sounded, and

a bullet whistled over the fallen man's back to find a target in the midst of the confused villagers. At the next moment the bronzed giant had drawn himself erect.

"Nao!" he shouted. "It is Bantan! Don't shoot any more."

Above the confusion of the howling villagers, the girl recognized the voice of Bantan. With a glad smile she lowered the automatic, which now was empty, and she took another step toward him. But then, so great the emotion she had been subjected to, the girl's senses reeled, and with a low moan she collapsed to the ground in a dead faint.

Bantan sheathed his dagger as he dashed toward the unconscious girl. Bending over her, he took the automatic from her lax fingers and slipped it into the belt about his waist. Then he gathered her into his strong arms, and with a single, backward glance at the still confused villagers, he dashed in the direction of the beach with his precious burden. By the time he had reached it, Nao was stirring. She murmured his name repeatedly.

"Bantan—Bantan—"

The bronzed young giant identified his canoe the girl had come hither in, and in another moment he had placed her gently within. Giving the canoe a shove into the surf he leaped in, and taking up the paddle dextrously mastered the breaking surf until presently they were in the calmer water beyond.

With a deep sigh of relief Bantan called softly to Nao, reclining in the bow, and he was rewarded to hear her sweet voice in answer.

PART III

CAPTURE — AND ESCAPE

The stars in the tropic heaven dotted the dark canopy above the vast expanse of the Pacific Ocean. The surface was calm. Hardly a breath of air stirred. The night was mild. A canoe was being speedily paddled from Ono Island. Some ten minutes had passed since the paddler had set the course eastward, for he was familiar with the planets and constellations in the heaven.

Having escaped certain death from the Ono village, Bantan was grateful they had not been given pursuit in the now fast-settling darkness. A number of times he had glanced to his rear, and there had been no sound of trailing canoes. It was possible the Ono warriors had realized the futility of giving chase to the escaping man and the girl who accompanied him.

Bantan's eyes were becoming accustomed to the darkness of night. He could distinguish the reclining figure of Nao, the Amo Island girl, who was now arising to a seated position. She sighed deeply.

"Nao," he softly called to her.

"Yes, Bantan?" she asked.

"You were a brave girl," he complimented her. "If it had not been for you I doubt that I could have managed to escape the Ono warriors. It is true at the last moment I managed to break the encircling vines that bound me when flames were billowing about me and the smoke was choking in my throat. The confusion that gripped the people at your appearance, discharging the automatic, is all that saved me. I owe you my life, Nao. But tell me, how did you manage to escape from the chief's daughter?"

Nao then told Bantan of his attraction to the princess of Ono Island, and how the latter had tried to bargain with her.

"I was to be her father's slave," she added. "When I asked about you, the chief's daughter said that was none of my business. She slapped my face and knocked me down. When she kicked me in the ribs—that was too much. I arose and leaped upon her, and in falling, she struck her head, rendering her unconscious. Then I realized my opportunity to escape was at hand. No one noticed me escaping from the village, so I went to the old hut. There I found two Ono boys examining the canoe. With a stick I knocked both of them unconscious and bound them with vines. I provisioned the canoe and waited for near dusk before setting out for the village landing. When I saw you bound to a stake and the flames leaping about you, I knew I had to save you from your plight."

"You remembered well what I explained about the automatic, Nao," he complimented her. "Had I not stumbled and fallen before you fired the last time, I might have been seriously wounded—perhaps killed. In the settling dusk I could not hope that you would have recognized me."

"When you shouted to me after I had fired," she murmured in trembling tones, "I realized how near I had come to shooting you. That was why I fainted."

"But everything will be all right now, Nao," he assured her. "This time I think nothing will prevent us from reaching Marja Island. There you will know the happiness that the people of the Beneiro and Marja

Islands are now living together in peace and harmony."

Nao sighed deeply.

"Though my father and mother shall miss me," she said, "I have the feeling I am going to love the father and mother you have known."

"You will, Nao," he answered. "And you will know the love of Wanya, who has been so like a sister to me."

A short silence ensued while Bantan continued to ply his paddle, propelling the light water craft with steady progress in response to his methodical strokes.

To the rear of the canoe Ono and Amo Island, together with the volcanic island of Aoono in the center, distance was being spanned with each passing minute. With fair weather prevailing, Bantan hoped to reach the atoll before the evening of the next day. It was his intention of paddling all night. In the early morning, when Nao waked, he would exchange places with her and obtain a few hours sleep. This he told her.

"When we reach the atoll we can rest there that night, the next day and night as well before resuming our way to Marja Island," he added.

Nao laughed lightly.

"The excitement of today has left me wide awake," she confessed. "I don't feel a bit sleepy."

The young giant realized he was hungry. He had not eaten since noon.

"You have some fruit in the canoe, Nao?" he asked.

He laid the paddle down while she gave him some. While he ate it he complimented her for having been so thoughtful to have provisioned the canoe.

"I realized that you would be hungry as I would be in the time that must pass before the atoll was reached," the girl answered. "Since I had the time, I thought it best to do so."

"I hope no sharks bother us as they did me when I came to Amo Island," Bantan added reflectively. "A couple of them were rather persistent then."

Nao stifled a gasp.

"I must remember not to let my hands trail over the side of the canoe," she said.

Having satisfied his hunger, Bantan took up the paddle and plied it with renewed vigor.

"Aoono has been cheated," the girl said after a short silence. "But I don't mind— do you?"

"Not at all, Nao," he replied. "I wonder if Amar was rescued before the storm struck the island?"

The girl shuddered at the mention of Amar's name.

"Something tells me that Amar will search for us," she said fearfully. "Knowing him as I do, I don't think we have seen the last of him."

Bantan shrugged his broad shoulders.

"What the future holds for us, Nao" he said, "we don't know. But why concern ourselves with that at the present?"

"That's right, Bantan," the girl agreed. She stifled a yawn. "I'm becoming sleepy after all."

Lying back and settling herself upon the pallet of grasses as comfortable as possible, the steady dip of Bantan's paddle and the sound of the wavelets against the side of the canoe was sufficient to lull the girl asleep.

When the paddler presently spoke to her in a gentle voice, and received no reply, he listened to her regular breathing. He was assured she slept soundly.

Keeping certain constellations before him, Bantan's methodical strokes propelled the canoe toward his distant goal unerringly. The air was not too cool, and for that reason the sleeper was not uncomfortable. The minutes passed into hours. The stars continued to rise over the eastern horizon, and accordingly, those over the western water line disappeared from view.

When several hours of unceasing paddling had passed, above the eastern horizon a dull glow announced the moon, several nights past fullness, would soon be appearing. With the passing minutes the dull glow increased in luminosity, and soon Bantan's eyes viewed the top edge of the fading disc. In due time the satellite had cleared the horizon, and the paddler looked at the scarred countenance. He thought it strange that nearly each month the Mistress of the Night passed through the phases of approaching her fullness, and then faded thereafter until the time came when her full glory had been attained again. For how many centuries this miracle occurred Bantan, of course, had no conception—nor is it likely more learned astronomers could hazard more than a conjecture.

The silvery effulgence of the oval satellite illuminated the gentle undulations of the ocean. The canoe followed a silvery, shimmering reflection upon the water. To the rear, the three islands in the west had converged into one, and a blur upon the horizon evidenced the distance Bantan had paddled since leaving Ono Island.

With the coming of sunrise, the paddler glanced to his rear and no longer could see the blur that represented the islands. Somewhat wearied now, he laid the paddle aside and reached for a plantain. While he ate it he looked at the still sleeping girl. She lay upon her back with her head pillowed upon her lustrous hair. Her hands were folded over her slow rising and falling bosom. Her features were composed, and as the bronzed giant looked at her, he realized how beautiful, even in sleep, Nao was. Her slim ankles were crossed.

Thinking of the exciting events of the past few days, Bantan could hardly believe them true. Yet he knew they were, for his feminine companion was here before him, composed in deep sleep. While he watched the girl, her eye lids twitched. She drew a deep breath, and exhaled slowly. Her moist lips parted then, and for some reason her regular breathing was interrupted. Her eyes opened for a moment and closed. For a full minute she remained motionless, as though her faculties were collecting the details she had recently experienced to bring her to the present moment. Nao's eyes then opened wide, and looked at Bantan, who was silently watching her. A smile touched her lips, and arising to a seated position, she stretched her arms upward.

"Have I slept all night, Bantan?" she asked as she stifled a yawn.

"You never woke once, Nao," he said with a nod.

"I must have been more tired than I believed," she admitted. "You have been paddling all night?"

"The islands we have left have disappeared beyond the horizon," he answered.

"Then you must be tired," she said. "I'll paddle while you sleep. Come, let's change places."

With care, so as not to overturn the canoe, the man and the girl alternated places. Before taking up the paddle, Nao dipped water from the side of the canoe and applied it to her face and neck. While Bantan reposed himself upon the pallet of grasses, warmed by the girl's body, Nao partook of some fruit for her matutinal repast. Then she took up the paddle and plied it, her strokes naturally not so powerful as Bantan's would have been, but the light water craft moved ahead on its course faithfully.

Nao looked with gentleness upon the now sleeping young giant. She could not picture with clearness what life would be upon Marja Island; but somehow her confidence in Bantan was sufficient to assure her she need not worry, for wherever he was would be reason enough for her happiness to be completer than it had been previously upon Amo Island. No warrior there could ever attract her as this handsome bronzed giant did.

The girl's reveries were rudely interrupted. A triangular fin appeared to be coming in the direction of the canoe. Nao had chanced to glance to her rear on the left side and she caught a glimpse of the tell-tale evidence of a shark's approach. The girl knew at once that it must have been attracted by the moving canoe. Perhaps the peels from plantains that she and Bantan had thrown overboard had lured the denizen of the deep from its lair. The shark now was some twenty feet from the rear of the canoe.

Nao never had been occasioned to do battle with a shark. She was positive she would not know how to fight one. Instinctively she knew Bantan would know what to do. Though he had been sleeping less than an hour she did not wish to waken him, but under the circumstances she had no choice.

"Bantan!" she called gently, though her voice threatened to rise in volume. "Wake up!"

As easily as he had fallen asleep, Bantan's eyes opened and he sat upright. Perhaps in his subconscious mind he had detected a note of concern in the girl's tones.

"What is it, Nao?" he asked.

"A shark is approaching the canoe," she said in a steady voice.

A grim smile touched the young giant's lips.

"I'll attend to it," he said, looking in the direction the girl indicated.

Quickly Bantan sought the automatic and the cartridge belt. He filled it with cartridges, then quickly knelt, his right hand clutching the automatic. The shark was veering in its course and now was drawing alongside the canoe with perhaps six feet intervening. Through the translucent water Bantan's keen eyes determined the gray shark was easily fifteen feet in length. Taking careful aim, he pressed the trigger repeatedly. Nao's features grimaced as several shots were discharged.

That the shark was hit by the bullets there was no question. At once the water churned as the wounded monster lashed its powerful tail. The canoe rocked as the waves washed against it with increasing size. Then Bantan discharged several more shots into the foaming water. The shark was wounded in several places and the churning water was becoming bloodied. The bullets could not have penetrated a vital spot in the shark's body, for the monster appeared goaded to madness. It swam a dozen feet ahead of the canoe with lightning-like speed, then it turned abruptly and sped at a right angle for about twenty feet before veering in its seemingly erratic course before taking another.

Nao had ceased to paddle and was staring wide-eyed at the wounded shark's actions. There was no terror in her dark eyes now. The Amo girl possessed courage; Bantan realized that as his eyes met hers assuringly. He smiled, and she responded in a like manner.

The bronzed young giant replaced the automatic in the bow of the canoe. The girl noticed his right hand was resting near his right hip where the handle of his steel dagger protruded from its sheath. At once a fear of Bantan's contemplated peril rose in her bosom.

"No, Bantan, you can't—you mustn't!" she cried. "I won't let you!"

His smile was grimmer as he removed his eyes from the seemingly pain-crazed shark that was swimming so erratically about the canoe.

"The shark's blood may attract others, Nao," he warned. "The quickest way to kill it is with my dagger, then we can hope to get away before other sharks bother us. They will be too busy feeding upon the carcass of their dead fellow to take notice of us."

A pitiful smile touched the girl's lips; her eyes were brave, but filled with concern for his safety.

"I wouldn't want anything to happen to you," she protested, moaningly.

His smile was comforting as were his words.

"I have battled sharks before, Nao," he said, "so have no fear." His eyes returned to the threshing shark, now some ten feet from the left side of the canoe. "It may decide to upset the canoe," he added. "I must prevent that."

A grim silence of a few moments intervened during which the girl hardly breathed, for she realized nothing she could say or do would alter the bronzed giant's decision. Her left hand pressed her breast as though she might ease the pounding of her heart. Her dark eyes seemed riveted upon Bantan's features, watching the changing expression in his dark eyes. The young man turned to her.

"Steady yourself, Nao," he cautioned. "I'm about ready to dive overboard."

The girl gripped a side of the canoe with each hand so tightly her knuckles gleamed white to the light of the sun that shone upon them.

The shark had come alongside within several feet, then with a surge of its powerful tail was turning. This was the moment Bantan awaited. He flashed a smile to the concerned girl, then dived into the churning water. The last sound he heard was the girl's voice uttering his name distressfully.

The moment the bloodied water engulfed him, Bantan's eyes were open and the grayish belly of the shark loomed before him. With powerful strokes of his arms and mighty thrusts of his legs in perfect time, he propelled himself alongside the moving monster of the deep. His arms went about it for anchorage, then his powerful legs followed, locking themselves about the cold, coarse form. Holding fast, his right hand then released itself and closed upon the handle of his dagger and withdrew it.

The pain-maddened shark threshed the water with its powerful tail and turned over, hoping to dislodge the man thing that clung so tenaciously to it. But Bantan was not to be dislodged. He pressed the dagger to the hilt into the shark's belly. For a moment a shudder wracked the giant fish. A moment later with redoubled fury its powerful tail threshed wildly, and it turned over and over repeatedly, pausing at intervals to swim forward with lightninglike speed. Suddenly it would stop, then dart to lower depths with the tenacious man thing still clinging tight and repeatedly plunging the dagger to its hilt in various parts of its belly.

Each plunge of the blade seemed to enrage the shark more so, and greater became its efforts to dislodge its tormentor. The blood spurted in gushing streams from the various wounds the dagger inflicted. By this time several minutes had elapsed, and Bantan's lungs were clamoring for renewed air. And then a final

Bantan Battles the Shark

plunge of the dagger pierced a vital spot, for the shark shuddered and seemed paralyzed. All indications of resistance were subdued. A final, spasmodic tremor pulsed through the cold body, and this was the sign Bantan awaited.

Knowing the shark was beyond hope to further harm him and the girl in the canoe, the bronzed giant released his left arm and his powerful legs unlocked from the inert form. One foot he placed against the still monster and shoved himself toward the surface. Through bloodied water he rose swiftly, his powerful legs threshing. To the relief of his starved lungs his head presently bobbed above the surface. Quickly he expelled the foul air from his lungs and gulped fresh air.

Treading water, Bantan replaced the dagger in its sheath, then looking about he saw that the canoe was some twenty feet distant. Nao had been watching therein with anxious, tear-filled eyes, hardly breathing. A smile of unfathomable relief appeared upon her worried face as she saw the bronzed giant's head bob above the surface.

Bantan smiled assuringly at the watching girl, then with strong, overhand strokes swam to the canoe. Reaching it, he placed his hands upon the gunwale.

"The shark is no longer able to bother us, Nao," he said, smilingly.

The girl's voice was so choked with emotion that she could not speak. She could only smile through the mistiness of her eyes.

Bantan then instructed her how to balance the canoe while he drew himself within without upsetting it. In another moment dripping wet he was seated within. He pushed his wet hair back from his forehead into pompadour fashion. Before him Nao knelt. Her

smile was brave and her praise for the bronzed giant
was clearly indicated in her dark eyes. She now found
her voice.

"What a brave thing to do, Bantan!" she murmured
with awe. "I have never known any Amo warrior who
willingly gave battle to a shark."

"Sharks have always been mortal enemies to me,
Nao," he said reflectingly. "Ever since they deprived
Ramo, my boyhood companion, of his life, I have despised them. I do not fear them. I hate them, and
where there is hate there can be no fear. That is why
I would rather leap to the attack than be forced to defend myself. I feel my chances are better to defeat
the monster."

"How can one be so brave?" the girl murmured
looking up at the heaven.

Bantan smiled with modesty and nonchalance.

"Now that the shark has been taken care of, Nao,"
he said, "I think I shall return to my sleep."

The bronzed giant curled upon one side, and even
while the girl was applying the paddle's first strokes
since her interruption, he was fast asleep. By the
manner of his regular breathing, Nao could determine
he had lost little time in doing so. With a shake of
her head she could only sigh.

"How can such a man be possible?" she asked herself.

With regulated strokes of the paddle, the Amo girl
paddled the canoe rapidly away from the vicinity of
the bloodied water to which, sooner or later, other
voracious creatures of the depths would come, attracted by the blood, and to feed upon the carcass of
the dead shark.

A couple of hours passed while Nao faithfully
paddled. Fortunately, no further sharks had appeared

to molest the two occupants of the canoe. Bantan had hardly stirred since falling asleep. As easily as he had fallen asleep, he awakened and appeared as fresh as though he had slumberéd an entire night through. As his eyes opened to behold the smiling girl, he, too, smiled.

"Hello," he greeted Nao.

The girl's smile became brighter, revealing her even white teeth that sparkled like pearls.

"You're wide awake already, Bantan?" she asked in surprise.

"After I bathe and have some fruit," he said, "I'll be ready to relieve you of paddling."

Some fifteen minutes later Bantan and Nao had exchanged places again, though the girl protested she was far from wearied. The bronzed young giant propelled the canoe with redoubled speed. The rising sun's rays were a source of annoyance, and he would continue paddling with head somewhat lowered. Only from time to time, shading his eyes as he peered ahead, would he scan the horizon to the right and left as well.

Nao's nimble fingers were busy at work with grasses, and in an incredibly short time she had fashioned a head covering with a visor attached to it. She had chatted with Bantan, meanwhile, and he didn't have the opportunity to mention out of curiosity what she was doing. Now, as she handed the head covering to him, he accepted it with thanks. When placing it upon his head—Nao telling him for what purpose the visor was—Bantan felt silly. Presently he discovered it was most appropriate, and he could paddle without having his head lowered, for his eyes were shaded by the visor.

"Wanya once fashioned a band for my forehead to keep the hair from my eyes, Nao," he said. "But this seems better, since it shadows my eyes from the sharp glare of the sun."

Nearing noon day, Bantan's keen eyes espied a blur upon the horizon slightly to the left. He called the girl's attention to his discovery. She, too, could presently see what he indicated.

"That should be the atoll," he said. "I hope the storm hasn't destroyed the shelter there."

While continuing to paddle, Bantan told Nao how he had unwittingly became lost upon the bosom of the ocean, finally reached the atoll, and made the acquaintance of a missionary by name of Father Lasance, the first white man he had ever known. He added that the missionary had taught him the tongue and ways of the white people. It was he who had told him that he must be a white man despite his bronzed body.*

"I shall always remember Father Lasance," he concluded.

It was late in the afternoon when the canoe beached upon the atoll near where the shelter had been constructed. Bantan and Nao stepped from the canoe, and the young man drew it close to the foliage.

"The atoll is very lovely, Nao," he said.

The girl inhaled deeply the fresh aroma of sweet-smelling flowers and growing vegetation, and exhaled slowly. Her eyes were sparkling.

"It is just like paradise," she murmured.

The aftermath of the recent storm was not so apparent upon the atoll as it had not struck with full force here as upon the Aoono Islands. Some branches had been torn from mother limbs, and numerous coconuts were to be found upon the ground. Bantan picked up several on the way to the shelter as, preceding the

---

*Note: See *"Bantan of the Islands"*

girl, he led the way. Nao followed closely, her eyes in rapt admiration as she looked at gorgeous flowers and luxuriant ferns.

"What a lovely island!" she exclaimed happily. "I could live here forever and never think of Amo Island."

"It is very lovely here, Nao," Bantan agreed.

Reaching the shelter, the bronzed young giant was relieved to observe it was none the worse for the tropic storm. Entering, with Nao close behind him, he saw that nothing had been disturbed since he had left it nearly a week before.

Bantan deposited the coconuts just within the door. Then he turned to the girl, who was appraising the interior of the shelter with apparent satisfaction.

"Do you like it, Nao?" he asked.

"This is very nice," she said with a smile.

"The missionary and I lived here for many moons before we were rescued by Mr. Brown and his daughter, who came from America in search of me," he replied. "At a later time we were marooned here and attacked by the Waneiro and taken prisoners. It was here——" He did not finish.

Nao looked at him questionably and she saw that faraway expression had again appeared in his eyes. With a shake of her head to banish the mistiness that momentarily blurred her vision, she uttered a little laugh.

"A different variety of fruit should be gathered, Bantan," she said. "Coconuts alone are not satisfying."

"I'll gather some at once, Nao," he responded. "Perhaps you may wish to clean up the shelter a little. It has been some time since any one lived here."

The Amo girl nodded.

"I'll do that," she assented with a smile.

While Bantan gathered a variety of fruits a short distance from the shelter, Nao attended to the house-cleaning. Old pallets of grasses, which smelled of staleness, were collected and carried outside, to be replaced with fresh grass and palm fronds. She even gathered a bouquet of frangipanis and placed them upon the table. The shelter's interior radiated with a freshness it had not known for many moons, thanks to the Amo girl's gift of appreciating a clean household.

Presently Bantan returned with arms ladened with a variety of fruits that were both appealing and appeasing to the eye and appetite.

"Before we eat, Nao," he suggested, "would you care to join me in a swim?"

The girl's dark eyes lighted with enthusiasm.

"Of course," she agreed.

They went to the beach and presently were indulging in a refreshing swim in the calm water beyond the surf. As carefree as children, they dove and swam beneath the surface, and when appearing, they would tread water and laugh and talk. Carefree though Bantan appeared, he always was on the alert for a tell-tale fin proclaiming a shark was near, and when swimming under water for that other vicious monster of the deep—an octopus. Almost reluctantly they quit the water to prepare the evening meal, for the sun was not far above the western horizon.

They ate at the table in the shelter, seated opposite each other. Though Nao's spirits were high, it was with a little dismay she saw that faraway expression creep into Bantan's dark eyes—indicative that his reveries were of the past again.

"Thinking of Mr. Brown and Leona, Bantan?" she asked naively.

Bantan's eyes met the girl's steadily for a moment and a quaint smile touched his lips as he nodded.

"I imagine they are back in America resuming their life from where they left off before taking a trip to the tropics," he answered. "I sometimes think of them and wonder if they give a thought of me."

The Amo girl shrugged her shoulders.

"And though you had the opportunity of returning with them," she added, "your choice was to remain in the tropics. Well, I, for one, am grateful you did."

There was nothing Bantan could say to this. He arose with a smile.

"I must get the automatic and belt of cartridges from the canoe, Nao," he said. "The firearms of civilized man must be given a lot of attention to preserve their usefulness."

She nodded.

"I'll clear the table and join you presently," she said with a smile.

In a few minutes the girl had joined Bantan at the edge of the beach, seating herself at his side, and helped him rubbing and polishing the mechanism.

"Tomorrow, Nao," he said, "I shall fashion a bow and more arrows. I'll teach you how to shoot arrows."

The girl's smile was eager.

"That will be fine," she said.

When the automatic was polished to Bantan's satisfaction, he refilled the magazine with cartridges. Nao watched him intently.

"I think I can do that," she said.

The bronzed young giant laughed and emptied the

magazine. He handed the girl the cartridges and the automatic.

"Let me see you do it, Nao," he urged.

With a little laugh of satisfaction, the girl from Amo Island replaced the cartridges in the magazine, as she had seen Bantan do, then she handed the automatic to him.

"Did I replace them right?" she asked.

He nodded and smiled.

"You learn very quickly," he commended.

She sat erect and a mock expression of egoism appeared in her eyes; then she laughed gaily at the wondering expression in her companion's eyes.

The sun was descending over the western horizon. They remained seated in the shadows at the edge of the foliage.

"Two suns ago at this time," Nao said in a low voice, "we were in a much different situation than now."

He nodded solemnly.

"That is true, Nao," he agreed. "I have been upon Amo Island and escaped with you, only to be captured upon Ono Island. Again we escaped. Had it not been for you—" He shook his head.

One of his hands sought the girl's, and finding it, clasped it gently in his. A soft glow of contentedness was to be seen in Nao's dark eyes as he looked at her that the settling dusk did not conceal. Though the bronzed young giant wanted to place an arm about her shoulders, draw her closer to him and rest his cheek against hers, for some inexplicable reason he did not do so.

They sat there in silence for some few minutes before he released her hand.

"I am weary, Nao," he confessed. "We should sleep sound tonight."

Arising, Bantan picked up the automatic and belt of cartridges. Together, he and the girl returned to the shelter. The automatic and cartridge belt was placed upon the table. In the settling dusk, Bantan gathered up half of the grass and palm fronds Nao had gathered.

"I'll sleep near the door," he said. He then indicated the small apartment that was partitioned in a corner of the shelter. "Leona occupied the apartment when we were marooned here," he added. "I'm sure you will be comfortable there."

The girl smiled and gathered the remaining grass and palm fronds.

"I'm sure I will," she agreed.

Bantan then arranged his sleeping pallet to his likening and closing the door, he lay down. In a few moments he was fast asleep.

In her apartment, Nao arranged her sleeping pallet and composed herself for slumber. But for some unknown reason sleep did not come to her at once. She lay awake in the darkness that had now settled, and whatever her thoughts, who might guess? But it was a contented smile that enwreathed her lips at last, and without knowing it, she fell into a deep, refreshing slumber.

The girl awoke first in the morning. Birds twittered noisily in the tree tops—perhaps that was what awoke her. Already the sun was well above the horizon. Arising, she peered through the opening of her apartment. Near the door, lying upon his back, she saw that Bantan was still fast asleep. Nao sighed as she approached the bronzed young giant. She paused beside him, then with a soft glow in her dark eyes, she

knelt and gently touched her lips to his forehead.
Then, with a blush suffusing her cheeks, she straightened, and with fast-beating heart, silently slipped out
of the shelter and went to the beach. There she
bathed, being careful not to wet her lustrous hair so
early in the day.

Returning to the shelter, she paused to pluck a lovely
frangipani flower which she affixed in her hair just
above her left ear. Again peering within the shelter
she saw that Bantan had now stirred to wakefulness.
Hearing the girl's soft laughter, he sat up quickly. He
smiled as he saw Nao looking at him from the doorway.

"You're up already?" he asked.

"Up and bathed," she answered with a nod. "While
you do so, I'll prepare the morning meal."

The bronzed young giant arose and shook his head,
banishing the last drugging influence of sleep from his
brain.

Later in the morning, with Nao accompanying him,
Bantan cut a sapling with his keen-edged dagger.
Testing it, he found that it was very pliable and just
what he wanted.

"This is fine, Nao," he said to the eagerly watching
girl. "Now I must wait for a sea gull. With its en-
trails I can complete the bow. While we wait, I'll
fashion some arrows."

Bantan handed the bow to the girl, and while he
proceeded to cut some smaller, straight saplings to be
fashioned into arrows, the girl tested the bow as she
had seen her companion do. She could understand
now what he meant when he said it was "fine."

Within a few minutes Bantan had returned to the
girl's side with a half-dozen smaller saplings in hand.
He indicated they would go to the beach. There he

picked up several stones, selecting those that were almost round and would easily fit into an almost closed
hand. These he placed at his right side, and motioned
to Nao to sit at his left.

While whittling on one arrow, and notching its end
v-shaped, time and again Bantan's keen eyes would
look about for the presence of sea gulls. Some few
minutes passed before one flew overhead, then circled
about, screechingly. The bronzed giant watched the
bird fly low over the gentle surf, then presently came
to land just above the point where the washing waves
laved the sandy beach. It stood staturesque, looking
toward the man and the girl seated at the edge of the
foliage.

Bantan now placed his half-finished arrow to one
side along with the dagger. His right hand groped
for a stone and palmed it. With a smiling glance at
Nao, he slowly arose, first to his knees, and then
reached an upright position. A good thirty feet intervened between him and the sea gull. It was a trifle
too far for a successful throw.

The sea gull stood there upon its webbed feet, its
baleful eyes never leaving the man and the girl. So
slowly and methodically Bantan moved, the sea gull
could not have noticed, for it surely would have taken
flight.

By this time Bantan had now taken ten short
steps in the direction of the bird. He stood poised,
his weight resting upon his right foot. Slowly his
right hand lifted with the smooth stone tightly clenched
therein.

Subconsciously warned, the sea gull screeched, and
spread its wings. It started to run laterally along
the beach preparatory to taking flight. There could
be no delay—this was the moment. The bronzed

giant's right hand came forward swiftly, releasing the
smooth rock. Without waiting for the stone to reach
its target, Bantan was dashing toward the moving
creature. So speedily he ran, he had taken several
strides when the missile struck one of the bird's wings
where it joined the backbone, damaging it beyond hope
of further use and resulting in much louder screeching
than before. The wounded sea gull flapped its unharmed wing vigorously with the result it fell over and
crazily staggered about the beach, screeching loudly in
pain.

In another moment Bantan's quick right hand
grasped the long neck, silencing the raucous sounds.
With a deft movement of his hand he snapped the
bird's neck. The feathered body became lax. The
young man then walked toward the smiling girl,
who had arisen to her feet. She was shaking her head
dubiously.

"I wouldn't have believed it possible," she remarked.

"I've done this before, Nao," he said; "so I knew
it was possible. And now comes the part I don't think
you would care to witness. While I am attending to it,
you may scoop a hole in the beach with my dagger
large enough to bury the bird after I am through with
it." He handed her his dagger which she readily accepted.

The girl nodded, and turning, knelt, and began to
scoop a hole in the sandy beach.

Meanwhile, Bantan disemboweled the sea gull, and
from its intestines selected what he wished to utilize.
From its belly he plucked a number of soft feathers.
By this time the girl had completed scooping out a
cavity of sufficient depth to accommodate the bird's
carcass. The bronzed giant deposited the remains
therein and covered it over, then he turned with a

smile to the girl, brandishing the piece of intestine.

"Now to finish the bow, Nao," he said.

They returned to where they had formerly been sitting.

Bantan notched the ends of the sapling that was to be the bow. Then he twisted the piece of intestine until it was the shape of twine. He knotted one end to a notched end of the bow. Bending the bow, he fastened the other end securely. A triumphant smile was upon his face as he looked at the eagerly watching girl.

"There, Nao, the bow is completed," he said. He pulled upon the bow string and it hummed as he released it.

The girl's eyes were bright as she watched Bantan.

"The feathers that you plucked from the sea gull's breast—" she then asked, "—for what purpose are they to be used?"

Bantan smiled as he picked up an arrow and fastened several feathers to its notched end.

"These guide the arrow in flight, Nao," he explained. "Watch, and I'll show you."

He placed the notched end of the arrow against the bow string, allowing the shaft to rest upon the bow against his thumb and forefinger. Standing erect, he drew his right hand downward as he aimed the arrow directly above him.

"I'll shoot it so it will land where it can be retrieved," he explained to the apparently excited girl.

The bow string twanged and the arrow sped upward in a straight course. All of fifty feet it went, then, its momentum spent, it came to a pause, and fell earthward. Bantan stood beneath it, and as it came within arms' length his deft right hand plucked it out of the air.

The girl laughed aloud with glee at the success of his catch.

Bantan approached with the bow and arrow, smiling.

"Now you may try it, Nao," he said.

Accepting the bow and the arrow with a smile, the girl duplicated Bantan's skill to perfection, even catching the descending arrow before it touched the beach, though she came near missing it.

Bantan smiled and nodded as he lauded her.

"You learn quickly, Nao," he said.

"With such a remarkable teacher," she added, "who would wonder?"

"If you wish to practice more," he added, "you may do so. I have more arrows to finish."

While the girl successfully continued to shoot the arrow, Bantan fashioned more from the slender saplings he had gathered. And so the balance of the morning was consumed. As they quit the beach to return to the shelter and make preparations for their noon day meal, neither thought to give a glance at the broad expanse of water beyond the beach.

Had they, they would have been surprised, for three canoes were being paddled in the direction of the atoll from the west. In two of them were four warriors plying paddles, and now were not many miles distant. The foremost canoe, somewhat larger than the two that followed, occupied six paddlers. In the bow, facing the atoll, sat a giant warrior of regal mien. His features were inscrutable, but in his glittering black eyes naked hate was clearly revealed. This was Amar, the son of the chief of Amo Island, and the one thought in his chaotic brain was—revenge!

For having defiled his sacred person, and besting him in fair combat, Amar had decreed that the handsome giant known as Bantan was to be tortured as no man

had ever been before at last a merciful death released
him of his agonies. As yet, Amar had not devised the
nature of the tortures to be administered to Bantan
when he was taken prisoner, but he had no doubts the
appropriate means would come to him in due time.
Never in his life had the chief's son been so affronted
—from his point of view—and his want of revenge
would not be satisfied until Bantan had died the tortures of a thousand deaths—more, if his giant constitu-
tion could endure it.

From the distance Amar's keen eyes had espied the
figures of a man and a girl upon the beach. His breath
quickened noticeably with the seething anger that
passed through his chaotic brain. Watching them intently, he was aware they did not glance toward the
water and observe the nearing three canoes. As the
man and the girl disappeared into the foliage, Amar
turned to the paddlers and urged them to make more
haste in their efforts to reach shore the sooner.

With the thought of Nao, who had accompanied
Bantan in his escape from Amo Island, Amar decided
she was unworthy of her birthright, and as her punishment, he decreed she would suffer the same fate as the
bronzed giant. An evil light appeared in his eyes as
he contemplated what else she would experience before
her death.

When Amar had been released from the bound condition Bantan had left him so that he and Nao might
escape without danger of immediate pursuit, the chief's
son had not even felt grateful that he had been rescued
from his plight and had managed to reach the shelter
of his father's hut before the tropic storm had descended upon the island in all its untamed fury. All
the while the storm had raged, Amar planned the
course he would take the next morning.

First, he inquired of his rescuers of the night before

how they had learned of his plight, and the finger of suspicion pointed at the father and mother of Nao. Next, he interviewed Maro and Luno, and by subtle questioning at first, then by dire threats, he learned that Bantan was taking Nao to Marja Island, far to the east, from which he had come. That was the information required. For the present the parents of Nao were promised absolution for their knowledge of Bantan's coming to Amo Island. At a later and more appropriate time, Amar had assured himself, they would be punished for withholding knowledge of the stranger's coming.

Amar then familiarized his father, Tomara, with the details of his plan for the recapture of the stranger and Nao, and the chief was in full accord with his only son's wishes. He promised his son that Maro and Luno would be kept under surveillance during his absence. When Amar was ready to depart early in the morning of the second day, accompanied by fourteen warriors, Tomara wished his son success in his venture.

The three canoes now sped in the direction of the atoll. Amar suspected the stranger and Nao were to partake of their noon day meal, and he was assured good fortune smiled upon him. While thus occupied they could easily be captured. In less than half an hour since seeing the man and the girl disappear into the foliage, the three canoes were beaching a short distance from where Bantan's canoe rested high up on the shore near the foliage. In silence the three canoes were drawn up on the beach.

In whispers, Amar instructed his men to separate and encircle the immediate vicinity. All were armed with spears, and stone daggers were sheathed at their right hips. With the utmost stealth they entered the foliage. Two warriors accompanied the chief's son, one to each side of him. Presently the shelter was to be observed. Amar nodded to each of the warriors. From within they heard the sounds of talking and laughter.

"They are partaking of their noon meal," he said in a whisper. "Their capture should be easy. They do not suspect they were followed."

Bantan and Nao were enjoying their noon day repast. The bronzed giant for the time being was not haunted by the ghosts of the past. The girl's good comradeship and vivacity dissipated thoughts of all other than the fact he and Nao were upon the atoll and apparently were getting along famously.

They had finished eating, but they still lingered at the table, looking across at one another, and speaking of trifling matters. It seemed both were under a spell because of the other, and each wished to prolong the spell to its utmost. A quizzical expression now appeared in Bantan's eyes as he looked at the girl. Her soft dark eyes did not waver.

"What is it, Bantan?" she asked. "You wish to say something?"

He nodded and a smile touched his lips.

"Nao, you seem to read my thoughts," he remarked. "Wanya, too, was like that."

The girl's smile revealed no jealousy because of his mention of his foster sister.

"I was just thinking," he said, and then hesitated.

"Yes?" Nao's dark eyes lost none of their glow.

"I was thinking and wondering," he continued, "if you have regretted knowing me, and because of me have left Amo Island—your father and mother, and your other friends."

The girl slowly shook her head in negation.

"Since we have come to know each other, Bantan,"
she confessed, "I have not regretted thus far. One
thing, I had the occasion to realize my foolish infatuation for Amar." She snapped her fingers as though to
dismiss the matter. "I know now I had been very
foolish to think of him at all. Our existence together
has been more exciting than I would have thought possible. We were nearly caught in a tropic storm that
doubtless would have taken our lives had we not been
so fortunate to be near Ono Island; and so we were
spared. Our capture by the Ono people seemed hopeless, but by a miracle we escaped. We have had much
excitement in the past few days," she concluded. "But
I'm sure our future will be a happier existence. As
for me, I could remain here forever. But that wouldn't
be fair to you, since your foster father and mother, and
your other friends are upon Marja Island. There I
hope to be accepted as one of them."

Bantan's smile became broader as the girl finished
speaking.

"You surely shall be accepted as one of them, Nao,"
he assured her. "After the dangers we have been
subjected to and have been spared, it must be intended that our future is to be a happier and more
peaceful one."

A quizzical expression now possessed the girl's dark
eyes. She appeared in deep thought.

"Yes, Nao?" he asked with a soft laugh. "You
wish to say something that disturbs you?"

She nodded and smiled. Then her smile became one
of fear, for looking beyond Bantan, who sat in line
with the opened door, she was paralyzed by what she
saw. She knew at once the revengeful Amar had come
in search of them. She obtained a glimpse of his
sinister face among the other warriors who peered

through the opened doorway at the rear of Bantan. The realization that her happiness was to be so short-lived seemingly stunned her. With a moan of despair she broke the seeming hypnosis that gripped her, but too late to warn Bantan, or even to be of assistance to him. At the next moment she was taken captive by one of the Amo warriors. Though she realized the odds were overwhelming, she thought of the auto-matic. Imprisoned as she was, she could not reach it.

Bantan had been aware of Nao's startled expres-sion, but before he could speak or turn about to see what was the object of the girl's fear, strong hands fastened about him, pinioning his arms to his sides. At once the bronzed islander realized the danger that con-fronted them.

Bantan was not to be taken a captive without a struggle. Surging to and fro, exerting his muscles to their greatest strain in an endeavor to be free of the steel-like hands that gripped him, he writhed mightily. So violent his efforts, grunts issued from his lips. The young giant managed to arise to his feet, pushing the rattan chair backward, and the table was rudely shoved ahead. At such a disadvantage and not able to see his captors, another mighty surge he made. One of his arms was freed, and as he turned to administer his wrath upon the captor who imprisoned his other arm, he was struck sharply upon the back of his head with the haft of a spear. The pain enraged Bantan. Still writhing mightily, successive blows were struck upon his unprotected head. The young giant's struggles became weaker. Then at last a final blow resulted in his muscles becoming lax. With a moan escaping his lips, he sank to the floor of the shelter, unconscious. Quickly Amar stepped to his side and relieved him of his steel dagger.

With tears in her eyes Nao saw the handsome bronzed giant repeatedly struck on the head with the haft of a spear, and as he collapsed she realized the futility of life's glowing promise.

Futility? The girl became possessed with a seemingly demoniac rage. She writhed and twisted, sought to bite and kick her captor, but he was a strong man. Strive though Nao did to win her release, she was doomed to disappointment, for her efforts to free herself availed her nothing. In despair, she became resigned to her fate. Dry, choking sobs found their way to her lips.

The first intimation Bantan had of returning consciousness was the realization his wrists had been bound tightly with slender, strong vines. As he opened his eyes and looked about him, he did not realize the identity of his captors until his eyes rested upon the hate-filled countenance of Amar, the son of the Amo Island chief. He realized now that Nao had spoken true words when she had warned him that Amar would not be the one to forget an injustice, and that he would trail his enemy until he eventually caught up with him.

Defiance blazed in the bronzed giant's eyes, but he uttered no word to Amar. The chief's son stood at his side, his hands clenched. His black eyes glinted malevolently.

"You did not think I would follow you, stranger," he hissed. "Know now that Amar does not forget an enemy while he lives."

Bantan's dark eyes still revealed his defiance, but he uttered no word.

Amar drew his sandalled right foot back and kicked the bound captive in the ribs.

"Take that, stranger," he muttered. "What the future holds for you is far from pleasant."

Still Bantan did not speak.

Amar again kicked him in the ribs—harder than previously.

The bronzed giant's dark eyes were narrowed to mere slits, and only with an effort did he repress the defiant words that were upon the tip of his tongue.

With a malevolent laugh, Amar turned from Bantan and approached Nao. As he neared her, the girl drew herself erect, with head lifted proudly.

"And you, Nao," he sneered, "you preferred to run away with the stranger. Do you know what your punishment shall be?"

"I do not regret what I have done," the girl stated in level tones. "If I had the opportunity, I would do so again."

Amar muttered a curse, and with vehemence slapped a side of the girl's face with an opened hand.

"You are insolent," he said in nasty tones. "As your punishment, I have decreed that you shall be tortured with the stranger. Your father and mother shall be made to witness your agonies, before they, too, are put to death as their crime for having concealed knowledge of the stranger's coming to Amo Island."

Instant tears appeared in Nao's eyes and she was greatly agitated.

"No, Amar," she begged, "do not make my father and mother suffer for my wrongdoing."

The chief's son laughed heartily in mockery.

"You are no position to tell me what to do," he answered.

Nao's cheek was red where she had been slapped smartly, but that did not hurt a part as much as the knowledge that her beloved father and mother were to be punished. Realizing her pleas were in vain, she subsided into stoic silence.

Amar now walked to Bantan's side, and glaring down at him, he again delivered a kick in the ribs with his sandalled foot. He muttered unintelligible words beneath his breath. Then he turned and paced about the shelter, inspecting it casually. He peered within the small apartment Nao had occupied during the night. Presently his eyes came to rest upon the automatic and the belt of cartridges, also the bow and the arrows, which were in a corner of the shelter. He picked them up, inspecting each article carefully.

Though he had never seen a bow and an arrow, he seemed to know for what purpose they were intended. Deliberately he placed the notched end of an arrow against the bowstring, and clasping the end with his thumb and two fingers, he tensed the bowstring several times, and then nodded. Grudgingly he admitted to himself this bronzed stranger was superior to him in regards to implements of war.

The automatic then claimed his interest. He lifted it, weighing it in one hand and then the other. He examined it carefully. He peered within the hollow tube, then examined the trigger and its guard. He steadied it with his left hand, and with his right sought to hold it as it should be. Steadying it in his right hand, the base of his thumb pressed against the butt, his forefinger tentatively touched the trigger. He was tempted to press hard upon it to see what would happen, but decided against such an act. With a knowing light in his black eyes he returned to the bronzed stranger who had been watching him intently. Bantan had been permitted to arise to a seated position. The bronzed skin covering his ribs was red where he had been kicked by the chief's son.

"What is this and for what is it used?" Amar demanded of the captive, brandishing the automatic before him.

Bantan shrugged his shoulders, not uttering a word.

Amar's anger was aroused on the instant.

"You won't tell me?" he shouted.

The bronzed giant merely shook his head. His coldly staring eyes were fixed on the chief's son.

Amar drew his right foot back, but as his eyes met those of the captive, the contemplated kick was not delivered. Muttering beneath his breath, he turned to the leader of the warriors.

"Ruma, we shall partake of fruit and then take up our return to Amo Island," he said in level tones of authority.

Bantan's ankles were bound, and then Nao was made to sit down, and her ankles were bound similarly. The Amo warriors then gathered fruits with which to satisfy their hunger, and in compliance with Amar's orders, more fruit was gathered and stored in the canoes for use upon their return to Amo Island.

While the warriors attended to these matters, Bantan and Nao, seated near each other, conversed in low whispers. The bronzed giant's features were impassive, and though the girl smiled bravely, he shook his head sadly.

"You should hate me very much, Nao," he said. "Had I not come into your life you would not be in this present trouble."

The girl's eyes glowed, and though she realized the hopelessness of their position, she was not reproachful.

"No, Bantan, I would not even dare hate you," she murmured. "You should never say anything like that again."

He shook his head sadly.

"I should have heeded your warning," he protested. "I should have been more alert. Having reached the atoll, I should have insisted on continuing to Marja Island this morning for our safety—especially yours."

"Nothing can alter that now, Bantan," she said.

The vines that bound the girl's wrists did not prevent her from placing her hands upon his, and the light that glowed in her luminous dark eyes was indicative of her feeling for him. Bantan was not blind to the expression in Nao's eyes. His heart warmed and a smile touched his lips.

"Before we were captured, Nao," he said, "you were about to tell me something."

With the recollection of that moment a shyness overcame the girl. A flush tinged her cheeks and her eyes dropped for a moment before his steadily regarding ones. As she presently raised her eyes to meet his again, his smile became more gentle.

"You do not have to tell me in words what my eyes see, Nao," he said. Her warm hands pressed his tighter in answer. In a whisper, as though what he was going to say was sacred, Bantan added: "And, Nao, I need not tell you in words what my heart holds for you. But know this—if through some miracle we escape our present, seemingly hopeless plight, I shall pass the balance of my life to make your happiness complete."

The girl sighed deeply and a gentle, sweet smile enwreathed her lips.

"To have heard you say that, Bantan," she murmured, "makes me regret I hadn't known you always. Though I would have preferred life with you and the fulfillment of happiness, if we are going to our death I am happy and proud that I shall be dying with you.

I know life without you now would be meaningless for
me."

It was at this moment that Amar entered the shelter
with a couple of his warriors.

"Unfasten the bonds about their ankles," he said
to them.

When the vines were unfastened, Bantan and Nao
were dragged to their feet and made to walk ahead of
the warriors. Out of the shelter they went toward the
beach. Amar instructed one of the warriors to gather
up the automatic and the belt of cartridges, also the
bow and the arrows. These were placed in the bow
of Amar's canoe.

After Bantan and Nao were told to step into Amar's
canoe, their ankles were again bound. The canoes were
then drawn to the edge of the water and launched into
the gentle surf. When the calmer water was reached,
the course was set and the return to Amo Island was
taken up.

The return trip was uneventful. The weather remained clear and no sudden squalls of wind interrupted
the steady paddling of the warriors. At intervals
Nao's hands were unfastened to allow her to bathe
and partake of fruit. No protest was offered by Amar
when the girl bathed Bantan's face and fed him. The
bronzed giant thanked her for attending to him.

For the most part during the trip, Bantan and Nao
were silent. But whenever their eyes met the understanding that existed between them was not to be denied and this made the trip more enduring. The
thought of what horrible fate they were going to was
obliterated from their minds. The present alone sufficed—they were together and alive. If they were to
die together—then nothing else mattered.

Though the Amo warriors had been wearied from

wielding their paddles from Amo Island to the atoll,
they had offered no protest at being compelled to return at once to their native island without a reasonable
reprieve. Like automatons they paddled the canoes
with brief relays during the balance of the afternoon,
that evening, and all the next day until late in the afternoon when the canoes neared the shore of Amo Island.

The three approaching canoes had been observed
when they were several miles distant. This information was relayed from one villager to another, so that
by the time the canoes were nearing the beach nearly
the entire village's huts were emptied of their occupants. They were present to greet the return of
Amar and his warriors with shouts of glee that the
stranger had been recaptured, along with Nao, who
had fled with him.

Proud indeed were the Amo villagers of Amar, the
son of Tomara, the chief and acknowledged deity, but
none was more proud than Tomara. He, too, was
among the welcoming villagers, standing at the very
edge of the washing waves, awaiting the moment when
Amar's canoe would beach. Amar had recognized his
father as the canoe was about to enter the gentle surf
and he smiled and waved to him. Tomara waved in
return.

The chief and his son dressed alike, and they closely
resembled each other in all respects with the exception that the father's greater age of some twenty years
identified their true status.

Through the gentle surf the foremost canoe, followed by the two accompanying ones, came to the shore
without mishap. At the same instant the prows touched
the sandy beach, several warriors drew them up on
the sand from the reach of the lapping water.

The two captives were made to stand upright and

the villagers shouted their derision at sight of them. The vines about Bantan's ankles were unfastened, as were those about Nao's as well. Two warriors gripped the bronzed giant's arms, and another the girl's. The two captives were then made to step out of the canoe.

Tomara placed an affectionate arm about his son's shoulders and congratulated him upon the success of his mission. Amar acknowledged his father's praise with a short laugh of satisfaction.

"We shall place the captives in the temple prison cell for the night, father," he then said. "There is no need of the council to meet and decide their fate. Since the stranger defied and attempted to kill me, I alone shall decide the manner of his torture and subsequent death."

"And the girl?" his father asked.

"She went willingly with the stranger," was the reply. "She has denied her birthright, and for that reason she shall be punished the same as the stranger."

Tomara nodded.

"It is well, Amar," he said with a nod. "Your decisions are just and fitting—as the decisions of a chief-to-be should."

At Amar's command the two captives were marched to the temple, which was located to the rear of the chief's quarters. It was there the council held their meetings and where Tomara was the acknowledged deity of the Amo villagers. In one corner there was a stoutly built apartment that had no windows—only a reinforced door. Into this prison cell Bantan and Nao were thrust and the door was slammed shut and barred beyond hope of escape. The air in the prison cell was stale and almost stifling. It was dark as Erebus.

As soon as the footsteps of the warriors had re-treated from the temple, Bantan whispered to his companion. In his voice there was a spark of hope.

"Nao, this is the moment I've waited for," he said with eagerness.

The fragrance of the girl at his side relieved the staleness of the prison cell.

"You have hope of escape, Bantan?" she asked with incredulity.

"First, we must free our wrists of our bonds," he said. "Use your teeth, Nao, as I shall use mine."

In silence, except for an occasional grunt of satisfaction that indicated their success was satisfactory, both attacked the vines that encircled their wrists. With the passing moments their sharp teeth worked unceasingly. A snip sounded and Bantan uttered a sigh. In a few more moments his wrists were free.

"My wrists are free, Nao," he announced. "How are you doing?"

"Almost free," she answered.

Bantan crouched and commenced a systematic search near the floor of the wall farthest from the door. At intervals he would tap lightly upon the wall. A hollow thud would indicate the space between the upright poles. Carefully checking, he discovered the upright poles were about a yard apart.

Meanwhile, Nao had completed removing the vines from about her wrists and she sought her companion in the Stygian gloom of the prison cell. The light tapping sounds he made guided her to him.

"What are you doing, Bantan?" she asked with curiosity.

"I have a plan, Nao," he said, his tones indicating his eagerness. "Once before, when I was a prisoner upon Waneiro Island, I succeeded in escaping from a

similar plight.   Perhaps we may do so again.   All I
hope is that we have the time without interruption."

"I'll help you," she volunteered.

"You won't be able to help me, Nao," he said "Just
hope that I'll be successful."

The girl laughed lightly.

"That won't be very difficult to do," she answered.
"But if it will help I'll hope very much that you are
successful."

Upon his knees in the darkness, Bantan's strong
fingers attacked the tough fibers of the thatched walls,
breaking each strand separately.   He was thankful the
thatched walls were dry, for the strands snapped without difficulty, whereas were they damp, it would have
been more difficult to part them.   With fingers that
had to see in the Stygian gloom, from one strand to
another his fingers went, breaking them in turn.   With
the passing minutes beads of perspiration gathered
upon the bronzed giant's forehead, and these he
brushed away with a forearm before the salty drops
might run down into his eyes and cause them to smart.
Each passing minute was not to go unrewarded, for
the tough fibers gave to the assaults of his strong
fingers.

While thus engaged, Bantan's ears were alert for
the sounds of passersby.   He assumed at this time the
villagers were partaking of their evening meal, for to
his sensitive nostrils was wafted the aroma of stewing
vegetables and the rather acrid odor of cooking fires.

It was not long before an opening was made in the
wall to permit fresh air to enter the staleness of the
prison cell, also to give Bantan an opportunity to look
outside.   To the rear of the temple the village lane
was deserted.   The bronzed giant's courage was renewed as he assiduously attacked the tough fibers with

his strong fingers. Though the ends were sore and some of the nails were broken, he realized if he and Nao did not make good their escape that night, there would be no hope for them on the morrow. This thought of salvation spurred him on.

As the darkness of night descended upon Amo Island, larger became the opening in the wall of the temple prison cell.

*   *   *

Meanwhile, Amar and Tomara were partaking of their evening meal. A servant attended to their wants. Kamara, the mother of Amar, had long since died and Tomara had not remated. The fact that he had a son who one day would take his place was sufficient.

While the chief and his son ate, the former asked Amar if as yet he had conceived a punishment to be meted the bronzed stranger and Nao. Amar had been meditating as his father spoke, and with a shake of his head he dispelled his reveries. He looked toward his father, and an ironic smile touched his lips.

"No, father," he answered, "as yet I have not determined the nature of the punishment to be meted to the stranger and Nao." Then he laughed bitterly. "But have no fear. What I conceive as their punishment will be deserving."

"During the day I heard rumors that Zama expects a council meeting so that he might have a word in judging the fate of the captives," Tomara said.

Again Amar laughed bitterly.

"The witchdoctor may one day overstep his authority, father," he answered with gleaming eyes. "The matter of the stranger and Nao is a personal one. It was I who was affronted by the stranger. Zama may be assured the captives shall be punished sufficiently before their death."

"My son, you speak as a true son of a chief should," his father said; then with a shake of his head, added: "But I know Zama even better than you. Zama takes pride in his office as a witchdoctor, and all of the villagers respect him. From the beginning of our history, the witchdoctor's word comes next to the chief —his wishes come before yours, Amar. I tell you this, my son, so that Zama will not be offended."

The expression on Amar's features revealed his dislike that Zama should have a say in the matter of the captives' punishment.

"Tomorrow we shall discuss the matters more fully, father," Amar said. "I am wearied now and shall retire to my quarters."

"Of course, my son," his father agreed.

"And tomorrow, father," Amar added, "I will show you the strange weapons the stranger had in his possession."

Tomara expressed delight in this, and then Amar bade his father good night and went to his quarters. He again examined with great interest the automatic, and the bow and arrows before at length preparing to retire.

*   *   *

In their prison cell Bantan was encouraged by Nao as he continued to sever the tough fibers of the thatched wall that barred their way to freedom. As the hours had passed, the aperture slowly, but surely, became enlarged in proportion so that the girl could worm her way through without too much difficulty even now, but before the passage of Bantan's broad shoulders would be possible, several hours of painstaking work was yet to be accomplished.

The hour of midnight had come and long since passed. For some time now there were no sounds from stirring villagers. All had retired long since. Occasionally a child whimpered. All bird and insect life had become quiescent. No breeze stirred the tree tops on the outskirts of the village. The barely audible sound of the surf was to be heard.

In his quarters, Amar had been wearied so that he had fallen asleep almost as soon as he lay down upon his pallet of sweet-smelling grasses. For several hours he slept before waking. Lying flat upon his back, his eyes opened wide and his ears were alert. Something was wrong. This he realized when a few minutes had passed. Ordinarily he slept the night through. He had never known the meaning of insomnia.

With the passing minutes and sleep did not weary his eye lids, he shook his head and sat upright. A peculiar snipping sound seemed to be the reason for his wakefulness. Listening intently, holding his breath that he might hear the better, again the snipping sound was to be heard. Arising and placing an ear close to the thatched wall, the snipping sound seemed telegraphed more clearly.

Amar shook his head. He could not understand the reason for the snipping sounds. Then, as though a bolt from the heaven had struck him, he thought of the two captives in the temple prison cell. Could it be possible the bronzed stranger in some way was gnawing an opening to freedom through the thatched wall of the prison cell? The supposition seemed absurd and Amar laughed. But for a moment only, for realizing the stranger was clever, there was a possibility he would try anything to gain the freedom of himself and the Amo girl.

With a decisive nod of his head, Amar sought his dagger belt and affixed it about his waist. He touched the handle with assurance, then without loss of time crept out of his quarters and entered the temple. By this time his eyes were accustomed to the darkness, and with no difficulty he made his way in the direction of the prison cell. No longer did he hear the curious snipping sounds that he had heard from his quarters.

There was a reason for that, for Bantan's alert ears had heard Amar the moment he had left his quarters and stepped into the temple. The bronzed captive had no knowledge of the nocturnal prowler's identity, but he suspected the snipping sounds had been heard and were being investigated. His sore fingers were given respite in the minutes intervening.

Whispering to Nao, he advised her a prowler was in the temple. Straining her ears, the girl could hear the stealthy footsteps that Bantan had heard previously. Nearer to the prison cell they came until presently the prowler was directly outside the door. Bantan could hear the prowler's silent breathing. He and Nao had arisen and they stood motionless in the silence of the Stygian gloom. One of the bronzed giant's arms was about the girl's shoulders protectingly. They breathed slowly, their ears alert.

Amar remained standing before the door of the prison cell with ears strained. From within he detected no sound. Minutes passed, then realizing his folly, the chief's son turned, and with the same stealth returned to his quarters and again prepared himself for bed. Lying upon his pallet of grasses, an hour passed during which he heard no repetition of the snipping sounds that previously had disturbed him. Then with

a sigh, his tired lids closed over his eyes and he was
fast asleep again.

It was about this time in the prison cell that Bantan
felt he had rested sufficient before completing the task
he had started hours ago. Peering through the aperture he saw that all was quiet outside. As he continued
breaking the fibers of the thatched wall, he spoke to
Nao in a whisper.

"Do you know where Amar's quarters are?"

The Amo girl admitted that she did.

"When we are free, Nao," he said, "I must go there
and obtain the weapons that were taken from us."

"To do so will be risky," the girl cautioned.

"Risky or not," he replied, "I can't go without them.
We do not know what other dangers might beset us.
To be unarmed is sure death."

The snipping sounds continued during the passing
minutes, and gradually the aperture became enlarged
Peering outside after an hour had passed, Bantan
observed the first streaks of dawn lighting up the
eastern heaven.

"I will have to hurry faster, Nao," he murmured.
"If we are to escape, we must do so before the villagers are stirring. You can easily slip through the
opening, but I know my shoulders will not yet pass
through."

Though his fingers were tired, and the ends raw and
with a number of broken nails, Bantan renewed his
attack upon the fibers of the thatched wall. Every
few minutes he would thrust his head through the aperture and try to worm his broad shoulders through, but
as yet he could not do so.

Without loss of patience his sore fingers renewed
the attack upon the thatched wall; but now the element

of time was going against him, and for that reason there was more need for haste.

Nao felt helpless. There was nothing she could do but gently encourage the bronzed giant to successfully overcome the obstacle that meant life and happiness for them.

At intervals Bantan continued to thrust his head through the enlarging aperture, then at last he murmured a sigh of relief. His giant shoulders could worm through the opening, and though the skin was broken in many places, from which blood oozed, he was relieved to know he was free of the temple prison cell. The darkness of night was fast turning to the gray of dawn as he stood outside in the village lane.

"Come, Nao," he whispered. "We haven't much time."

In another moment the smiling girl had followed through the aperture in the wake of Bantan. Her slimmer shoulders had not been touched by the broken fibers of the thatched wall.

"Show me how to reach Amar's quarters," he urged.

In a few moments Nao had led Bantan to a thatched door; she indicated it led to Amar's quarters.

Bantan hoped the door had not been latched from within. The Gods of chance favored him, for the door was unlatched. Wearied as Amar had been the previous evening, combined with his keen interest in the weapons he had taken from the bronzed captive, was the reason he had neglected to lock his door.

Drawing the door open noiselessly, Bantan stepped within. The dusk of early morning lighted the interior of Amar's quarters sufficiently for him to distinguish objects. As he might have suspected, his weapons were near the side of the sleeping Amar.

As silent as a shadow, the bronzed giant crept

toward them. Not for an instant did his eyes leave the sleeping figure who lay flat upon his back, deep in sleep. Bantan earnestly hoped Amar would not waken, for he wished no further trouble with the chief's son at the present. Even though his ribs were still sore where Amar had kicked him, he felt no animosity toward him. All he hoped was to repossess his weapons and leave Amo Island without further trouble. Were he alone it might be another matter; but with Nao's safety in the balance, he did not wish to jeopardize her further.

Approaching the pallet of grasses where Amar slumbered, Bantan reached the desired position where he might gather his weapons. He went down upon one knee. The steel dagger he sheathed first. Then he placed the belt of partly used cartridges over his left shoulder. The bow and the half-dozen arrows he clutched in his left hand. As his right hand closed about the butt of the automatic, his alert ears caught the broken rhythm of the sleeper's breathing.

As though warned by a subconscious sense, Amar's eyes opened wide. In the grayness of dawn, the first intimation that something was wrong was the observance of the opened door. Quickly he sat upright, and simultaneously Bantan straightened to his full height.

An exclamation of bitter hatred was unmasked upon Amar's features as he recognized the identity of the prowler in his quarters.

"You!" he snarled. "I don't know how you managed to escape from the temple prison cell, but you will not live long to enjoy your freedom."

With his words, Amar leaped toward Bantan with outstretched hands.

The bronzed giant had no alternative but act upon the spur of the moment. His right hand clutching the automatic was raised and he swiftly brought it forward, smashing Amar upon the side of the head just above the left ear with a dull thud. The flesh was cleaved to the bone and blood spurted. With a moan, the chief's son tottered upon rubbery legs. His eyes closed and he slumped to the floor, unconscious.

Bantan looked at the inert form with no trace of emotion. Without delay he quit Amar's quarters to rejoin Nao outside in the graying dawn. The girl smiled as she saw that he had repossessed his weapons.

"Amar waked, and I struck him upon the head with the automatic," Bantan explained. "He lies unconscious upon the floor. Come, we must get to the landing and be off without delay in one of their canoes."

"He isn't dead?" the girl asked anxiously.

He shook his head.

"I don't think so," was his reply.

"If he recovers," she murmured, "greater will be his desire for revenge. Another time, should we be in his power, no mercy shall be spared us whatever."

While they spoke, they were hastening through the deserted village lanes in the direction of the landing. There a canoe was selected. Bantan deposited his weapons in the bow, and ascertaining a paddle was therein, he drew it to the water's edge. In another moment Nao had stepped within. The bronzed giant then shoved the canoe into the gentle surf and leaping in, took up the paddle, and with dextrous strokes guided it to the calmer water beyond.

Nao was looking at him with a smile of incredulity.

"I can hardly believe our good fortune, Bantan," she murmured.

A grim smile touched his lips.

"Do you realize we have no provisions, Nao?" he asked. "We cannot make the trip to the atoll without them. It looks as though we must circle the island and make a landing and provision the canoe for our trip to the atoll."

"You know best, Bantan," the girl answered.

Quickly Bantan altered the prow of the canoe, and with powerful strokes propelled it southerly until they had reached a position beyond observation from the landing. The prow was turned toward the shore and in a few minutes the canoe was beached.

Bantan and Nao quickly gathered an assortment of fruit and returned to the canoe, placing it in the bow. The canoe was then drawn near the edge of the washing waves, and Nao stepped within. As the bronzed giant was about to push it into the gentle surf, from the direction of the Amo village they had recently quit there rose a great commotion. The young giant looked at the girl, and she nodded solemnly.

"Amar has been found," she murmured; "else he was not badly injured and, recovering consciousness, has roused the villagers to give us pursuit."

Bantan's features were grim and he appeared in deep thought.

"What shall we do now?" Nao asked, rousing him from his deep thought.

"That is what I am thinking of for our future safety, Nao," he answered. "To remain here is dangerous, and to try and reach the atoll now would surely result in our recapture, for Amar will have warriors paddle there. If they do not sight us on the way, he may have them remain there for a while in the hope we will come later if we manage to elude capture. The only solution to our problem, therefore, is for us to go to Ono Island again, and hope we can remain there undiscovered for several suns. By watching for returning canoes of the Amo villagers, we will know when it will be safe to return to the atoll and trust no further dangers beset us."

Nao thought of Lori, the Ono princess, and how she was infatuated with Bantan. With perhaps a twinge of misgiving, she acquiesced to his suggestion.

"We will have to be very careful and keep constant watch while upon Ono Island," Bantan cautioned. "But we should be able to do that all right. The Ono villagers will not expect us to return there after our recent escape. Therein lies our only hope of survival. Do you not think I am wise in my decision?"

Nao smiled and tried to banish the thought of Lori from her mind.

"Let us hurry before we are apprehended," she said.

With a nod, Bantan launched the canoe into the gentle surf and presently was guiding it in a southerly course in the calmer water beyond the surf. Circumnavigating Amo Island, when the canoe reached a point nearest Aoono Island beyond which Ono was to be seen, the bronzed giant reset the canoe's course, and now was leaving Amo behind. With powerful strokes the canoe fairly leaped across the intervening distance in response to the paddler's anxiety to reach the fancied security of Ono Island.

"So far all is well, Nao," Bantan said with a smile.

The girl had been looking up at the volcanic cone with awe, and the young giant's words roused her from her reveries. She smiled as she indicated the volcano.

"What a huge mountain!" she exclaimed. "I have never been so close to this barren island in all my life."

Bantan's eyes swiftly swept the towering volcanic cone with interest. It seemed strange that nature should provide two islands, each lush with vegetation, at the side of this barren volcanic island. He had no means of knowing the long-ago eruption of the volcano that had resulted in the huge island dividing itself. He made no comment as they were circumnavigating the barren island, but time and again his eyes would sweep its surface with awe. And then he espied the cavern upon the southwestern side above a rock shelf.

"Look, Nao!" he exclaimed, and he pointed with an indicating hand toward the object of his discovery. "Do you see that cavern?"

The girl's eyes followed his direction, and she, too, saw what he did.

"Do you suppose we might land and seek sanctuary there?" she asked. "Then we would have no need of worry from either the Amo or Ono villagers."

Bantan nodded.

"We could hide in the cave by day," he mused. "At night we could go either to Amo or Ono Island for fruits. Yes, I think it would be best we land there."

With his words, he altered the course of the canoe, and headed the prow for the sanctuary of the cave on Aoono Island. Minutes later the canoe neared the slightly sloping rock shelf, and Bantan permitted the canoe to come to an easy landing. As the prow scraped against the rock shelf, he placed his paddle in the bottom of the canoe and agily leaped out. Steadying the canoe, he held it while Nao stepped outside. He drew the water craft higher up on the rock shelf, and looked toward the cavern. It was some twenty feet from where they had beached.

The light of the early morning was sufficient to reveal the interior, the opening of which was some six feet in width and twelve in height. Standing at the entrance, the bronzed giant and the girl peered with wondering eyes to behold the cavern extended all of

fifty feet into the bowels of the mighty volcano. Some
seaweed and crab shells littered the floor, which fact
indicated the incoming tide must extend this far. The
cavern was either a flaw in the mountain or the result
of erosion, rain, tide, and wind. It seemed most
feasible for the fugitives to seek sanctuary therein
until they felt the time was reasonably safe to return
to the atoll, and from thence to the safety of Marja
Island.

Bantan looked at Nao after they had surveyed the
interior of the cavern, and as their eyes met, it was the
girl who spoke first.

"We should be safe here, Bantan," she said.

He nodded in approval.

"I'll bring the canoe within from possible detection
by a passing search party," he said.

Suiting his words to action, Nao, meanwhile, prepared what fruit they would eat. As they partook of
it, a smile lighted the wearied features of the bronzed
giant.

"You are smiling," the girl said with an amused expression in her dark eyes.

"I was thinking," he said with a nod. "Thinking
how fortunate we have been thus far. We are always
in danger and somehow manage to escape."

"And I wonder," she added, "if we are always going to be so fortunate in making our escape from
dangers."

He shook his head, as a smile touched the corners of
his lips.

"Anyway, we are safe now," he assured the girl.
"The Amo warriors would never suspect we have
sought sanctuary upon this rock island. I wonder what
they will think when the days pass and they don't find
us?"

The girl shrugged her shoulders. Then she stifled a yawn with a dainty hand.

"After I have slept a little while I may be able to think more clearly," she answered.

"That's how I feel," he agreed.

Dry seaweed was gathered and carried to the rear of the cavern. The rock floor was reasonably dry—testimony that no recent high tides had deposited water therein. Spreading the dry seaweed upon the rock floor to their satisfaction, Bantan and Nao lay down upon their respective pallets. The last thought in their mind before sleep overtook them was the fact they had again managed to make an escape from a precarious situation.

What the unknown future might hold for them, they gave not a thought. The present alone sufficed. They were safe.

What more could they ask of a benevolent fate?

PART IV

SANCTUARY ON AOONO ISLAND

Centuries ago, the Aoono Islands of today had been one large island. Directly in its center loomed a barren volcano. Many hundred feet above the tallest coconut trees it towered. Indeed, there were times when the cratered top was enwreathed with low-hanging clouds. Its fissured sides made it possible without too much difficulty to scale one's way to the top of the lofty crater.

In stately majestic regalness the volcano had stood throughout the centuries from time's beginning when the structural topography of the earth had been fashioned. Occasionally, then, deep-throated rumblings had been heard from its bowels. The island would tremble, and all bird and insect life would become quiescent in fear of the unknown, cataclysmic forces that might be unleashed from the earth beneath.

Only once had this concealed force burst free of its incarceration. It had been horrible—would have been more so had the island been inhabited by people. The great island had shivered and shook repeatedly for hours. Then the entire mass convulsed fearfully. The east and west side of the island parted from the base of the mighty volcano. As though mighty hands had been at work, the two masses of land were drawn a half-mile from the mother parent. Light tidal waves had followed this disturbance.

Sulphuric flames and smoke had erupted from the yawning crater, casting a pall upon the surrounding land and water, and blotting out the light 'from the equatorial sun for many hours.   Molten lava had flowed down the sides of the fissured volcanic cone to be engulfed into the raging water with drum-splitting reports.   Hissing water at a boiling pitch lifted high, and steam rose swiftly upward to the very top of the belching crater.

With increasing violence the volcano's eruptions had continued.   The two islands convulsed fearfully, and it was of little wonder nature's disturbance did not cause them to sink beneath the ocean.   Their structure must have been of the same ruggedness as the volcano's base, for each survived the awful convulsed movements.

The long-pent forces at length reached their peak, then gradually subsided.   At greater intervals the volcano belched, then at last the rumblings, deep throated in the bowels of the earth, commenced to cease.   The boiling lava no longer flowed down the barren slope, but that there was turgescence therein was apparent, since the crater continued to smoke.

For days the sulphuric fumes rose into the blue heaven.   Then a mighty tropical storm had raged. Rain fell in torrents.   When the storm had passed, a mist rose from the yawning crater for several days, then presently this ceased.

The volcano had become stilled.   For many centuries it had been so since its first eruption—but would it remain quiescent until the end of time?

Who could tell?

Many centuries had passed, and vegetation, bird, and insect life had flourished again upon the east and west island.   In the wake of this had come one of the many migrating Polynesian tribes to take up their existence in this region.

*   *   *

The sun was several hours high and his rays passed beyond the range of penetrating the mouth of the cavern in the volcano upon Aoono Island. For that reason the semi-darkness of the cavern's interior induced sleep to the bronzed giant and the girl who reposed upon respective pallets of seaweed.

Nearly five hours had passed since they had fallen asleep. Deep and refreshing was their slumber, for neither had closed their eyes during the past twenty-four hours. Inside the volcano's cavern the atmosphere was of a degree that was neither too cool nor warm, and for that reason the two sleepers were not uncomfortable. Had their sleeping pallets been of softer and finer textured grasses there was no doubt they would have been much more comfortable.

The sleeping girl was the first to awaken. She arose to a seated position and looked about her in the semi-gloom of the cavern. Several yards from her she saw the bronzed giant still sleeping. He was lying upon his right side, somewhat curled forward with knees flexed. A smile touched the girl's cheeks. Rubbing her arms vigorously for a few moments, and pushing her lustrous hair over her shoulders, she arose to her feet.

She stole quietly to the sleeping giant's side. She knelt and peered down at his handsome features, composed in refreshing sleep. With a smile she gently touched her lips to his left cheek. Though the sleeper's rhythmic breathing was interrupted for a moment, he did not waken. With a long-drawn sigh and stirring a little, the sleeper's regular breathing was resumed.

The girl then arose to her full height and softly stole away on tip toes. Approaching the mouth of the cavern, she paused and peered outside before ven-

turing into the open. For long moments she stared
across the intervening sun-kissed water to Ono Island.
Her sharp eyes could detect no sign of a villager upon
the beach. Then she looked to right and left, but there
was no canoe to be seen upon the shimmering water.
With a nod she stepped outside, and with care because
of the uneven footing, she walked along the rock shelf.

In another moment she had entered the water and
swam about for several minutes before returning to
the cavern. Looking within, she saw that the bronzed
giant still slumbered. Sitting upon her haunches just
within the mouth of the cavern, she ran her fingers
through her wet, lustrous hair, arranging it as best
she could without the use of a comb.

Within the cavern the sleeper now stirred to wakefulness. Arising to a seated position, he looked about
in the semi-gloom. He espied the girl seated near the
cave's opening. In another moment he had approached
her as she sat with back turned toward him. Her at-
tentive ears had been aware of his stirring, and just
as he paused behind her, she turned with a smile.

"You are awake at last," she said.

"You always seem to waken before me, Nao," he
answered with a shake of his head.

"And I've had a swim, too," she added.

"Then I'll have a swim, too," he said.

"I'll prepare some fruit and will be waiting for you,"
the girl added.

"You saw no sign of any one, Nao?" he then asked.

"I especially looked toward Ono Island," she replied with a shake of her head.

"That is good," and with his words the bronzed
giant stepped forward.

Cautiously Bantan looked about before stepping out
into the bright sunlight. Moments later he was ap-

proaching the water's edge. To the right and the left
he looked at the shimmering water for sign of a canoe;
then toward Ono Island his dark eyes rested for long
moments. Satisfied that there were no chance ob-
servers, he then entered the water and swam leisurely
for several minutes before returning to the cavern.

During his short absence Nao had obtained fruit
from the canoe's bow and had prepared it. As Bantan
entered, she beckoned to him to join her at breakfast.

As they ate, squatting upon their haunches, Bantan's
eyes roved about the cavern. As they presently rested
upon the girl, who had been silently watching him in
curiosity, he spoke.

"Did your people ever mention anything about the
volcano being active?" he asked.

The girl shook her head.

"Nothing has ever been said about the volcano,"
she replied. "Always has Aoono stood like a silent
sentinel between the two islands. 'Silent sentinel' is
what the word Aoono means."

Bantan nodded and made no further comment rela-
tive to the volcano, and their conversation drifted to
other channels. Having finished their meal, as a tidy
housewife would, Nao gathered the refuse and deposited it into the water outside. Returning to the
cavern where the bronzed giant was still seated, the
girl smiled as she seated herself near him.

"Our enemies are now to each side of us, Bantan,"
she remarked. "I wonder what they would think were
they to know of our present, close whereabouts?"

"It's not what they would think, Nao," he added;
"it's what they would do. Our present freedom would
not be for long."

"To be free means a lot to a person, doesn't it?" the
girl said seriously.

He nodded with a grave expression upon his face.

"I never had the occasion to realize how precious freedom was until I knew you," she added. "The freedom of one's village is one thing. To be free, even though among other people, is another. I have come to realize this during the past several suns."

"Doctor Hunter taught me the real meaning of freedom," Bantan said in answer. "When the Japs came to Marja Island and made slaves of the villagers, it was then I really understood what freedom meant. When we reach Marja, then we will realize it all the more."

An expression of wistfulness appeared in the girl's lovely dark eyes.

"I am longing for that day," she said. "But that won't be possible for several suns yet, will it?"

He shook his head regretfully.

"Perhaps longer than that," he answered. "It is possible Amar will instruct warriors to remain upon the atoll to await our eventual return. It will not be too difficult for us to remain here so long as we are un-discovered. Each night we can go either to Amo or Ono Island for fruits. We will not find the time too long."

She nodded and smiled with a flush mantling her cheeks.

"Wherever you are, Bantan," she confessed, "is reason enough for me to be happy. Even if we were compelled to remain in this cavern the rest of our lives, I wouldn't mind too much."

The bronzed giant's arm went about Nao's shoulders and drew her close to him. Their cheeks pressed the other's.

"I feel that way, too, Nao," he murmured.

For long minutes they remained thus, one of the

girl's slim arms going about his shoulders. No words were spoken. There was no need for words. As though their thoughts originated from one source, they were content in being this close together. But at last with a sudden fear in her bosom, the girl spoke.

"I would be so much happier if only I knew my father and mother were not to be punished for having withheld knowledge of your coming to Amo Island," she said wistfully.

Bantan was silent a few moments before speaking.

"It would be dangerous to go to Amo Island and search the village—even at night," he said. "But I can understand your fears, Nao. I would feel the same concern for my foster father and mother were they in danger. Perhaps tonight I may risk going there and, if I can find them, persuade them to come with me."

The girl's troubled eyes brightened with joy.

"Oh, if only that could be!" she exclaimed. "How happy it would make me!"

Upon the impulse of the moment, Nao pressed her warm lips to Bantan's cheek. Then, at once, though her cheeks were flushed and her eyes were bright, she became humble and contrite.

"Forgive me," she said in a low voice. "I didn't mean to be so impulsive."

"Of course I forgive you, Nao," he said with soft laughter. "You have committed no wrong. There isn't anything, I'm sure, that I wouldn't forgive you. If it makes you feel better I'll kiss your cheek as you did mine."

With his words the bronzed giant pressed his lips to the girl's burning cheek, and as he drew his head back and met her eyes, he saw that hers were shy. Her left hand pressed her bosom as though to stifle the pounding of her heart. In her thoughts the realization was apparent that it was the first time a man had ever kissed her—even upon the cheek—and she was amazed at the tingling sensation that pulsed through her. Her maidenly shyness prevented the answering of the question: What would happen to her were Bantan to place his arms about her, hold her close, and press his lips warmly to hers?

Realizing the girl's embarrassment, Bantan averted his attention from her and looked out at the shimmering surface of water that spanned Aoono and Ono Islands. His dark eyes lighted with interest, for he saw a canoe being propelled by two paddlers. From where they had come, the bronzed giant had no means of determining; but at least he might watch and see where they were going.

"Look, Nao," he said to the girl. "There is a canoe with two paddlers."

The girl was happy there had been something to dispel the embarrassment she had experienced, and with an expression of concern upon her still flushed features she drew near her companion and looked in the direction he indicated.

"It is difficult to discern whether they are Amo or Ono warriors," she said. "Unless I am mistaken the canoes of the two islands are very much alike."

"We'll watch from the concealment of the cavern, Nao," he said, "Perhaps we may determine where they are going."

"My people do not often paddle on this side of Aoono," the Amo girl said. "It is possible our escape from the village may have induced them to search for us—at Amar's command."

Bantan chuckled at the mention of Amar's name.

"His head must hurt this morning," he remarked.

Nao did not join in her companion's sense of humor. The thought of her father and mother at Amar's mercy was of deep concern to her.

"I hope Amar spares my father and mother until they can be rescued." she said with a little shudder.

Bantan's compassion was apparent. He reached out and rested a gentle hand upon the girl's shoulder.

"If it is possible, Nao," he assured her, "I'll rescue them this very night."

Bantan's eyes again sought the canoe. They brightened at what he saw beyond. Emerging from the shoreline of Ono Island was another canoe. This surely was from the Ono village. It was apparent the paddlers sighted the other canoe, and without hesitation their course was set to intercept it. The bronzed giant now had reason to guess the first canoe, much nearer Aoono Island than the Ono, was from Amo Island.

As the more distant canoe drew closer in the passing minutes, the two watchers in the cavern saw that it was manned by four paddlers, and they were plying their paddles with a seeming frenzy. As yet the two paddlers in the nearer canoe were not aware of the farther one that approached from Ono Island, for their paddle strokes were leisurely.

"The two Amo warriors are in trouble, Nao," Bantan observed. "Do the warriors of Amo and Ono Island fight whenever they meet?"

The Amo girl nodded.

"It has always been that way," she answered sadly. "Sometimes, after such killings, the relatives of the slain will go to the island of their enemy under the cover of darkness, and slay some of their enemies. Then, in turn, relatives of those slain, will go to their enemy's island for a similar reason. It has been many moons now since revengeful deaths have occurred. But from what we see is about to happen, I'm afraid more revengeful deaths shall occur."

The bronzed giant shook his head.

"I can't understand why people of neighboring islands cannot live in peace with one another," he said. "Why must there always be killing among human beings? I can understand people defending their freedom against an invader, but the killings you speak of, Nao, are useless."

The girl nodded and a faint smile touched her lips.

"I guess they don't know any better," she replied. "Perhaps they need some one like you to show them a new way to live."

Bantan's features were serious.

"I would like to play that part, Nao," he answered. After a moment's silence, he exclaimed: "Look! The Amo paddlers are now aware of their enemy."

Nao looked with renewed interest.

It was true. The pursuing Ono canoe was within a hundred yards from the Amo canoe before its occupants were aware that pursuit was being given them. It was apparent they had reason to fear, for they were outnumbered four to two. They were not so brave that they felt equal to engage their hereditary enemies in battle, for now they plied their paddles with a frenzy that knew no equal.

The four paddlers of the Ono canoe increased their speed more so, and thus the chase commenced, with the pursuing canoe quickly overtaking the Amo paddlers.

Bantan and Nao could still watch from the concealment of the cavern without exposure to themselves. Wordlessly they viewed the chase. Within minutes the two Amo warriors laid down their paddles and took up their spears, for they realized they could not hope to outdistance the enemy.

Two of the Ono warriors exchanged paddles for spears while their two companions maneuvered the canoe alongside the enemy's. Upon their knees all warriors remained so that their actions might not upset their respective water craft. Four spears parried in the passing minutes without injury to any, for each warrior was capable of defending himself. A thrust by an Amo was made, and a parry by the opposing Ono followed. Repeatedly this was performed, and after some ten minutes had terminated, the two Ono warriors bearing paddles now placed them in the bottom of the canoe and took up their spears. The engagement was being prolonged beyond time of their likening, and with their assistance the conflict should be ended within minutes. Two Ono warriors now engaged a single Amo, and the thrusting and parrying of spears became more furious.

From around the westerly side of Aoono Island another Amo canoe with two warriors plying paddles appeared. Almost at once they espied the battling warriors. Upon the instant they increased the tempo of their strokes and their canoe leaped in response as they hoped to render assistance to their fellows before they were overwhelmed.

Bantan and Nao caught sight of the Amo canoe.

"Now the battle will be even," Bantan said with a grim smile.

"If they can reach their companions before they are defeated," the girl agreed.

"I think they will," he observed. "The two Amo warriors are giving a good account of themselves against their odds."

The Ono warriors had become aware of the nearing

Amo canoe with reinforcements. In a frenzy they sought to overwhelm their lesser numbered opponents. But the two Amo warriors, aware of the assistance coming to them, took new heart and warded off the spear thrusts of their enemy with dexterity.

The two Amo warriors in the approaching canoe shouted words of encouragement to their outnumbered fellows.

Over anxious, one of the Ono warriors thrust fiercely with his spear and missed his target. The momentum of his lunge was not checked in time. The canoe rocked. The other three warriors endeavored to balance it at once, and in this they were successful. Their attention detracted for brief moments was sufficient for the two opposing warriors to take advantage.

One of the warriors thrust with his spear and the point pierced the left chest of one of the Ono warriors. With a shriek of mortal agony, the Ono warrior was dragged to his feet clutching his chest as the spear was withdrawn. Crimson spurts of blood were emitted from the mortal wound, covering his hands and running down his body in rivulets. Attaining an erect position, his legs at once became lax. Without a further sound he toppled over backward into the water, not even rising to the surface once.

The canoe started to rock, but it was quickly settled by the remaining three warriors. With grimness they attacked their foe. So savage the attack following the death of one of their comrades, one of the Amo warriors lost his balance in defending himself, and toppled over backward with a splash. As he did so, the canoe rocked and perilously came to a point of capsizing.

At the next moment the three spears of the Ono

warriors were directed at the lone Amo, and the only way he could avoid a mortal injury was to fall flat. As the spear points passed over his naked back and were withdrawn, he at once arose to his knees and thrust with his own spear. One of the Ono warriors was disabled as the spear point penetrated the muscles of his right chest just under the arm pit. A howl of pain was emitted from his writhing lips.

The Amo warrior who had toppled into the water had now swum to the side of the canoe, and holding it steady while he treaded water, he uttered words of encouragement to his valiant companion. At the next moment he was vilifying the Ono warriors.

The nearing Amo canoe was reason for the Ono warriors to redouble their attack upon the lone Amo warrior, for they realized with the advent of the newcomers in the conflict they would be outnumbered, and they had no stomach for that. More frenziedly the two uninjured warriors sought to overwhelm their single opponent. It was evident the Amo warrior was anxious to survive, for he parried and thrust with his spear savagely, even as the two Ono warriors sought earnestly to overwhelm him. Since he was more on the defensive than offensive, the Amo warrior was successful for the time being in thrusting aside the spear thrusts of the two Ono warriors. It was a question how long he might survive the savage attack.

It was at this juncture the nearing Amo canoe circled about the Ono canoe and the efforts of the paddlers became more intense. There was no question of any intention that prisoners were to be taken, for each spear thrust was aimed to kill, not wound.

The wounded Ono warrior, though suffering from his flesh wound, transferred his spear to his left hand, and thrust at one of his enemies. In this move he was

not adept, for he missed widely.   At the next moment
an Amo warrior in the rescue canoe thrust at him
while he was off balance, and the spear point passed
through his heart.   An agonizing moan escaped the
lips of the doomed warrior, and he toppled over backward into the engulfing water—a crimson blotch
marked the surface where he had plunged.

Now the Amo warriors had the advantage with two
of the Ono warriors having been dispatched. While the
two newly arrived Amo warriors engaged the two Ono
warriors in combat, the Amo warrior who had toppled
into the water unhurt informed his companion to steady
the canoe while he drew himself within.   In another
moment he had done so.   Rearming himself with his
spear, he and his companion joined in the battle with
the two remaining Ono warriors.

Outnumbered four to two, the Ono warriors defended themselves as best they could, but the end was
inevitable.   First, one received a mortal wound, and
within a minute the other succumbed to another spear
thrust.   Both toppled into the water with moans, a
blotch of blood marking the surface where they had
disappeared.

Their enemies defeated, the victorious Amo warriors took possession of the Ono canoe which had not
overturned.   In accord and without delay, they returned to Amo Island to report the success of their engagement with enemy warriors.

Bantan and Nao had watched the battle with interest.   Now that it had terminated in victory for the
Amo warriors, the bronzed giant turned to face the
girl.

"And that is that, Nao," he said with a shrug.

The girl merely nodded.

Bantan's brow furrowed, giving evidence to his deep thought.

"Does it seem strange to you, Nao," he said then, "that the two Amo canoes should be upon this side of Aoono Island?"

"It could be possible that the Amo warriors were searching for us," she answered.

"That is what I was thinking," he agreed, nodding his head slowly. "And yet, what could be the reason the canoe from Ono Island appeared when it did?"

Nao's eyes contained the wisdom of the sages.

"Perhaps they were looking for us as well," she replied. "We escaped from their island, too—you remember?"

"Only too well," he said. "Several warriors were killed. I suppose they would wreak vengeance upon us, were we recaptured."

Nao nodded slowly, but said nothing.

Bantan seated himself near the mouth of the cavern and appeared in deep thought again. Presently the Amo girl seated herself near him, and she, too, appeared to be thinking as seriously as her companion. The bronzed giant looked intermittently in the direction of Ono Island—as though he anticipated seeing another canoe round the island shore.

When half an hour had passed, Bantan's dark eyes brightened. From the same direction the first Ono canoe had appeared, a second now was to be seen. He called Nao's attention to it, and the girl, too, watched in silence as the canoe reached a distance where the paddlers could be distinguished. This time there were four warriors in the canoe. They plied their paddles rather briskly. When they reached a point directly opposite Aoono Island, they paused for some few minutes, shading their eyes from the glare of the sun

and the shimmering water, to look toward the volcanic
island.   Without further delay they resumed their
circumnavigation of Ono Island.

A little while later the two watchers in the cavern
saw the Ono canoe disappear around the southerly end
of the island.

"That is that, Nao," Bantan murmured.

The girl smiled and nodded.

"When the four Ono warriors who were killed by
the Amo warriors are known to be missing," she added,
"then there will be more slaying."

"Perhaps much trouble between the two islands may
delay any punishment that might be meted to your
father and mother," Bantan said with encouragement.
"Trouble between them will be to our advantage."

The girl's eyes brightened and a wistful smile appeared upon her face.

"We can hope so anyway," she said.

The afternoon passed without further canoes from
either island being sighted.   After they had eaten an
early evening meal, Bantan cached the automatic, belt
of cartridges, and bow and arrows where they could
easily be found.   He was ready to go to Amo Island
in the hope of locating Nao's father and mother.
Nothing had been said as yet that he was going alone.
The canoe was drawn from the cavern along the rocky
shelf to the water's edge.   The bronzed giant looked
at Nao in the dusk of the early evening.   Her very attitude was sufficient for him to understand that she
intended accompanying him.

"Do you think it wise that you go with me, Nao?"
he asked.

The girl's eyes were immediately filled with hurt at
the thought of being separated from him, even if for
only a few hours.

"I would rather be with you, Bantan," she said hardly above a whisper. "While you are seeking my father and mother, I can gather fruits and softer grasses."

"It shall be as you say, Nao," he answered, nodding his head.

Presently, with Nao seated in the bow, Bantan was paddling the canoe around the easterly end of Aoono Island. Twinkling stars were now appearing in the dark canopy above as he headed for Amo Island, hoping to beach the canoe as near the landing as was possible. Above the village a reddish glow suffused the heaven. Exultant shouts could be heard.

"The villagers must have a bonfire, Bantan," Nao whispered. "There must be a celebration of some kind tonight."

"Perhaps they are celebrating the killing of the four Ono warriors," he answered.

"That must be the reason for their exultation," the girl agreed. In her heart she feared it was the celebration preceding the torture of her father and mother. She earnestly hoped not, and it was comforting to know such knowledge would be apparent in a short while.

Under Bantan's expert guidance the canoe rapidly approached the shore near the landing. He had learned from Nao that no guards were kept posted there, but in view of the possibility of a want of revenge from the Ono warriors, there was the probability they might have guards posted for an indeterminate period.

As the canoe beached, Bantan's keen eyes, long since accustomed to the darkness, scanned the shore. No indication of guards was evident, so the canoe was drawn close to the edge of the foliage. Nao followed in silence. Since the bronzed giant knew the location of the hut Nao had occupied with her parents, he needed no further instructions from her.

Leaving Nao to the duties she had to perform, Bantan stealthily approached the landing, keeping close to the foliage. The glow of the bonfire was reflected through the village lanes, casting grotesque shadows all about. The exultation of the celebrators was louder as he neared the edge of the village.

With his keen eyes alert and ears strained for any unusual sounds, Bantan then advanced to the rear of the hut Nao's parents occupied. He stole around the rear to the side where the door was located, and he at once noticed the guard who stood before it. With relief, he knew Nao's parents still lived and was not the reason for the present celebration, for no guard would have been stationed outside their hut were it otherwise.

The Amo guard stood with a spear in hand, leaning against the door. He was facing slightly away from the direction the nocturnal prowler had appeared, and for this Bantan was grateful. He stealthily advanced toward the guard. He hoped he would have no difficulty with the Amo warrior, but he was prepared for anything that might occur. The guard appeared to be interested in the village celebration, and for that reason his auditory organs were dulled. His hearing would have to be acute indeed, for Bantan moved as silently as a shadow.

The first intimation the guard had of the presence of any one near him was when an arm slipped about his neck, preventing an outcry. The guard dropped his spear and flailed his arms, for he was not to go down without a struggle. One of his clenched fists struck his unknown assailant in the stomach. Though Bantan grunted, his tightening arm about the Amo warrior's neck did not relax.

Presently the guard's struggles became weaker, then at last he went limp. Ascertaining the Amo warrior was not shamming, Bantan stood over him for a full minute. There was no question the guard was unconscious. The glow from the bonfire in the village spread in the heaven above as more firewood was heaped upon it. The shadows cast by the leaping flames were of all shapes and descriptions, and seemingly alive.

Without further hesitation, the bronzed giant went to the door and found that it was latched. He opened it and peered into the Stygian gloom within. He could see nothing, but from a corner he was positive he heard a gasp.

"Maro! Luno!" he called softly.

For a moment there was absolute silence from within. Then a low voice spoke.

"Who is it that speaks?"

"Nao feared for the safety of her father and mother," he replied. "I am the stranger with whom she left this island. I have come to rescue you both."

"Luno and I are bound," Maro answered. "We are being held prisoners until Amar decides what manner of torture we are to be subjected."

Bantan entered the hut. The voice of Maro served to guide him to Nao's bound parents.

"Where is Nao now?" the mother of the girl asked with anxiety.

"She is near the beach—awaiting our return," Bantan answered.

"Where are you going to take us?" Maro then asked.

"We have been hiding in a cavern on Aoono," was

the reply. "Nao would be very happy to have you come with us. Later, I shall take you to Marja Island, from which I came. There, you both will be welcomed in friendship and be permitted to live in peace and happiness." He added in extenuation: "I've re-gained my lost memory. My name is Bantan."

As he spoke, Bantan severed the bonds from Maro's wrists and ankles, being careful not to cut the skin. Then he groped in the darkness to cut Luno's bonds as well. Nao's parents arose to their feet a little un-steadily, for the bonds about their ankles had been somewhat tight and the circulation had been restricted. Each briskly rubbed their lower legs and presently felt much better.

"Come, let us go to the beach where Nao awaits us," Bantan then said.

Maro and Luno followed their rescuer out of the hut. Bantan noticed that the guard was still inert. All carefully avoided tripping over him. In another moment they had skirted the side of the hut and were on their way to the beach. Maro paused there to snatch up a paddle from a canoe. Along the beach at the edge of the foliage they passed, and within a few minutes had reached the canoe. Nao had completed provisioning it with fruits, and soft grasses had been gathered as well. She was awaiting their coming.

Nao and her mother embraced warmly, then the girl turned to her father and threw her arms about his neck, murmuring soft words of gratefulness that they had been unharmed.

Meanwhile, Bantan drew the canoe to the water's edge. Nao and her parents followed, taking their places as the bronzed giant held the canoe. He was last, giving it a shove into the gentle surf.

With the light water craft loaded beyond capacity,

Bantan and Maro paddled carefully so as not to capsize it. Several times water washed over the gunwale, but fortunately the calmer water was reached before the canoe shipped much more. Thereafter the light water craft rode fairly well, but its progress despite two paddles being plied was not as speedy as when Bantan and Nao had come hither.

When the canoe was several hundred yards from shore, the din in the Amo village ceased except for spasmodic shouts.

"The guard has recovered his senses and must have announced the escape of the prisoners," Bantan said to his companions.

"I hope they don't follow us tonight," Nao murmured.

"I do not think we need have any fear of that," Bantan added. "They wouldn't know where we were going, nor could they follow us at night."

Maro and Luno heaved a sigh of relief. Though Nao was silent, in her heart she hoped the morrow would not be calamitous because of Bantan's rescue of her parents.

The volcanic cone silhouetted against the canopy of stars was Bantan's guide, and in due time the canoe was paddled around the eastern side of Aoono Island. With a little difficulty the rock shelf was located and the canoe was beached there.

After all had disembarked, Bantan and Maro drew it within the cavern's mouth. Nao and her mother brought forth the grasses from the canoe's bottom and in the darkness they spread it in pallets for sleeping.

The parents of Nao had not eaten that evening, and while they partook of fruits, they expressed their gratitude for having been saved from unknown tortures. When asked of their whereabouts since escaping from

Amo Island, Nao told her parents of their brief adventure upon Ono, where Bantan had recovered his lost memory. She also told how they had reached the atoll, but the following day Amar and his warriors had captured them and brought them back to Amo. She added how they had managed to escape from the temple prison cell and that they had sought sanctuary in this cavern on Aoono, and thus far had been unapprehended.

Bantan remained near the mouth of the cavern, watching for indications of pursuit while Nao spoke with her parents. But as the time passed and there was no evidence of being followed, it was decided all would retire for the evening, for they were tired. Ensconcing themselves upon the fresh pallets of grasses, their sleep was refreshing.

Bantan slept nearer the mouth of the cavern than any of the others. Almost each hour that passed found him wide awake. Arising softly so as not to disturb the others, he would go outside and look out at the darkened water for long moments. His ears would strain for the possible sound of paddles dipping in the water. Satisfied each time that he could neither see or hear anything alien to their safety, he would return to his pallet of grasses and the next minute was fast asleep again.

The sun was just clearing the eastern horizon when he woke the last time. Despite the half-dozen wakings during the hours of the night and early morning, the bronzed giant felt surprisingly fit. Perhaps the bed of softer grasses may account for this. He remained awake now, though Nao and her parents slumbered peacefully. Moving stealthily, he ventured outside the cavern. He stared for long moments in the direction of Ono Island. Then he ventured into the water for a hasty swim that was very invigorating, for the water was somewhat cool this early in the morning.

Returning to the mouth of the cavern, he squatted there, basking in the warm rays of the rising sun. So silent the morning was, Bantan's ears, always alert, became aware of a thrumming sound now issuing from the direction of Ono Island. At first he could not be sure. The longer he listened, the more positive he became that it was the beat of tom-toms that he heard.

It was evident that the Ono villagers were to seek vengeance upon the Amo villagers in return for the death of four of their warriors.

As he sat there, the passing minutes revealed a number of canoes appearing from around the shore of Ono Island, and all were filled to capacity with warriors.

It was at this time Nao awoke. At once she looked toward the mouth of the cavern where she saw Bantan's attention fixed upon the shimmering water intervening Aoono and Ono Islands. Quickly she arose and came to the bronzed giant's side.

"What is it, Bantan?" she asked.

"The Ono warriors are going to seek vengeance for the death of their companions," he answered.

"Attacking the Amo village so early in the morning will be disastrous for those who used to be my friends," the girl said then.

Bantan nodded.

"The element of surprise is always advantageous," he agreed.

Maro and Luno, the parents of the girl, now awoke. At once they became aware of the attention of Bantan and Nao. They lost no time in joining the two watchers at the mouth of the cavern. The girl pointed toward the many canoes coming from Ono Island.

"The Ono warriors are going to attack the Amo
village," she said to her father and mother.

An ironical smile touched the lips of her father.

"I may be considered a traitor," he said; "but I
hope the Ono warriors are victorious in the battle."

Bantan was not surprised that Maro expressed himself thusly. Whatever loyalty he may have known
toward the Amo ruler could not exist after the im-
prisonment of him and his mate with the threat of torture and eventual death.

"It is regrettable that I can't join the Ono warriors
in their battle with the Amo warriors," Maro added,
after a short silence had passed.

As the canoes approached nearer the end of Aoono
Island, Bantan counted them. In all there were thirty,
and in each four warriors paddled. Even from the
distance the bronzed giant saw that the warriors had
applied war paint to their features. He smiled to his
companions.

"This is one battle we cannot engage in or even
watch," he remarked.

In single file the Ono canoes were approaching
Aoono Island, and when reaching the easterly end, they
then proceeded in double file. More quickly did they
ply their paddles, and the canoes forged ahead faster.

While the Ono canoes were passing by, a mad
scheme was in the process of evolution in Bantan's
brain. Since he and the others could not be present
at the coming battle, why not take advantage and
watch the proceedings—even from a distance? He
turned to Maro.

"Have you ever been to the top of the volcano?"
he asked.

The Amo native nodded.

"Not for a long time," he answered.

"There is a way to go up the side?" Bantan asked further.

"Upon the other end of the island, long ago there was hewn a stairway," was the reply.

A smile touched the bronzed giant's lips.

"After we have eaten, Maro," he suggested, "suppose we go to the top of the volcano and watch how the battle fares between the Amo and Ono warriors?"

A knowing smile touched the lips of the father of Nao.

"Since we can't take part in the battle," he said, "we can at least watch it. Nao and her mother wouldn't be interested, so they can remain here. They should have much to talk about while we are away."

Nao shivered involuntarily, for she had heard what her father and Bantan discussed. She drew near them with a smile.

"You both intend to go to the top of the volcano?" she asked.

The bronzed giant and Maro nodded in unison.

Again the girl shivered.

"I am afraid of going very high and mother feels the way I do," she said. "We'll be glad to remain here while you two do so."

Bantan and Maro partook of a substantial breakfast from the variety of fruits. By the time they had finished eating, the last of the Ono canoes had passed the easterly end of the island on their way to attack the Amo village.

"Come, Maro," Bantan said, arising. "Let us be on our way."

The face of the girl's father lighted with a grim smile as he joined the bronzed giant.

Without too much difficulty they picked their way along the base of the volcano until they came at last

to the westerly end.   A crude stairway had been hewn
up the side of the towering cone to the very top of the
crater.   Bantan had no means of estimating the height
from base to apex, but it looked considerable.   He
looked to Maro.

"It is quite high," he said.   "Do you think you can
make the climb?"

The Amo native's grim smile was the answer as he
nodded.

"Lead the way, Bantan.   I will be right behind you.
I may be a little soft, but I will be able to make the
climb."

Bantan smiled and started to climb the stairway up
the sloping surface with Maro following closely.   Up,
up, up the two went—a hundred, two, three, four
hundred feet.

The bronzed giant paused at this stage and looked
down at Maro who was close behind him.   The Amo
native's face was streaked with perspiration, but his
smile was eager.   Bantan perspired some, but not near
so much as the older man.

"Getting tired, Maro?" the younger man asked his
companion.

A shake of the head was the answer.

"Let's go a little faster," Maro urged.   "We don't
want to miss any more of the battle than we have to."

In the minutes that passed, the two continued their
way up the stairway without further hesitation.   By
this time Bantan's breath became a trifle labored,
whereas Maro, being older, fairly panted.   Stub-
bornly he was determined, however, to continue the
way, and maintained his place just below the leader.
The two climbers were grateful the steps hewn into
the volcano were of sufficient depth to make their hand
and footholds quite secure.

At last they were on the final stage of their climb to the top. A hundred feet more was all they had to cover. Again Bantan and Maro rested, regaining their spent breath. The former was now perspiring quite freely. Looking down at the shimmering surface of the water to his right, Ono Island seemed to have shrunk considerably in size from this height. From above the village, which could plainly be seen, wisps of smoke rose into the still, morning air. The villagers who had not joined the armada on their way to Amo Island looked small and insignificant as they moved about the seemingly miniature village. Their village idol was most imposing, however.

Rested, Bantan and Maro resumed their way upward, and at last the bronzed giant reached the apex of the volcano to find a ragged shelf fully ten feet in width surrounding the crater. Into the depths he peered, but could see nothing in the inky darkness of the bottomless pit below. He turned to give the panting Maro a hand, and in another moment the Amo native was resting upon the shelf, drawing deep, labored breaths into his starved lungs.

Bantan's massive, hairless chest rose and fell noticeably as he slowly breathed the fresh air and almost reluctantly exhaled. Already he had ceased to perspire. He turned now and his interest was directed upon the seemingly miniature Amo Island. His sharp eyes distinguished the Ono warriors who had already beached their canoes. A number of warriors were going from one Amo canoe to another and were slashing the bottoms to guard against an immediate pursuit. The main body of warriors were gathered near the foliage, evidently awaiting instructions from their leader.

The bronzed giant turned to the now more easily breathing Amo native.

"Look, Maro," he said, "we are in time to witness
the battle which will soon occur."

Smiling as he shook his head a trifle, Maro turned
about so that he could view Amo Island.

"The climb up the side of the volcano was more difficult that I anticipated," he said. "Our descent will
be easier, however."

"That is so, Maro," Bantan agreed.

When the canoes were damaged to the satisfaction
of the Ono leader, Maho, he waved a hand. The warriors were in accord and followed him into the village.
Their shouts were to be heard by the two watchers
upon the top of the volcano. A grim smile touched
Maro's lips, whereas Bantan's features were calmly
composed.

With the unheralded entrance of the Ono warriors
into the village, pandemonium ensued among the
Amo villagers. Women shrieked in terror. Children
cried. The warriors, old and young, hurriedly procured their spears and sought to defend themselves and
their families. Some were successful—others were
not. The unfortunate ones went down in injury or
mortal death from a spear thrust.

About the village temple, Tomara and Amar, the
latter with a bandaged head, gathered warriors about
them to make a determined stand against the attackers.
Warriors upon each side dropped to the ground,
wounded and dying.

Though the two forces were evenly matched, the
Ono warriors had the advantage of the surprise attack, and more of the Amo warriors were injured and
lost their lives than the attacking forces. It was fortunate for the Amo villagers that the Ono warriors
were not intent upon complete invasion and subjuga-
tion of their hereditary enemies, for their surprise at-

tack could well have been a means of doing so. Their
attack had merely been one of revenge for the deaths
of the four Ono warriors on the previous day.

For many, many moons the Ono warriors had had
no occasion to quarrel with their neighbors, even
though ill feeling had been in existence since that last
quarrel for supremacy some few centuries ago. The
families that had come to live upon Ono Island and
had built their homes and took up their living there
had not sought further intercourse with the other
families that had triumphed and remained upon Amo
Island.

For several centuries had the state of ill feeling
existed between the two islands with only minor raids
upon the other. But at no time had one or the other
islanders made a determined effort to invade and con-
quer and subjugate the other. Perhaps the thought
had not occurred to the leaders of either island. They
had been content to revenge, and take revenge in return whenever the occasion arose, and let matters stand
as they were. In this way each island prospered as
it would, and to all intent and purpose every one was
happy and contented that it should be thus.

And so it was when an hour had passed, the leader
of the Ono warriors felt the resistance of their foe
stiffen, and his own warriors were suffering more injuries and deaths. Sufficient satisfaction had been obtained for the death of the four Ono warriors, so he
lost no time in passing the word among the warriors
that they were to withdraw in order.

Maho, the leader, was a master strategist in the art
of withdrawing his warriors without too many injuries
and deaths occurring. The dead and more seriously
wounded were transferred ahead of the withdrawing
warriors to the canoes beyond the landing. There, all

canoes were in readiness to leave the island, with the dead and more seriously wounded equally distributed so as to make the return to their island easier for the warriors that would wield the paddles.

As the Ono warriors rode in the safety of their canoes in the calm water beyond the gentle surf, the Amo warriors would have followed and continued the battle. Discovering that their canoes had been damaged beyond hope of immediate repair, they uttered howls of rage in their disappointment because of the inability to continue the conflict.

Upon the shore Amar, with his father, Tomara, the chief, shook their fists threateningly at the departing canoes and vowed an early reprisal in return for the attack of their hereditary foes.

* * *

Atop the volcano on Aoono, Bantan and Maro had been interested spectators of the attack upon Amo by the Ono warriors. Time and again they had commented briefly as the attack progressed, and now at the orderly retreat of the Ono warriors, the bronzed giant shrugged his shoulders. He had been somewhat disappointed in the battle. He turned to Maro.

"The battle is over now," he said. "Have you rested sufficient to descend the volcano?"

The Amo native nodded and smiled.

"It will be easier descending than when we came up here," he answered. "Luno and Nao will be wondering how the battle fared. Lead the way. I'll be right behind you."

The bronzed giant approached the edge of the volcano and turning facewards to it, sought with his feet the roughly hewn stairway. Locating it easily, he started to back down. In another moment Maro was

following him as they descended the side of the volcanic cone. On the descent they did not find it necessary to rest as when ascending, since considerably less
effort was required. So rapid their descent, they
reached the base of the volcano by the time the Ono
canoes had passed the easterly end of Aoono.

Bantan and Maro waited until the canoes were well
on their way to Ono Island before they returned to
the cavern. Already the foremost canoes were rounding the shoreline of their island. A few minutes later
the bronzed giant nodded to his companion. With
Bantan in the lead, they lost no time in taking up their
way.

Nao and her mother were happy at the return of
the two men. Naturally they wanted to know about
everything. In turn, Bantan and Maro spoke of their
ascent of the volcano and from its top they had witnessed the battle in the Amo village.

"The Ono warriors obtained the revenge they
sought," Maro was saying. "They even slashed the
bottoms of the Amo canoes so as not to be pursued
for the present."

Nao's eyes lighted with pleasure at hearing this.
She looked toward Bantan. A warm smile touched
her lips as she rested a gentle hand upon his arm.

"Does that mean that we can soon leave for Marja
Island?" she asked.

Bantan shook his head sadly.

"I have a feeling Amar previously sent warriors to
the atoll," he replied. "They would be waiting there
to capture and return us again to Amo Island.
Another time we might not be so fortunate as we were
the last time we escaped."

The girl nodded slowly.

"Knowing Amar as I do," she added, "that is what

he would do.   But how long do you suppose the Amo warriors will wait for our coming to the atoll?"

"We should wait at least seven suns before attempting to return to the atoll before resuming our way to Marja," he answered.

Maro drew near at hearing this.

"With two paddles, Bantan," he said, "we would have no need of stopping at the atoll. We could paddle in relays, and in that way neither of us would be too tired. You need only to set the course for me, and I could follow until you relieved me."

"There is a question of being able to provision the canoe with sufficient fruits to last us," the bronzed giant added. "It is not pleasant to paddle when one is hungry. However, we shall think of the matter carefully, and perhaps within a day or so we can decide the best course to take. It is not pleasant to think of enemies to each side of us. I know the peace and happiness that awaits us at Marja is to be envied, but the thought of possible recapture by our enemies makes me hesitate to risk the safety of all of us."

Luno nodded to her mate.

"He speaks wisely," she said. "I, for one, dread to think what Amar would do to us should we be recaptured again." She shook her head sadly. "He is a very wicked man. Woe befall the Amo villagers when he becomes their chief and god."

Maro nodded as he spoke.

"Something tells me that Amar would not rule long," he said. "I have overheard much, but commented little, that Amar is not very well liked. Tomara should not have permitted his son to have influenced him as he has since emerging from boyhood."

"And to think," Luno added, "Maro and I hoped

the day would come when Nao might become Amar's mate and be the future queen of the island."

The girl shuddered.

"All that is past," she said with relief. "It seems like a horrible dream. But then, I was not the only girl in the village who hoped to be a queen. It was natural for any girl to feel that way."

* * *

Upon Amo Island following the surprise raid by the Ono warriors, the dead were hastily buried with no ceremonies. The wounded were cared for in their respective huts by the immediate members of their family.

Upon the beach under the supervision of Amar, the damaged canoes were undergoing repairs with feverish haste. The chief's son vowed the Ono village would know and long remember his wrath.

* * *

Meanwhile, upon Ono Island, the villagers were exultant that the deaths of their four warriors had been avenged. Roko, the chief, and his daughter, Princess Lori, together with Kolo, the witchdoctor, and Maho conferred, and it was decided that there would be a celebration that night in the village owing to their successful raid upon the Amo Island village.

When their conference had ended, Lori sauntered alone from the village. Reaching the beach, she strolled in a southeasterly direction, coming at last to an enviable spot where it was shady. There she sat beneath a puka tree, and for long moments looked toward Aoono Island. In the past she had come often to this identical spot, but the burning curiosity now in her mind had been absent upon those previous occasions.

Lori Thinks of Bantan

Bantan—the white prisoner—where had he gone with the Amo Island girl? Since their escape, this question repeatedly had been asked of herself, and for an answer there had been none forthcoming.

What a perfect specimen of manhood Bantan was! As the princess clearly visualized the bronzed giant's handsome features her heart accelerated, and her breathing was faster. A pleasing sensation of warmth pervaded her entire being. What a perfect mate he would be for her, she mused. He was by far more preferable than Amar, the son of the Amo Island chief. Bantan seemed possessed of all the attributes a woman longed for in a mate.

Though the princess and Amar had been secretly meeting for many moons, always in her heart Lori rebelled that they must meet in that manner. The fact that the inhabitants of their respective islands were not on friendly terms made it impossible that they meet in public. Now that there was serious trouble between the two islands, further meetings would be impossible. The fact that the princess had known of the existence of Bantan banished the thought of any further interest in Amar from her mind. It were as though he never existed.

Seated there, basking in the shade of the puka tree, Princess Lori realized there was no end that she wouldn't go to attain the satisfaction of her curiosity.

Comparing in her mind the Amo girl and herself, she felt even without the title of a princess, her physical charms should command Bantan's attention far more than the Amo girl. In all respects she outclassed Nao.

Lori's well shaped hands went to her rounded neck which she touched gently, and then they caressed the smooth bronzed skin to the halter that covered her firm, full breasts. These she touched lovingly and then clasped gently. As she uttered a sigh and her figure seemed to stiffen momentarily, she released her breasts and permitted her hands to pass down her ribs to the flatness of her abdomen. Then her hands caressed her well rounded thighs lingeringly and passed down her plump legs to rest upon her well developed calves.

The princess then lay back suddenly, and covered her closed eyes with her hands as though to better visualize the handsome bronzed giant. Her reveries seemed so real it were as though she saw him approaching with a smile upon his lips and a warm glow in his dark, smoldering eyes.

Lori stretched her arms upward with beckoning fingers to extend an invitation for him to come into them and bury his face upon her bosom. Her heart beat fast and the blood coursed madly through her veins. Her body arched gracefully and then she closed her arms about the imaginary form of Bantan. Her lips parted and a deep sigh of contentment was emitted from them.

"Bantan! Bantan, my lover!" she murmured with writhing lips. "I am yours for the taking. Hold me close and shower my willing lips with loving kisses!"

For long moments the moist lips of the princess puckered and relaxed as though she truly were kissing, and was being kissed, by a lover. Her lithe form seemed to tremble in reaction to her emotions. A long sigh escaped her lips, and she lay still, almost with the stillness of death. Save for the rhythmic rise and fall of her bosom, one would have believed the girl had succumbed to her emotions.

When some few minutes had passed, the princess stirred and sat up. Her eye lids opened, but for long moments her eyes seemed glazed. Then at last with

a shrug of her shapely shoulders, she dispelled the reveries that had claimed her.

Lori's attention became focused on the present world
rather than the imaginary one that had temporarily
claimed her. Again she shrugged her shoulders. Her
eyes rested upon Aoono. Though she had looked at
the volcanic island countless times in the past from
this same spot, now she viewed it again with a curiosity that had never appealed to her previously.

Her dark eyes looked admiringly at its lofty peak,
and then followed the sloping sides to the base. About
the base facing her the eyes of the Princess Lori slowly
traversed. Then at last they rested upon the cavern
that was clearly to be seen. A mad hope instantly occurred to her.

Suppose Bantan and Nao had sought refuge therein?

For long moments Lori gazed in the direction of
the cavern, and then at last she nodded her head de-
cisively. Arising to her feet, she set her footsteps
in the direction of the landing. The burning curiosity
within her would not be satisfied until she had convinced herself that Bantan and Nao were, or not, seeking refuge therein.

Many of the villagers were enjoying a siesta and
for that reason very few were about. No one was
at the landing when the princess reached there. Without delay she sought her canoe, and in another moment
had drawn it to the edge of the water and launched
it into the gentle surf.

Lori was an expert paddler and in a few minutes
the canoe was gracefully riding the calm water beyond
the surf. During the passing minutes the princess
plied her paddle steadily and the canoe responded
nobly. In the girl's mind the single thought persisted:

If only Bantan were to be found in the cavern on

Aoono Island! The fact that the Amo girl was, in all probability, with him was the only discordance that troubled the princess. However, that would be taken care of in due time. Lori was a woman, and as such she felt capable of coping with that situation when the time came. Her first impulse now was to ascertain the handsome bronzed stranger was to be found.

*   *   *

Within the cavern where Bantan and Nao were seated, talking quietly, it was the girl's keen eyes that first sighted the canoe rounding the shoreline of Ono Island.

"Look, Bantan!" she said, pointing at the object of her discovery.

The bronzed giant's dark eyes at once detected the lone canoe and, too, he observed it was manned by a single person.

"There is only one paddler, Nao," he announced.

Maro and Luno drew near with the announcement of a canoe making an appearance.

"A canoe approaches?" the father of the girl asked.

Bantan nodded slowly.

"And from its course I would say it was headed for this island," he added.

The truth of his words were ascertained, since the canoe's prow was in a direct line with the cavern. During the passing minutes the watchers observed that its course did not deviate an iota.

"The paddler is a woman," Bantan announced presently, for his keen eyes observed the long hair flowing about the paddler's naked shoulders.

"A woman!" Nao exclaimed. In her heart she knew there existed only one woman who would be rash enough for this venture. That one was the Princess

Lori! "It must be Lori," she muttered with glinting eyes.

"If she comes here," the bronzed giant added, "our near future will have its complications."

"What would we do with her?" the girl asked.

He shrugged his shoulders.

"If our safety is to be assured," he answered, "we would have to hold her prisoner until we were ready to leave for Marja."

"In that event," Nao added, "we would have to leave soon."

"Why do you say that, Nao?" Bantan asked.

"The princess would be missed," the girl replied. "Naturally, a search would be made for her."

"That is right," he agreed, nodding. Then, with a shrug of his broad shoulders, added: "We'll have to attend to that detail when the time comes. There is a chance she may not come here."

Nao looked out at the approaching canoe which now was scarcely several hundred yards from Aoono.

"I hardly think so," she said. "The canoe is unquestionably headed for this island."

Bantan nodded again.

"You are right," was all he said.

Nao's keen eyes were intently studying the features of the paddler. Even from the distance there was a seeming familiarity about the woman, and while the thought seemed fantastic, the Amo girl was positive in her identification of the woman paddler. She now nodded her head in assurance.

"Unless I am very much mistaken, Bantan," she said slowly, "I have every reason to believe Lori is the paddler in the canoe."

An expression of annoyance crossed the bronzed giant's features.

"Why are you so sure, Nao?" he asked.

With an effort the girl masked her dislike for the princess of Ono Island. She forced gaiety in her tones.

"She was stricken by you," she said smilingly. "Now she is searching for you."

Bantan's brow furrowed.

"If it is Lori," he answered, "that will mean we can wait no longer than tonight before leaving this island. When she is known to be missing, the villagers will lose no time in searching for her." Now he smiled. "Her canoe will be the means of having sufficient provisions to take us to Marja without stopping at the atoll and risking capture by Amar's warriors, who must certainly be waiting there for us."

Maro and Luno smiled and nodded to one another.

"As I said before," the father of the girl said, "with the two of us paddling, we can easily reach our goal."

"That is true, Maro," Bantan answered.

As the bronzed giant's eyes rested upon the features of the woman paddler, they now lighted with recognition. It was Lori, the princess of Ono Island. Nao was right. He turned to the girl with an apologetic smile.

"You were right, Nao," he admitted. "It is Lori who is paddling the canoe."

"I knew I was right in identifying her," the girl said with a nod.

"The capture of the princess means I will have to go to Amo Island later on for provisions," he added. "The Amo warriors will be too busy repairing their canoes to notice me, so I should be successful in that venture. Now, when Lori beaches her canoe and approaches the cavern, you, Maro and Luno, be upon one side of the entrance. Nao and I will be upon the

other. If the princess approaches nearest you, Maro,
seize her. If she is nearest us, I shall do so."

Maro and Luno nodded and drew to one side of
the cavern's mouth, while the bronzed giant and the
Amo girl went to the other. In silence all watched the
nearing canoe.

The princess gave a final stroke with her paddle,
then placed it in the bottom of the canoe as the prow
neared the rock shelf before the cavern at the base of
the volcano. The moment the prow grated against
the solid bottom Lori quickly stepped forward and
with agility leaped out of the canoe, keeping a hand
upon the bow. She drew it a short ways from the
water's edge. Straightening, she drew an arm across
her slightly perspiring forehead, then without hesitation approached the mouth of the cavern. She strained
her eyes to peer within the semi-darkness of the interior, but saw nothing to give her alarm.

Careful of her footing, the princess was looking toward the cavern's floor as she entered. She had taken
several steps when a pair of strong arms encircled her,
pinioning hers to her side. The scream of terror that
issued from her lips echoed through the stillness of the
cavern. At the next moment Lori was struggling her
utmost to be free of the powerful arms that imprisoned
her, but in vain were her efforts.

"Be quiet, Lori," a voice said to her. "No harm
shall befall you."

As Bantan spoke he relaxed his grip upon the princess so that she could turn and look up at the features
of her captor. As she recognized Bantan, she sighed
with relief.

"I came in search of you, Bantan," she murmured.
"Since first seeing you when you were a prisoner in
our village, I have not been the same."

Speaking as she did, the princess had thought they
were alone, and for that reason she did not see Nao
as she drew away from the wall near where Bantan
had been standing. The Amo girl confronted Lori
as she finished speaking. She had heard what she had
said, and now a derisive sneer possessed her otherwise
sweet features. Before Bantan could speak, Nao did
so.

"Ever since you were a little girl, Lori," she said,
"all you had to do was snap your fingers and your
wishes were gratified. You would have seen Bantan
sacrificed to a fiery death, and you would have rejoiced
more so if I had been sacrificed as well."

Lori appeared horrified by the girl's accusation.

"That is not true!" she exclaimed "I wanted to stop
the fiery sacrifice—believe me—but my throat was paralyzed and I could not speak. Please believe me, Bantan." And with her concluding words, the princess
turned appealingly to the bronzed giant. He had released her, though one hand still rested upon her shoulder. She clutched his arm. "You must believe me, for I
speak the truth. Doesn't coming here in search of you
prove that?" It was an humble plea that could not be
denied.

Bantan's features were inscrutable, but there was a
softening in his dark eyes that reflected a wavering of
his resolve.

The princess now observed Maro and Luno as they
approached from the opposite side of the cavern. She
looked at them questionably, then turned to Bantan.

"And who are these two?" she asked.

"The father and mother of Nao," he answered.
"They are to accompany Nao and me to Marja Island
where they shall know the peace and happiness my
people dwell in. Amar has condemned them to tor-

ture and death. We witnessed the slaying of the four
Ono warriors, and we also saw the surprise attack the
Ono warriors made upon the Amo village and the dam-
age done to their canoes. I have the feeling after
Nao and I escaped from Amo and sought refuge here,
Amar dispatched warriors to the atoll to await our
coming to be recaptured.

"Now, with your coming, Lori, we have no need of
being compelled to stop at the atoll for provisions.
Your canoe shall be the means of storing the provisions we require. We will have to take you to Marja
with us. There I shall leave Nao and her parents.
But I will return with warriors and take you back to
your island, then I shall settle my scores with Amar.
You will not be ill-treated if you promise to go with
us willingly and cause no trouble. What is your answer, Lori?"

The princess of Ono Island had never been accustomed to being told what she should or could do.
It had always been she who had given the orders, and
they had been executed without questioning. Though
at first she felt her sensibilities shocked to be spoken
to in the manner this handsome bronzed stranger spoke
to her, for some reason Lori did not seem to mind
that she took orders from him. A gentle smile touched
her lips, and a strange glow appeared in her dark eyes.

"I am your prisoner, Bantan," she answered in a
low, husky voice. "I feel I have nothing to fear. I
shall be grateful for whatever consideration you may
defer upon me."

Bantan's dark eyes met those of the princess for
a long moment. He could read no guile in hers. He
shrugged his shoulders.

"I am not going to bind your wrists as I might,

Lori," he said. "I am going to accept the word of a princess."

"Thank you," Lori said in that same low tone.

Bantan turned to Maro.

"Drag her canoe into the cavern," he directed.

As the father of Nao nodded and turned to execute Bantan's bidding, the bronzed giant turned to Nao. The Amo girl was inwardly furious at his humane treatment toward the princess of Ono Island, but she masqueraded her feelings with excellent self-control.

"I am giving Lori into your charge, Nao," Bantan said solemnly. "As a princess, she is entitled to a certain measure of respect and consideration." As he spoke, the bronzed giant looked toward Lori, who acknowledged with a warm, friendly smile. Then he reverted his attention to the Amo girl, and added: "You will do this as a promise to me since the safety of all of us may depend upon your consideration."

The tightened lips of the Amo girl relaxed and she managed a genuine smile.

"I cannot forget the manner in which I was treated when I was Lori's prisoner," she answered. "But I will do as you ask, Bantan."

"Now that that is settled," he said with a smile, "we shall eat. Then I must go alone to Amo and provision the canoe for our trip this coming evening."

After they had partaken of their noon day repast, Bantan was relieved. Upon a number of occasions he had been aware that Lori was watching him with strangely glowing eyes. Once he looked toward Nao, and though no words were spoken, he was aware that she, too, had noticed the marked attention the princess had been paying him. It made him feel uncomfortable to know that two young women, both beautiful, were vying for his favorable attention. He arose with a shrug of his broad shoulders. Nao followed him silently as he drew the canoe in which the princess had come here outside the cavern. Lori watched them, but no changing expression was to be observed in her dark eyes or upon her features.

"Be careful, Bantan," Nao murmured. "I know I do not have to tell you that, for you know only too well the safety of all of us depends upon you."

The bronzed giant turned and smiled assuringly.

"Nao, you know I will be careful," he answered. He rested a gentle hand upon one of her slim shoulders. "And," he added, "you need not be jealous of Princess Lori."

The Amo girl flushed deeply, acknowledging her guilt.

"I don't like the way she looks at you," Nao murmured with sharply drawn breath. "It is as though she is biding her time. Remember, Bantan, I am a woman, and a woman knows another far better than a man might."

"That is true, Nao," he said chidingly in a gentle voice. His hand dropped from her shoulder and sought one of hers which he clasped warmly. "I won't be longer than necessary. With your father and mother see that Lori doesn't get away."

"She won't get away," Nao promised.

Bantan launched the canoe, leaped in, and took up the paddle. He looked back at Nao and waved, to which she responded in a like manner. He looked ahead and plied the paddle with steady, rhythmic strokes. The canoe skimmed across the shimmering water around the end of Aoono, then its course was set for the southerly tip of Amo Island—the farthest distance from the village.

Without mishap the bronzed giant beached the canoe

in a slight cove, and drew it close to the foliage. He
noticed the profusion of brilliantly colored sea shells
on the beach. Thinking of Nao, he decided to gather
enough to fashion a necklace for her. He was positive
it would please her. And so he did, and in less than
half an hour he had threaded them with some twisted
tough grass. With a smile touching his lips he placed
it in the bow of the canoe.

Without further delay Bantan gathered a variety of
fruits that would last until Marja Island would be
reached. Fortunately there was a profusion of these
within easy reach, and he transported them to the
canoe with arms ladened to capacity each trip.

The last incursion into the foliage that he made took
him farther from the beach than any of his previous
trips. Already the afternoon was half spent. Until
now he had heard nothing or seen anything unusual to
mar his otherwise successful trip to Amo.

With his arms full of melons on this last trip, Bantan was returning to where his canoe was beached—
a distance of nearly a quarter-mile. He had not proceeded far when he stepped into a clearing. Almost
instantly, upon the opposite side, appeared three Amo
warriors. They were armed with daggers which they
clutched in their right hands, and advanced menacingly toward him.

The three Amo warriors had been searching for a
resinous substance with which to repair their damaged
canoes. It was apparent they had heard the crackling
of foliage, and they had decided to investigate. At
sight of the bronzed giant, whom they recognized, they
knew what they must do, and for that reason they were
prepared to take him captive, if possible. Amar, the
chief's son, would reward them handsomely if they

brought him to the village a captive, for all knew of
Amar's hatred for the bronzed stranger.

In that brief moment Bantan observed the three
Amo warriors, he knew he would have to fight his
way through them to reach the shore and the waiting
canoe. At once he dropped some of the melons he
carried, but the others he retained. He hurled these
in turn at each of the enemy, hoping to confuse them
for the moment. Two of them were recipients of the
juicy fruit, but the third timely ducked. The melon
sailed over his head. Toward him, drawing his steel
dagger as he moved, Bantan leaped. So swift his
movement, the Amo warrior went down before the
force of his overwhelming lunge. No damage had
been inflicted by their daggers; there was no need of
the bronzed giant's dagger inflicting a mortal wound
upon his opponent, for in falling the back of the Amo
warrior's head came in sharp contact with the bole of
a tree, rendering him unconscious.

Quickly realizing his enemy would be in no position
to harm him, Bantan arose from the prostrate form
and turned to give battle to the other two Amo warriors. They had now wiped away the pulpy mass that
had spattered their features, and once again were prepared to meet the enemy stranger. Snarling epithets
issued from their lips because of the insult they had
been subjected to. The two warriors nodded to each
other, then one started to circle about Bantan.

Each warrior brandished his stone dagger menacingly. The bronzed giant looked from one to the other
with eyes that gleamed. He was estimating his
chances, as the two warriors drew farther apart. They
did not realize that in separating their chances of
overwhelming the enemy were lessening with each
passing minute. As the distance increased between

Bantan and the two Amo warriors, the gleam in the bronzed giant's dark eyes was a satisfactory one.

Bantan stood in the center of the clearing—to each side of him the enemy warriors had drawn to the very edge. A distance of some ten yards separated each from the enemy they hoped to capture alive, if possible. Before the Amo warriors made a move to attack him, the bronzed giant leaped toward one with his dagger hand ready.

So swiftly he moved, he had covered the short distance before the other warrior started in his wake. Bantan slashed with his dagger as he neared his foe. At the last moment the Amo warrior twisted to one side to avoid the bronzed giant's thrust. Not anticipating the enemy's split-second move, Bantan missed; but so quick his nerve reflexes, his left hand flashed out and gripped the wrist of the enemy's dagger hand. Though unable to immediately check his lunge, Bantan half turned the warrior around. Tripping, the Amo warrior went down. Instantly Bantan released the dagger hand of his foe, and retarding the momentum of his lunge, he turned quickly, and sprang toward the remaining warrior who was closing in upon him.

Again the bronzed giant's right hand was lightning-like in its movement, and this time he was more successful. His keen blade slashed the warrior's left shoulder near the neck, and blood spurted forth. With a howl of pain, the Amo warrior would have been content to slink away; but at the next moment Bantan's clenched left hand lashed into the fellow's stomach, knocking the wind from him. Gasping, and clutching his stomach, the Amo warrior stumbled backward and fell upon his back, writhing in pain upon the ground.

Bantan turned to the second warrior who had now leaped to his feet and was bent upon attacking him.

In the center of the clearing they came to hand grips, each clutching the wrist of the other's dagger hand. The bronzed giant lost no time in starting to force his opponent backward. In this manner, step by step, he forced the Amo warrior to the very edge of the clearing. Then, with a quick right foot extended behind his foe, Bantan tripped him. As the warrior fell, the bronzed giant kicked the dagger hand, and the stone dagger went flying into the tangled mass of foliage.

This warrior temporarily out of the battle, Bantan turned quickly to the other two warriors. The first, who had struck his head against the bole of a tree, had now recovered his senses and was advancing toward Bantan with outstretched hands. He had lost his dagger, but his rage was reflected upon his snarling features.

Bantan quickly sheathed his own dagger, and met the fellow upon equal terms. For a moment they sparred and then came at each other with fury, gripping each other's arms. The Amo warrior was slightly larger than Bantan, and as they came to hand grips, the bronzed giant realized the greater strength of his foe. In seeking to force him backward, he discovered he was not equal to the task. His first engagement with the fellow had been a successful one for Bantan because of the suddenness of his attack.

But now, upon equal terms, the Amo warrior was pushing his opponent backward. Strive though the bronzed giant did to halt his backward retreat, to no avail was his strength. Bantan could employ craft when necessary. He had been pitted against many foes in the past and he knew many methods of strategy to be employed.

He suddenly relaxed his resistance now and dropped to the ground at the same moment. The Amo warrior's forward thrusting, suddenly meeting no resistance, caused him to stumble. Bantan drew his knees to his chest, and with his feet cushioned his opponent's fall. Then, as lightning, his knees became powerful springs that recoiled. With his feet against the Amo warrior's hips, Bantan straightened his legs in a mighty effort, releasing the warrior's wrists whose grip upon Bantan was likewise released. Fully ten feet into the air he catapulted, and so great his surprise he was helpless to prevent his fall upon the flat of his back. The shock resulted in temporary helplessness. In another moment the agile Bantan had pounced upon him and repeatedly thudded the back of his head against the hard ground, rendering him unconscious.

Quickly regaining an upright position, the bronzed giant's glaring eyes looked about at the three prostrated Amo warriors. None had stirred as yet. Realizing the safety of those in the cavern on Aoono Island depended upon him, without a moment's hesitation the victor of the fray crossed the clearing nearest the shore where his canoe was moored, and he disappeared into the tangled mass of foliage.

By the time Bantan reached the cove, from the distance he heard shouts and the crackling of underbrush. The Amo warriors he had defeated were pursuing him. The handsome reward Amar would offer them for the stranger's capture still tempted their courage.

Without a moment's delay, Bantan drew the heavily ladened canoe to the edge of the water and pushed it into the gentle surf. Quickly leaping within, he plied the paddle with expertness to presently reach the calmer water without mishap. At this moment the three Amo warriors burst out of the foliage and ran to the very edge of the beach. They shook their fists and uttered howls of rage because their quarry was escaping and they were powerless to give chase.

Bantan gave a single glance in their direction. A grim smile touched his lips, but with a shrug of his shoulders he again looked ahead, and continued to ply his paddle, setting the course for Aoono Island.

PART V

The Word of a Princess

As the canoe, provisioned with fruits, neared the
westerly end of Aoono Island—Ono Island to be seen
beyond—Bantan shaded his eyes time and again to
look toward it with the hope he would be able to
reach the cavern and cache the canoe therein without
detection from a chance observer upon that island.
Now that he had the means providentially provided
for the return to Marja, he did not wish his plan to be
fouled.

Rounding the end of Aoono, his vigilance was
seemingly rewarded, for the canoe and its lone occupant were not detected by any one upon Ono.
Strangely, the bronzed giant gave no thought of the
three Amo warriors he had battled, little realizing at
the present what perils the near future might hold for
him and his companions. Looking toward the bow
where the necklace of pretty sea shells reposed, the
lovely features of Nao rose within his mind.

The canoe was maneuvered to a gentle stop at the
edge of the rock shelf. Bantan quickly disembarked.
At the next moment Nao had come to him. A smile
of welcome was upon her lovely features. Smilingly,
he reached within the bow and brought forth the necklace. The girl's eyes radiated at sight of it.

"Remembering you had none, Nao," he said, "I
took the time to gather the pretty shells and fasten
them together. Let me fasten the necklace about your
neck."

The girl sighed deeply as he did so. Fondling the shells with her fingers, Nao's eyes were warm as she looked at the bronzed giant.

"I should know it was silly of me to feel jealous of Lori," she murmured.

He smiled assuringly. Then, quickly, he looked toward Ono Island.

"We mustn't remain in the open, Nao," he said.

Laying hand upon the bow, Bantan drew the canoe within the entrance of the cavern. Nao assisted him in this. They were greeted by the girl's smiling parents. Princess Lori remained a short distance from them, but her dark eyes glowed at the return of the handsome bronzed giant.

"Did you have any trouble?" Maro asked.

Bantan shrugged his shoulders and smiled.

"Three Amo warriors attacked me as I was carrying the last armful of fruit to the canoe," he replied. "I managed to defeat them—but only by attacking them first."

The girl's father could not restrain his enthusiasm.

"You defeated all three of them?" he asked with amazement.

"By attacking them one at a time I managed to do so," was the answer. "Had I waited for all three of them to attack me, I might not be here now."

Maro and his mate looked at Bantan with incredulity, but their daughter smiled proudly as her fingers pressed the necklace Bantan had fashioned for her.

"The princess is still with us?" Bantan asked, turning to Nao.

"She is still with us," the Amo girl replied with a slight frown. "She hasn't spoken a word. She has remained upon a pallet of grasses all the while you were gone—just as she is now." In a whisper she added: "Perhaps she regrets having come here."

The bronzed giant shook his head in gentle reproach.

"Her coming, Nao," he said in a low tone, "provided the means for us to return to Marja. We should feel grateful to her."

The girl frowned momentarily, but managed a smile.

As Bantan approached Lori, she arose to her feet with a smile and leaned against the wall. Her dark eyes revealed no fear, though her bosom heaved noticeably.

"I trust you were not ill-treated during my absence," he said to her.

The princess shook her head, the smile lingering upon her lips.

"No," she answered, "I was not ill-treated. Thank you for being so considerate by not binding my wrists and ankles."

"I accepted the word of a princess that you would not cause us any trouble," he said in a low voice. "Presently we shall sail for Marja Island—and we must take you with us. You have my word that no harm or otherwise ill-treatment will come to you. We must get to Marja to ensure the safety of Nao and her parents. There you will be shown every consideration until the time you are returned to your island."

"You need not take me to Marja," Lori said, meeting his eyes steadily. "I would not cause any interference in your plans." She shrugged her shoulders. "I think very highly of you, and even though a princess cares for some one who can't return her affection, there isn't much I can do about it."

With a shrug of her shoulders the princess looked at him with forlorn eyes for a long moment, then lowered her head in evidence of her hopelessness.

Bantan's eyes softened as he looked at the dejected princess of Ono Island. Only too well was he aware of her beauty, and there was no questioning her sincerity. He straightened and shook his head, knowing Nao came first in his heart.

"Rest further until we are ready to depart, Lori," he said. "It may be possible I will decide to do as you request. For some unknown reason I feel I can trust you." With a deprecating smile he added: "Why— I don't know, yet I do."

A smile touched the lips of the princess and her eyes glowed strangely. It seemed a long moment passed before she spoke.

"Thank you," she murmured. "If you don't mind, I'll take my pallet of grasses farther back in the cavern so as to be alone and reflect upon the generosity of my noble captor."

He nodded and shrugged his shoulders. The princess stooped and picked up her pallet of grasses and without another word walked regally toward the rear of the cavern. There she placed the grasses upon the floor and flung herself thereupon and buried her face in her arms.

Bantan returned to Nao and her parents near the mouth of the cavern. Looking toward the shadowed recesses of the rear, he could see the princess lying there. Turning to Nao, who was watching Lori curiously, he smiled.

"Anything wrong?" Nao asked with concern.

He shook his head.

"If you had been born a princess, Nao," he said with a gentle smile, "you would understand her better."

The Amo girl sighed and shrugged her shoulders.

"I suppose it is difficult for a princess to be a prisoner," she answered. "But we can't take her to Ono Island now. If we did, we would undoubtedly be pursued."

"She asked that she be taken to her island before we leave for Marja," he admitted. "I told her I would consider her request."

Nao shrugged her shoulders, but made no comment.

"I suggest we get some rest until shortly before sundown," he said.

Maro and Luno, who had been standing nearby, went to their pallets of grasses and lay down. Nao went to hers and did likewise. But Bantan seated himself and rested his back against the wall. He did not close his eyes even though he felt a trifle wearied. He tried to visualize the near future upon Marja.

When he arrived there with Nao and her parents he could almost read the silent reproach in Wanya's dark eyes when she would look upon the Amo girl and learn of her feeling for Bantan. With a sigh the bronzed giant banished those thoughts and once again looked toward the rear of the cavern. Lori had not stirred from her prone position. Once again he looked a short distance to his right where Nao reposed. As thoughts of Leona Brown, and Kalma, the Marja Island goddess, passed in procession across the screen of his recollection, to be followed by Wanya's haunting dark eyes, he shook his head again and tried to banish all such visions from his mind.

* * *

Meanwhile, the three warriors with whom Bantan had battled upon Amo Island, had watched the direction the giant stranger had paddled his canoe, and when it disappeared around the westerly end of Aoono, one turned to the others.

"Now we know where they are hiding," he said.

"Come, let us lose no time going to Amar and tell him."

"But, Roku," one protested, "what good is it when we have no canoes to follow?"

"Amar may still reward us for telling him of the whereabouts of Bantan, the girl, and her parents, Mayu," was the reply. He looked to the third member of the party. "What do you say, Ulin?"

The warrior nodded eagerly.

"By this time I'm sure there may be some of the canoes sufficiently repaired to paddle to Aoono Island," he said. "Come, let us lose no time in returning to the landing and inform Amar of the whereabouts of the escaped prisoners."

In accord, the three warriors broke into a run. Quickly they sped along the beach.

Superintending repairs upon the damaged canoes, Amar's attention was called to the appearance of the three running warriors when they were still some distance away. His eyes glittered angrily as he saw they were returning empty-handed, whereas they should be returning with more pitch with which to repair the damaged bottoms of the canoes. Presently his expression became curious because of the unusual haste the three warriors approached. When they drew near he spoke to them sharply.

"What is the reason for such haste and returning empty-handed?" he demanded.

Mayu was the spokesman.

"We have fought with the stranger—" he said, pausing to gasp for breath.

Amar's black eyes glittered with the hate he harbored for the giant stranger from faraway lands.

"The three of you failed to capture him?" he almost shouted in rage.

Sheepish expressions overtook the faces of the three warriors.

"He is an unusual man, Amar," Mayu murmured. "We tried to capture him, but he was too much for us."

"What was he doing upon this island, Mayu?" Amar then demanded.

"He was gathering fruits," was the answer. "He outdistanced us, after we fought with him, and reached his canoe before we could overtake him. We watched him paddle away—"

"Where did he go?" Amar asked, breathing hard, his black eyes gleaming with unsuppressed hate.

"He rounded the westerly end of Aoono Island," was the reply. "It is possible that he, Nao, and her parents have found refuge there."

A knowing smile touched the thin lips of the chief's son.

"Of course—the cavern!" he exclaimed.

Inwardly he upbraided himself for failing to think of such a possibility. He looked about quickly in an effort to determine how many canoes had been safely repaired thus far. Four of them were ready for launching. No time was to be lost. Vengeance toward the Ono villagers could wait for the time being. Quickly Amar made known his plans. He selected eleven of the stoutest warriors to accompany him, and without delay the four canoes were launched into the gentle surf. In each, three warriors took their places with paddles in hand, including Amar. They wielded them mightily so as to sooner cover the intervening distance to their objective.

While enroute, Amar made plain his plans to the warriors in his canoe, and this information was passed along to the occupants of the others. Soon they were beaching upon the westerly end of Aoono Island. Taking the lead, the chief's son cautioned his followers to extreme care.

Rounding the end of the island and keeping close to the base of the extinct volcano, they soon approached the cavern. At the side of the entrance, Amar peered into the semi-darkness of the interior. He espied the two canoes upon the opposite side—one appeared empty, while the other, nearest the entrance, was fully ladened with fruit.

Stretching a little farther so as to look upon the side nearest him, his blood instantly boiled at sight of Bantan scarcely ten feet from him, seated upon a pallet of grasses and resting his back against the wall. Nearby, lying upon similar pallets of grasses, he observed Nao, and just beyond her, two others whom he believed to be her parents. He did not look the entire length of the cavern to the rear wall, for he believed these four were the sole occupants.

Amar turned to his followers and indicated their quarry was within. Then, with a concerted movement, the eleven Amo warriors, led by the chief's son, dashed into the cavern.

Bantan's reveries were rudely interrupted by the sounds of many hasty sandalled footsteps upon the rock floor. Quick though he moved, he had hardly reached his full height before overwhelming numbers leaped upon him and forced him to the floor without an opportunity of defending himself.

Nao uttered a cry of fright, instantly arousing her dozing parents. Though the girl managed to gain her feet, at the next moment she was made a prisoner by a stalwart warrior. Her father and mother did not have time to gain their feet before they, too, were rudely seized and made prisoners.

From the rear of the cavern, Princess Lori heard
the scuffle at the entrance. Looking up, she was a silent
witness to the proceedings occurring there. Not recognizing the identity of the attacking warriors, she did
not wish to reveal herself until she was certain who
they were—whether friend or foe.

Though Bantan had been forced to the floor beneath
the weight of overwhelming odds, he lashed out with
mighty arms and powerful legs. He had the satisfaction of kicking two of his attackers, and his mighty
hands lashed at two others. With less hands gripping
him now, he managed to arise to his knees, swinging
his powerful arms to and fro, warding off any further
attempt to imprison him. Though a heavy body
landed upon his back, forcing a grunt from his lips,
he shrugged himself mightily, freeing himself temporarily of the foe. Despite the grappling arms about
him he managed to draw himself to an erect position
again.

A gleam of rage possessed his dark eyes at recognition of Amar, and with a demoniac surge of strength
he swung a mighty blow at his enemy. Amar stepped
back nimbly, the intended blow just missing him. As
Bantan sought to follow up with a second one, a heavy
body leaped upon him from behind and an arm locked
about his neck, choking him.

Bantan's flailing arms could not touch his new adversary, and as he tried to shake him loose, other hands
gripped his ankles. Swaying to and fro as a madman
might, and repeatedly shaking his shoulders, he felt his
strength slipping away into nothingness. A thundering
roar increased in tempo as his starved lungs clamored
for more air. He summoned whatever reserve
strength was his to command, but the supreme effort
resulted in oblivion. He was aware of the sensation

of falling forward and multicolored stars blazed before him.

The roaring sound in Bantan's ears subsided at last, and after what seemed an eternity he opened his eyes. He was lying flat upon his back. His wrists had been bound with strong vines. Looking upward, he saw Amar looking down at him with an ironical smile upon his thin lips. A triumphant gleam possessed his glittering black eyes.

"This time, stranger," he hissed, "you shall not escape. By the sacred bones of my ancestors I swear it!"

The bronzed giant then looked about curiously. He saw Nao being held prisoner. Her parents were likewise captives. The whereabouts of Princess Lori puzzled him. Once again he looked at Nao, and her despair was clearly indicated. Before he could smile assuringly to her, Amar spoke curtly to his warriors.

"Come, let us return the prisoners to Amo."

Bantan was dragged to his feet. Where he had lain, his steel dagger remained. It had come loose from its sheath in the scuffle, and it lay there unnoticed. So overjoyed at the recapture of the escaped prisoners, Amar gave not a thought of the automatic, belt of cartridges, and the bow and arrows that previously had attracted his attention.

The captives were marched out of the cavern and around the end of Aoono Island to where the canoes were beached. A prisoner was designated to each canoe, being made to sit in the bow. Bantan was made to sit in the canoe Amar occupied.

During the return trip to Amo, the chief's son could hardly remove his gloating eyes from the bronzed giant. Though Bantan's eyes were defiant, Amar was not worried. This time, for a certainty, the white

stranger would no longer be a threat to his supremacy
and peace of mind, for already his torture and eventual
death was being conceived in the cunning mind of the
chief's son.

"Look about you, stranger," Amar taunted in
sneering tones. "This is the last day that you shall
live. And know this and think of it as you may, that
Nao shall first entertain me before she follows you to
her death. Her parents shall watch her die later, and
when they hear her screams for mercy they will regret
the day she was born. Last of all they, too, shall
die!"

The bronzed giant's features indicated no inkling
of the rage that was aroused within his breast. As yet
he had not tested the strength of the vines that bound
his wrists. The time had not come for that. He considered leaping out of the canoe, but with his wrists
bound, he realized such a bid for freedom would be
foredoomed to failure.

Suffering in silence, and suppressing his rage only by
magnificent self control, the short trip to Amo Island
was endured. Tiny beads of perspiration upon Bantan's brow indicated the mighty effort of will power
being employed in mastering his hate for Amar.

Several times he looked over a shoulder at the
trailing canoes. Nao was in the one following, and her
head was bowed, giving evidence of her despair. Maro
and Luno, her father and mother, being in each of the
other two canoes, were likewise dejected. The bronzed
giant's eyes met those of Maro, but no expression of
hope was exchanged by either.

Villagers gathered upon the Amo Island beach,
awaiting the return of the canoes. From the distance
they could see that the escaped prisoners had been recaptured. Great was their joy that this was so.

Tomara, the chief, had been informed of Amar's departure, and he, too, had come to the shore to await the return of his son with the captives.

Loud was the cheering as the canoes drew near the beach. In turn, Amar's canoe in the lead, the four of them were beached. The forlorn captives were made to disembark.

Amar turned to the populace and, raising his hands, stilled their joyful shouts.

"Tonight the prisoners shall taste the torture and death they have escaped once before," he announced. "This time there shall be no escape for them. By the sacred bones of my ancestors I promise this."

The villagers shouted in their exultation.

Tomara drew near his son with admiration beaming in his eyes.

"Our ancestors would indeed be angry were we to fail them this time," he said.

A grim smile touched the corners of Amar's thin lips.

"We shall not fail our ancestors this time, father," he answered with a resolute nod.

Without delay the prisoners were marched into the village to the temple prison cell. The wall adjacent to the village lane that Bantan had laboriously cut through to effect his previous escape with Nao had been repaired. At the door the ankles of each were bound with slender vines, and in turn, they were thrust within to fall helpless upon the floor. The door was closed and barred. Stygian gloom enveloped the prisoners. A guard was detailed to remain outside, and another was stationed in the village lane to further safeguard the prisoners from possible escape.

In the inky darkness of the prison cell, the silence was broken only by the labored breathing of the captives. Maro and Luno, whispering to each other, had wormed their way to the side of the other. The woman was sobbing silently and her mate endeavored to console her with words of encouragement.

Meanwhile, Nao called softly to Bantan, and guided by his voice in answer, she crept toward him upon hands and knees, drawing herself at his side and managing to reach a seated position with their naked shoulders in contact. Though the girl inwardly was horrified at their predicament, her voice was very brave as she spoke to the bronzed giant.

"There isn't much hope for us this time, is there, Bantan?" she murmured.

He had been silently testing the strength of the vines that bound his wrists. His chest expanded and the muscles of his arms bulged to his mighty effort. A harsh expulsion of repressed air now escaped his lips.

"The vines are much stronger than they appear, Nao," he remarked.

Once again he strained mightily to snap the encircling vines, and when his effort was without reward, the voice of the girl again was to be heard.

"There isn't much hope," she murmured in a resigned tone.

At thought of what Amar had told him in the canoe concerning Nao's near future before her ultimate death, a wave of compassion welled within Bantan's bosom. He would not tell her and thereby allow her to be oblivious to the greater mental suffering she would have occasion to experience. He realized it would be better in these last hours that he told her how much he loved her and his deep regret that they could not live to enjoy the promise of future happiness that might have been theirs.

His warm cheek rested against hers, and as the girl
sighed deeply, his lips found her willing ones. As
they pressed together, she snuggled closer to him.
With the parting of their lips, she sobbed silently.

"Oh, Bantan! Bantan!" she moaned. "What have
we done to deserve this cruel fate?"

"Be brave, Nao," he whispered. "We are still alive
—and together."

"But for how long?" was all she could ask hopelessly.

He kissed her upon a cheek, then her forehead.
Lifting her head, Nao's lips sought his, and though
sobs choked in her throat and her bosom heaved to her
pent emotions, her lips remained fastened upon his
almost frenziedly. Tears from her eyes moved in
rivulets down her cheeks. Presently, when their emotions were calmed, their lips parted reluctantly and
their cheeks rested against the other's.

"Nao," he whispered, after a few minutes of silence
had passed.

"Yes, dear," she answered.

"Do you realize Princess Lori was not taken captive
when we were?" he reminded her.

Within his breast a mad hope had taken root, and
the slender thread of hope it offered was not to be extinguished in their present, seemingly hopeless plight.

The girl caught her breath.

"That is true," she replied. "Lori was at the rear
of the cavern. Amar and his warriors did not see her.
They could have no reason to believe she would be
with us."

"There is the hope within me that she will immediately return to Ono Island," he murmured. "Our
canoe and hers were left behind. There is the possibility, upon returning to her village, that she might

inflame the warriors to return to Amo and rescue us."

Realizing Lori's infatuation for Bantan, in the girl's heart such a hope as he nurtured could not be fully appreciated.

"Even if what you suggest could be possible—and the Ono warriors were in time," she said, "do you suppose she would care what my fate was, or that of my parents?"

Nao's words were not idle ones, and Bantan realized how very right she could be. It had been a nice thought to believe a possibility, and now with the realization of its hopelessness, the bronzed giant dismissed it from his mind.

"Nao," he whispered with eagerness. "Try and gnaw through the vines about your wrists, as I shall."

"What good would it do even though we freed ourselves of our bonds?" she murmured in apparent dejection. "We can't hope to escape from this prison cell again. We wouldn't have the time."

"It is a nice feeling to have our hands and feet free of bonds," he reminded her.

Without further words Bantan's strong white teeth were gnawing at the strands of vines that encircled his wrists. When the girl heard him engaged thusly, she, too, did likewise. Calling softly to her parents of what she and Bantan were endeavoring, they, too, began to gnaw at their bonds, hopeless though it seemed.

How much time had passed, the four captives had no means of computing.

In the village, after the evening meal had been prepared and eaten, increased activity was to be heard. More sounds of footsteps—some in apparent haste— were to be heard in the lane adjacent to the prison cell. Greater became the chatter of voices.

In the center of the village a huge bonfire was burning to provide illumination. Nearby a smaller fire was blazing. Over it suspended upon a spit was an earthen pot in which a resinous substance was boiling and the aroma emanating from it was not unpleasant. Near this, stakes had been driven into the hard ground in the form of a rectangle—one stake at each corner. To each stake a slender vine had been attached.

Within the temple prison cell, Bantan succeeded in gnawing through the vines that bound his wrists. In another moment his strong fingers were working at those about his ankles and it was not long before he had released them. In the darkness he turned to Nao. She had freed her wrists, but her ankles were still bound. This she told the bronzed giant when he asked how she was faring.

"Let me unfasten them, Nao," he said.

With his words he knelt before the girl and felt for her ankles. He drew upon the vines gently until the slack was obtained upon one of them. He fastened his teeth upon it, and one bite was sufficient to sever it. Then he unwrapped them from about the girl's slender ankles and tossed them to one side. He quickly massaged the chafed flesh until the skin glowed.

Arising to his feet, as the girl did hers, though the Stygian darkness was impenetrable as far as vision was concerned, instinct seemed to guide the bronzed giant and the Amo girl. Though no words were spoken— only their labored breathing being heard—their arms went unerringly about the other and their bodies drew close as their lips sought the other's, and remained pressed together for what seemed a blessed eternity.

The sound of footsteps outside the cell door was to be heard. Their lips parted with reluctance and their arms released the other. Nao smothered a gasp.

Quickly her right hand moved to the right side of her bosom and, a moment later, to the left.

"They are coming for us!" she murmured fearfully.

He drew her to his side and placed a protecting arm about her shoulders, but remained silent.

The latch was lifted and the door opened. Outside, three warriors in addition to the guard stood. One held a burning torch. The light penetrated the inky darkness of the interior. The warrior discerned Bantan with an arm about the girl protectingly. Her fearful eyes seemed blinded by the leaping flames from the burning torch. The warrior beckoned to the girl.

"Come," he said. "Amar wishes to speak to you."

Realizing for what reason the chief's son wished to "speak" to Nao, Bantan's arm tightened more so about the girl's shoulders.

Nao turned to her protector with a wan smile, though a spark of hope burned in her dark eyes.

"Perhaps I can convince Amar of his wrong," she said in a brave tone of voice.

Bantan's features became grim.

"I have my doubts, Nao," he said, his voice quivering in rage. He turned to the warrior holding the blazing torch. A mad hope had been instantly conceived in Bantan's breast. "Tell Amar to come after Nao in person."

The warrior merely gaped at the bronzed giant for a moment. Then with annoyance he turned to his two companions who were armed with spears. A stone dagger was sheathed at their right hip.

"Amar said to *bring* the girl to him if necessary," he said with emphasis. He laughed as though the matter were a joke. "He said nothing about coming after her, otherwise we wouldn't be here."

At a nod from the warrior bearing the burning

torch, the two warriors who had accompanied him stepped within the prison cell with menacing spears and approached Bantan and the girl. Their spears were pointed at the bronzed giant.

"Release her," one said in tones that were meaningful, threatening.

Bantan instinctively tightened his arm about the girl's shoulders. His sharp eyes were determining the chances of attacking the two armed warriors. He looked toward Maro and Luno. Their wrists were free of their bonds, but their ankles were still securely bound. He could expect no assistance from the father of the girl—that he realized at once. Once again his defiant eyes met those of the two warriors who threatened him with their spear points. One of the warriors—the same who had spoken a moment before —placed the point of his spear against Bantan's chest.

"Release the girl," he warned; "else I'll plunge the spear into you."

Meeting the warrior's determined eyes, the bronzed giant could well realize the threat was not an idle one. His left arm dropped from about Nao's shoulders. The girl sighed with relief, and looking up at him smiled bravely.

"I can take care of myself, Bantan," she murmured. "I have no fear of Amar."

Standing upon her tip toes she brushed his cheek with her lips, then turned toward the two warriors. Her shoulders were squared and her queenly head was held high as she stepped away from Bantan.

The bronzed giant's defiance melted and his features writhed with the inner pain that convulsed him at the realization of the fate the girl was unknowingly going to at the mercilessness of the chief's ruthless son.

"Nao, Nao!" he shouted hoarsely.

The Amo girl had taken several steps, but now halted with a shudder wracking her shoulders. She looked back and smiled unflinchingly at the bronzed giant through the tears that threatened, then once more she moved forward toward the door of the prison cell.

The spear point pressing Bantan's right chest did not relax as determinedly he leaned forward. The skin was broken and warm blood oozed about the point that had probed it.

With anguish mirrored in their eyes, the father and mother of the girl remained motionless as their daughter neared them. She paused momentarily to smile down assuringly that she was able to take care of herself. As she stepped out of the prison cell into the temple, the two warriors with their spears still threatening Bantan withdraw cautiously. Their eyes never for a moment were removed from the captive.

Each step backward they took, Bantan took one forward. His hands clenched and unclenched repeatedly; the muscles of his biceps bulged in evidence to the stress of emotional conflict waging within him. His features writhed with the indecision that thundered within him, and his eyes seemed almost wild.

For a brief moment the bronzed giant halted as though frozen into immobility. Then, as his entire being trembled, his eyes closed. As they opened again a seemingly maniacal light blazed in the dark depths, but that brief moment he had hesitated was sufficient to prevent the execution of the mad plan that had evolved within him. As he leaped forward, the door of the prison cell slammed in his face and the bar was dropped into place.

With a surge of redoubled strength Bantan heaved his shoulder with his entire weight behind the move.

The door shuddered, but withstood his grim assault. Again and again he hurled his weight at the door, but the stout bar and hinges held firm.

At last realizing how powerless he was to batter the door open, Bantan then sank to his knees. With a violent shake of his head he flung himself upon the bare floor of the prison cell, and in the Stygian darkness buried his face in his arms. He was oblivious of the near presence of Maro and Luno. His breathing was labored, and his ears were tense—hoping he might not hear the sound of Nao's voice, uttered in distress, knowing as he well did, the "reception" she was to receive in Amar's quarters.

To the bronzed giant's side in the darkness of the prison cell crept Maro and Luno, his cell-mates, and though each in turn tried to speak to him, he did not pay any attention. The father of the girl was most persistent, and at last Bantan uncovered his face and arose apathetically to a seated position.

"What is it, Maro?" he asked with a trace of annoyance in his tones.

"You need not be so alarmed about Nao's fate," the father of the girl said in a low voice. "Each young woman of the village carries a satchet of poison that is easily within reach should the occasion demand. Amar shall never defile her, for she would take her life first."

"True as that may be, Maro," Bantan replied. "Amar must have similar knowledge, and he would prevent the fulfillment of such designs upon her part."

"You do not know Nao as well as her father and mother," was Maro's assurance. "She takes great pride in her respect. No man could ever force unwelcome attentions upon her."

Bantan's giant shoulders shuddered. In that brief moment of silence he heard Nao's voice raised in distress. Upon the instant he leaped to his feet and hurled his weight desperately against the door—again and again —and though the door shuddered to the impact of his weight, the hinges and the stout bar did not give way.

Standing there in the Stygian darkness, his massive chest heaved convulsively and his labored breathing rasped in his throat. Then—his keen ears tensed.

What else was it he heard that was reason for a mad, almost inconceivable hope rising up within him?

*   *   *

When Nao was led to Amar's quarters, to all outward appearances she was calm and unafraid. Her left hand pressed her left breast where her fingers could feel the satchet of poison through the thin material that covered it. It was comforting to know death was far more preferable than to be a victim of the vicious lust of the chief's cruel son.

In her heart the girl knew Bantan would forgive her—as he had forgiven Kalma, the Marja Island goddess—if she chose self-destruction rather than to live —if only for a few hours, with the fearful knowledge her purity had been defiled. The thought of death had never occurred more seriously to Nao as being so real as at the present moment. She knew death in one form or another was eventual, and knowing there was no hope of escape in her present circumstances, the horror of death was banished from her mind. Even though she took her own life, she would do so with the profound feeling that her spirit would be reunited with Bantan's in that world beyond the grave to which he, too, would presently make his advent.

While passing through the temple to the quarters Amar occupied, Nao's fingers covering her left breast were inserted beneath the halter. Just below the soft mound the satchet nestled. She involuntarily shivered as her cold fingers came in contact with its warmth, and a sigh escaped her lips as the satchet was withdrawn and she palmed it, closing her fingers over it tightly.

The three warriors accompanying her were not suspicious that the girl pressed her left breast, for it was common knowledge that the women of the Amo village concealed a satchet of poison beneath the right one. Perhaps their attention was centered upon the activities of her right hand rather than the left.

Long ago the young women had adopted this practice for fear that their enemies—the Ono warriors—might attempt to defile them, and this teaching of self-destruction in preference to the other more disgraceful one had been instilled in their minds when very young. By the time adolescence was reached, and the maidens wore halters to cover their swelling bosoms for modesty's sake, each and every girl had been thus prepared to accept death rather than the unwelcome attentions of an enemy and be compelled to live with the enduring shame forever in her mind.

In the history of the Amo village, two such incidents had been recorded. When the bodies, cold in death, had been found, and the satchet of poison had been known to be missing, it was readily understood the girl's sacrifice had not been in vain. The elegance of the funeral preparations could have been no greater than a most renowned individual might have anticipated at death. Fasting and penitence by the immediate family was strictly invoked for a period of nine moons, and thereafter it was believed the soul of the deceased girl had taken residence upon a star in the heaven. The more popular the girl of such circumstances the more brilliant the star she occupied forevermore.

With the thought of her religious duty in mind, Nao now realized how often she had admired a certain lovely yellow star that was to be observed in the western heaven. Though the Amo girl did not know her astronomy, it was the planet Venus of which she was thinking. Upon countless occasions in the past she had remained upon the beach alone in the early evening and had watched the soft luminance of this planet. In her way of thinking she thought how wonderful it would be that she might dwell there in spirit after her earthly existence had ceased. Now, with the imminent realization of this dream coming true, she hummed softly to herself.

The party had now reached the door to Amar's quarters. One of the warriors stepped forward and opened it. He turned to the girl with expressionless features and indicated for her to enter.

Raising her head proudly and squaring her shoulders, Nao looked from one warrior to the other two in turn. Her dark eyes flashed their scorn. With a slight nod she stepped across the threshold. Looking across the apartment she saw Amar reclining upon a couch, watching her with glittering black eyes in which welled his vicious lust for her. She recoiled momentarily at the sight of the mocking smile that possessed his features. A bandage was still about his forehead, covering the broken flesh upon the temple where Bantan had struck him with the butt of his automatic.

Behind her Nao heard the door close. With a resolute shake of her head, the long, lustrous hair extending below her shoulders swaying, she raised her head and her scornful eyes met those of her gloating captor.

"How could a chief's son stoop so low!" she exclaimed.

The gloating smile upon Amar's face vanished instantly to be replaced with bitterness. He quickly arose from the couch, his tanned features drained of color to reveal his unconcealed displeasure.

"You should talk—" he snarled "—making love in secrecy to the first stranger who came to our island—even to the point of implicating your father and mother who, by the law of the Amo people, must die for their part in your unholy pact with the white stranger."

"And what of you, chief's son that you are?" she demanded. "A fine example you save set—sneaking off in the darkness of night to curry favor with Princess Lori of Ono Island. I have heard that you have done that."

The rage that overcame Amar knew no bounds. Such accusations, though true, had not been anticipated from this hitherto quiet and refined Amo girl.

"How would you know about my actions?" he snarled, taking several aggressive steps toward the girl.

"The night that the stranger spared me from injury and possible death from the attacking wild boar," she answered. "I had followed you to the landing and saw you launch a canoe and paddle in the direction of Ono Island. Since I was a very young girl until the time I entered the adolescent stage I looked up to you with reverence, hoping the day would come when you might look upon me with favor. I didn't know the real you, Amar, and only in recent moons did I suspect your true nature. After knowing Bantan—and were I in the position—I wouldn't exchange one of him for as many of you as there are stars in the sky."

Amar fairly shook with the rage that possessed him. He stood with hands that clenched and unclenched.

His lips were tight lines. His glittering black eyes were sullen now, and as they rested upon Nao shiftingly, he noticed her left hand was clenched, whereas her right hung lax at her side. As crafty as he could be ruthess, the chief's son took several tentative steps toward the girl who stood her ground unflinchingly with his closer proximity. The scorn in her dark eyes had not lessened. A cunning expression now replaced the sullen one of a moment previous, and into Amar's eyes a look of bewilderment appeared.

"Nao, I never realized that you thought of me so highly," he murmured in awed tones. "How *could* I know when such interest remained concealed?"

The girl watched him with no change of the cold expression that glared in her eyes. She made no effort to speak.

Amar lifted his eyes to the ceiling.

"How could my ancestors blind me to the beauty of this Amo girl who has revered me for many, many moons?" he asked in a soft tone of voice that was embellished by his supplicating posture, for now he raised his arms.

Nao was unimpressed by Amar's mockery of the dramatic. A shiver quaked her entire being as she realized how kind words from him into her gullible ears less than a quarter of a moon ago might have altered the entire course of her life—for better or worse who might conjecture? But all that was in the past. The girl had no ears for any who might falsely profess their romantic interest in her after making the acquaintance of the inimitable Bantan. With the very thought of the bronzed giant a sensation of ecstacy stirred within her and the realization was apparent that so long as she lived her heart belonged to him.   While enchanted by her reveries, Nao was caught off guard.

With a lightning-like movement, Amar had leaped to her side and grasped her left wrist, imprisoning it with the tightness of a vise.   Simultaneously the other hand clamped upon her right shoulder in a crushing grip.   Her left hand, seemingly paralyzed, dropped the satchet of poison.   With a triumphant laugh Amar kicked it to one side.   He then quickly spun the frail girl about so that one arm encircled her while the other went about her neck.

"You were even prepared to take your own life, Nao," he taunted her.   "You would have cheated me of this last opportunity to shower you with my long-deferred attentions."

Looking into the lust-filled black eyes of her gloating captor, the girl's terror mounted.   Though she realized how futile it was, she uttered a piercing scream of distress, then with tooth and nail attempted to free herself of her captor's clutches.   But Amar was powerful and the girl's struggles only infuriated him more so.

Though one of the girl's hands was free and she slapped her captor's face, his left hand about the nape of her neck drew her face close to his, now flushed with conquest.   With a mocking laugh his foul lips sought and covered her unwilling ones.   Those moments of agony were suffered by the helpless girl because she had no other choice, and she was nauseated by the contact of his lips upon hers.

Struggling with every ounce of strength she managed to free her lips from his, and with her free hand she raked one side of his face with her finger nails.   With a curse because of the pain he suffered, in a fit of uncontrollable rage Amar slapped the girl's face with

Nao Is Slapped by Amar

the palm of one hand with such force that Nao felt her senses swooning. Before she could fall to the floor, the chief's son swept her into his arms and bore her toward the couch.

Panting more from suppressed emotion than the effort required to carry the frail girl in his arms, Amar deposited Nao's lax body upon the couch. He straightened for a moment to look down gloatingly upon her helplessness. To his ears then there came above the ordinary sounds in the village punctuating shouts louder than the others that fairly pierced the ear drums. With annoyance he thought some of the younger warriors, in anticipation of the approaching sacrifices, were getting out of hand.

Once again he looked down at the helpless girl with burning eyes of naked lust, and as he moved toward her the shouts in the village outside became more numerous. Blood-curdling screams were emitted from the throat of a pain-crazed warrior, and then more excitement of a similar nature prevailed in the ensuing moments. To his ears came the sounds of hurrying footsteps outside in the village lane.

With a curse, Amar removed his eyes reluctantly from the helpless girl upon the couch and hurriedly walked toward the door of his quarters. He opened it and stepped upon the threshold. Looking down the village lane in the direction of the beach from where the most confusion seemed to issue, he was amazed to observe the shadowed forms of warriors in apparent engagement with enemy warriors. He could hear their spears clash and the curses that were showered at one another. Could it be the Amo village was being attacked a second time in the same day by the Ono warriors?

Quickly looking up the village lane, he saw other

warriors armed with spears hurrying in the direction of the fighting forces. He called to an approaching warrior.

"What is the trouble near the beach?" he demanded.

"The Ono warriors are attacking the village!" the warrior replied. "Quick, Amar, come and lead us victoriously in repelling their attack."

With a muffled curse, the chief's son turned and re-entered his quarters. He looked toward the still unconscious girl for a brief moment. With a shake of his head he quickly sought his spear. Without hesitation he joined the battling warriors in the village lane.

In the passing minutes Nao recovered consciousness. She opened her eyes in amazement. To her ears came the sounds of conflict in the nearby vicinity of the temple. Looking about her in wonder, she saw that she was alone. Amar must have gone to join the Amo warriors in the fighting that had taken place in the village near the beach.

Arising from the couch, she was eternally grateful to the divine Providence which had spared her from Amar's evil designs. The side of her face still smarted where the chief's son had slapped her, and though her head felt heavy from its effects, she was alert otherwise and was not to overlook this chance opportunity to make good her escape from the immediate vicinity.

There was no question the attacking foes of the Amo village could be other than the Ono warriors. Into the girl's mind flashed the possibility that Bantan had mentioned when in the temple prison cell, and whether or not it was the likely answer, Nao was nevertheless grateful that the attack had been so timely.

Approaching the door of Amar's quarters, she opened it cautiously and peered out into the adjacent village lane. Belated warriors were still dashing from the furthermost village huts in the hope of stemming the tide of battle that seemed to be going against the Amo defenders, for they were steadily being forced backward from the direction of the beach. The bonfire in the center of the village illuminated the village lane, lending grotesque shadows as more shouting warriors dashed on their way to join the fray.

Without hesitation Nao stepped outside and closed the door behind her. She had no difficulty in locating the door of the temple, nor was she apprehended or molested by any of the Amo warriors that passed her. Pushing the door of the temple open with caution, she peered within and found that it was empty. Two urns near the center of the temple containing a resinous substance into which a wick had been placed was burning. The flickering light revealed no guard was stationed before the door of the prison cell. In all likelihood he had gone to join the fighting forces in repelling the Ono attack. Closing the door behind her, Nao stepped forward quickly, and reaching the prison cell she withdrew the stout bar and flung open the door.

"Bantan! Father and mother!" she cried.

The girl had hardly spoken when Bantan's giant figure loomed before her out of the darkness behind him, and enveloping her in his mighty arms, smothered her lips with kisses. When he released her moments later, concern was to be detected in his grave eyes.

"I heard you scream, Nao," he said. "Did Amar harm you?"

The girl smiled as she shook her head.

"The sounds of fighting and shouting in the village near the beach must have attracted his attention and he went to investigate," she answered.

His concerned eyes noted her flushed cheek where the chief's son had violently slapped her.

"Your cheek, Nao," he murmured, reaching out a hand to caress it gently. "Did he strike you when you resisted him?"

The girl nodded.

"I became unconscious as a result," she admitted. "When I recovered my senses, Amar was gone."

A grimness flashed through Bantan's dark eyes.

"Amar shall pay dearly for striking you, Nao," he vowed.

Maro and Luno, the girl's parents, appeared from the darkness of the prison cell with an expression of amazement upon their faces.

"What could have happened?" Maro asked.

Bantan and the girl turned to them. Nao went to her mother and the two embraced warmly.

A triumphant smile came upon the bronzed giant's features, for to his ears the nearing battle in the village recalled to mind the thought of what Princess Lori might do. At the time he had mentioned it, it had been the hopeless expression of a drowning man grasping for the proverbial straw in a vain hope of rescue.

"It must be as I mentioned, Nao," he said. "Princess Lori must have returned to Ono Island and inflamed the warriors to attack the Amo village with the hope of sparing us from torture and death at Amar's bidding."

Nao shook her head and a mistiness appeared in her dark eyes.

"Spare us from Amar—and then what?" she asked, hesitatingly.

The bronzed giant had no answer for Nao's question.

"Come," he said, beckoning; "since we have been so fortunate to have gained our freedom, let us see if we can preserve it. Follow me."

Bantan went to the door of the temple, and opening it a trifle, peered outside.

The Amo warriors had been forced to retreat from the beach where the battle had first begun with the discovery of the surprise attack. Quickly the word had spread that the Ono warriors were again attacking the village and all the Amo warriors available had hurried to stiffen the resistance. The battle was now raging in earnest in the village lane just outside the temple. Spears were clashing in the ill-lighted lane. Amar was now in the front ranks shouting to his warriors to repel the enemy.

From the doorway, Bantan could distinguish the chief's son as well as hear his stentorian voice. He was tempted to dash out into the midst of the battling warriors and thrust himself through to Amar's side; but the thought was futile, for such a rash act would be suicidal. He closed the door and turned to Nao and her parents.

"The battle is raging just outside," he said. Then directing his attention to Nao. "Is there any other way out of the temple?"

The girl shook her head ruefully.

"None that I know of," she replied.

Bantan turned and opened the door a trifle again to peer outside. The Amo defenders were being forced backward, for now they were beyond the temple and only their attackers were visible through the crack in the doorway.

Once again Bantan closed the door, and turning, informed his companions of the progress of the battle in the village lane.

"If only I had the automatic that is in the cavern on Aoono Island," he said with a rueful shake of his head. "I could shoot our way clear to the landing."

Nao drew near him with a wistful smile and rested a gentle hand upon his arm.

"You would be rash enough to do something like that," she remarked.

He smiled and once again opened the door to look outside. Among the rear guard of attacking forces, the bronzed giant was surprised to observe a young woman with a spear in hand was now approaching the temple door. Looking carefully, the firelight from the center of the village fitfully lighted the village lane, and as Bantan's keen eyes studied the young woman's features he recognized her as none other than Princess Lori. His mad hope that she might inflame the warriors of her village to attack the Amo village and "rescue" him and his companions was a reality. As he looked in her direction he saw her motion to four warriors armed with spears to join her.

Quickly Bantan closed the door and turned to his companions.

"It is true!" he murmured. "Princess Lori and four of her warriors are approaching the door of the temple."

As he uttered the last word, the door opened and a warrior stepped across the threshold with a spear poised to cast if necessary. Bantan and his companions had drawn back several steps. Recognizing the former captives of the Ono village, the warrior entered, followed by his three companions. Princess Lori entered last. As she looked at Bantan a smile touched her lips and her dark eyes glowed strangely. She sighed audibly.

"I had hoped I would be in time, Bantan," she said. "Oom has favored me."

A smile touched the lips of the bronzed giant.

"You have come to rescue us?" he asked.

The princess nodded.

"For what other reason would I have accompanied my warriors, Bantan," she said, "if it wasn't to be assured of your safety, and your companions as well?"

The bronzed giant stepped forward with a smile of gratitude upon his features. The spears that menaced him were lowered as the princess shook her head to her warriors.

"How can I thank you, Lori?" Bantan asked simply. She smiled enigmatically.

"You treated me with respect when I was your prisoner on Aoono Island," she replied. "The least I could do to show my appreciation when I saw you captured by the Amo warriors under Amar's command was to hope I would be in time to save you. That has been accomplished. Come, let us return to the beach before the Amo warriors succeed in turning the tide of battle. When we are safely there I will dispatch instructions that my warriors are to retreat in order."

Bantan turned to Nao and her parents, and in another moment they had left the temple and were passing down the village lane in the direction of the beach. Several warriors holding torches revealed the canoes of the Ono were in order and ready for launching. Princess Lori turned to the four warriors who had accompanied them.

"Two of you return to the fighting warriors and pass along the word that they are to retreat," she instructed them. "We have accomplished our objective."

With nods, two of the four warriors broke into a run, leaving their two companions with the princess and her rescued captives. Bantan was about to question his savior of the attitude of the warriors of the Ono village when she inflamed them to rescue the cap-

tives in the Amo village, but Lori interrupted his trend
of mind.

"Come, Bantan," she said, "let us take to the canoes
and be ready when the warriors return. Each of you
take your place in the bow." In a whisper, her lips
close to the bronzed giant's ear, she added: "You
must enter the same canoe I occupy. There is something I wish to tell you."

Not a little puzzled, Bantan stepped into the canoe
the princess indicated. As he looked toward Nao,
the light of the torches revealed her disappointment
that they were not to share the same canoe. He flashed
a smile to the dejected girl and nodded assuringly.
Though the girl's features affected a similar smile, the
droop of her shoulders revealed she was confused and
unhappy.

Bantan and the princess had hardly taken their places
when warriors from the scene of fighting in the center
of the village came hurrying to the beach. They
selected places in the canoes already partly occupied,
and at a word from Lori, launched them into the gentle
surf to presently reach the calmer water beyond.

The leader of the Ono warriors was the same Maho,
who had led the warriors to attack the Ono village
that same morning. Master strategist that he was, at
night Maho performed even better than in the daylight, for fewer warriors suffered injury. Those that
had been seriously wounded—numbering a dozen—
and three had been killed outright—had been previously transported to the waiting canoes. The torches
were extinguished as the last of the retreating warriors leaped into the waiting canoes, and the return
to Ono Island in the darkness of early evening was
taken up. The stars were their guide.

Upon the shore of Amo the unhappy warriors at

whose head Amar stood, with his father, Tomara, shook their fists in unmitigated rage at the departing canoes. Howls of anger from the disappointed warriors were loud and threatening. Woe befall the Ono village in the near future was the vow in each heart.

The steady dip of the paddles and the occasional groan of a wounded warrior was all that was to be heard in the enveloping darkness as the victorious Ono warriors returned to their island.

In the bow of the foremost canoe that Princess Lori occupied with Bantan and four paddlers, a silence had prevailed for a few minutes. Lori inclined now toward the bronzed giant with accelerated breathing, and reaching out in the darkness one of her soft warm hands found one of his.

"It must seem strange to you to be rescued by the very warriors who were to put you to death a few short suns ago," she murmured for no other ears than his to hear.

"It seems unbelievable, Lori," he answered. "Tell me, were the warriors of your village unwilling to go to our rescue?"

In the darkness he could not read whatever expression overcame the features of the princess, but he did hear the slight gasp that caught in her throat, and when she spoke he wondered at the trembling of her whisper. Her hand gripped his hard momentarily to give evidence of her emotions.

"They do not suspect my true purpose," she said.

The bronzed giant was puzzled by the true meaning of the answer the princess had given. A chill raced through him.

"Do you mean, Lori," he asked, "that the warriors believe we were rescued so that they might again sacrifice us by fire?"

The princess was agitated and her hand clutched his nervously.

"You must show no fear," she murmured. "Nor should Nao and her parents. As the princess of Ono Island, my word will be strongly in your favor. When I tell my father and Kolo, the witchdoctor, how you respected me when I was your captive, I'm sure everything will be all right."

"I hope so, Lori," Bantan murmured fervently.

In his heart misgivings were present. Had he and his companions been rescued from one perilous position to be transported to another as equally dangerous? He consoled himself that Nao at least was not to be subjected to the indignities that had threatened her upon Amo Island, for upon Ono there was no one like Amar to force his unwelcome attentions upon her. But with the thought there came to his screen of recollection what Nao had told him about Lori's father desiring her as a slave. That fate would be as equally despicable.

As a result of such unpleasant cogitations Bantan became silent, for he was convinced the future was far from bright. The fact that the princess still clasped his hand was not warming to him, for the full realization was apparent that she was only one in the inhospitable village that he might call friend—and the only reason for her friendliness was the fact she was infatuated with him. Should she make demands upon his affection—and he spurned her as he was fully determined to do—how easily her infatuation might turn into unmitigated hatred and a want of revenge be demanded in satisfaction to her rejected suit.

In due time the canoes were rounding the westerly shore of Aoono Island, and in the darkness Bantan looked at the towering volcano silhouetted against the stars. With the thought that his weapons had been cached in the canoe he had filched from the Amo village when he and Nao had escaped from the temple prison cell, he wondered if Lori had emptied her own canoe of the fruit he had provisioned it, or had she taken the other. It would do no harm to ask her.

"Lori," he whispered.

"Yes?" she asked, leaning toward him.

"When you left Aoono Island," he said, "did you take your canoe, or the one I had?"

"Mine was full of fruit," she replied. "I didn't empty it, so I took yours."

"Then you must know about my weapons that were in it," he said.

"I placed them in my hut," she answered. "Your dagger, so unlike the stone ones my warriors have, I also picked up and placed it with your other weapons. You must tell me about them later."

"Amar was very much interested in them when he captured us upon the atoll," he added. "He must have forgotten about them in the excitement of recapturing us in the cavern."

"They shall be restored to you—if all is well," she said.

The words "if all is well," uttered after a brief pause caused a strange chill to race through the bronzed giant. It was gratifying to know where his weapons were, but for some unknown reason he had occasion to wonder if he would be in a position to claim them again.

"Later, Bantan," the princess said, with a trace of eagerness in her tones, "you will show me how the weapons are used?"

"Of course, Lori," he answered.

After a brief silence the princess spoke again.

"By what names are the strange weapons called?"

Bantan described the weapons by their name and how each was used.

Lori seemed excited.

"Yes," she said presently, "you must show me."

The bronzed giant, with heavy heart, promised to do that.

Looking to his right he saw that the looming volcano upon Aoono Island, silhouetted against the stars, was gradually drawing away, and soon now the canoes should be nearing the Ono village beach. The sound of the gentle surf served to guide the paddlers around the bend of the shoreline. The eyes of all, accustomed to the darkness by this time, presently were aware of the landing. From the village beyond the glow of cook fires was to be seen.

As the canoes were beached, several old warriors appeared from the village carrying torches. Women and children followed, and cheered the return of the princess and the warriors. When they presently learned of the successful mission, loud was their exultation.

Bantan, Nao, and her parents drew close together after disembarking from the canoes. They were not favorably impressed with this reception. But Lori, the princess, came to the bronzed giant's side and whispered for him to inform his companions they need not be afraid.

"Trust me," she murmured. "For the sake of appearances, you, Nao, and her parents are to be marched into the village as prisoners. All of you will be confined in a single prison hut. But know that the promise of a princess is not easily broken. You will have faith in me?" It was an humble plea that Lori made.

Bantan shrugged his broad shoulders. One of his

hands groped for Nao's and he clasped it assuringly.
After all, he reasoned with himself, they were no
worse off than when in the Amo village. There always was that glimmer of hope, however faint, that
the princess could spare them. As the matter now
stood they had no choice but to hope that Lori could
intercede in their favor.

"We have no choice but hope your mercy for us will
not go unrecognized, Lori," he said to the princess.

Bantan turned to Nao and her parents.

"You have heard the princess," he said in a low
voice. "Under the circumstances we have no other
choice."

Nao's hand clasped his and she smiled bravely.

"We understand," she murmured. "We can be no
worse than when we were upon Amo Island." With
the thought of Lori's father she repressed with an effort the shudder that otherwise would have gripped
her.

Warriors with their spears in hand gathered about
them.

"Come," the princess said. "Let us enter the village."

With no protest, the "rescued" captives were
marched into the village. The women and children—
those especially who had suffered the loss of a beloved
one—shook their fists threateningly and voiced their
anger at the prisoners.

Meanwhile, the wounded were given assistance by
other warriors, while the dead were carried to their
huts so that their immediate relatives might mourn-
fully prepare them for burial the following day.

The captives were confined in the same prison hut
that Bantan had previously occupied.

"I will have my slave girl bring you fruit," the princess promised as they entered the hut.

Then the door was closed and barred. A warrior was stationed outside on guard.

True to the promise of Lori, Sela, her slave girl, presently brought fruit to the captives. While they partook of it, Bantan nodded his head.

"This proves Lori's sincerity," he said.

Nao and her parents agreed with the bronzed giant, and in their hearts they tried to hope with the same fervor that Bantan did that the word of a princess was to be regarded highly.

Without loss of time, Maho had gone to the chief's hut and informed him of the success of their mission. He added how many warriors had met their death, and enumerated the warriors who had been more or less seriously wounded.

"In view of this, Maho," Roko said, "the celebration planned for tonight shall be postponed until tomorrow night. You will inform the villagers of this change of plans."

"That I will do, my chief," the leading warrior replied respectfully.

"Inform them that tomorrow night the rescued captives shall be bound to stakes and sacrificed to a fiery death to add to the victory celebration," the chief stated.

Bowing in respect, Maho left the chief's hut.

Meanwhile, the princess lost no time going to the hut of her father who eagerly awaited her return. As she entered he sighed, then curiosity overcame his features.

"I have learned of the successful mission that has been conducted, my daughter," he greeted her. "Maho has been here and just left."

The princess shuddered.

"That is why I have come first to you, father," she said. "I have instructed Sela to summon Kolo."

A worried expression had overcome Lori's features.

"Father," she said, "I have an unusual request to make of you."

"Yes, Lori," was the reply. "What is it?"

"The captives are not to be harmed, father," the princess said in a level tone. " When I was their prisoner upon Aoono Island, they treated me with respect. They did not bind my wrists and ankles. They must not be harmed. I have given my word to them that I shall intercede for their liberty."

Roko was infuriated. His dark eyes flashed coldly.

"My daughter, you forget they killed several of our warriors when they made their previous escape from the village." he said. "Others were seriously wounded and three killed when they were rescued from the Amo village tonight. Their immediate relatives will demand revenge, and the only satisfaction I can give them is to have the prisoners burned at the stake."

"But, father," Lori pleaded, "doesn't it matter that they treated me, your daughter, with respect when I was their prisoner after their horrible treatment by us?"

Roko laughed sardonically. His dark eyes glowed with cunning.

"Lori, you are safe now—that is all that matters," he reminded her. "Even though you promised the captives you would intercede for them—does that mean anything? Do you think that I, the chief, would even consider acceding to such foolishness?"

Lori's features revealed her hopelessness. Her dark eyes were misty.

"I gave them the word of a princess that I would

intercede for them," she said in a monotone; and she repeated this.

Roko's dark eyes were merciless.

"Lori, ever since your mother died," he said in cold tones, "you have made me heed your every beck and whim. Secretly I have learned of the ridicule the villagers hold for me because of this. I am the chief of the village, and as my daughter, from now on you shall do as I say. You have pled for the prisoners and I deny your request. I have no doubt that Kolo will feel as I do. The prisoners must die!"

It was then that the door opened and Kolo, the witchdoctor, entered. He bowed to the chief first, then to his daughter. With measured steps he walked toward them. His features were impassive, though his glittering eyes became soft as they rested upon Lori. The princess turned to him with a hope in her heart that he might help her.

"Kolo, is there mercy in your heart?" she asked with threatening tears.

The witchdoctor's smile was a mask to his true emotions.

"I love you as though you were my own daughter, Lori," he answered.

"Listen to me, Kolo, and hear my plea," the princess entreated.

The witchdoctor turned wondering eyes to the chief. Roko's features were expressionless. Kolo again looked at the unhappy princess.

"What is it that troubles you, Lori?" he asked in a voice that was gentle.

"I have asked my father that the captives are not to be harmed, Kolo," she said.

As Lori spoke, the import of her words made the witchdoctor apparently freeze. He drew himself to his full height of better than six feet, and his features became very stern.

"You plead for the captives, Lori?" he asked with surprise. "Oom forbid that you, the daughter of our chief, could hope to be lenient toward the captives who insulted Oom once before by escaping the fiery death ordained for them."

"But, Kolo," the girl interceded, "when I was their prisoner today they did not ill treat me. I was regarded with respect—the respect a princess might command. But I was in no position to demand respect, and yet it was accorded me—because I was a princess."

"The relatives of those who have died because of the prisoners demand satisfaction, Lori," Kolo reminded the girl. "Oom would never look down upon us with favor were we to shirk the duty that is ours to perform." Turning to the chief, he asked: "What have you to say, my chief, in regard to the captives?"

Roko looked disdainfully at his daughter. His dark eyes were not softened by her pleading ones.

"They must die!" he answered curtly. "I have said this to Lori, but because of a foolish infatuation she has for the bronzed stranger, she would selfishly deny the want of revenge which our villagers are entitled to, and she would ungraciously flaunt her indiscretion to Oom."

Kolo slowly shook his head.

"As your father, the chief, states, and in which I agree, Lori," he said with austerity, "the captives must die by fire!"

The princess buried her face in her arms and wept. Her shoulders quivered. The witchdoctor approached the sobbing girl and for a moment his heart softened. He placed a hand upon her naked shoulder and patted it gently. Then he shook his head again.

"Lori, you do not act like a princess," he softly reproached her.

The girl continued to sob for another minute before her quivering shoulders stilled. She arose. She dried her wet eyes with her lovely tresses. She looked first to her father, then to Kolo. She smiled sheepishly.

"I should be ashamed," she said in a low voice. "Excuse me while I go to Oom and beg forgiveness for my strange way of thinking."

So sincere the expression upon her face, her father was deceived. As the girl left the hut, Kolo, the witchdoctor, watched her with a peculiar expression of contrition in his dark eyes. He turned to the chief with lips pursed.

"Lori acts strangely because of the bronzed stranger," he remarked.

Roko laughed derisively.

"Since the death of her mother, Kolo," he said, "Lori has had her own way too much." He was thinking of Nao as he spoke. "I realized this recently, and decided she was to heed me in the future rather than I should heed her. It is quite a shock to her to know her wishes have not met with my approval. But I'm sure after the prisoners have been sacrificed she will come to her normal senses again. Then I shall broach the subject that she should mate with some stalwart warrior of the village for the sake of posterity."

The witchdoctor smiled and cleared his throat.

"That is something I have long wanted to discuss with you, my chief," he said, drawing himself erect. "I am not old, and since the death of my mate many moons ago, leaving me childless, I would mate again."

Roko stared at Kolo. The witchdoctor must at least be as old as he. When they were boys, how well he remembered that Kolo always outstripped him in whatever contest was held. As a boy, naturally, he had become chief following his father's death, and Kolo became a witchdoctor. Roko had many reasons to respect him. Now, indeed, what could be more appropriate that Kolo became the mate of his daughter? As these thoughts passed through the chief's mind, his features revealed, first, his surprise, and then with the gradual awakening to its possibilities, his pleasure. He looked up at the patient features of the witchdoctor.

"Kolo, forgive me for being so absent-minded in the past," he murmured. "Because of your age I had never considered you as a fitting mate to my daughter. But why not? As you say, you are not an old man. You and I are about the same age, and I do not *feel* old. There is no reason why you should feel otherwise. I shall speak to Lori about you. She should feel honored to know that you would happily mate with her."

A gentle smile touched the lips of the witchdoctor and his dark eyes glowed strangely.

"Just the thought of my union with Lori makes me feel like a youth, my chief," he remarked.

Roko smiled but said nothing.

"Forgive me, my chief," Kolo then said, "I must retire to the sanctuary of my lonely hut to reflect upon the possible joys of the near future."

With Kolo's departure, Roko went to his couch, and lying down, placed his hands beneath his head. A contented expression enwreathed his features. For the first time in many, many moons he was at peace with himself. In reflection, when Lori was mated to Kolo, he felt it might be appropriate that he, too, selected a maiden from the village and mate with her to bring untold happiness in the later years of his life.

*   *   *

When the princess left her father's hut her lips were drawn in tight lines. A glance about the village revealed the women were preparing the evening meal over cook fires, and their families were nearby awaiting the time to eat. For that reason she did not encounter any one as she went to the nearby Oom, idol of the Ono village.

Before the deity of the village, Lori went down upon her knees. Folding her hands respectfully upon her bosom, she raised her head and her eyes looked upward at the separate deities until the darkness above enveloped the others she couldn't see. Her lips did not move, nor was there a prayer voiced in her heart for Oom's forgiveness that she thought strangely for an Ono princess.

Where she should be exultant that the escaped captives were again prisoners of her people—thanks to her—to the contrary, the princess was sad. Until recently she scarcely had reason to be sad over anything, however important or trivial. Deep in her heart was the realization her love for Bantan could never be returned; but for some unaccountable reason she was keenly aware that she could not hate him since it was apparent his heart belonged to the Amo maiden. She envied Nao, it is true, for the blessed opportunity to be so fortunate to be loved by the giant stranger; and though she envied the girl she realized she could not hate her—even though they both were women, and she was a princess. How quickly she would exchange places with the Amo girl if such could be a possibility.

While Lori knelt there in apparent communion with Oom and, for her, such strange thoughts were pulsing through her, in the shadows of a nearby hut a silent figure had appeared and watched her with palpitating emotions. Deep was the breathing of this individual and with reluctance he exhaled. Time and again he would shake his head.

At long last, with a convulsive shake of her shoulders, Lori arose to her feet. A final look she gave at the village idol, then turning about, set her footsteps toward her own hut.

The silent figure in the shadows of the nearby hut watched her sorrowfully—almost hoping she would linger longer. With a sigh he returned to the sanctuary of his lonely hut to reflect upon the beauty of the Ono princess and how the very sight of her stirred his blood to youthfulness.

*   *   *

In the prison hut following the meal Sela, Lori's slave girl, had brought them, the captives remained in silence for a while save for desultory conversation. Time and again Bantan would approach the barred window and look out into the village, hoping the firelight from the various cook fires would reveal the princess walking in his direction. He seemingly looked in vain.

Outside, the guard remained at his station.

Each time that Bantan approached the barred window, Nao would be at his side. In her heart she could realize his mounting tension.

"It looks hopeless, Bantan," she murmured, reaching for one of his hands.

He shrugged his broad shoulders.

"It is not very hopeful, Nao," he agreed. "Anyway, we are still alive. For the present that is all that matters." Then, with a shake of his head, he added: "I can't explain it, but somehow I am convinced that Lori shall not fail us in our hour of need."

Nao caught her breath in her throat, for she remembered only too well how vicious the princess could be.

"I hope you are right," she said with a little quiver in her voice.

Turning away from the window, with Nao at his side, the two returned to the far side of the prison hut where Maro and Luno were seated, offering in low tones what consolement they might to each other. Bantan and the girl seated themselves nearby.

Outside, from time to time the movement of the guard was a source of irritation to the bronzed giant. The Amo girl was aware of this, for every time the guard moved, Bantan would seemingly start with ears that strained. Perhaps he hoped too much for Lori to come—a hope that waned as the minutes dragged into long hours.

The parents of the girl presently slept with their backs against the wall, remaining seated. Bantan remained awake in a similar position, though Nao, at his side, leaned against him and her head rested upon his shoulder. She, too, drowsed. In compassion, the bronzed giant placed an arm about the girl's shoulders, and though half asleep, she snuggled closer to him, mumbling something beneath her breath that he could not distinguish with clarity.

Some little time had passed when to Bantan's keen ears there came the soft, stealthy sounds of sandalled feet approaching the rear of the prison hut—directly in a line where he sat. Nearer they came until at last they stopped just outside the wall. The bronzed giant's keen ears could hear the labored breathing of the prowler outside. He heard the barely audible sound of things being placed gently upon the ground. Light, groping hands touched the thatched wall of the prison hut. A whisper was heard—his name. At once he recognized the identity of the one outside. It was Lori, the princess!

"Yes, Lori?" he whispered through the stoutly thatched wall.

The princess muffled a sob in her throat before she spoke.

"Listen carefully to me," she murmured.

"I am listening, Lori," he answered.

Nao waked and at once was aware Bantan was communicating with someone outside the wall. She sought one of the bronzed giant's hands and pressed it to let him know she was awake.

"I have begged my father, the chief, and Kolo, the witchdoctor, to spare all of you," Lori was saying. "They have decreed death for all of you by fire at stakes tomorrow night. May Oom forgive me, but I cannot let you die. I have your dagger with me. I shall cut a small hole in the wall and give it to you. Do you think you can cut a larger one to permit the passage of your body and the others with you?"

"I'm sure that I can, Lori," Bantan replied.

The princess pressed the keen-edged dagger into the wall near Bantan's side and eased it down a few inches, then across a similar distance. Upward she forced it, and then across again. The patch of wall was removed.

"Here is the dagger," she said.

The dagger was then extended handle first through the aperture. The bronzed giant felt for it and as his hand clasped the handle he sighed. He placed his mouth to the aperture.

"Lori," he whispered.

"Yes?" the princess asked.

"I am eternally grateful to you." As he spoke,

Bantan reached a hand through the aperture and the warm hand of the princess found his.

"The other weapons that are yours are also here outside the wall," she whispered. "Be careful when you go to the beach. There are two guards stationed there. More than what I am doing I cannot do. I hope you are successful, and that you and Nao are very happy afterwards."

Bantan swallowed a lump of gratitude. He drew Lori's hand through the aperture and gently pressed his lips upon its back. He heard the princess muffle a sigh.

"I must go now," she said.

"I'll never forget you, Lori," he said with solemnity.

Then, releasing her hand, he heard her steal away. Bantan turned to Nao.

"Now, to cut our way to freedom," he whispered.

Without loss of time the keen blade was gently forced through the thatched wall. With brief pauses, to ascertain the guard stationed outside was not aware of the cutting of the fibers, in the passing minutes Bantan's dagger cut vertically along an upright beam, then horizontally from one beam to the other, which was about a yard apart. Then upward the blade was gently forced, and then once again sideways. The severed panel was removed, and an aperture was revealed of sufficient space to permit the passage of Bantan's broad shoulders.

While the bronzed giant had been thus engaged, Nao had waked her father and mother, and in a whisper informed them Bantan was making it possible for them to escape from the prison hut. They were overjoyed to know that they might be free again. As they gathered joyfully around him, he spoke to them in a whisper, advising what procedure they were to follow to make good their escape. He slipped the dagger in its sheath.

In turn, with Bantan in the lead, the prisoners slipped through the aperture. Outside, the bronzed giant felt about with tentative hands for the weapons Lori had placed there. He found them without difficulty. He slipped the cartridge belt with its holstered automatic over his head, allowing it to trail over his left shoulder. He handed the bow and arrows to Maro. Quickly they looked to right and left while Bantan determined the nearest way to the beach.

There was little activity in the village. The cook fires were fast dying, and from his place of observation, Bantan wisely decided they would have to slip from the shadows of one hut to another with the hope they would not be detected by the guard in front of the prison hut. He was the first to make a move.

Across a distance of twenty feet he crept, silent as a shadow, reaching the sanctuary of the hut across the village lane. Bantan beckoned to Nao. She followed, as did her mother, and last of all, Maro joined them. Creeping around this hut, they looked in the direction of the next. From within came the sound of a wounded warrior, moaning in pain. Almost immediately words of consolement were uttered by his mate.

From this second hut Bantan and his companions went to the next, and in turn other huts were passed until they reached the edge of the foliage which bordered the village. Keeping in line, with the bronzed giant leading, they cautiously stole toward the beach. Hut after hut was passed until they had reached the last one. At the edge of the foliage they paused while Bantan strained his eyes, now becoming accustomed to the darkness. With a little difficulty he observed

the two guards seated upon the bottom of an overturned canoe—at the opposite end of the beach! They
were armed with spears, and doubtless stone daggers
were sheathed at their hips. They were talking in low
voices.

"Now is the time," Bantan whispered to his companions. "Maro, you and I shall carry the canoe to
the water's edge. Nao, make sure you obtain two
paddles. We shall take the last canoe upon the outside edge of the beach. Maro, give Luno the bow and
arrows to carry."

In a few moments the two men were carrying the
canoe to the edge of the beach. Nao and her mother
moved cautiously, the former having obtained two
paddles. The canoe was gently placed in the water.
Bantan and Maro held it while Nao and her mother
stepped within. The bronzed giant then removed the
cartridge belt from about his neck and with care placed
it into the canoe. At a whisper from him, Maro stepped within and took up one of the paddles to be in
readiness. Bantan shoved the canoe into the gentle
surf, and leaping in, took up the second paddle. With
sweeping strokes, both men were extremely careful to
avoid striking the sides of the canoe and thereby alert
the guards upon the beach of their escape.

Breathless minutes passed and with each stroke of
the paddles, the canoe forged through the gentle surf
to presently reach the calmer water beyond. Nao
heaved a sigh of relief.

"I can hardly believe we are free again!" she murmured.

"But we are, Nao," Bantan quickly assured her.
"And this time we have the generosity of a princess
to thank."

"You seemed to know Lori would keep her word,"

the girl remarked. "I'll be contrite and thank her for her assistance. But, where are we going?"

The bronzed giant was looking at Aoono, silhouetted against a starry canopy. A smile touched his lips.

"First, we are going to the cavern on Aoono," he said. "Lori said her canoe filled with fruit was left there."

"That is true," Nao admitted.

"This very night we are going to start for Marja Island, with the hope nothing prevents us from reaching our goal," Bantan stated.

Nao and her parents uttered a deep sigh. It would be a blessing to be free of constant danger and live a normal life again.

PART VI

The End—And the Beginning

The night was dark as Erebus. The distant light from the stars offered scant illumination to the surface of the mighty Pacific Ocean beneath. The rhythmic dip of the two paddles wielded by Bantan and Maro propelled the canoe they had filched from Ono Island in the direction of the looming volcano upon Aoono which was silhouetted against the starry canopy. This was their first temporary stop, for a canoe ladened with fruit awaited them in the cavern, and this was a necessity for their trip to Marja.

Nao and Luno, her mother, were indeed happy that at last their perils of recent days were terminated, and happiness and peaceful living was to be their reward when they would reach Marja within a few days. The Amo girl now had reason to be grateful to Princess Lori for being instrumental in paving their way to freedom. She spoke quietly to her mother who was seated just ahead of her.

"At first Lori had given me every reason to hate her," she was saying. "Her infatuation for Bantan was the reason she could not see us sacrificed. I am very grateful to her, and I hope very much she is not punished if it is discovered that she aided us to escape."

"I have known many villagers that way, Nao," her mother answered. "They usually had some good in them. The only one I know who was not blessed with good graces is Amar. From the time he was a child, he was to be despised."

"And to think I hoped the day would come when I might have been his mate," her daughter murmured with a shiver. "I hope I never see him again—"

"*I* hope to see him again," Bantan interrupted the girl. "I have scores to settle with him. The fact that he slapped you is reason enough for his death, let alone the threats he made to me. When Amar and I first met in combat I realize now I should have done as you insisted."

"Do you mean," Nao asked, "that at a later time you intend to seek Amar and settle scores with him?"

"That I do," he replied.

"When we reach Marja," the girl suggested, "why don't we forget that Amar ever existed?"

"Thought of him would ever be in my mind," he answered. "If a man is to be happy he cannot have disturbing thoughts in his mind."

The girl sighed audibly.

"I can understand that you are determined," she said; "so let us forget Amar for the time being. Shall we?"

"We shall," was his reply.

The canoe now was nearing Aoono. Already the lapping wavelets against the rocky shore could be heard. Bantan's keen eyes, accustomed to the darkness by this time, were directed intently upon the looming mass just ahead. He spoke quietly to Maro.

"Paddle easier—we are almost there."

By dragging his paddle in the water, Bantan served to brake the canoe's speed in the passing moments with the result the prow came to rest with gentleness on the rock shelf. Quickly all disembarked. Bantan and

Maro drew the canoe a short ways from the water's edge.

Nao was enthusiastic.

"We are this much nearer our goal!" she exclaimed.

"We were once before," Bantan reminded her.

"But this time we cannot be so unfortunate as before," the girl added with a laugh. "Somehow I feel it. Already I am looking forward to meeting your foster parents—and Wanya. I wonder," she added, "how she will receive me?"

This last was uttered more to herself than her companions. But Bantan had heard her dropping voice, and he shrugged his shoulders as Wanya's features were mirrored in his mind. Without answering Nao, he and Maro carefully walked toward the cavern with groping hands. In the darkness they felt about for the canoe that had belonged to Princess Lori, and which had been provisioned with fruit earlier that afternoon. It was Bantan's groping hands that first touched it. The pleasing aroma of the fruit had been attracted by his keen nostrils and guided him to the canoe.

"Over here, Maro," he asid.

In another moment Nao's father had joined the bronzed giant.

"It's smell should have led me here, Bantan," he remarked with a chuckle.

"That is how I found it so soon," was the answer.

Laying hand upon the canoe, the two men drew it out of the cavern toward the edge of the water where Nao and Luno were awaiting them.

The girl's keen ears had been attracted by a sound from the direction of Ono Island while Bantan and her father had gone into the cavern, and she had asked her mother to strain her ears, as she did again. There had been no repetition of the sound she believed she had heard. She joined the bronzed giant then and spoke to him concerning it. He listened intently for a few moments, but heard nothing unusual. However, his curiosity was aroused.

"What did it sound like, Nao?" he asked.

"Like a paddle striking the side of a canoe," she answered.

"I don't understand how any one could be following us," Bantan added. He turned to Maro. "Listen carefully and see if you can hear anything."

Tense moments passed while not only the girl's father strained his ears, but all three of them, in an effort to determine if Nao's hearing had been correct at first. In the pitch darkness that enveloped the water between them and Ono Island there was no hope of being able to discern anything. Presently Maro shrugged his shoulders.

"I can't hear anything," he announced.

"Nor I," Bantan added. "Now, comes the problem of attaching the canoe provisioned with fruit to ours so that we might tow it."

"Our pallets of grasses in the cavern!" Nao exclaimed. "Mother and I should be able to weave the grass into strong strands even in the dark."

"Good!" Bantan said. "Come, Maro, let us go after some."

In another moment the two men returned to the cavern, and groping within, presently came upon the pallets they sought. Gathering several of them, they returned to the two women and deposited them in the canoe they had recently filched from the Ono village landing.

"While you and father were gone, Bantan," Nao

said with evident apprehension, "I heard the same sound as before—only this time nearer."

"And I heard it, too," her mother hastened to add.

"You both are sure?" the bronzed giant asked with concern.

Mother and daughter agreed there had been no mistake this time.

In a whisper, Bantan suggested Nao and Luno start weaving strands from the grasses. Turning to Maro, he added that he accompany him.

"We are going just a short distance," the bronzed giant said to the mother and daughter. "We want to concentrate our attention upon the sounds you both have heard."

Bantan and Maro carefully picked their way across the rock shelf until they were about fifty feet from where the cavern was located. They looked with straining eyes into the impenetrable darkness that intervened to Ono Island, while their ears were intent to detect any unusual sounds that might indicate all was not well.

A long minute passed while they stood there, but nothing out of the ordinary came to their attention. Another minute passed while they were motionless, hardly breathing. Bantan earnestly hoped Nao and her mother had not heard anything that would inter- rupt their plans to return to Marja.

Suddenly his even breath caught in his throat. To his ears came the sound—not too far away—of a paddle gently striking the side of a canoe. His groping hand rested upon Maro's shoulder.

"Did you hear that?" he whispered.

"I did," was the reply. "It is as Nao and her mother said."

"Some one is paddling toward Aoono," Bantan said

in a convinced tone. "Listen again carefully for the sound of a paddle dipping into the water."

Again their ears strained. Sure enough, they could hear a methodical dip dip dip of a paddle.

"From the sound, Maro," Bantan then said, "I would say there was only one paddler in the canoe."

"That is right," was the reply. "Who can it be?"

The bronzed giant shook his head and uttered a barely audible "Sh-h-h!" He was straining his ears again to determine the exact position of the nearing canoe. It seemed to be coming directly toward them. This fact he made known to Maro.

Instinctively Bantan's right hand went to his hip and his fingers closed about the handle of his dagger. He did not withdraw it from its sheath. Without warning at the next moment a dark object grated upon the rock shelf with an unexpectedness that surprised the occupant of the canoe, for a muffled cry was uttered by the paddler—a voice that was unmistakably feminine —as she managed to regain her equilibrium which had been nearly upset.

"Who are you?" Bantan demanded, stepping forward and laying a hand upon the bow of the canoe.

A sigh of relief was uttered by the woman paddler. She lay her paddle down and in another moment disembarked. Even before she spoke, the aroma of perfume emanating from her announced her identity to Bantan's keen nostrils.

"Lori," she whispered softly. "I come to you with a plea for mercy."

As the princess spoke, her hands groped for one of his. Finding it, she clasped it tightly with a frenzy that amazed him.

"But why have you followed us, Lori?" he insisted. "We are eternally grateful that you provided us the

means of escaping certain death from your people."
As he spoke, Bantan could not see Lori's features with
clearness, but he was aware of her agitated breathing.

"You must let me go with you, Bantan," she begged.
"My slave girl overheard my father and Kolo, the
witchdoctor, talking. She hurried to me and informed
me that Kolo wishes to mate with me. I should be
honored, but Kolo is old enough to be my father, and
I do not love him. Rather than be forced into such
a loveless mating, I realized I couldn't remain in the
Ono village. I knew you would stop at Aoono for
the provisioned canoe, and I was hoping I would be
in time. At the beach I eluded the two guards and
launched a canoe. Take me with you and the others,
I beg of you, and let me start a new life upon Marja
Island."

As he listened to the princess, a wave of compassion rose in Bantan's breast. His free hand covered
hers that clasped his other hand.

"I can't refuse you, Lori," he said. "We owe you
our lives, and for that reason alone I cannot see you
be made to enter a loveless mating. I'm sure upon
Marja you could not be less happier." Turning to
Maro, he spoke. "Drag Lori's canoe to the cavern."

With Lori at his side, Bantan returned to where
Nao and her mother were weaving strands of grasses.
The two women had heard a canoe being dragged upon
the rock shelf and their curiosity was aroused. Presently Bantan and Lori came to them, and though they
were not clearly distinguishable in the inky darkness,
the two women knew a stranger had joined them.

"Who is it?" Nao asked.

"Your ears did not deceive you, Nao," was Bantan's
reply. "Lori has come and wishes to accompany us
to Marja."

"Let me explain, Nao." In an agitated tone of voice that revealed her emotional stress, Lori told the Amo girl what she had already told Bantan. She concluded simply: "As a woman, you would not wish to be forced into a loveless mating with a man old enough to be your father, so you surely must understand how I feel."

"We owe you our lives, Lori," Nao said in a softened tone of voice. "There is no reason why you cannot come with us."

"Thank you, Nao," the princess replied. "I'm sure you shall never regret it. Since I have willingly left the island where I was a princess, it would be kind of all of you to forget that I was a princess and just call me Lori. I think I would like it better."

All agreed to respect Lori's wishes. When inquiring what Nao and her mother were doing, and she was told, Lori offered her apologies that she was unable to help them owing to a lack of knowledge of such practical things. She expressed the hope that Nao and her mother would teach her in the future the many useful duties a girl should know so that one day she might be a worthy mate to some warrior of the island to which she was going as a total stranger.

"Wanya, my foster sister, will be happy to help you, Lori," Bantan added. "You will like her as you both have so much in common."

"I can't be worse off anywhere than upon Ono Island," was her reply. "I promise I will try and be patient with the new life I have chosen."

In the passing minutes the industrious fingers of Nao and her mother continued to weave grasses into a sturdy, slender rope, and presently they announced they should have sufficient length for their requirement.

The two grass ropes were approximately ten feet in length. Bantan, with two ends and handing the other two to Maro, twisted them together for double strength. One end was fastened to the bow of the provisioned canoe. The paddle that was in the canoe in which Lori had come to the island was placed in the provisioned one in the event one of their paddles might break. The bronzed giant expressed his regret that they must leave the canoe concealed in the cavern, but he did not wish to be burdened with it, since the one containing fruit was sufficient to tow and would retard their progress as it was.

"Perhaps some warriors from Ono Island might come and find it," he commented. Turning to Maro. "Hold the provisioned canoe while I place the other in line," he said.

When this was done, he turned to the three women and bade them enter, advising in a low voice where to take their places, so that he and Maro might have suf-ficient room to ply their paddles. Four people could be very comfortable in the canoe, but the addition of Lori made quarters a trifle cramped. Bantan, how-ever, was not reproachful of her presence, for had it not been for her they would not now be preparing to return to Marja. In silence, Nao, Luno, her mother, and Lori, took their assigned places.

"Now, Nao," he directed, "take up a paddle and hold the canoe steady while I attach the grass rope to the stern."

In a few moments this was attended to. Bantan then bade Maro take his place near the bow, while he stepped into the aft portion of the canoe. Paddling easily, they gently took up the slack upon the grass rope. Then, at a word from Bantan, they plied their paddles in unison, and the trailing canoe followed obediently as they drew away without mishap from the rock shelf of Aoono Island, for the water was calm. After paddling a few minutes and the canoes were a sufficient distance from the volcanic island, Bantan informed Maro the course they were to keep. With the passing minutes Aoono was being left behind.

Bantan studied the star-shot heaven, and checking carefully the various constellations, with the Southern Cross to his right, he observed a star of the first magnitude that was rising over the eastern horizon. This was to be his guide until another might later rise above the waterline.

After several hours of continuous paddling, the younger man urged Maro to desist and obtain some sleep. Already the three women were asleep and all were thankful the evening was fairly mild. The father of Nao insisted he was far from tired and sleepy, but after more persuasion from Bantan, with a little reluctance he put aside his paddle. Making himself as comfortable as circumstances would permit, he presently slept.

As an automaton, Bantan continued to paddle alone, keeping the trailing one in tow with the attached grass rope as taut as possible so as to avoid any unnecessary jerking upon it that might snap it without warning. Hour after hour, thereafter, he wielded his paddle with methodical strokes that did not seem to tire his mighty arms. As the time passed new stars appeared above the eastern horizon toward which distant Marja was the goal.

In due time the moon, well past her full stage, rose above the water, and as Bantan looked up at the earth's satellite, his curiosity was again aroused that the moon passed through the various stages she did. Her silvery light lessened the darkness of the early morn-

ing, and now for the first time the paddler could look
at the occupants of the canoe as they slumbered.

Lori, the self-renounced princess of Ono Island, was
curled in the bow, with her knees drawn up to her
bosom. Her face was pillowed upon one arm while
the other covered her features. Just behind her, in
an inverted position, Maro was sleeping, he, too, curled
with his head near his mate's. Luno was in a similar
position, one of her arms about Maro's neck. Nao,
nearer Bantan, was curled upon her right side, and her
fair features with her lustrous hair pillowed the side
of her head. She was sleeping peacefully. The
bronzed giant looked at them all in turn, then with a
shrug of his shoulders, paused in his steady paddling.
He was becoming hungry and must have sustenance.

He drew the trailing canoe alongside and reached
in for some fruit. His continuous paddling during the
night thus far had consumed much energy that he must
needs renew. Several plantains and figs he ate, then
once again resumed paddling, his hunger satisfied for
the time being. His first strokes were easy until the
slack in the grass rope attached to the trailing canoe
was taken up, then his paddle strokes were more firm.

In due time, as the partly eaten moon rose higher in
the eastern heaven, the first streaks of dawn appeared.
When another hour had passed and the bosom of the
gently heaving ocean was more clearly revealed, Bantan paused in his paddling to look to his rear for sight
of the Aoono Islands. A faint blur upon the distant
horizon was all that could be seen of them, and this
great distance testified to the constancy of his effort
during the long hours of the night.

It was now that Nao heaved a deep sigh, and stirring, she awoke. Aware of the girl's movements, Bantan looked at her with gentleness. As her eyes pres-

ently opened and she looked up at the bronzed giant, the Amo girl smiled and arose to a seated position with care so as not to waken the other occupants in the canoe.

"It is morning!" she exclaimed, rubbing her arms vigorously for a moment, then smothering a yawn.

"It is, Nao," he replied with a nod. "We are quite a distance from the Aoono Islands. They can hardly be seen now."

The girl looked beyond him and she could barely distinguish the blur that represented the Aoono Islands upon the distant horizon. Then directing her attention upon him once again she smiled pensively and slowly shook her head.

"You have been paddling all night while we slept, Bantan," she said. "You must be very tired."

A gentle smile touched his lips.

"A little," he admitted.

Lori was next to waken. She was stirring in the bow, and opening her eyes, she was surprised to observe daylight. Wincing a trifle, for she was unaccustomed to such cramped quarters, she looked toward Bantan and Nao. She managed a smile as she drew herself to a seated position. She rubbed the small of her back and then her arms. Quickly she arranged her lovely hair as best she might and allowed it to trail over her shoulders. Even thus early in the morning Lori was beautiful to behold.

"We'll only have one more night to sleep in the canoe, Lori," Nao said. "If we could be sure no Amo warriors were upon the atoll, we could stop there this coming night and there would be no need of being cramped in this canoe."

"We'll manage somehow, Nao," was the smiling

reply. "At least we have the thought of Marja to look forward. That is something."

Maro and Luno woke now, and they, too, stretched and eased their stiffened muscles.

"At least we can be grateful we are still alive," Maro remarked good naturedly.

All agreed the father of Nao spoke with logic.

While they ate of fruit from the trailing canoe, their plans for the day were discussed. Bantan instructed Maro to continue paddling in the face of the rising sun, and by late afternoon—perhaps much sooner—the atoll should be sighted.

"Lori and I shall help father," Nao said. "In that way we can make it easier for all of us."

"Even I can paddle," the mother of the Amo girl said eagerly.

"Before we start," Nao said, "mother and I should fashion a grass hat with a visor to protect father's eyes from the blazing sun."

Maro protested that he did not require such protection, but his daughter had her way in the matter. Shortly, when her father was induced to don the crude grass hat, he was forced to admit the visor provided fine protection from the brilliant rays of the sun.

Bantan exchanged places with Lori, and curling himself in the bow he presently was fast asleep. Meanwhile, as the hours passed, the other four occupants took turns at paddling. Beneath the hot, brassy orb the canoe, with the provisioned one trailing, moved across the gently heaving surface of the mighty Pacific.

Occasionally a sea gull winged its way overheard from the east, and flying fish arose from the surface to flit through the motioness air to plop back into the water at varying distances. Porpoises appeared at intervals to sport upon the surface and feed upon the

smaller marine life. Dreaded sharks were not to be
seen, thus with favorable conditions, all was well.

Bantan slept soundly until midday when he awoke
to find the other four occupants partaking of their
noon repast. Sitting upright with a smile, he massaged his arms and legs in turn and was aware he felt
surprisingly fit. Shading his eyes with his hands he
looked at the brassy sun to determine the time of day.

"It is noon day," he annouced. Then he looked to
the east, allowing his eyes to shift a trifle to the left,
and then to the right. In this direction was the blur
upon the horizon that proclaimed their course had been
reasonably calculated under the existing circumstances.
The atoll was in sight. He indicated it with a hand
as he spoke. "The atoll can be sighted now."

Not one of the others had observed the blur as yet,
but with Bantan's announcement, and looking in the
direction he pointed, they could distinguish it. Sighs
of relief were uttered by the three women, while Maro
upbraided himself for his failure to observe the distant
atoll before now.

"I am a poor navigator," he remarked.

"At least we have maintained our course fairly well,"
Nao added with a smile to her father.

"Yes, you have all done well while I slept," Bantan
replied. "By late afternoon we should be passing the
atoll. We should paddle slower now so as not to be
readily seen in the event Amo warriors are stationed
there. I have a strange feeling Amar has sent warriors there to await us."

After eating some fruit and feeling more refreshed,
the bronzed giant again exchanged places with Lori.
Bantan and Maro continued to paddle with easy
strokes.

Mile after mile was covered during the passing

hours and the atoll, still far to their right, drew nearer. It was Bantan's deliberate intention of keeping a considerable distance from it. Were they discovered and given pursuit by Amo warriors waiting there for them, with the coming of darkness he felt they might elude their pursuers, and have no difficulty in reaching Marja the following day.

The sun, a blazing ball of fire, was about two hours from setting as the two canoes were abreast the atoll with a mile intervening.

Nao looked at the atoll with regret, thinking of the too brief, happy hours she and Bantan had passed there before their capture by the ruthless Amar and his warriors. What wouldn't she give to spend the night there instead of being cramped in the canoe. She consoled herself that at some future time Bantan might take her there again— perhaps when upon their honeymoon. Sighing, the Amo girl was about to reluctantly remove her eyes from the atoll when from the foliage darted a number of warriors bearing two canoes which they launched into a gentle surf and immediately started to ply their paddles with seeming frenzy.

"Bantan!" she cried. "Amo warriors upon the atoll have seen us and are paddling in our direction."

The attention of all was instantly arrested. Without difficulty they could see the two canoes had now reached the calmer water beyond the surf and were headed in their direction. A grim smile touched Bantan's lips as he lay aside his paddle and reached for the belt of partly used cartridges and the holstered automatic. He withdrew the automatic and in another moment was examining the clip to ascertain it was filled to capacity.

Maro removed his eyes from the distant canoes and

looked toward the younger man. Instantly he suspected his intentions.

"You intend to battle with them, Bantan?" he asked with a twinkle in his dark eyes.

As her father spoke, Nao removed her eyes from the two canoes, and as she saw the automatic in Bantan's hand, she, too, at once knew what he intended. Their eyes met.

"It would be more comfortable to pass the night in the cabin on the atoll," he said with a smile. "Had the warriors not sighted us and we were permitted to go our way, we would have done so. Since they have discovered us and wish to intercept us, why should we run away? I have the means here to discourage them."

Knowing the potency of the automatic, Nao smiled. She felt no apprehension in allowing the two enemy canoes come closer. She turned to her mother and Lori with a proud smile.

"Bantan is right," she said with confidence. "With his weapon in hand we have nothing to fear from the enemy."

Maro and Luno had never witnessed the potentialities of civilized man's methods of warfare, whereas Lori had some understanding of its death-dealing from afar. Naturally all three were interested to witness such proceedings.

As the minutes passed the two enemy canoes drew nearer. The paddlers now could be more easily distinguished. Four warriors were in each canoe. Looking to the shore of the atoll, Bantan could see no others there, so it was evident these eight warriors were all that Amar had dispatched with the hope of trapping the fugitives were they to pass or stop at the atoll.

Exultation was to be glimpsed upon the dusky faces of the Amo warriors. They looked upon the recapture of the fugitives as a relatively simple matter. They did not pause to wonder why the occupants of the canoe supinely remained there and made no effort to get away. They seemingly awaited their capture as though they realized the futility of making any endeavor whatsoever.

The grim smile upon Bantan's lips did not alter as the canoes drew still closer. Silence seemed to grip each of the occupants, but a smile touched the lips of Nao, for her confidence in the bronzed giant's ability was not to be doubted.

Still closer drew the canoes of the Amo warriors; and now, when within a couple hundred yards from the fugitives, the first promptings of a doubt assailed Hamar, the leader, that all was not as well as he might assume. The fugitives were giving up too easily. Having witnessed the bronzed stranger's previous resistance in the face of greater odds, Hamar could not understand why he was seemingly giving up so easily now. And while the leader pondered upon this, with no decrease of speed the two canoes were propelled toward the canoe containing the fugitives.

As yet Bantan had not revealed the automatic he clasped in his right hand. With glinting eyes resting upon the approaching canoes, time and again he would speak to the other occupants of the canoe, assuring them there was no reason for alarm. His forefinger pressed the trigger gently.

"The leader seems a little puzzled that we have made no effort to get away," he murmured. "Perhaps he doesn't know about this weapon and the death it is capable of dealing."

"He wouldn't know, Bantan," Nao reminded him. "The only time it was used was in the Ono village when

I went to your rescue while you were bound to the stake."

"That is so," he agreed with a nod. "He shall soon learn."

The two canoes were now about a hundred yards from the one containing the five fugitives.

Maro shook his head hopelessly.

"I feel so helpless," he remarked.

Bantan assured him he had no reason to feel that way, as the weapon he possessed was sufficient to defeat the enemy.

Seated in the bow, Lori was pale, and her hands were pressed against her bosom as though to stifle the fear that all might not go as well as Bantan anticipated. Strangely, she had ample faith in Bantan, but the numbers of the enemy made her wonder that he would be able to slay them all.

Once, as Bantan's eyes averted from the approaching enemy, they rested upon Lori. The Ono girl smiled in an effort to masquerade her fear, but the bronzed giant was not deceived.

The mother of Nao was palpably frightened even though her daughter, and her mate, Maro, attempted to bolster her waning courage.

More puzzled was the expression upon Hamar's features as his canoe reached a distance of fifty yards from their quarry. Then his better judgment came to the rescue.

"Cease paddling," he bade his companions. "Something is wrong. The wily stranger must have some manner of trick he intends using against us."

As he spoke, his companions ceased paddling. Hamar continued to look at the defiant bronzed stranger. At that moment a hollow tube rested above the edge of the canoe at Bantan's side. And, as the

leader of the Amo warriors looked, a sharp report was
to be heard accompanied by a flash of flame and blue
smoke. A half-uttered gasp was stifled in Hamar's
throat as he fell backward with blood streaming from
a tiny, gaping hole in the center of his forehead.

The amazement following the shock of the sharp
report from the automatic made Maro and Luno
fairly shriek with joy as they saw the leader of the
Amo warriors fall backward. Lori's dark eyes opened
in silent wonder and then glowed with pride as she
looked toward the bronzed giant. Nao merely smiled
with confidence.

An ironic smile touched Bantan's lips now as he
steadily held the automatic and his forefinger was ready
to apply pressure to the trigger again.

The three Amo warriors in the leader's canoe were
amazed to know Hamar had been killed from afar by
an unseen missile. The foremost of the three warriors, after examining Hamar and realizing he was
dead, arose to an almost upright position and shook
his clenched hands angrily at Bantan.

Once again the hollow tube spat flame, smoke, and
death, as a second bullet penetrated the warrior's left
chest. As he swayed uncertainly, too late were his
companions to catch him or steady the wildly rocking
canoe. As the stricken warrior toppled over the side,
the canoe was overturned, and the remaining two warriors were dumped unceremoniously into the water
along with the corpse of Hamar.

The three women shrieked their delight at this
catastrophe to the enemy. No change of expression
crossed Bantan's features as he looked toward the remaining canoe. The four warriors therein had been
frightened by the sharp reports that dealt death to
two of their companions, and as the canoe was over-

turned, they realized they must tax their efforts to reach the canoe of their quarry and come to hand grips with the bronzed stranger who was responsible for the deaths of their companions.

Arising to the surface, the two warriors, who had been the survivors of the overturned canoe, shouted encouragingly to their companions in the second canoe to close with the author of their indignity.

Deliberately Bantan awaited the propitious moment, then his forefinger pressed the trigger of the automatic. The foremost warrior in the second canoe released his paddle, and he fell backward with a howl as a bullet shattered his right shoulder near the neck, and from which blood copiously flowed.

The three remaining warriors bent low and plied their paddles furiously in an effort to ram the canoe they were nearing.

Bantan instantly became aware of the enemy's intention.

"Quick, Maro, start paddling," he directed. "They intend to ram us."

In another moment Maro was plying his paddle with hasty strokes in an effort to avoid the speedily approaching enemy canoe.

Bantan still held the automatic steady, and now, to better his aim because of the partially concealed foe, he arose to a crouched position. The enemy canoe was barely fifteen yards from them. Intermittently the leading warrior would raise his head to sight their objective, then he would quickly lower it and transmit his directions to his companions.

The second time he lifted his head was the last. A bullet from Bantan's automatic caught him upon the side of the forehead near the temple. He collapsed without a sound.

Paddling furiously, Maro succeeded in turning the
canoe about so that it faced the oncoming Amo one
with its two paddlers. As it passed with a scant few
feet intervening, the two Amo warriors dropped their
paddles and seized their spears. In one motion they
arose and hurled them without specific aim at the occupants in the canoe opposite them.

As the same moment Bantan's automatic spitefully
spat flame and death. The two warriors dropped,
mortally wounded.

One of the hurled spears passed to the right side of
Bantan, missing him by a scant six inches. The second,
an instant later, buried itself into Nao's bosom. The
force shattered her spine, and the bloody point protruded through her back.

A muffled cough escaped the girl's writhing lips as
her hands instinctively fastened upon the shaft just
below her left breast. An agonizing expression possessed her dark eyes as she looked toward Bantan, and
for a fleeting moment all the love her heart contained
for him relieved the agony of her eyes. Then, as a
bloody froth issued from her parted lips, she fell backward with unseeing eyes into the arms of her mother.
Instantly Luno was overcome with grief as she realized her only child had passed from the present world
— her lax body was evidence of that. She shrieked in
horror one moment, then at the next she clasped her
daughter's head and pillowed it against her bosom,
meanwhile uttering endearments as tears flowed from
her eyes.

Maro ceased paddling at once and turned to his mate
to console her as best he might.

In the bow Lori's eyes were instantly filled with
tears and her features were deathly pale as she leaned

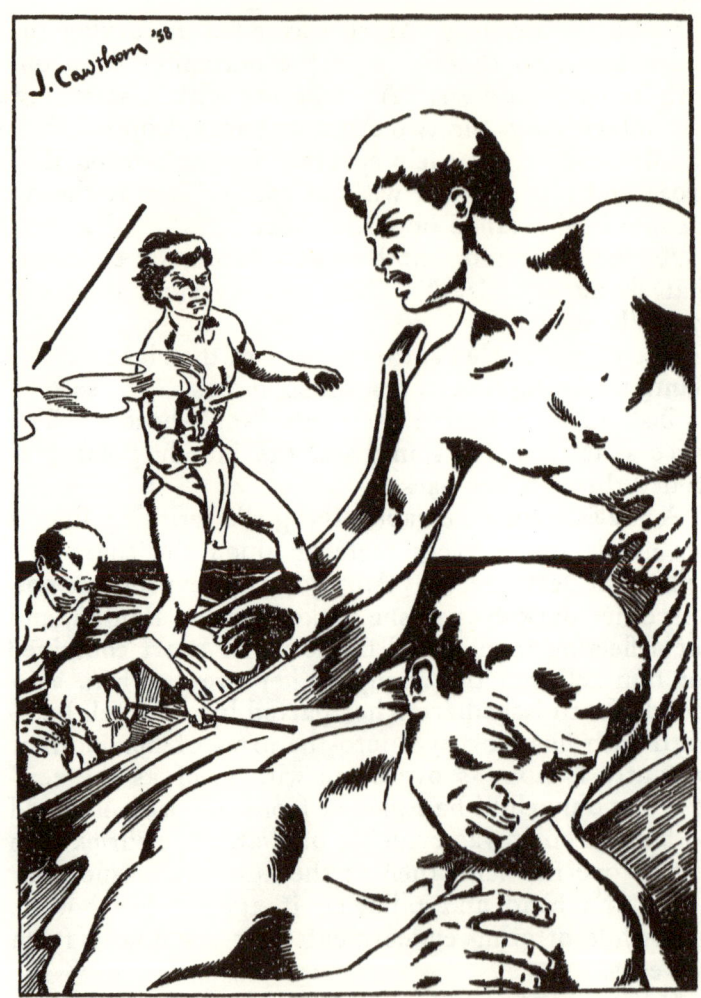

Bantan's Automatic Spat Flame and Death

forward to look at the unfortunate Amo girl whom she had come to respect very highly.

Though his lips quivered, Bantan's features were impassive. His dark eyes bore the expression of a man bereft of all that life could hold dear for him. So shocked by what had befallen Nao, he released the automatic from nerveless fingers. The weapon dropped into the water with a splash and sank beneath the surface. As though in a trance, the bronzed giant slumped to his knees and reached for the girl's hands that clasped the spear even in death.

"Nao!" he moaned. "Nao, speak to me!"

The girl's eyes were closed, and not a flicker of the lids was apparent. Where the spear had passed through her bosom blood was slowly oozing about the shaft, staining the breast covering.

Bantan's lips pressed the back of the girl's hands repeatedly, then he drew them to his cheeks. Once again he looked at her with haunting eyes.

"Nao!" The single word with ineffable tenderness was uttered from a heart that was sad and the emptiness of which made him realize the futility of speaking further to her since she had passed from the present world.

Raising agonized eyes to the other occupants of the canoe, he then looked toward the atoll.

"Maro, paddle to the atoll," he said in a listless voice. "Nao loved it. She would be happy to know she will be buried there."

In silence, the father of the girl picked up his paddle and plied it mechanically. Sorrow was mirrored in his eyes, and a mistiness therein appeared that blurred the atoll.

Screams were then heard from the vicinity where the first canoe of the enemy had been overturned. A

swirling of water proclaimed sharks had scented blood
and were feasting. The two Amo warriors who had
been swimming about could not be seen now. The
voracious sharks had claimed them.

None of the denizens of the deep molested the canoe
that was being paddled toward the atoll. In silence all
remained, except for the choking sobs issuing from the
lips of Luno. With compassion, Bantan grasped the
handle of the spear that transfixed his beloved one.
Closing his eyes and with contorting features—as
though the pain were his—he gently pulled upon the
shaft. When it was free his eyes opened and he stared
dully at its bloody point. Almost savagely he hurled
it into the water, realizing it was the instrument that
had deprived Nao of her life. With consoling words
to the mother of the girl, he took the slain girl from
her and cradled the still form in his arms, her cheek
pillowed against his broad chest. And thus he held
her, unmindful of the blood that streaked upon him,
and with eyes unseeingly before him until the canoe
reached the shore of the atoll.

Quickly Maro stepped out and steadied the canoe
while Luno and Lori disembarked. Then, last, with
Nao in his arms, Bantan stepped out upon the sand.
Maro drew the canoe a short ways up on the beach
then detached the grass rope from the trailing one, and
also drew it alongside the other.

Meanwhile, carrying Nao's body in his arms, and
followed by the silently weeping mother and Lori—
she, too, misty-eyed—the bronzed giant went directly
toward the cabin. Near the door, in reverence he
laid the deceased girl upon a carpet of soft under-
growth. As he arose, Maro hurried to join the party.

"We shall bury her nearby, Maro," Bantan said in
a low voice. Turning to Luno and Lori he nodded

toward the still body, and spoke hardly above a
whisper: "Prepare her for burial."

Selecting a place near the cabin, the bronzed giant
bent, and with his dagger commenced to dig in the soft
soil, while Maro in silence heaped the loosened earth
to one side. In the passing minutes the cavity became
deeper.

The sun was hovering over the horizon when the
last handful of dirt was placed upon the grave. Luno
and Lori placed flowers upon the heaped mound. They
stood in silent communion for several minutes. Bantan raised his head to reveal agonizing eyes from which
tears had welled and rolled pathways down his bronzed
cheeks.

"There is the cabin to occupy for the night," he said
to his companions. "I do not feel like going to sleep
just now. I wish to be alone for a while."

Lori timidly approached the bronzed giant in compassion.

"Bantan, I am truly sorry for you," she murmured.

Though he did not answer, his suffering eyes met
hers and acknowledged his appreciation. Without a
word he slowly walked to the beach. He drew the two
canoes near the edge of the foliage from the possible
reach of an incoming tide. At the beach, standing in
water reaching to his waist, he washed away the blood
that had dripped from Nao's mortal wound.

Returning to the canoes, he stepped into the empty
one and seated himself in the aft portion. For long
moments he looked in the twilight of early evening
toward the bow. He could almost see Nao with
laughter upon her lips and a twinkle in her dark eyes
looking toward him. With a low moan escaping his
lips, he bowed his head and clasped his face in his
hands. Only the God Who had created him could

know the torturing thoughts that coursed through him.

Minutes passed unheedingly into an hour. With the sinking of the sun twinkling stars appeared in the darkening canopy above. In the west, high above the horizon, the planet Venus—where Nao's religious belief hoped her spirit would go when her earthly existence had terminated—seemed to radiate greater brilliance than ever before.

When at last Bantan raised his face from his hands, and his eyes looked heavenward, the luminance of the evening star arrested his attention almost immediately. Though Nao had never confided to him her religious beliefs concerning the spirit after life had departed from the earthly form, in a strange way he now wondered of the possibility of the transmigration of Nao's spirit to that distant planet. At least, he hoped such might be true, for Nao—as Kalma, the Marja Island goddess—was deserving of a worthy place in the world beyond the grave.

Seemingly mesmerized by the soft radiance of the planet Venus, in the minutes that passed Bantan seemingly relived each and every moment he had passed in the company of the Amo girl from the time he had first spared her from injury and possible death when a wild boar had attacked her until the moment of her unfortunate death. Then, with a shake of his head, without knowing what he did, he arose and stepped out of the canoe. His lagging footsteps took him to her grave, and there he slumped to his knees. With bowed head he remained silent in his sorrow.

After some time had passed a silent figure appeared from the cabin. Going first to the beach and not finding Bantan there, the seeming apparition then went to Nao's grave to find the bronzed giant humbly kneeling there in his deep grief for the passing of his sweetheart.

With a choked sob in her throat, Lori drew near Bantan and placed a gentle hand upon his shoulder, arousing his numbed faculties from the seeming lethargy that enveloped him. His nostrils, attracted by the perfume emanating from her, informed him of her identity.

"Come, Bantan," she said in gentle tones. "Nao would not be happy to know you grieved so."

Without protest—dazed by his deep grief—the bronzed giant slowly arose to his feet. With an arm linked in his, Lori walked at his side to the cabin. Just within the door she made him lie down upon a pallet of grasses. The former princess of Ono Island caressed his brow tenderly, and her maternal instinct quite evident, she murmured soft words of comfort to him.

"Sleep, Bantan," she murmured. "Peace will come to relieve your sadness. Sleep now."

Strangely calmed by Lori's soft voice, Bantan closed his eyes, and unaware of the transition he immediately fell into a deep sleep. He was first to awaken in the morning. Brilliant sunshine poured in through the latticed window facing the east. The noisy twittering of birds in the tree tops grated upon his sensibilities, for with waking there returned to him the recollection of Nao's death. The one thought: "She is dead! She is dead!" constantly echoed chaotically in his brain.

Arising to a seated position, he looked about and saw that Lori, still asleep, lay upon a pallet of grasses not far from him. Remembering her tender solicitude of the previous evening in the darkest hour of his grief, Bantan's dark eyes softened. Beyond her, the father and mother of the slain girl lay side by side, fast asleep.

Arising to his feet, the bronzed giant quietly left
the cabin and his footsteps led him to Nao's grave.
The flowers placed upon it by her mother and Lori
were still fresh. Hardly knowing what he was doing,
he gathered more and placed them upon the mound.
For long moments he stood there with bowed head
and his thoughts of Nao were sorrowful indeed.

The aroma of perfume emanating from none other
than Lori aroused him to the fact he was not alone.
Turning, he saw that the former princess of Ono
Island stood in silence just behind him. Compassion
for him was clearly revealed in her soft dark eyes which
also were misty. Without a word and a gentle smile
of solicitude for him touching her lips, she stepped forward. Instinctively one of the her hands rested upon
one of his arms. Though he was aware, he did not
seem to mind Lori's presence.

"Poor Nao," he murmured; his broad shoulders
drooped and he shook his head sadly.

Lori's hand pressed more firmly upon his arm as
though in answer for words that she could not utter.

"She would have been so happy this morning," he
said a moment later. And then with a resolute nod
of his head, he added: "I guess it just wasn't to be."

Lori still remained silent, but her soft dark eyes
were very misty.

From the cabin the voices of Maro and Luno could
now be heard.

With a shake of his head to dispel the sorrowful
thoughts that were his, Bantan squared his giant
shoulders. He turned to Lori.

"Come, let us make preparations for the morning
meal," he said. "We have considerable paddling before we reach Marja Island."

Maro and Luno were greeted quietly, and without

delay the morning meal was prepared and eaten. While doing so, Bantan spoke of their plans for the day, and ended by saying:

"In advance, I assure you of the friendship of the Marja and Beneiro people."

Shortly afterward preparations were made for the trip. Fruit was gathered and placed in the single canoe they were to take. Before leaving the atoll, all assembled in final respect at Nao's grave for a few minutes in silent farewell. When they presently returned to the beach where their canoe was in readiness, the eyes of all were a trifle misty to know they were leaving Nao behind.

Bantan did not forget to include his bow and arrows, and when the canoe was out beyond the gentle surf, it was then he recollected the loss of the automatic. However, there were others upon Marja Island in the hut of his foster parents so its loss was not too great. It has served its purpose.

The bronzed giant and Maro paddled without haste, and within a few hours a blur upon the eastern horizon proclaimed their objective was already in sight. With the passing minutes the island became more distinguishable. In due course of time the canoe passed through the gentle surf and was nearing the beach.

Several villagers had observed the canoe when some distance from shore and they had informed others of their discovery. Many warriors, women, and children were gathered at the shore, awaiting the beaching of the canoe. When it presently became known that Bantan was in the canoe, great was their joy. Their natural curiosity was aroused because of his companions, but they were positive of their worthiness else they would not be with him.

Beneiro and Skilda, foster parents of Bantan, were among the foremost to greet the returning bronzed giant, as were Trayman and Reela, his mate. In turn, Bantan introduced each of his companions.

"Friends of Bantan are our friends," Beneiro said to them with a smile.

"Where is Wanya?" Bantan asked of his foster father.

The chief shook his head.

"Wanya acts strangely in your absence," he replied. "She often goes to the lagoon to be alone with her thoughts."

"She is too much alone, father," Bantan said. With a meaning look to Lori, he added: "Wanya is hereafter to take charge of Lori, and she will teach her the ways of a village maiden so that she might be a worthy mate to some warrior of her choosing in the future."

The mother of Wanya smiled and nodded her head knowingly.

"Bantan knows what is best for his foster sister," she said.

"Come to our hut, all of you," Beneiro urged. "Bantan must tell us where he has been."

Later, the bronzed giant had told his foster parents of his whereabouts and of his hopeless love for the Amo girl, Nao. His parents shook their heads and expressed their sorrow because of his bereavement.

It was arranged that Maro and Luno were to have a small hut to themselves, and the feeling of welcome extended to them by the villagers with whom they came in contact made them realize the truth of Bantan's promise of the friendship that would be theirs in the village of his friends.

At last, shortly before sundown, Wanya returned

to the village. Being told of Bantan's return by the villagers she met, the eyes of the Beneiro princess were filled with joy as she entered the hut of her parents. At sight of Bantan she lost no time in going to him, and though she noticed Lori, for the time being she paid no attention to her. The bronzed giant might have suspected Wanya's actions, but his foster sister did not hesitate. He arose to his feet, and at the same moment Wanya flung her arms about his neck and kissed him repeatedly until he managed to free himself of her overwhelming embrace. Her too evident love for him somewhat embarrassed Bantan. Holding her at arms' length, though she strained to be nearer to him, he shook his head reprovingly.

"Calm yourself, Wanya," he gently upbraided her. "Can't you see we have a guest?"

His foster sister frowned and looked toward the beautiful Ono girl.

"Who is she?" she asked with furrowed brows.

"Her name is Lori," he answered. "She comes from Ono Island, far to the west. Were it not for her I would not be here now."

"Why have you brought her here?" Wanya asked. "Are you in love with her?"

Bantan smiled apologetically to Lori.

"You must overlook what Wanya says, Lori," he said. "Had she been here when we arrived, she would understand how much I am indebted to you. But she will realize when I tell her." Then turning to Wanya, he added in a low voice: "Listen to me carefully."

Briefly he told her of his adventures since the last full moon, and when he had concluded, Wanya appeared very contrite.

"And, Wanya," Bantan added, "there is something I want you to do."

His foster sister merely nodded her head meekly.

He told her that he wished her to take care of Lori and teach her the duties a maiden should know. Because of his indebtedness to the Ono girl, Wanya promised to do as he requested.

"Are you going to remain with us now, Bantan?" she asked with hope expressed in her dark eyes.

He shook his head uncertainly.

"I have a score to settle with one called Amar," he replied. "After that—I don't know."

Lori was to remain in the hut of Bantan's foster parents, sharing Wanya's apartment. As they were preparing to retire, the Ono girl spoke to Wanya.

"You care very much for Bantan."

Wanya smiled sadly.

"Ever since I was a little girl," she answered. "Bantan always considers me as a sister to him, and for that reason he has never returned my love."

"The moment I first saw him I was aware of a change in me," Lori admitted. "But he was in love with Nao. I did not have a chance. Even with Nao dead, I still do not feel I could ever find a place in his heart."

"Tell me about Nao, Lori," Wanya said.

In hushed whispers Lori told Wanya of Nao, the Amo girl, and how she had met her death and was buried on the atoll near the cabin.

*   *   *

Bantan passed the evening in the hut of Trayman and Reela, his good Marja friends. They had been very happy, as were all the surviving Marja villagers to have made their home with the surviving Beneiro villagers following their encounter with the invading Japanese.

Before they retired for the evening, Trayman and Reela importuned the bronzed giant to relate his adventures upon the Aoono Islands, and this Bantan did in part. When he mentioned the name of Nao, the Amo Island girl, his dark eyes would be sad. But when he spoke the name of Amar, a glint of determination was to be observed therein.

"And with Amar I have scores to settle," he concluded.

"Do you want any one to go with you, Bantan?" Trayman asked. "I'm sure there would be many Marja and Beneiro warriors who would be willing. I, for one, would be happy to accompany you."

Bantan smiled deprecatingly.

"Thank you, Trayman," he said with a quiet smile. "I feel the matter is personal. I would rather go alone. It may seem strange, but it is true. Since the death of Kalma, whom you both know I loved most dearly, I do not seem to be the same. Nao was a fine girl and I would have been happily mated to her. But since she is no longer of this world, my happiness with her cannot be fulfilled."

"But the other young girl that came with you, Bantan," Reela ventured with a smile. "As the suns pass perhaps she might interest you."

He shrugged his shoulders.

"And there is Wanya," Trayman added. "Her love for you never seems to cease."

"Poor Wanya," Bantan murmured. "If only I could dispel the feeling of 'brother' toward her, I'm sure she would make a worthy mate. At the present, however, my thoughts of Nao would not permit me to feel I might love another so soon."

*   *   *

Late the following forenoon Bantan and Wanya went swimming a short distance from the landing, and when they returned to the shore to dry and bask in the sun, the Beneiro princess became very humble. She reached for one of his hands and covered it with hers.

"Bantan, why don't you act like the other warriors of the village?" she asked.

He regarded her questionably.

"In what manner, Wanya?"

"You've known for how many moons I've lost count how I have felt toward you," she answered with serious eyes. "When a suitable period of mourning has passed because of Nao, why don't you mate with me? I'm sure I could make you happy in every way possible."

He shook his head slowly.

"Do you forget that I am of white birth?" he reminded her.

She frowned and tears came into her eyes.

"But what difference does that make?" she asked. "Nao was a native girl. You are still a man—and it should be normal for a man to want a mate and have children."

The trace of a smile touched the corners of Bantan's lips.

"Perhaps it is because I am a white man that I am not permitted to mate with a native girl, settle down, and rear children," he answered. "When I do feel that way toward a girl—Kalma and Nao, for instance —some dire fate overtakes them, and I am alone again."

The Beneiro princess regarded him seriously.

"Would mating with me be so terrible to you, Bantan?" she asked.

He smiled good naturedly and covered her hand

resting upon his with his other.

"Perhaps had you not been so persistent, Wanya," he answered, "I might have found myself pursuing you. You are very beautiful and I know you so very well. But the fact that we were brought up together as brother and sister makes me realize too much brotherly feeling toward you. I cannot seem to change this feeling."

"But I don't feel like a sister to you, Bantan," she protested. "Why you should feel the way you do I can't understand."

"Neither can I," he replied.

"Even last night Lori admitted she cares a great deal for you," Wanya added.

"I suspected as much," he said in answer. "But my heart cannot respond now. Even poor Nao suspected Lori was casting a spell over me. One's heart in the matter of love is difficult to explain," he added. "I know only this: at present my heart is filled with sadness because of Nao's passing, and hate toward the one who was indirectly responsible. When this score is settled the hate will be gone; then, with the passing suns, the sadness will lessen. After that—who knows?"

"When do you intend to leave, Bantan?" Wanya asked after a short silence had prevailed.

He shrugged his shoulders.

"At least not before as many suns as the fingers upon one hand," he answered. After a brief pause, he added: "Perhaps two hands."

"Will you tell me when you go?" she asked. "You did not say when you left before."

He regarded her with an enigmatical smile.

"Perhaps." Then looking up at the sun, high in the heaven, he arose to his feet and drew Wanya to hers. "Come, it is nearing noonday. Already I am hungry. You must not let Lori do all the work in preparations for the noonday meal."

Arm in arm they returned to the village.

*   *   *

·With the passing days Bantan joined the other villagers in their occupations of fishing, gathering fruit, and working in the community garden. In appearances he appeared as happy as the others in these menial tasks.

Wanya and Lori, sometimes one or the other, and not infrequently both, sought his companionship, for each cared a great deal for the bronzed giant. They seemed content in just being in his presence. The renounced princess of Ono Island seemed very happy in her new existence, even though she spoke but little; but whenever she saw Bantan her dark eyes were filled with a longing that was too obvious of her feelings for him.

Some of the younger, unmated Beneiro and Marja warriors were instantly attracted to Lori, and in the passing days vied with one another in seeking to win her interest. The Ono girl never voluntarily sought to injure their vanity, but having eyes for none but Bantan, her aloofness soon discouraged their suit.

One day while strolling along the beach, Lori was a considerable distance from the village landing when Bantan was seen coming from the opposite direction. At sight of the renounced princess of Ono Island the bronzed giant's eyes lighted with pleasure. A ready smile came to the girl's lips as she continued to walk with quickening steps toward him. As they confronted each other they spoke pleasantly.

"You are going for a swim, Lori?" Bantan then asked.

"I had been thinking of doing so," she replied with a smile.

He shook his head warningly.

"It is not wise to go swimming alone and unarmed, Lori," he said. "Sharks or an octopus may await a victim."

"Several of the Beneiro and Marja warriors have asked me to go with them, Bantan," she answered; "but I declined with thanks." The girl flushed as she spoke.

"I had been thinking of taking a swim, Lori," he added. "Perhaps you will permit me to accompany you?"

"I would be delighted," she said with a sweet smile.

Without hesitation they walked to the edge of the water. Awaiting the break of a favoring swell, with a nod to each other, they plunged into the gentle surf. As their heads broke above the surface, they commenced to swim with methodical strokes toward the calmer water beyond which they reached with no difficulty. Bantan observed that his companion was very adept at swimming. While they treaded water he spoke to her.

"You swim very well, Lori," he commended. "Nao too, was a fine swimmer. In the past Wanya and I often went swimming. She is like a fish in the water."

"Swimming is the only thing I do well, Bantan," the Ono girl replied. "But under Wanya's tutelage I hope to do many things better as the suns pass. I dive and swim under water well, too. Watch me."

As the girl spoke a mischievous light was to be detected in her now vibrant dark eyes. In another moment she dove beneath the surface and remained for several minutes while Bantan, treading water, watched for her reappearance. Presently her head broke above the surface, and at sight of the worried expression upon his features she laughed gaily.

"I was worried about you," he said with an admonishing shake of his head.

With a laugh Lori dove again, and this time was beneath the surface even longer than before. Fearing something might have happened to her, Bantan drew himself beneath the surface, and with eyes opened, looked for the Ono girl. With powerful strokes of his arms and vigorous kicks of his sturdy legs he drew himself through the translucent water to the very bottom of the ocean floor, a distance of at least thirty feet. There was no sight of Lori, search as he did.

Varied underwater plants of fanciful colors were to be seen, and numerous small fish swam about, unconcerned by the stranger in their watery domain. A sea cucumber hovered near some rocks covered with lichen. A giant condor eel looked out from between two rocks, ever wary to catch a passing morsel of daintiness.

Near a group of boulders the swimmer observed a grayish giant clam—*Tridacna gigas*—with its jagged jaws wide open, and from which was emitted an almost steady stream of water. It must weigh all of several hundred pounds. Bantan had not seen any of these giant mollusks since his childhood days. He had nearly lost his leg at the time, and well he remembered the occasion. He knew they were living creatures with respect for nothing. As a man he had yet to test his strength against the jagged jaws that could imprison a foot and render a victim helpless.

The swimmer was relieved that Lori was not to be seen. He decided to return to the surface. His lungs were clamoring for renewed air by the time his head broke above the undulating water.

Meanwhile, Lori had returned to the surface, and finding Bantan not there, she again dove. This time she swam in another direction to the very ocean floor near where a group of boulders were to be seen. From the direction she approached, the girl did not see the grayish giant mollusk ensconced near them, thus as she passed closely above she had no means of being forewarned of the lurking menace there. At one moment she was swimming along easily close to the giant jaws. One kicking foot just missed the tendrils that were outthrust, but the other kicking foot touched them. Instantly they enfolded about her foot, drawing it within the already closing jaws.

Lori realized now that Bantan's warning of danger was not to be minimized. Unarmed, she could do nothing to battle this monster of the ocean floor.

"Bantan! Bantan!" the words in her heart were murmured in a vain possibility that through mental telepathy he might become aware of her peril.

But Lori was not to give up without a struggle. She was composed of sterner material. With rejuvenated strength in her arms, though her lungs were clamoring for renewed air, she strove mightily to free her imprisoned foot from the clutching jaws. With her other foot she beat a tattoo upon the cold shell. The pain that she suffered was excruciating. In a brief instant it seemed a million thoughts raced across her screen of recollection. Aware of a roaring tempo in her ears, she felt the strength draining from her body. The last fleeting recollection she had was of something approaching her, then her senses swooned.

Bantan returned to the surface. He could see that Lori was not there. With the recollection of the opened giant clam lying upon the ocean floor, he filled his lungs with air. Drawing his keen-edged dagger

he speedily returned whence he had just come. With
a start, his searching eyes espied the girl in the clutches
of the mollusk there. Quickly he swam to her, and
with his dagger sought to sever the muscles of the
giant clam that had closed the jagged jaws about the
girl's foot.

Bantan's dagger slashed and plunged repeatedly to
each side of the girl's trapped foot. Then, feeling he
could do no more in that manner, he quickly sheathed
his dagger. His strong hands fastened upon the edges
of the giant mollusk. His biceps bulged in evidence to
the strain he subjected them, hoping to pry the jaws
sufficiently apart to release the girl's imprisoned foot.

Unconscious as she was, Lori had slumped across
Bantan's back. Aware of this, he straightened as the
jaws slowly were forced apart, and the girl's bleeding
ankle was freed. Quickly, then, he released the jaws
of the mollusk, and turning about, enveloped the limp
girl in one arm. With his free hand, accompanied
by his kicking legs, he pulled himself upward through
the translucent water.

Reaching the surface, Bantan held the unconscious
girl's head above water. Upon his back he plied his
free hand in sweeping strokes that propelled him and
his burden shoreward. As his feet touched the sandy
beach, he swept Lori's limp form into his arms and
carried her to the very edge of the foliage where, in
the shade, he placed her upon the sand. She still lived
—of that he had been aware—for her bosom rose and
fell almost spasmodically.

Without loss of time he examined her bleeding ankle.
The flesh had been bruised. With careful fingers he
felt of the bones, hopeful that none had been broken
or crushed.

Lori regained consciousness, meanwhile. Her

breathing rasped in her throat. A fit of coughing overtook her for a few minutes. Quickly Bantan straightened and at once raised the girl to a seated position,
forcing her head forward while he thumped her upon
the back with an open hand to assist her in expelling
the water she had swallowed. Then, at last, though
pale and trembling, but quite weak, she seemed normal.
Her dark eyes were filled with tears as she looked up
at her savior.

"Forgive me, Bantan," she begged. "I don't know
how to thank you. I was very near death."

He nodded solemnly.

"You feel all right now, Lori?" he asked with concern in his voice.

She merely nodded her head, then once more raising her head slowly, her entreating eyes sought his.

"Tell me you aren't angry with me," she murmured,
imploringly.

He smiled, shaking his head slowly.

"Of course not, Lori," he assured her. "I saw the
giant clam when I went to the ocean floor in search of
you. When I returned to the surface to warn you, and
you were not there, I lost no time going down again
to find you trapped by the giant clam. Your foot must
be painful."

"It is, Bantan," she confessed. Her dark eyes still
rested upon his without wavering. "I have you to
thank for my life. How can I ever repay you?"

The bronzed giant was aware of a peculiar sensation in his breast, but with the thought of Nao flashing
through his mind, he shook his head. He quickly arose
to his feet with a deprecating smile and extended a hand
to the girl.

"Come, Lori, see if you can bear your weight upon
your injured ankle," he said.

As the girl rose to her feet with his assistance, she winced as she bore her weight upon her injured ankle. Her free hand reached for his shoulder to brace herself. She shook her head and the pain she suffered was mirrored in her dark eyes.

"I can't walk on it, Bantan," she murmured, lifting the injured foot from the beach.

"I'll carry you, Lori," he said.

In another moment he swept her into his arms. One of hers went about his neck.

"I'm sorry to cause you this trouble, Bantan," she murmured, as he started along the beach in the direction of the village.

A smile touched the bronzed giant's lips as he looked at her. In that brief moment her dark eyes were imploringly seeking to transmit her wishes to him —that he cover her willing lips with kisses. Hers were puckered and awaited his with eagerness. The fleeting glimpse of her eyes enlightened Bantan of her wishes, but the features of Nao interposed upon his memory, and whatever inclination was in his breast was smothered into extinction in due respect to the Amo girl he had so recently loved and had been devotedly loved in return. Removing his eyes from hers, he looked ahead, and from time to time at the sandy beach, so that his feet might not come in painful contact with some of the stones that were strewn there or to step upon a sharp-edged sea shell, many of which littered the sand.

Bantan carried the injured girl to the apartment Wanya shared with her and there he gently deposited her upon the pallet of grasses that was hers. Fortunately Wanya was at home, and with her mother, she followed her foster brother into her apartment. Both mother and daughter attended to Lori's injured ankle, bathing it carefully and applying a healing ointment to the broken skin before wrapping it up in cool leaves.

As the Ono girl told of Bantan's magnificent deed in her behalf, the glow in her eyes did not escape Wanya's attention. She could easily determine Lori's heroic measure of Bantan. But the palpable glow in her eyes undeniably foretold something else to the more sophisticated Beneiro princess, and with this realization a strangeness overcame her that made her reticent. But, Lori, in her joyful blandishments of Bantan's daring, did not observe the changing expression of his foster sister. During the passing days she became aware of Wanya's peculiar attitude, and then she realized why this was.

*　　*　　*

Ten days had passed since the death of Nao, the Amo girl, and the sadness in Bantan's heart had lessened to some degree. At the death of Kalma, the Marja Island goddess, moons ago, so, too, had the passing time alleviated his suffering.

All of this day a strange uneasiness had coursed through the bronzed giant's being. For hours during the afternoon he had sought the sanctuary of the lagoon to be alone with his cogitations.

Too well was he aware of the love of Lori for him. Since he had spared her from the vicious jaws of the giant clam, and the Ono girl had proclaimed his bravery to the villagers with whom she later came in contact, only too well were they aware of the love of the renounced princess of Ono Island for the bronzed giant. Knowing, too, of the long devotion of Wanya for her foster brother, the villagers were in a quandary as to which of the two girls Bantan would choose to be his mate. Many felt Wanya unquestionably would be the lucky one; but there were others who were more skeptical—thinking the chances of Lori were very good.

That same morning Beneiro had talked quietly with his foster son—had urged him to take a mate and settle among them with the intention of rearing strong sons and worthy daughters to take their place upon the island when the father and mother had passed on to another world.

"Father, I feel I am somewhat of a disappointment to you and mother in such matters," Bantan had answered. "What it is that prevents me from doing so, I cannot explain. I know Wanya would make me a fine mate, and it would make you and mother very happy to know we became mated. I also know of Lori's love for me, and I believe she, too, could make me, or any other warrior, very happy. Perhaps it is because I was born of white parents that makes me hesitant to mate with a native girl. It is true, I would have mated with Kalma because she was half white, but circumstances intervened, and I was denied such happiness I might have shared with her. And then there was Nao. I have every reason to believe I would have mated with her. But again circumstances have intervened and she lost her life. First, before I think of mating and settling down, there is the matter of settling scores with Amar. After that, perhaps I might be ready to do so."

Beneiro had nodded his head in understanding.

"Your life is your own, Bantan," he had said. "I do not wish to tell you how to live it. Many times I have wished you had never known you were of white birth, for then you would have been more like the other warriors of the village. But you are of white birth, and you know best what you wish to do. She, who has always been as a mother to you, and I have often talked of you, hoping for the best where your happiness is concerned. When you have settled your scores with Amar, feel free that the hospitality of Marja Island always welcomes you, for in our hearts you are one of us."

And so this afternoon at the lagoon, Bantan lay upon his stomach with his face pillowed upon his hands. The water shimmered before him, and occasionally sea gulls flew overhead ever in search of food. The bronzed giant's cogitations were varied.

His heart softened as he thought of Wanya and Lori, and with the added memory of Nao, a stranger thought occurred to him.

He had found unusual adventure upon the Aoono Islands. For a certainty there must be countless other islands beyond. Upon them what other adventures might he experience? What other type of people might he come in contact? The thought in itself was alluring, almost beckoning.

With a shake of his head he realized he would never rest content until his scores with Amar had been settled. What his future actions might be—time would determine. There was no sense in planning a future when so many factors might intervene and alter the entire course of his life.

He felt sufficiently rested now to make the return trip to the Aoono Islands upon the following day. Why he had delayed so long was a matter that now puzzled him. He would stop at the atoll to pay his respects at Nao's grave, and thereafter resume his way.

And while Bantan planned thusly, unknown to him, Wanya had come to his sanctuary—which also had been hers during his absence. For several minutes she had watched him in silence with a lovelight glowing in her dark eyes, almost hesitant at disturbing his reveries. Then, with a resolute nod of her head, she walked toward him upon tip toe. Before he was aware of her presence, she flung herself beside him with a laugh.

"Don't mind me, Bantan," she said as he looked with surprise at her. "Whenever you come here alone, I know you are planning something."

He smiled good naturedly and placed an arm about her shoulders.

"Wanya, you still seem to know what is happening in my mind, don't you?" he said.

"Having been around you so long, Bantan," she answered, smiling prettily, "I know you very well."

He nodded, then his bronzed features become sober.

"Yes, Wanya," he said, "I am planning my return to the Aoono Islands tomorrow to settle my scores with Amar."

"Would you like company?" she asked blandly. "I can paddle very well, as you must know."

"No, Wanya," he answered, shaking his head. "I don't wish to subject you to the possible dangers that may be encountered."

"We have shared many dangers in the past," she reminded him. "I would not hesitate to share them in the future with you."

He again shook his head.

"No, Wanya," he insisted, "I *must* go alone. If there was any one I would prefer to accompany me, rest assured, it would be you. I know it was mean of me to go away and not let you know, as I did the last time; but this time, knowing the possible dangers that might await me, I must be alone."

"And when you have settled scores with Amar—" Wayna added "—what then?"

"I shall return here," he answered. "Where else would I go?"

The Beneiro princess regarded him gravely. She slowly shook her head.

"You do not speak convincingly, Bantan," she said. "Knowing you as I do, at the least excuse you would continue elsewheres where you might hope there would be new adventures—and possibly romance. Oh, why are you not content to remain here?"

He shrugged his shoulders. Looking up at the sun, he removed his arm from about Wanya's shoulders and arose to his feet with alacrity.

"The afternoon is well along," he remarked. "I must look at my canoe and ascertain it is in good condition for my trip."

He extended a hand to Wanya and helped her to her feet. With a laugh the Beneiro princess flung her arms about Bantan's neck. Before he could prevent she kissed him upon the lips. As he disengaged her arms and looked at her with perplexity, she smiled a trifle shyly.

"That was to wish you good luck," she said in a way of explanation for her unexpected act. "A hope is also expressed that you will hurry back again—to me."

*   *   *

That night the moon was full. Resplendent in all her glory, the Mistress of the Night rose above the horizon of water, reflecting upon the undulations of the mighty Pacific Ocean.

After the evening meal Bantan wandered alone to the deserted beach and there seated himself upon the bottom of his overturned canoe. He looked with pensive eyes at the beauty of the evening.

The bronzed giant recollected other similar evenings when a full moon looked down upon him—once when he acknowledged his love for Leona Brown upon the atoll, and the second time upon this island when he had declared his love for Kalma, the island goddess. With a sigh he shook his head.

To his keen nostrils then there came the scent of perfume that to his knowledge only Lori was known to wear. He turned and beheld the renounced princess of Ono Island standing near him. The soft effulgence of the full moon shown upon her. She appeared to be agitated, for her bosom rose and fell noticeably, and her lips were trembling.

"Wanya told me you are leaving in the morning, Bantan," she said in quivering tones. "She also said you were coming back after settling scores with Amar. She seemed to express her doubts that you *would* be returning. You *are* coming back, Bantan?"

As she spoke, Lori drew nearer and the pleading in her dark eyes was revealed by the brilliant moon-light.

"I shall return," he answered. "You should not be alarmed at the thought of my going. Perhaps during my absence, it may help you to concentrate upon some of the other younger warriors."

The girl clasped her hands to her bosom. Her eyes were misty as she replied:

"Not while I know you are alive and shall return, Bantan."

He smiled gently with compassion.

"Be seated, Lori," he said, indicating his side.

With a shy smile she came to him and seated her-self. He turned to her gravely.

"Lori, I must tell you something about myself," he said in a low voice.

The girl smiled more openly now and her glowing eyes rested upon his handsome features.

"Wanya has told me much about you, Bantan," she hastened to reply. "Hardly a day passes but I learn more. I cannot tell you of the joy that is mine to know new things about you. I almost envy Wanya for having known you so much longer than I."

He nodded agreeingly.

"Wanya is a fine girl, Lori," he said. "I love her very much, but not in the manner she wishes. Too long have we been like brother and sister—as I believed we were for a long while. She tells me she had loved me even when she was a little girl. Toward her I cannot feel other than a brother might."

The eyes of Lori glowed warmly as she continued to study his handsome features. How hopeful she was that he might tell her that he loved her.

"From the moment I first saw you, Bantan," she said in a low tone, "I was aware of a change in me. If it isn't love for you that I feel in my heart, then there can be no such thing as love."

"Lori, I think very highly of you," he admitted. "But I'm sure I do not love you at the present time. The thought of Nao is still with me."

Lori's smile was of patience. Impulsively she reached for one of his hands and clasped it in hers. She raised it to her lips and kissed its back. She looked up at him then with humbleness.

"I would wait forever for your love, Bantan," she murmured. Then, as a choking sob was uttered, she arose quickly and dashed back to the village before he could prevent.

Shaking his head, he remained there for a long while before at last retiring.

*   *   *

The sun was several hours high the following morn-

ing as Bantan plied his paddle with the atoll as his first
stop.   To his rear Marja was gradually becoming
smaller upon the horizon.

In the bronzed giant's thoughts were the visions of
Wanya and Lori who had been among those who had
wished him well and a speedy return.   The two girls
had uttered only a few words before he had launched
his canoe into the gentle surf, but their haunting eyes
had spoken a great deal.   With a shrug of his giant
shoulders he dispelled thought of them and concentrated upon the memory of Nao who lay cold and
still in a flower-decked grave upon the atoll.

The sun was well past his zenith when the bronzed
paddler, carefully scanning the shore for possible sight
of enemies, and seeing none, beached his canoe.   He
drew it within the concealment of the foliage, then with
hand about the handle of his sheathed dagger, he approached the nearby cabin.   Entering it, he observed
that it was precisely as it had been left nearly two
weeks before.

In compassion he approached Nao's grave.   The
flowers that covered it were withered.   Bantan tossed
these to one side and gathered fresh ones and again
decked the grave.   Sitting near it, he remained there
until nearly sundown.   After partaking of fruit, he
gathered sweet-smelling grasses with which he formed
a new pallet.   With no difficulty he fell asleep.

Some time during the early hours of the morning he
awoke to hear a distant rumbling.   The atoll and the
cabin trembled.   When the sound persisted and the
shaking of the cabin did not abate, he quickly arose
and went to the door, thinking a tropical storm was
brewing.   To his surprise, the heaven was clear and
the moon was high.   Without hesitation, Bantan then
went to the beach.   He listened intently in an effort to

determine the location of the distant rumblings. They
seemed to be coming from the west. Looking in that
direction, the distant heaven seemed red, as though fire
was belching up at it. Now he noticed that the waves
were washing up on the beach angrily. With the
passing minutes the surf increased in turbulence. The
atoll still trembled.

Bantan thought it wise to draw the canoe closer to
the cabin because of the possible danger of an excep-
tional, high-rising tide. This he did, then once again
returned to his sleeping pallet to resume his interrupted
slumber.

The sun was several hours high when he awoke, and
above the noisy twittering of birds in the nearby tree
tops, he could still hear the angry surf as the water
smashed against the beach. The atoll no longer
trembled. From the cabin door he looked out at the
disturbed ocean, and he could easily determine something had occurred during the night to ruffle its seren-
ity, but what he had no means of knowing. Straining
his ears he could not hear the distant rumbling that
had aroused him in the early hours of the morning. In
his mind there was no connection with that sound and
the disturbance of the ocean at the present time. He
did know, however, he would have to postpone his
plans for continuing his way to the Aoono Islands for
another day at least.

And so he did, noticing as the day drew to a close,
the ocean surface was considerably calmer.

The following morning he launched his provisioned
canoe into a more gentle surf than the previous day,
and seemingly tireless in his motions, he paddled all
day and into the early evening before laying aside his
paddle to sleep.

Again the following morning after partaking of

fruit, he resumed his methodical paddling with the knowledge it should not be long before he would sight the lofty volcano upon the horizon toward which the canoe was moving speedily.

Mile after mile was covered as the sun rose steadily into the azure heaven toward his zenith, and Bantan's searching eyes were still unrewarded by sight of the volcanic cone he felt should have been sighted ere now. The thought was in his mind that during the night while he slept the canoe might have drifted considerably off course in the grip of an erratic current, and that his goal lay either to the right or left horizon.

To his puzzled eyes now there was seen floating upon the undulating surface all sorts of debris—as from an island village that had been swept by a mighty tidal wave and had left nothing behind. Bits of rattan furniture, pieces of thatched walls and roofs, dried grass, and fruit was seen. Upon some of the debris sea gulls had come to rest, but as the canoe approached they spread their wings and arose with raucous screams and flew away to rest upon other floating debris.

Bantan paddled toward a portion of thatched roof, and as he drew near it sulphuric fumes assailed his delicate nostrils. Now, suddenly, the picture became clear to him.

The volcano upon Aoono Island had erupted, and the villages upon both Amo and Ono Islands had been fired. Following the eruption, all three islands had sunk beneath the surface and all living beings had either perished, or had taken to canoes and were adrift somewhere upon the mighty surface of the Pacific. The question was: Had they the time to make their escape from this doomed region? The floating debris was all that remained now.

Bantan continued paddling—why, he did not know.

The farther the canoe progressed the more debris was to be observed. The absence of floating dead bodies was easy to determine—the voracious denizens of the deep must have feasted well—unless, of course, the islanders had managed to flee in their canoes.

An hour before sundown Bantan was paddling more slower and he was looking down at the water. Through the translucent depths some ten feet beneath him he saw the edge of a ragged crater—the mouth of Aoono that had previously towered so high above the surface. Inactive for countless centuries, mighty forces long held pent, had at last surged upward from the bowels of the earth and wreaked havoc upon all three islands. Sinking beneath the surface—each a part of the mother bed—all had been engulfed and a minor tidal wave had resulted in aftermath.

Looking about slowly, Bantan shook his head. This was the end of the Aoono Islands and their inhabitants. In a vague way he again wondered if any had survived, and if so, where were they now?

Since none had reached the atoll far to the east, was it possible that they might have knowledge of islands to other points of the compass to which they may have gone? The thought that Amar had possibly survived the eruption of the volcano and the subsequent sinking of the islands aroused Bantan's curiosity to such an extent that he felt he should continue paddling to the west to ascertain such a possibility. Looking in that direction in the face of the setting sun, he was aware of a mighty force within him that impelled him to follow.

The bronzed giant looked at the fruit remaining in the bow of the canoe. He decided there was sufficient for about four days—by partaking of it sparingly. That would permit another day's paddling to the west,

and if no other islands were sighted by nightfall, he
could return to the atoll without danger of being
weakened by privation, and then back to Marja.

Once again he looked toward the setting sun, and so
great the attraction to follow, with resolution apparent
in his very movements, he gripped the handle of his
paddle tightly and plied it with seemingly renewed
strength. The canoe swiftly moved forward—as
though eager to be on its way—to what unknown
destination?

(The End)

www.ingramcontent.com/pod-product-compliance
Lightning Source LLC
Chambersburg PA
CBHW032242010726
47494CB00002B/586